NEWBU
BURN 2

CHIP ZDARSKY
JACOB PHILLIPS

ALLISON O'TOOLE
EDITOR

IMAGE COMICS, INC. · Robert Kirkman: Chief Operating Officer · Erik Larsen: Chief Financial Officer · Todd McFarlane: President · Marc Silvestri: Chief Executive Officer · Jim Valentino: Vice President · Eric Stephenson: Publisher / Chief Creative Officer · Nicole Lapalme: Vice President of Finance · Leanna Caunter: Accounting Analyst · Sue Korpela: Accounting & HR Manager · Jim Viscardi: Vice President of Business Development · Lorelei Bunjes: Vice President of Digital Strategy · Emilio Bautista: Digital Sales Coordinator · Dirk Wood: Vice President of International Sales & Licensing · Ryan Brewer: International Sales & Licensing Manager · Alex Cox: Director of Direct Market Sales · Margot Wood: Vice President of Book Market Sales · Chloe Ramos: Book Market & Library Sales Manager · Kat Salazar: Vice President of PR & Marketing · Deanna Phelps: Marketing Design Manager · Heather Doornink: Vice President of Production · Ian Baldessari: Print Manager · Drew Gill: Art Director · Melissa Gifford: Content Manager · Drew Fitzgerald: Content Manager · Erika Schnatz: Senior Production Artist · Wesley Griffith: Production Artist · Rich Fowlks: Production Artist · Jon Schlaffman: Production Artist · IMAGECOMICS.COM

9

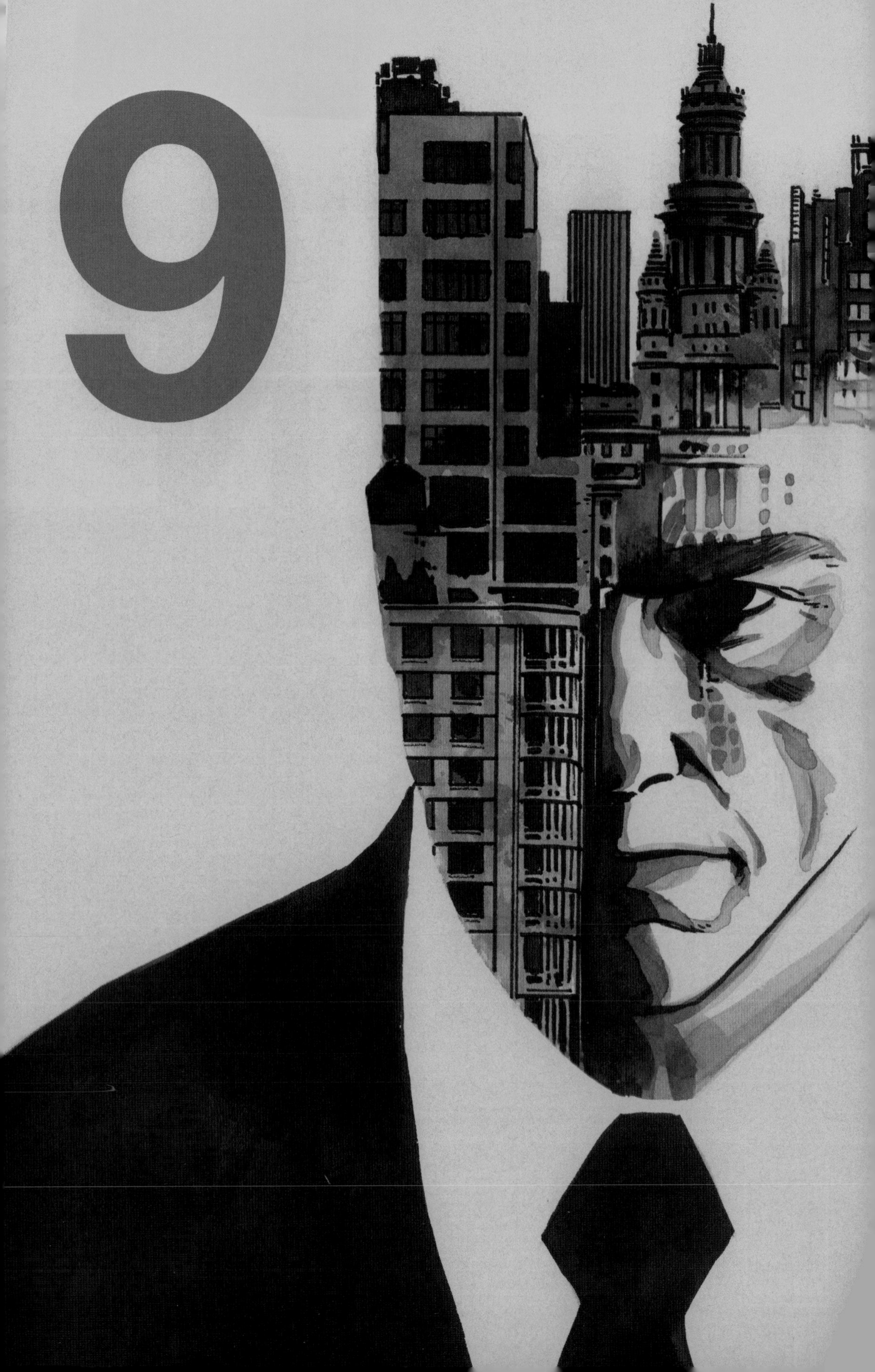

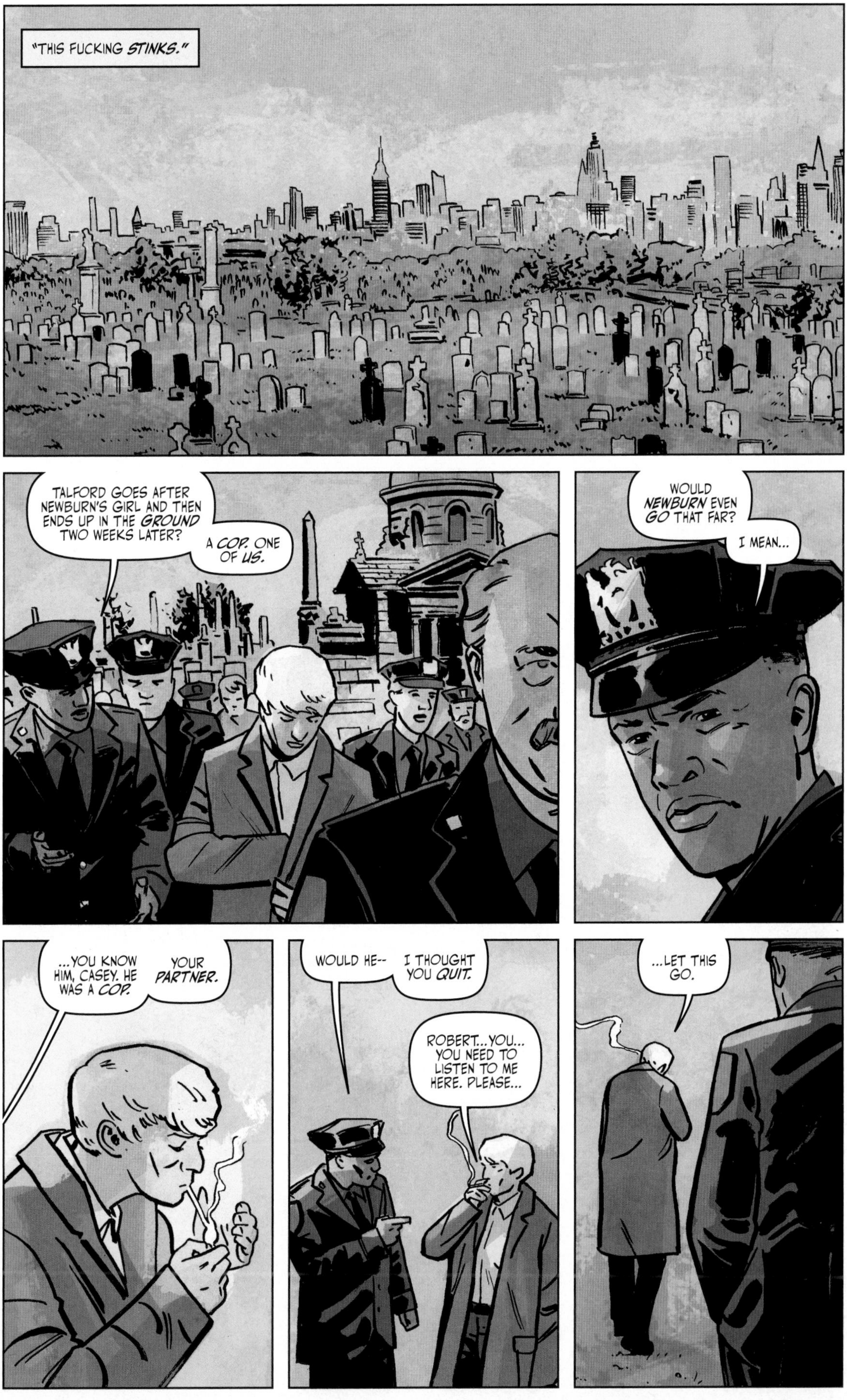
"THIS FUCKING STINKS."
TALFORD GOES AFTER NEWBURN'S GIRL AND THEN ENDS UP IN THE GROUND TWO WEEKS LATER?
A COP. ONE OF US.
WOULD NEWBURN EVEN GO THAT FAR?
I MEAN...
...YOU KNOW HIM, CASEY. HE WAS A COP.
YOUR PARTNER.
WOULD HE--
I THOUGHT YOU QUIT.
ROBERT...YOU... YOU NEED TO LISTEN TO ME HERE. PLEASE...
...LET THIS GO.

EMILY'S JOURNAL
08/01/22

It's been a time.

I'm still processing, still trying to find the space to breathe and think, but for now I'm safe.

It was an accident. Years ago I killed Mario Albano, the nephew of Michael Albano, the head of a crime family. I did it while defending my friend, Sydney Talford. Talford went on to become a cop, then went into debt to Russian mobsters.

It was our secret. Until he sold me out to the Albanos.

Thankfully, Newburn managed to pin it on a guy named Shigeyuki Shiroo, who gladly took the fall as it was preferable to his true crime: the murder of his boss, the head of the NYC Yakuza.

Life has never been uncomplicated, but I'm wondering how long I can do this for.

And how much debt I'm willing to be in to Newburn.

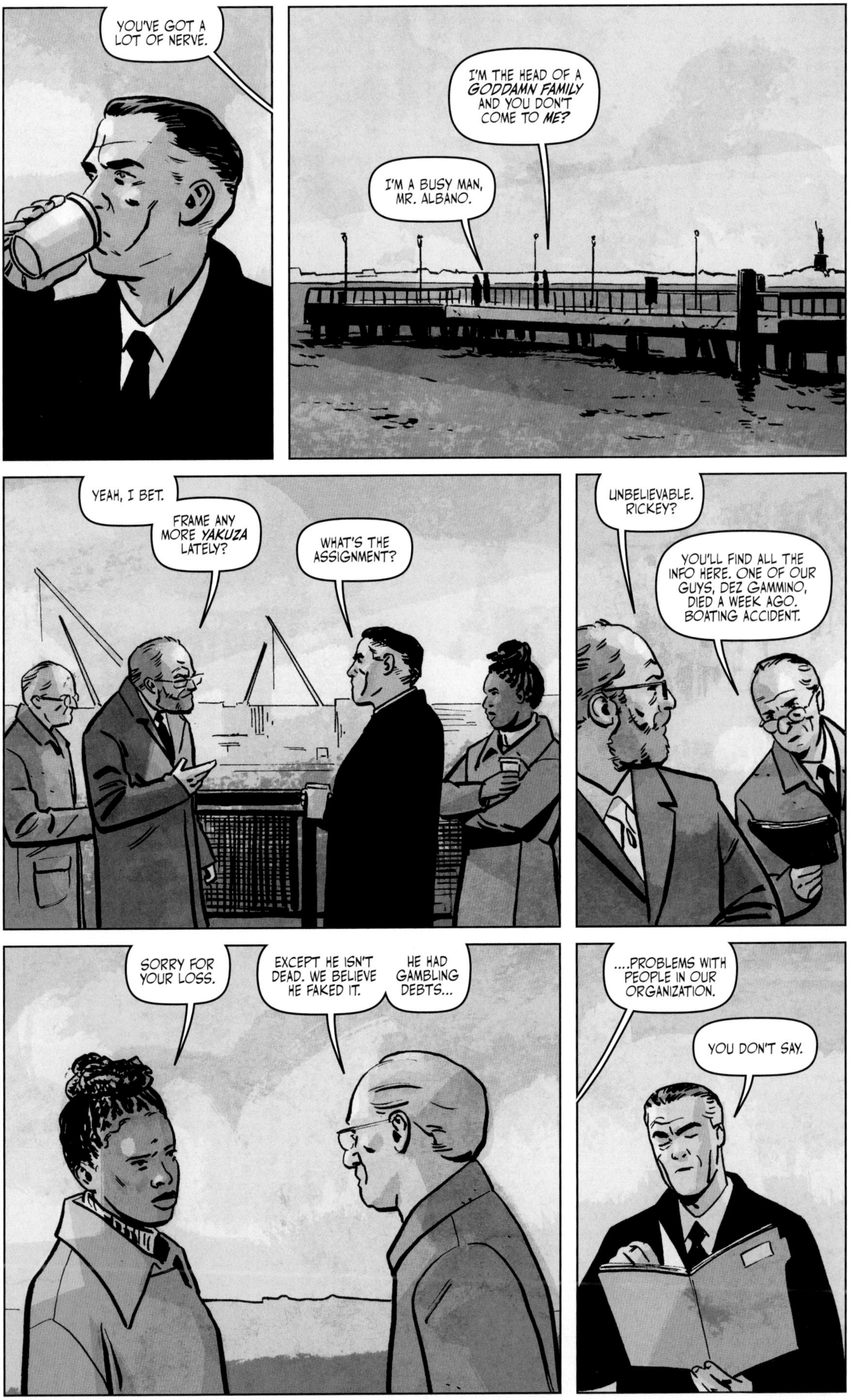
YOU'VE GOT A LOT OF NERVE.
I'M THE HEAD OF A *GODDAMN FAMILY* AND YOU DON'T COME TO *ME?*
I'M A BUSY MAN, MR. ALBANO.
YEAH, I BET.
FRAME ANY MORE *YAKUZA* LATELY?
WHAT'S THE ASSIGNMENT?
UNBELIEVABLE. RICKEY?
YOU'LL FIND ALL THE INFO HERE. ONE OF OUR GUYS, DEZ GAMMINO, DIED A WEEK AGO. BOATING ACCIDENT.
SORRY FOR YOUR LOSS.
EXCEPT HE ISN'T DEAD. WE BELIEVE HE FAKED IT.
HE HAD GAMBLING DEBTS...
....PROBLEMS WITH PEOPLE IN OUR ORGANIZATION.
YOU DON'T SAY.

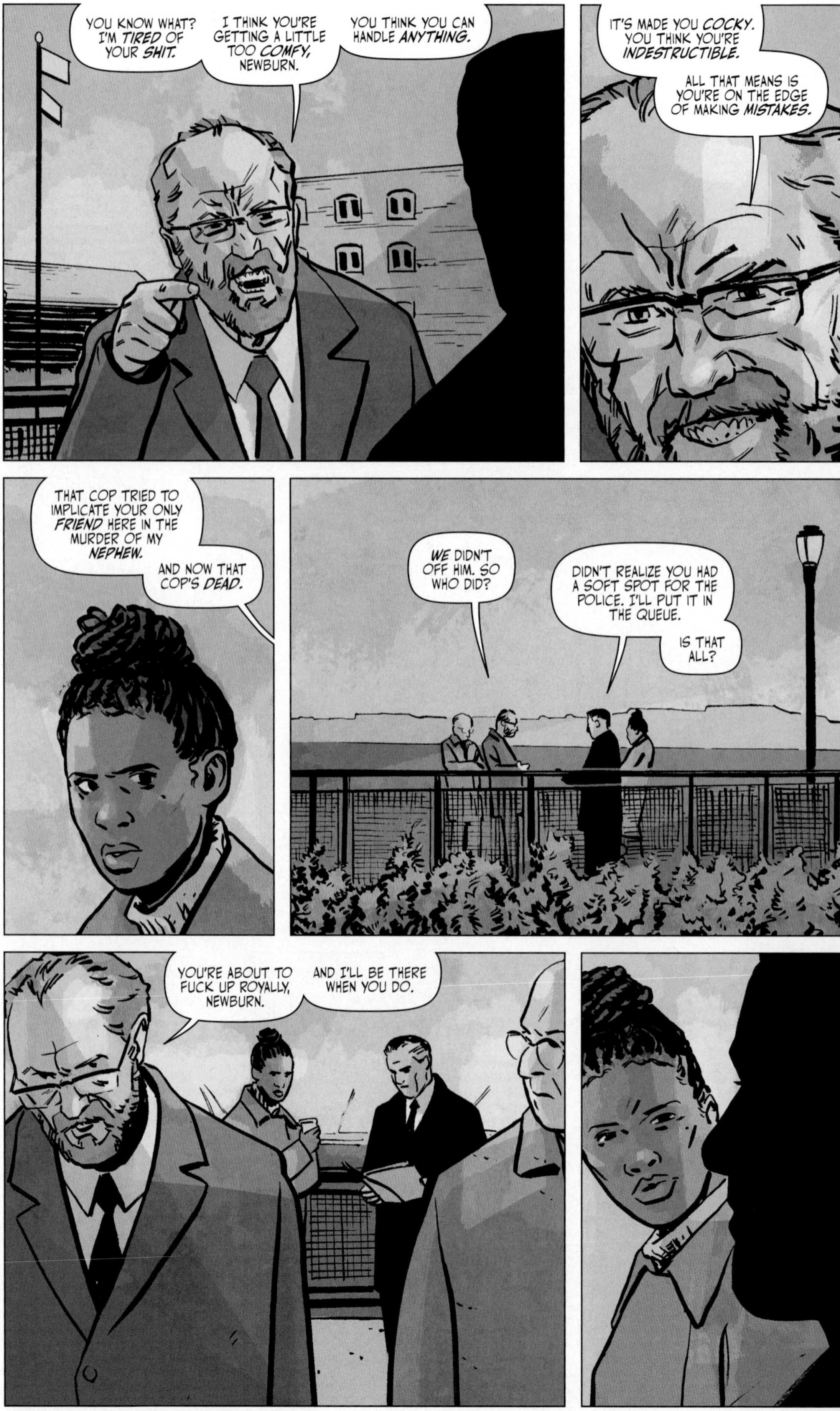

YOU KNOW WHAT? I'M TIRED OF YOUR SHIT.
I THINK YOU'RE GETTING A LITTLE TOO COMFY, NEWBURN.
YOU THINK YOU CAN HANDLE ANYTHING.
IT'S MADE YOU COCKY. YOU THINK YOU'RE INDESTRUCTIBLE.
ALL THAT MEANS IS YOU'RE ON THE EDGE OF MAKING MISTAKES.
THAT COP TRIED TO IMPLICATE YOUR ONLY FRIEND HERE IN THE MURDER OF MY NEPHEW.
AND NOW THAT COP'S DEAD.
WE DIDN'T OFF HIM. SO WHO DID?
DIDN'T REALIZE YOU HAD A SOFT SPOT FOR THE POLICE. I'LL PUT IT IN THE QUEUE.
IS THAT ALL?
YOU'RE ABOUT TO FUCK UP ROYALLY, NEWBURN.
AND I'LL BE THERE WHEN YOU DO.

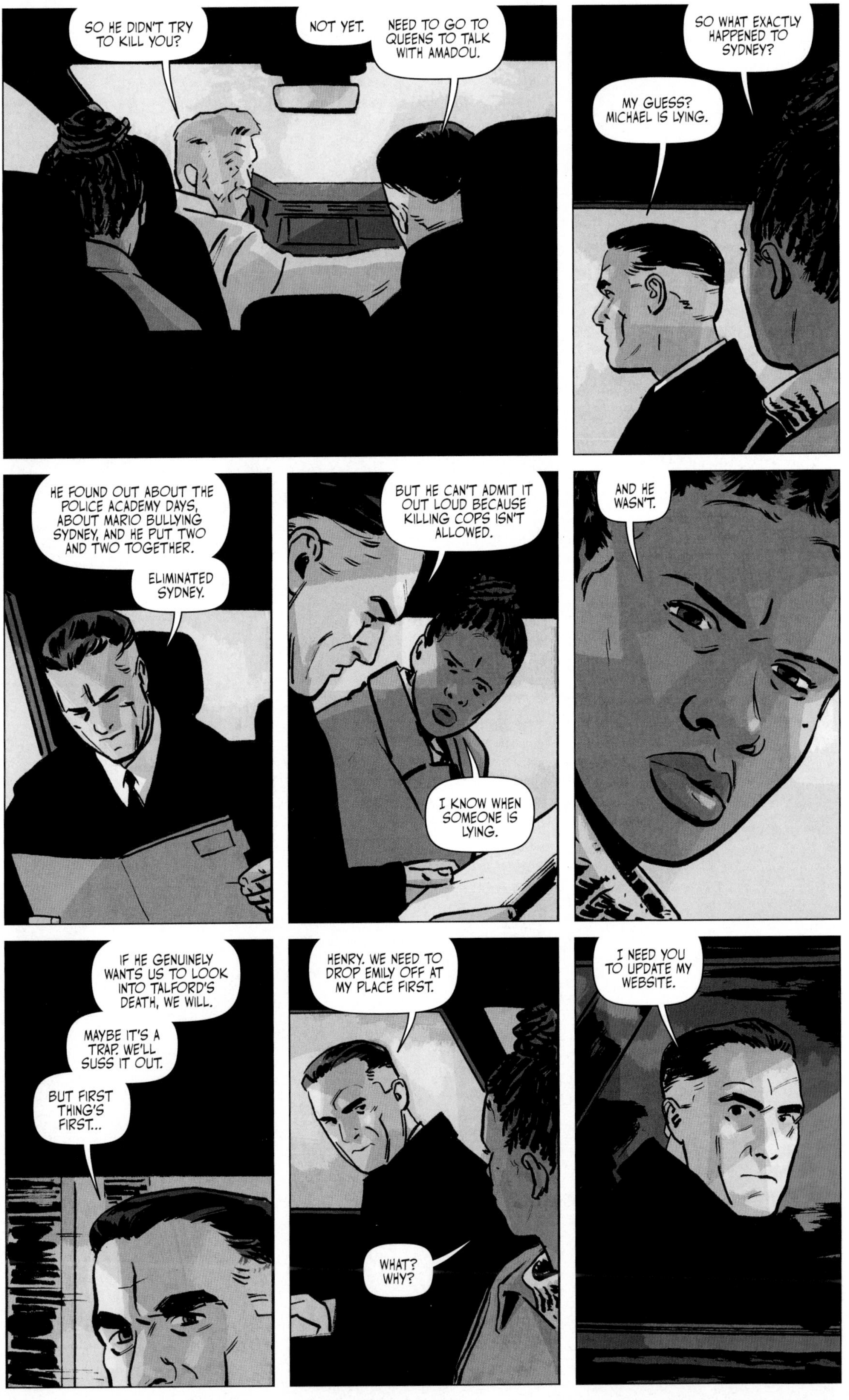
SO HE DIDN'T TRY TO KILL YOU?
NOT YET.
NEED TO GO TO QUEENS TO TALK WITH AMADOU.
SO WHAT EXACTLY HAPPENED TO SYDNEY?
MY GUESS? MICHAEL IS LYING.
HE FOUND OUT ABOUT THE POLICE ACADEMY DAYS, ABOUT MARIO BULLYING SYDNEY, AND HE PUT TWO AND TWO TOGETHER.
ELIMINATED SYDNEY.
BUT HE CAN'T ADMIT IT OUT LOUD BECAUSE KILLING COPS ISN'T ALLOWED.
I KNOW WHEN SOMEONE IS LYING.
AND HE WASN'T.
IF HE GENUINELY WANTS US TO LOOK INTO TALFORD'S DEATH, WE WILL.
MAYBE IT'S A TRAP. WE'LL SUSS IT OUT.
BUT FIRST THING'S FIRST...
HENRY. WE NEED TO DROP EMILY OFF AT MY PLACE FIRST.
WHAT? WHY?
I NEED YOU TO UPDATE MY WEBSITE.

EMILY'S JOURNAL
08/03/22

Sydney Talford is dead.

What Newburn says makes sense, that the Albanos did it. And maybe my proximity to Newburn is keeping me safe from them and their suspicions.

But something's not sitting right. Michael Albano is easily read. He grew up with a grimy silver spoon in his mouth, being the heir apparent to his father's empire. He says what he thinks, he's got little use for lies except the smirking ones he tells police where they're in on the joke.

So if he's not lying... then what exactly happened to Sydney?

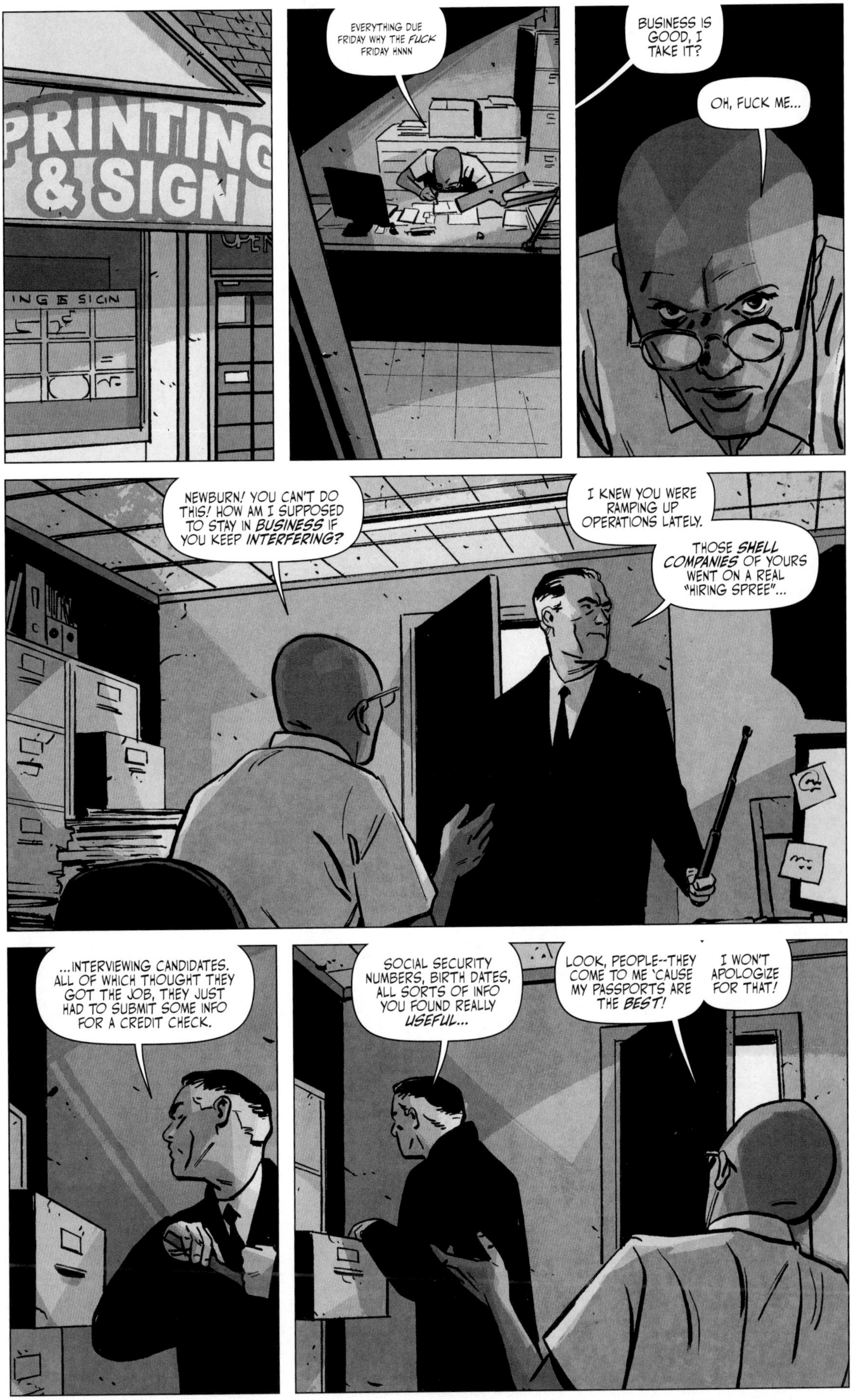
PRINTING & SIGN
EVERYTHING DUE FRIDAY WHY THE FUCK FRIDAY HNNN
BUSINESS IS GOOD, I TAKE IT?
OH, FUCK ME...
NEWBURN! YOU CAN'T DO THIS! HOW AM I SUPPOSED TO STAY IN BUSINESS IF YOU KEEP INTERFERING?
I KNEW YOU WERE RAMPING UP OPERATIONS LATELY.
THOSE SHELL COMPANIES OF YOURS WENT ON A REAL "HIRING SPREE"...
...INTERVIEWING CANDIDATES. ALL OF WHICH THOUGHT THEY GOT THE JOB, THEY JUST HAD TO SUBMIT SOME INFO FOR A CREDIT CHECK.
SOCIAL SECURITY NUMBERS, BIRTH DATES, ALL SORTS OF INFO YOU FOUND REALLY USEFUL...
LOOK, PEOPLE--THEY COME TO ME 'CAUSE MY PASSPORTS ARE THE BEST!
I WON'T APOLOGIZE FOR THAT!

I APPRECIATE YOUR PROFESSIONALISM.

DEZ GAMMINO NEEDED A NEW LIFE. I WON'T EXPECT YOU TO TELL ME IF HE WAS HERE, JUST...

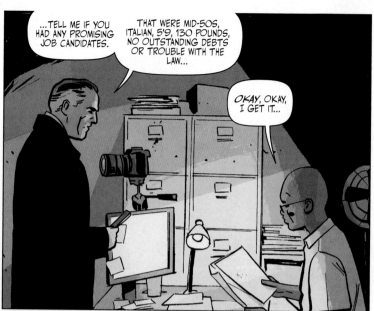

...TELL ME IF YOU HAD ANY PROMISING JOB CANDIDATES.

THAT WERE MID-50S, ITALIAN, 5'9, 130 POUNDS, NO OUTSTANDING DEBTS OR TROUBLE WITH THE LAW...

OKAY, OKAY, I GET IT...

...JUST DON'T LET THIS GET BACK TO ME, YEAH?

I WON'T. BUT YOU SHOULD STICK TO HELPING HUSBANDS LEAVE THEIR FAMILIES...

...AND STAY AWAY FROM DEALING WITH THE CRIME SYNDICATES.

YOU'RE ONE TO TALK. WORD ON THE STREET IS *THE BLACK CASTLE* ISN'T TOO HAPPY WITH YOU THESE DAYS.

IS THAT SO?

YOU'RE A *COOL CUSTOMER*, MAN. BUT NOBODY'S INDISPENSABLE...

...ESPECIALLY WHEN DEALING WITH THE *FAMILIES.*

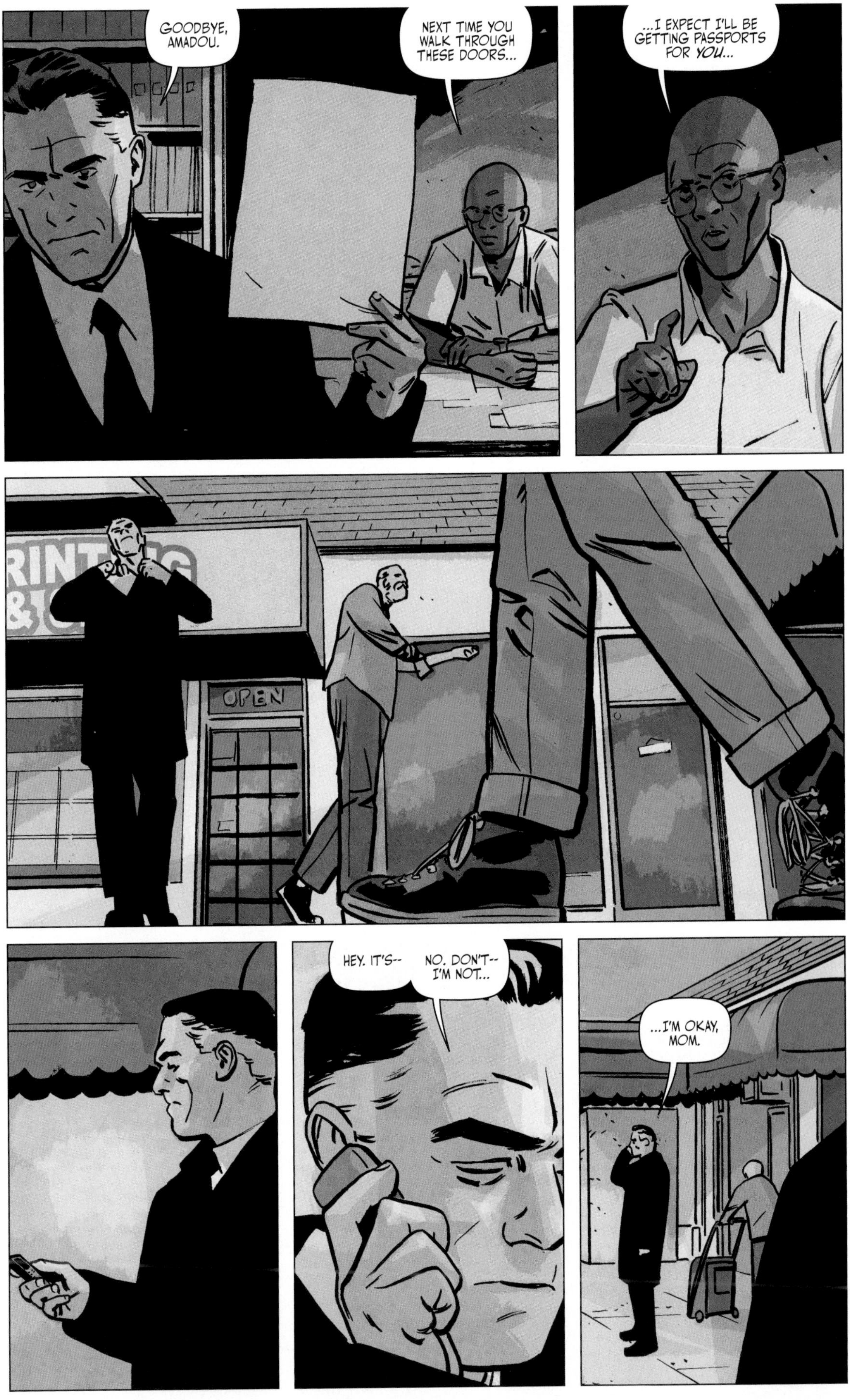
GOODBYE, AMADOU.
NEXT TIME YOU WALK THROUGH THESE DOORS...
...I EXPECT I'LL BE GETTING PASSPORTS FOR *YOU*...
PRINTING &
OPEN
HEY. IT'S--
NO. DON'T-- I'M NOT...
...I'M OKAY, MOM.

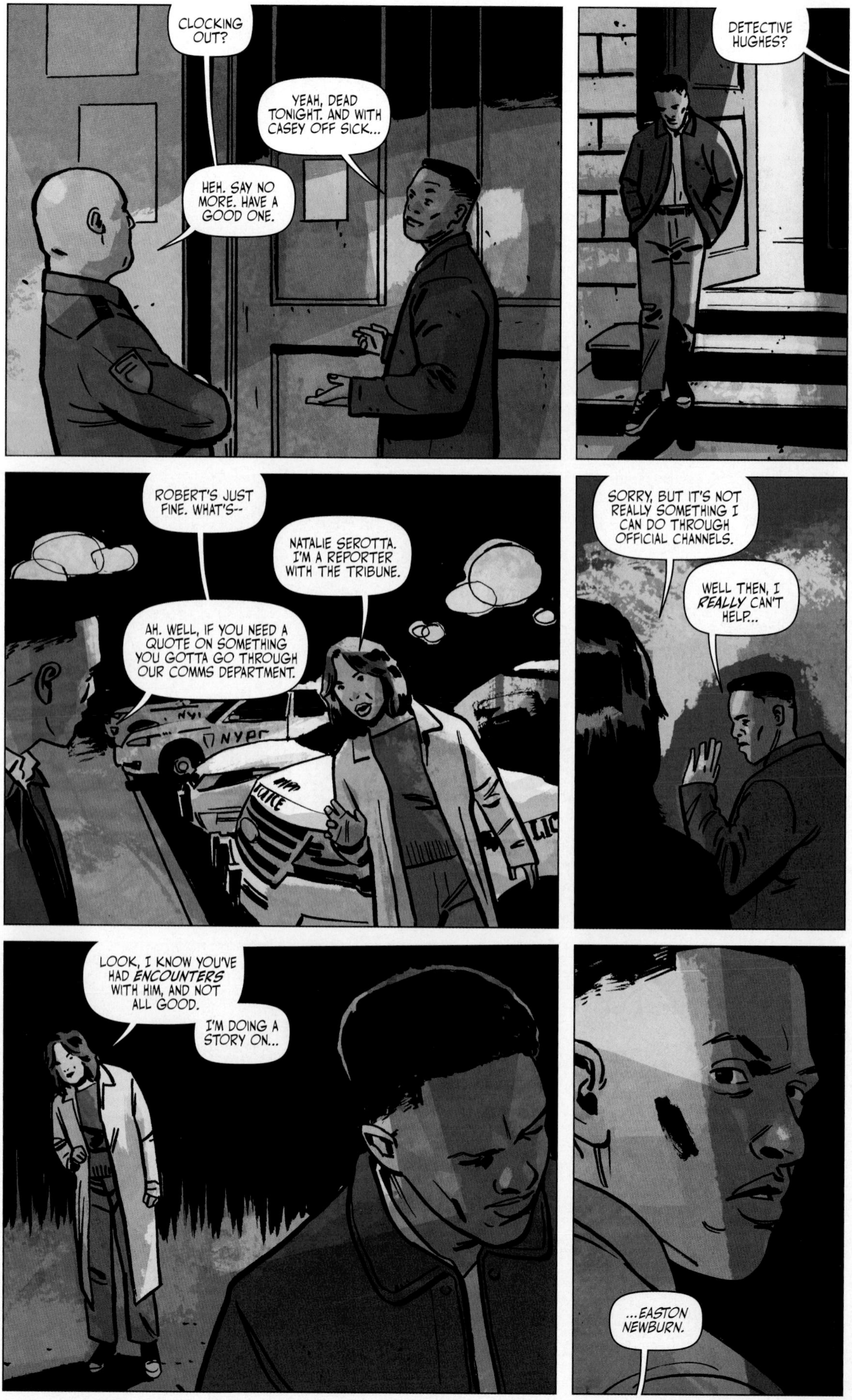
CLOCKING OUT?
YEAH, DEAD TONIGHT. AND WITH CASEY OFF SICK...
HEH. SAY NO MORE. HAVE A GOOD ONE.
DETECTIVE HUGHES?
ROBERT'S JUST FINE. WHAT'S--
NATALIE SEROTTA. I'M A REPORTER WITH THE TRIBUNE.
AH. WELL, IF YOU NEED A QUOTE ON SOMETHING YOU GOTTA GO THROUGH OUR COMMS DEPARTMENT.
SORRY, BUT IT'S NOT REALLY SOMETHING I CAN DO THROUGH OFFICIAL CHANNELS.
WELL THEN, I *REALLY* CAN'T HELP...
LOOK, I KNOW YOU'VE HAD *ENCOUNTERS* WITH HIM, AND NOT ALL GOOD.
I'M DOING A STORY ON...
...EASTON NEWBURN.

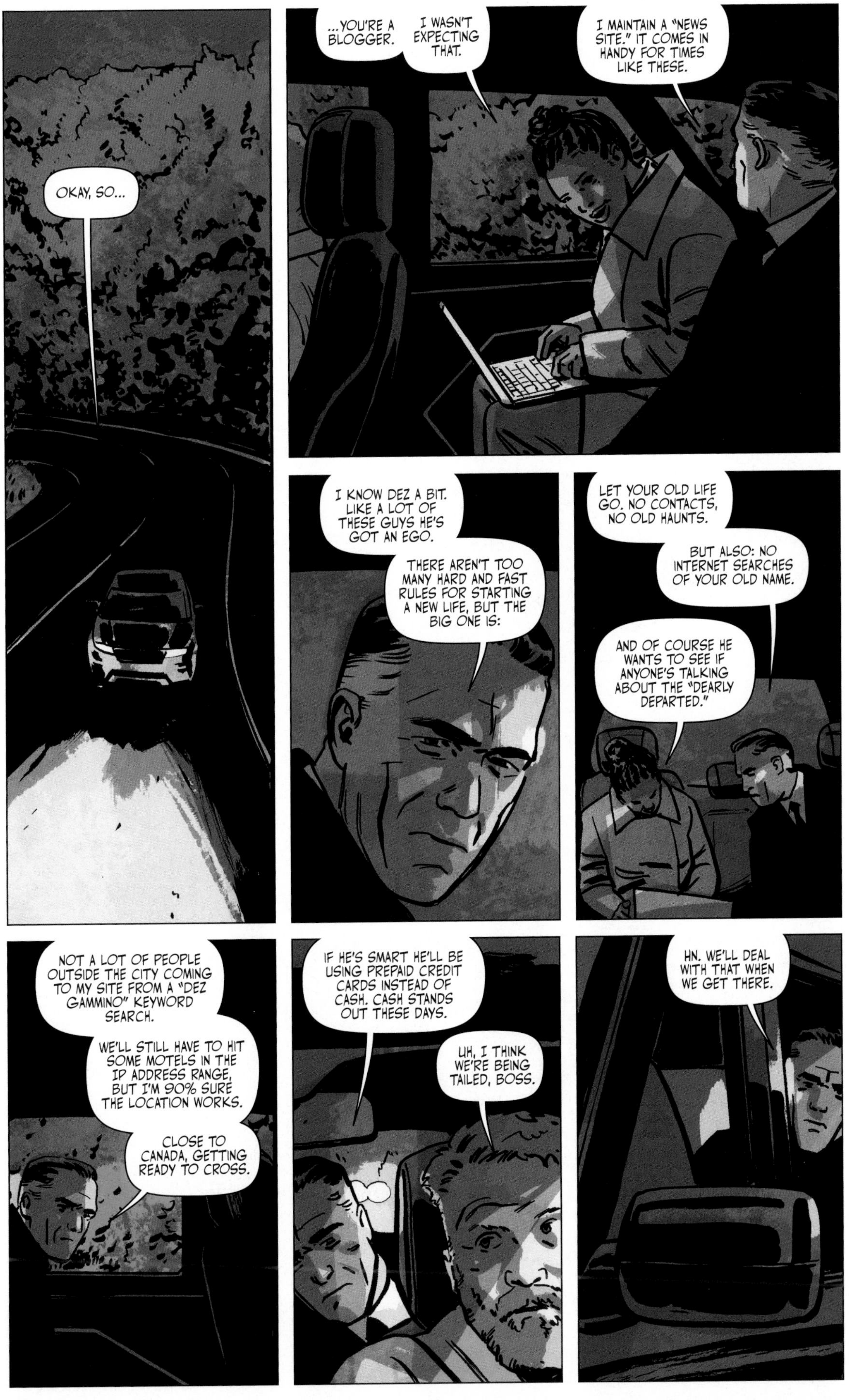
OKAY, SO...
...YOU'RE A BLOGGER.
I WASN'T EXPECTING THAT.
I MAINTAIN A "NEWS SITE." IT COMES IN HANDY FOR TIMES LIKE THESE.
I KNOW DEZ A BIT. LIKE A LOT OF THESE GUYS HE'S GOT AN EGO.
THERE AREN'T TOO MANY HARD AND FAST RULES FOR STARTING A NEW LIFE, BUT THE BIG ONE IS:
LET YOUR OLD LIFE GO. NO CONTACTS, NO OLD HAUNTS.
BUT ALSO: NO INTERNET SEARCHES OF YOUR OLD NAME.
AND OF COURSE HE WANTS TO SEE IF ANYONE'S TALKING ABOUT THE "DEARLY DEPARTED."
NOT A LOT OF PEOPLE OUTSIDE THE CITY COMING TO MY SITE FROM A "DEZ GAMMINO" KEYWORD SEARCH.
WE'LL STILL HAVE TO HIT SOME MOTELS IN THE IP ADDRESS RANGE, BUT I'M 90% SURE THE LOCATION WORKS.
CLOSE TO CANADA, GETTING READY TO CROSS.
IF HE'S SMART HE'LL BE USING PREPAID CREDIT CARDS INSTEAD OF CASH. CASH STANDS OUT THESE DAYS.
UH, I THINK WE'RE BEING TAILED, BOSS.
HN. WE'LL DEAL WITH THAT WHEN WE GET THERE.

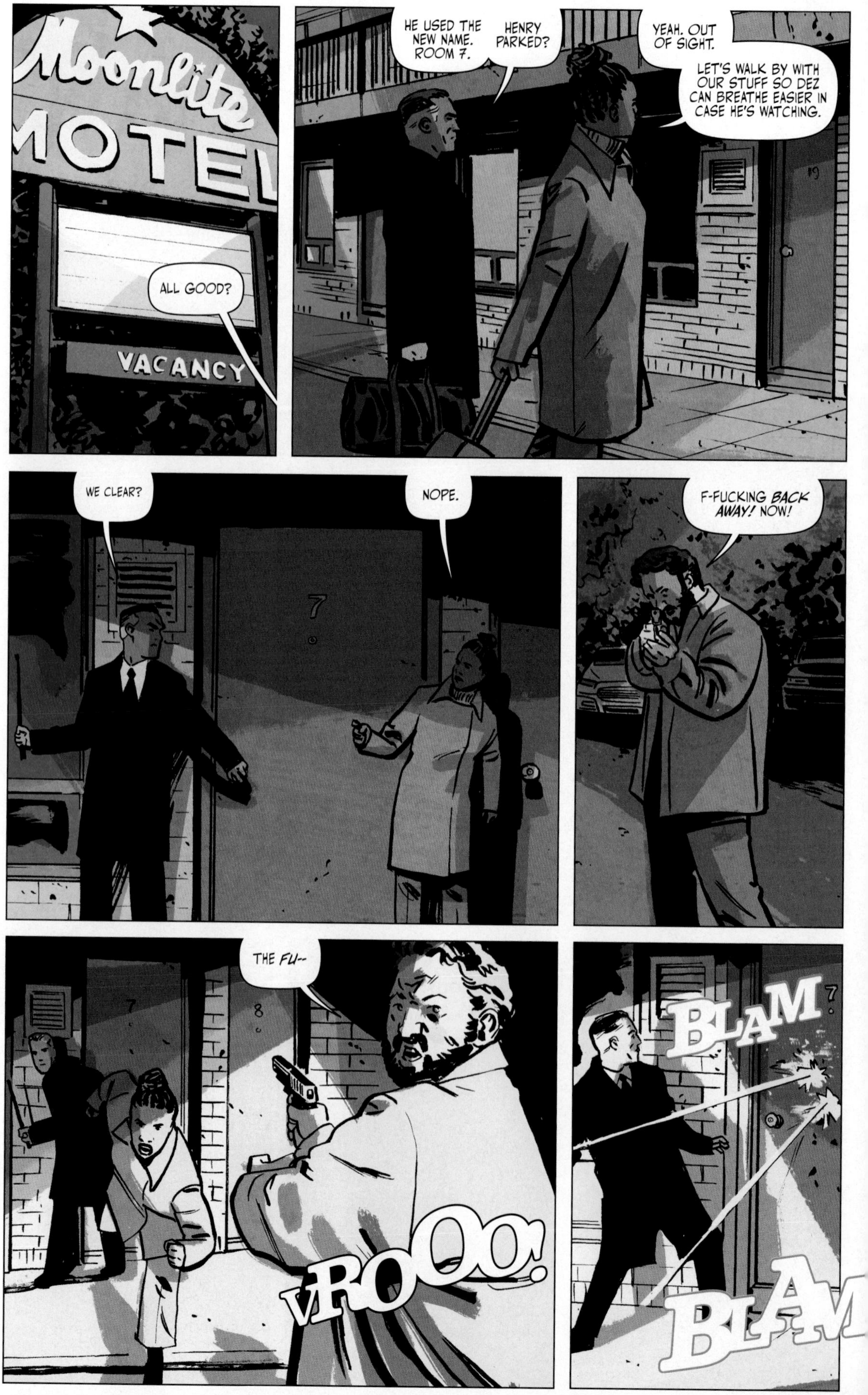
Moonlite
MOTEL
VACANCY
ALL GOOD?
HE USED THE NEW NAME. ROOM 7.
HENRY PARKED?
YEAH. OUT OF SIGHT.
LET'S WALK BY WITH OUR STUFF SO DEZ CAN BREATHE EASIER IN CASE HE'S WATCHING.
WE CLEAR?
NOPE.
F-FUCKING *BACK AWAY!* NOW!
THE *FU*--
vROOOO!
BLAM
BLAM

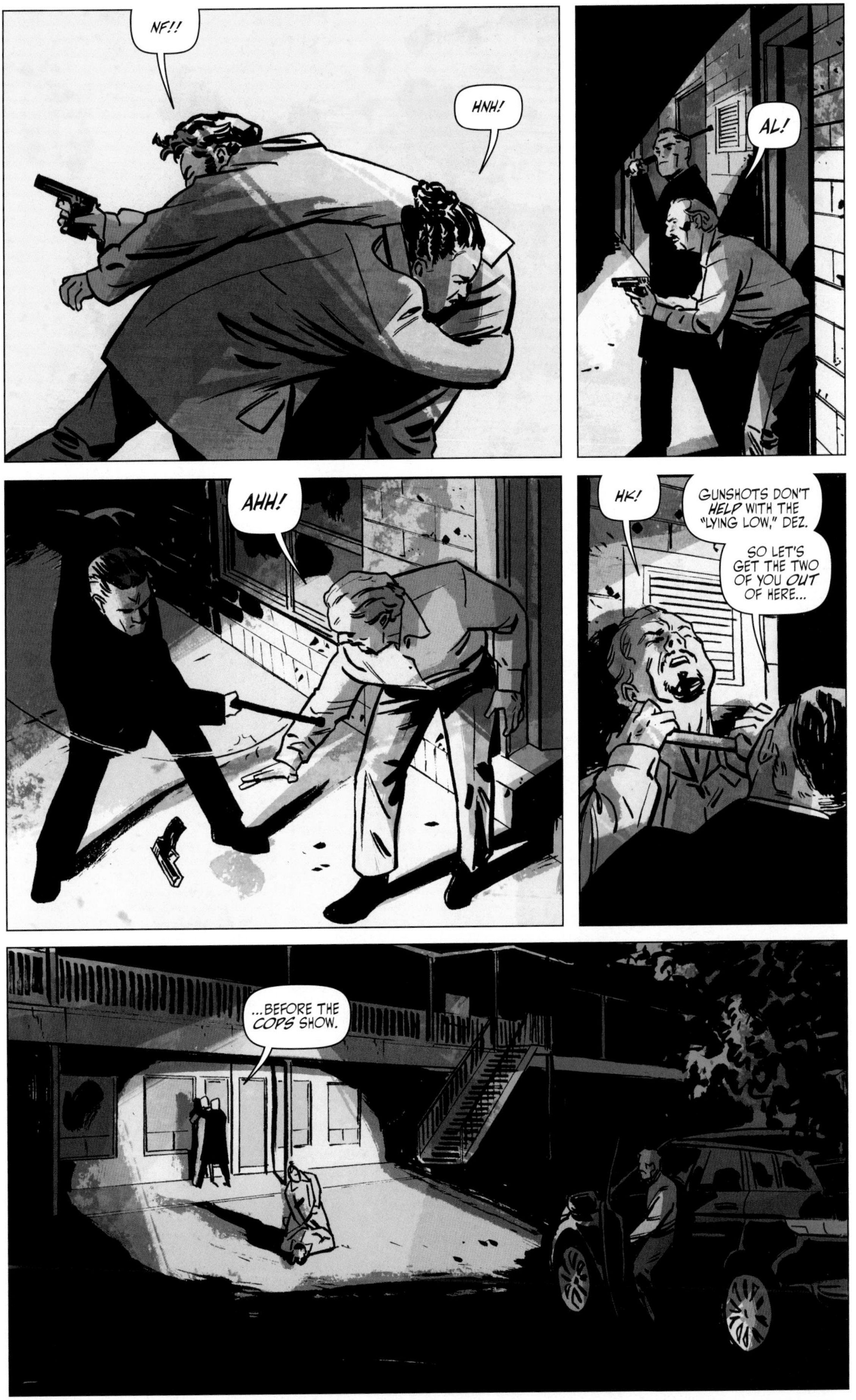
NF!!
HNH!
AL!
AHH!
HK!
GUNSHOTS DON'T HELP WITH THE "LYING LOW," DEZ.
SO LET'S GET THE TWO OF YOU OUT OF HERE...
...BEFORE THE COPS SHOW.

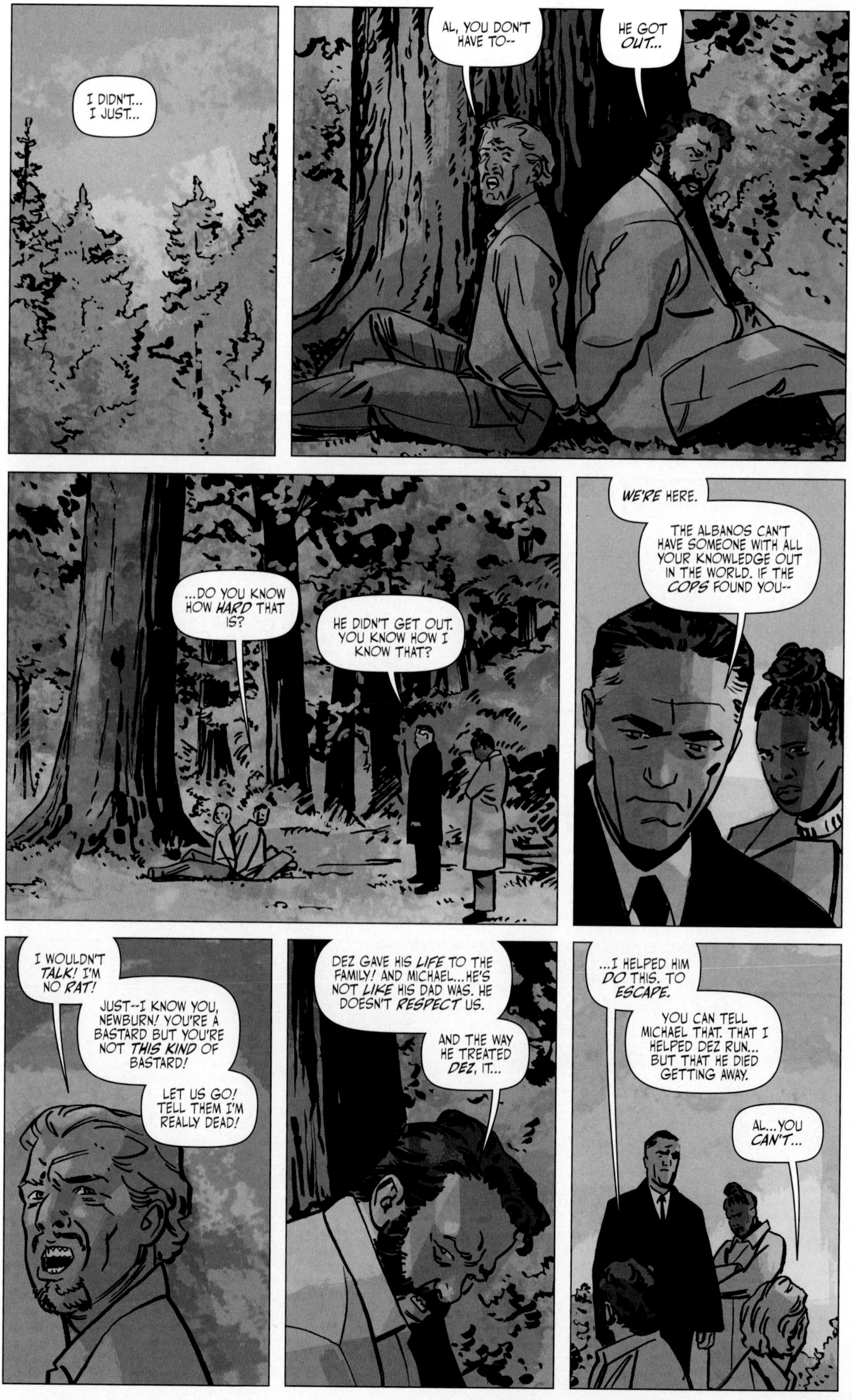
I DIDN'T... I JUST...
AL, YOU DON'T HAVE TO--
HE GOT OUT...
...DO YOU KNOW HOW HARD THAT IS?
HE DIDN'T GET OUT. YOU KNOW HOW I KNOW THAT?
WE'RE HERE.
THE ALBANOS CAN'T HAVE SOMEONE WITH ALL YOUR KNOWLEDGE OUT IN THE WORLD. IF THE COPS FOUND YOU--
I WOULDN'T TALK! I'M NO RAT!
JUST--I KNOW YOU, NEWBURN! YOU'RE A BASTARD BUT YOU'RE NOT THIS KIND OF BASTARD!
LET US GO! TELL THEM I'M REALLY DEAD!
DEZ GAVE HIS LIFE TO THE FAMILY! AND MICHAEL...HE'S NOT LIKE HIS DAD WAS. HE DOESN'T RESPECT US.
AND THE WAY HE TREATED DEZ, IT...
...I HELPED HIM DO THIS. TO ESCAPE.
YOU CAN TELL MICHAEL THAT. THAT I HELPED DEZ RUN... BUT THAT HE DIED GETTING AWAY.
AL...YOU CAN'T...

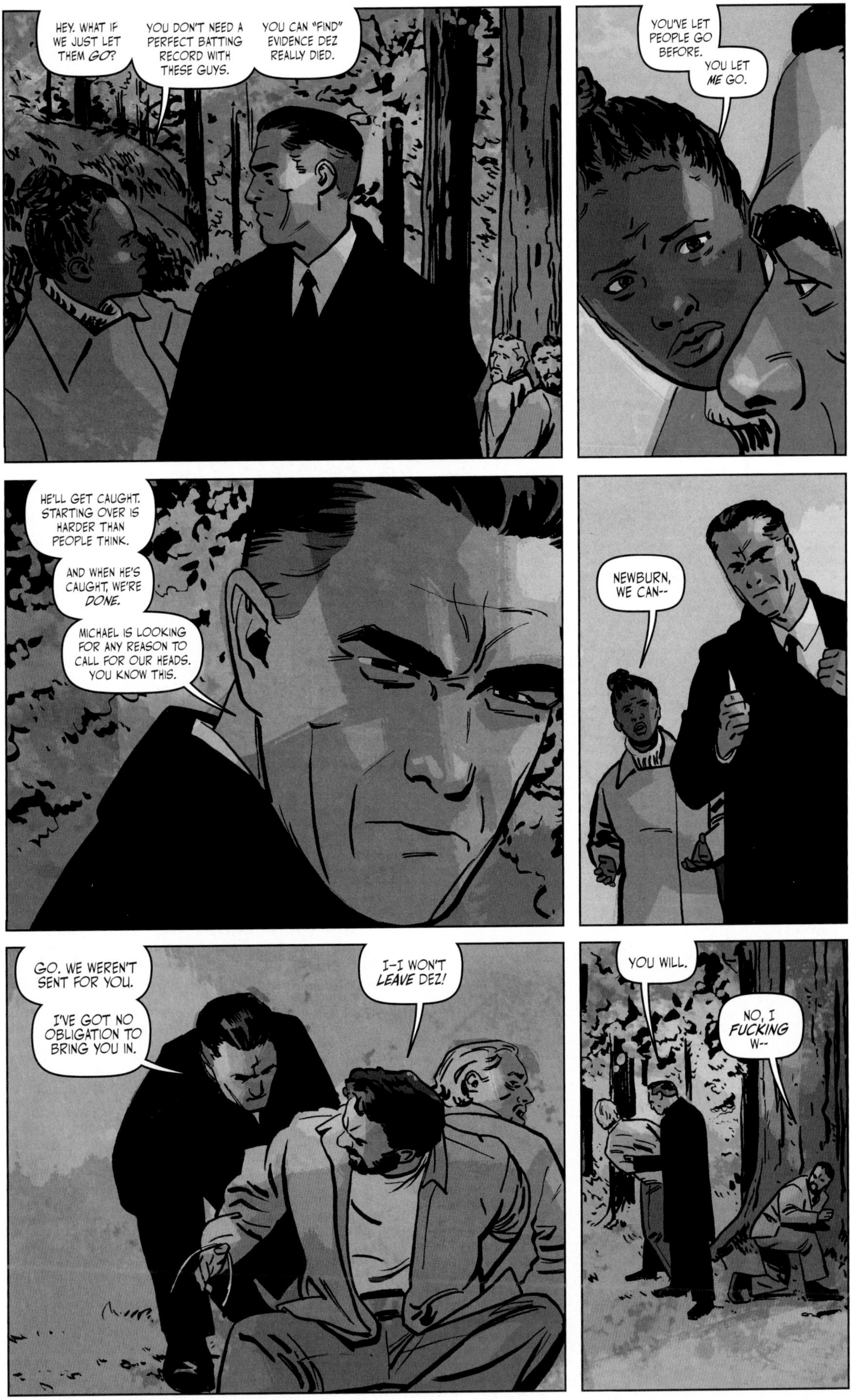
HEY. WHAT IF WE JUST LET THEM *GO*?
YOU DON'T NEED A PERFECT BATTING RECORD WITH THESE GUYS.
YOU CAN "FIND" EVIDENCE DEZ REALLY DIED.
YOU'VE LET PEOPLE GO BEFORE.
YOU LET *ME* GO.
HE'LL GET CAUGHT. STARTING OVER IS HARDER THAN PEOPLE THINK.
AND WHEN HE'S CAUGHT, WE'RE *DONE*.
MICHAEL IS LOOKING FOR ANY REASON TO CALL FOR OUR HEADS. YOU KNOW THIS.
NEWBURN, WE CAN--
GO. WE WEREN'T SENT FOR YOU.
I'VE GOT NO OBLIGATION TO BRING YOU IN.
I-I WON'T *LEAVE* DEZ!
YOU WILL.
NO, I *FUCKING* W--

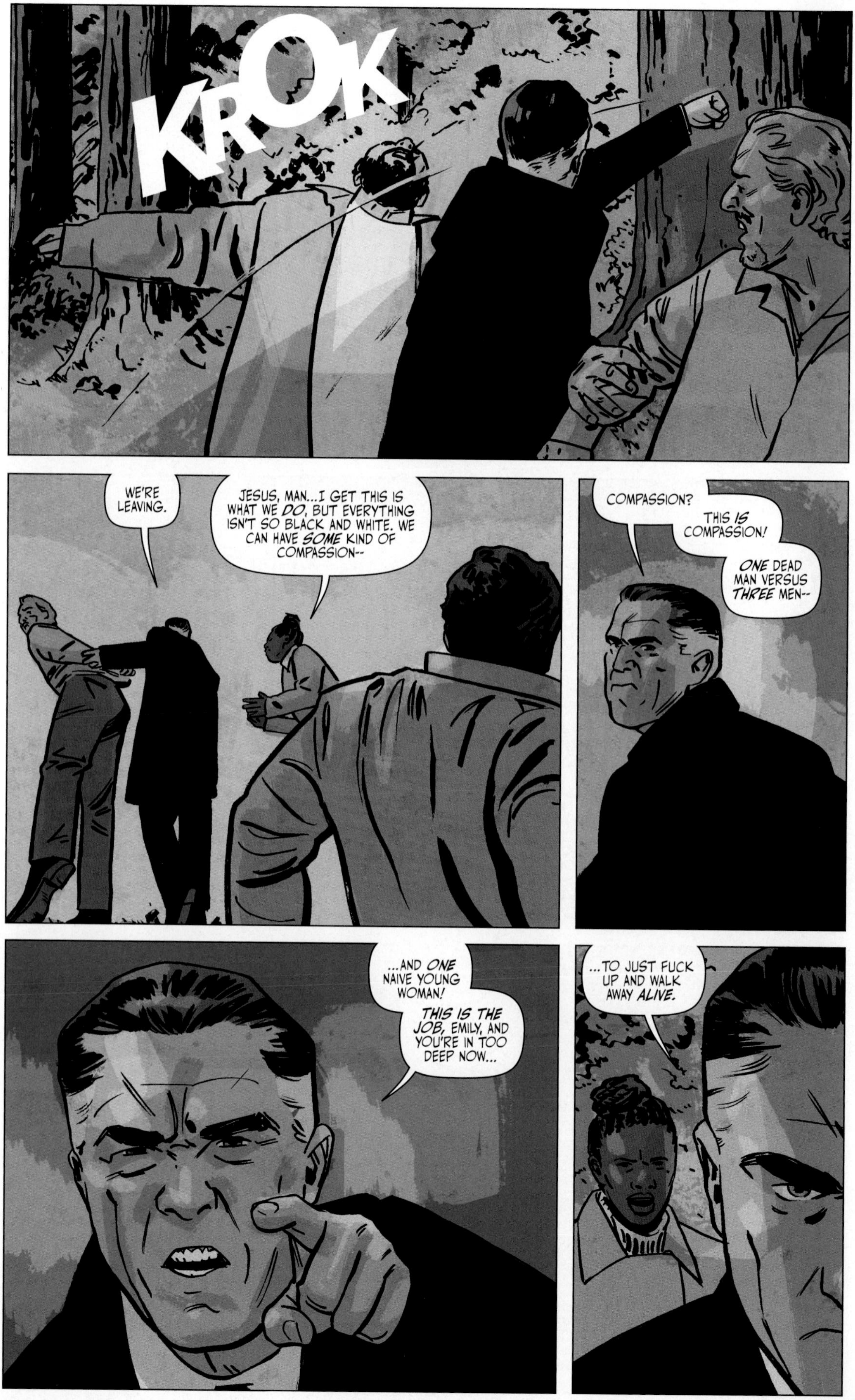
KROK
WE'RE LEAVING.
JESUS, MAN...I GET THIS IS WHAT WE DO, BUT EVERYTHING ISN'T SO BLACK AND WHITE. WE CAN HAVE SOME KIND OF COMPASSION--
COMPASSION?
THIS IS COMPASSION!
ONE DEAD MAN VERSUS THREE MEN--
...AND ONE NAIVE YOUNG WOMAN!
THIS IS THE JOB, EMILY, AND YOU'RE IN TOO DEEP NOW...
...TO JUST FUCK UP AND WALK AWAY ALIVE.

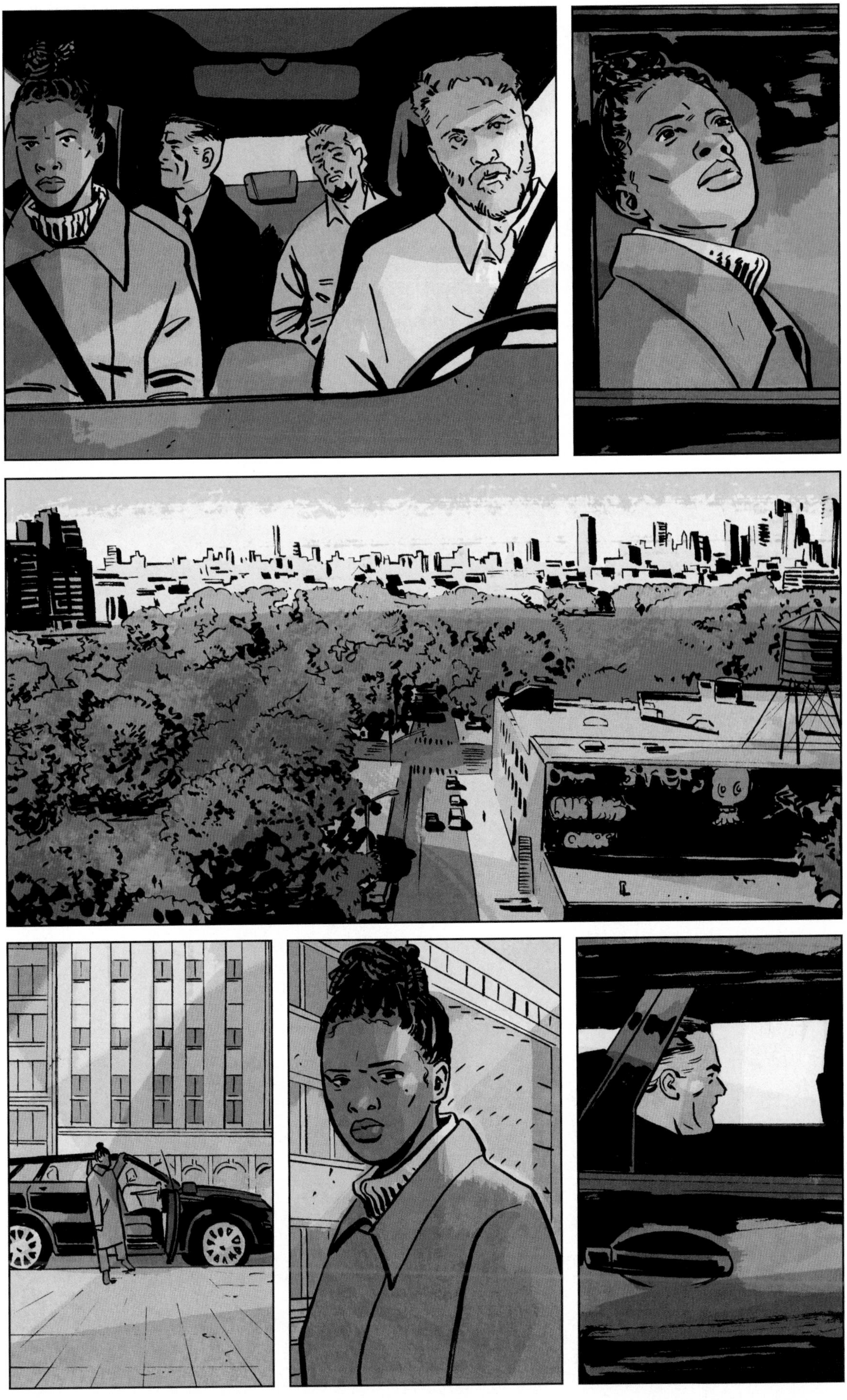

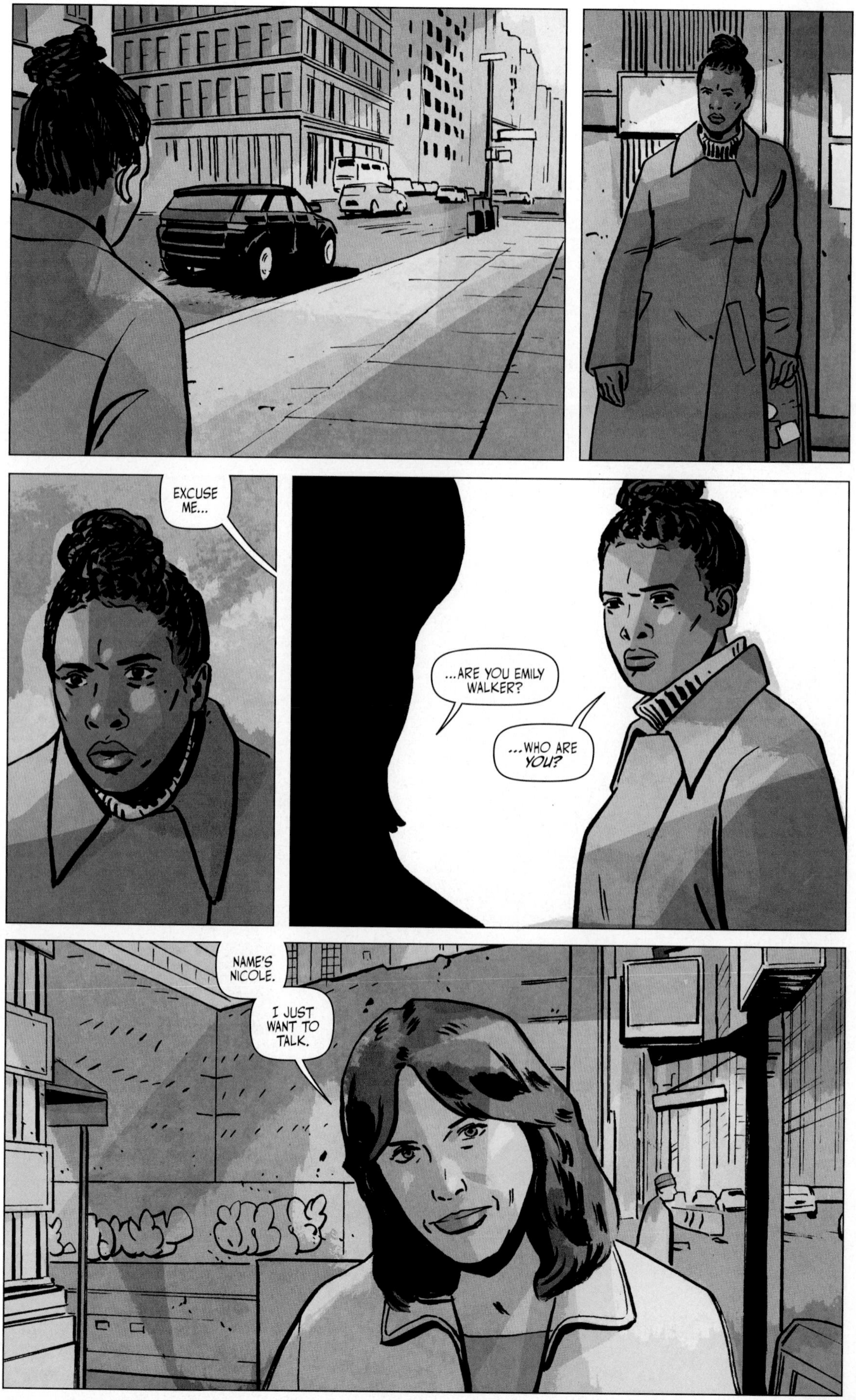
EXCUSE ME...
...ARE YOU EMILY WALKER?
...WHO ARE YOU?
NAME'S NICOLE.
I JUST WANT TO TALK.

10

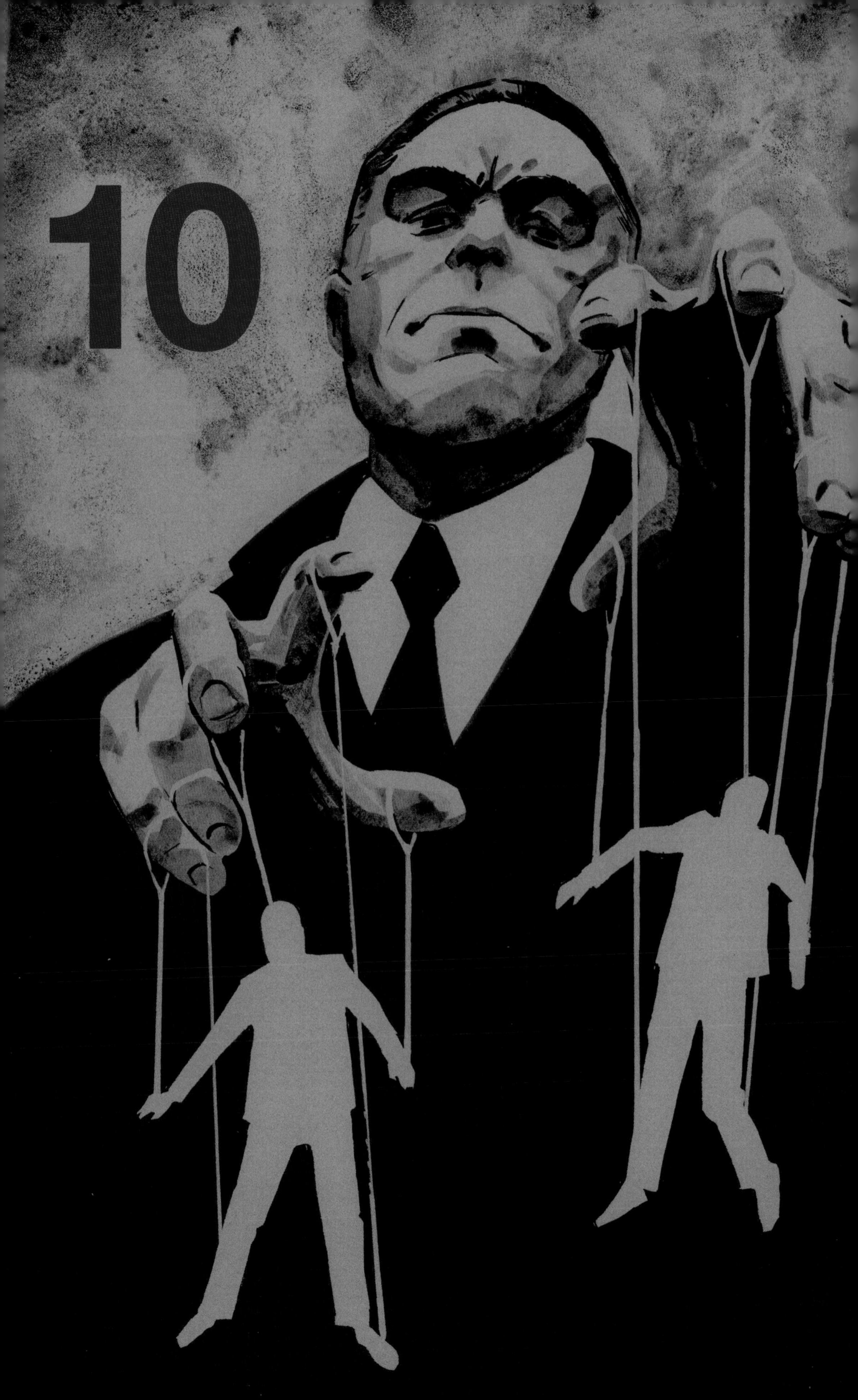

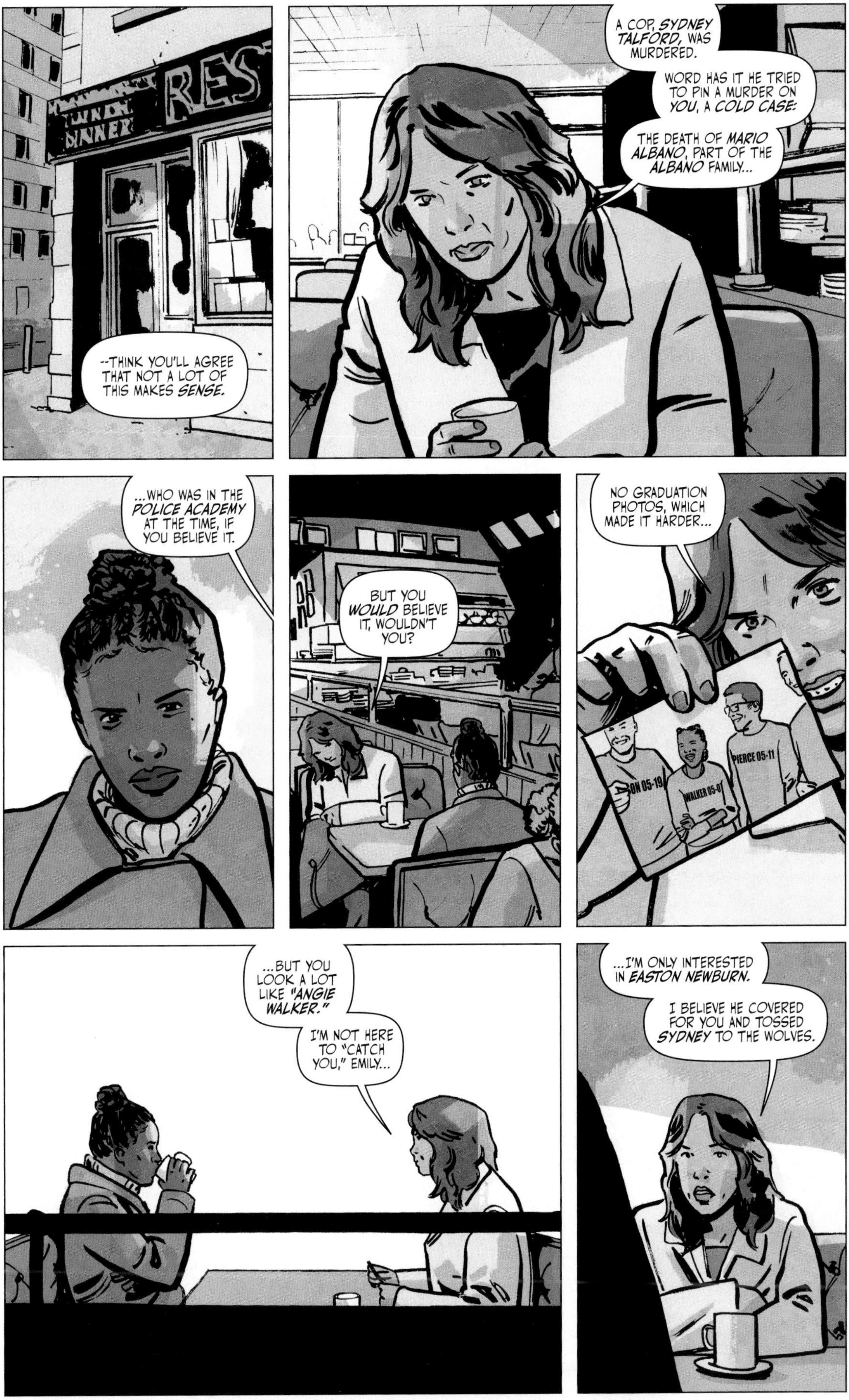
RES
DINNER
--THINK YOU'LL AGREE THAT NOT A LOT OF THIS MAKES SENSE.
A COP, SYDNEY TALFORD, WAS MURDERED.
WORD HAS IT HE TRIED TO PIN A MURDER ON YOU, A COLD CASE:
THE DEATH OF MARIO ALBANO, PART OF THE ALBANO FAMILY...
...WHO WAS IN THE POLICE ACADEMY AT THE TIME, IF YOU BELIEVE IT.
BUT YOU WOULD BELIEVE IT, WOULDN'T YOU?
NO GRADUATION PHOTOS, WHICH MADE IT HARDER...
SON 05-19
WALKER 05-07
PIERCE 05-11
...BUT YOU LOOK A LOT LIKE "ANGIE WALKER."
I'M NOT HERE TO "CATCH YOU," EMILY...
...I'M ONLY INTERESTED IN EASTON NEWBURN.
I BELIEVE HE COVERED FOR YOU AND TOSSED SYDNEY TO THE WOLVES.

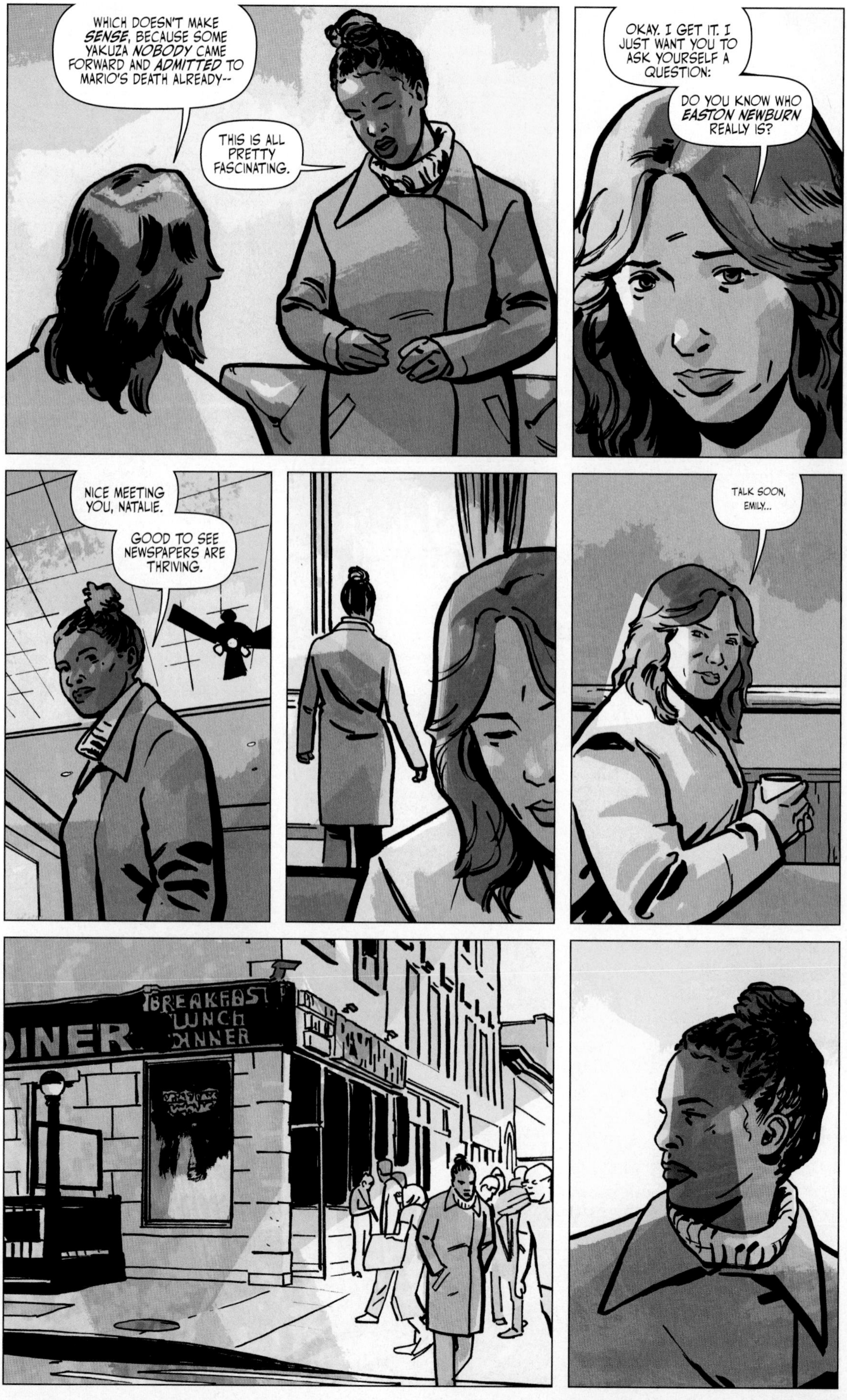

WHICH DOESN'T MAKE SENSE, BECAUSE SOME YAKUZA NOBODY CAME FORWARD AND ADMITTED TO MARIO'S DEATH ALREADY--
THIS IS ALL PRETTY FASCINATING.
OKAY. I GET IT. I JUST WANT YOU TO ASK YOURSELF A QUESTION:
DO YOU KNOW WHO EASTON NEWBURN REALLY IS?
NICE MEETING YOU, NATALIE.
GOOD TO SEE NEWSPAPERS ARE THRIVING.
TALK SOON, EMILY...
DINER

EMILY'S JOURNAL
08/05/22

This is bad.

I believe her that she's only interested in Newburn, but if things start to unravel then I'm going down too. Or, in place of. Newburn's too damned smart to get tossed in prison unwillingly.

Would he let me take the fall? I mean, everything sprung from my involvement in Mario's death. He'd have every right to.

When it comes down to it...

...is Newburn my friend?

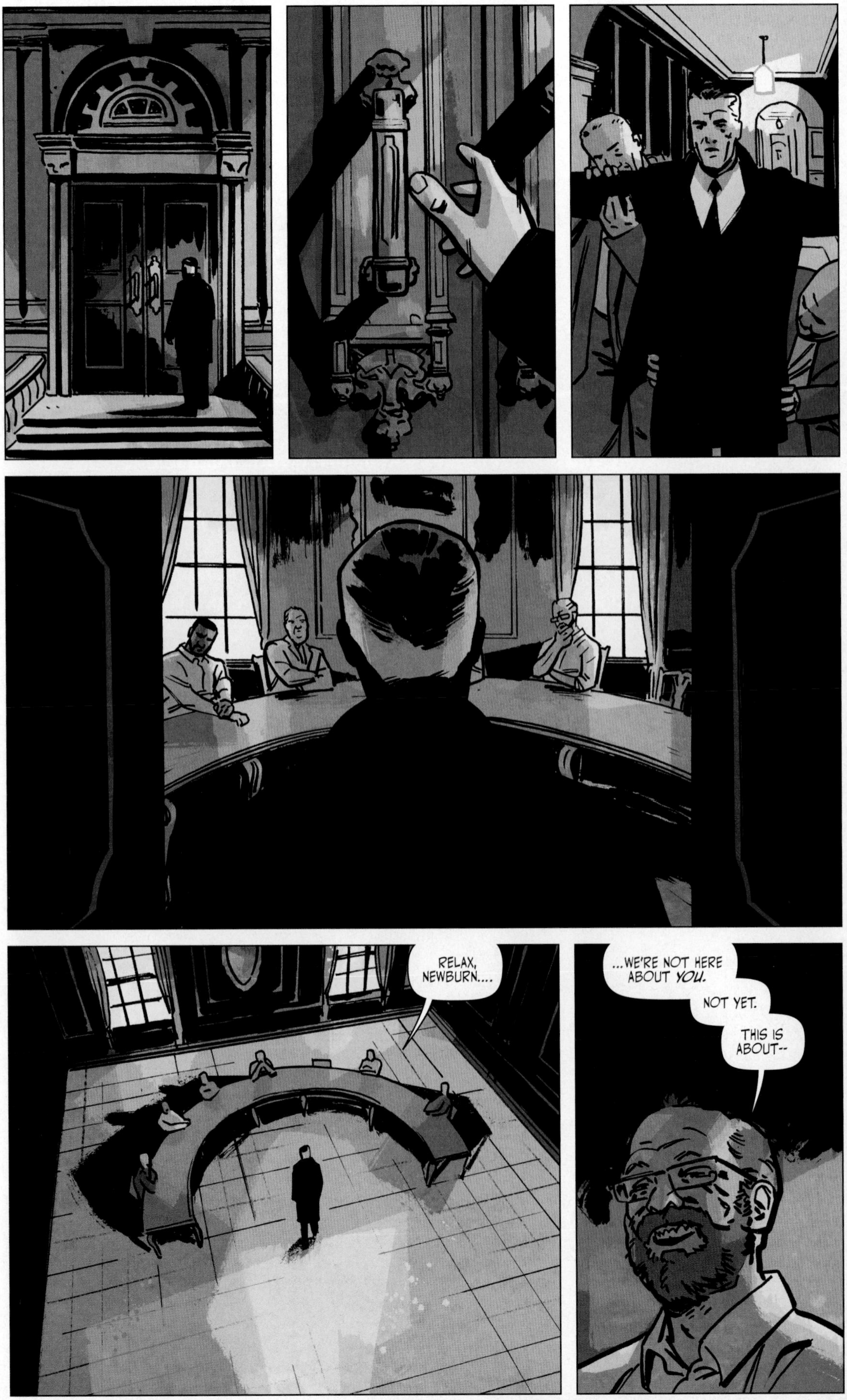
RELAX, NEWBURN....
...WE'RE NOT HERE ABOUT *YOU.*
NOT YET.
THIS IS ABOUT--

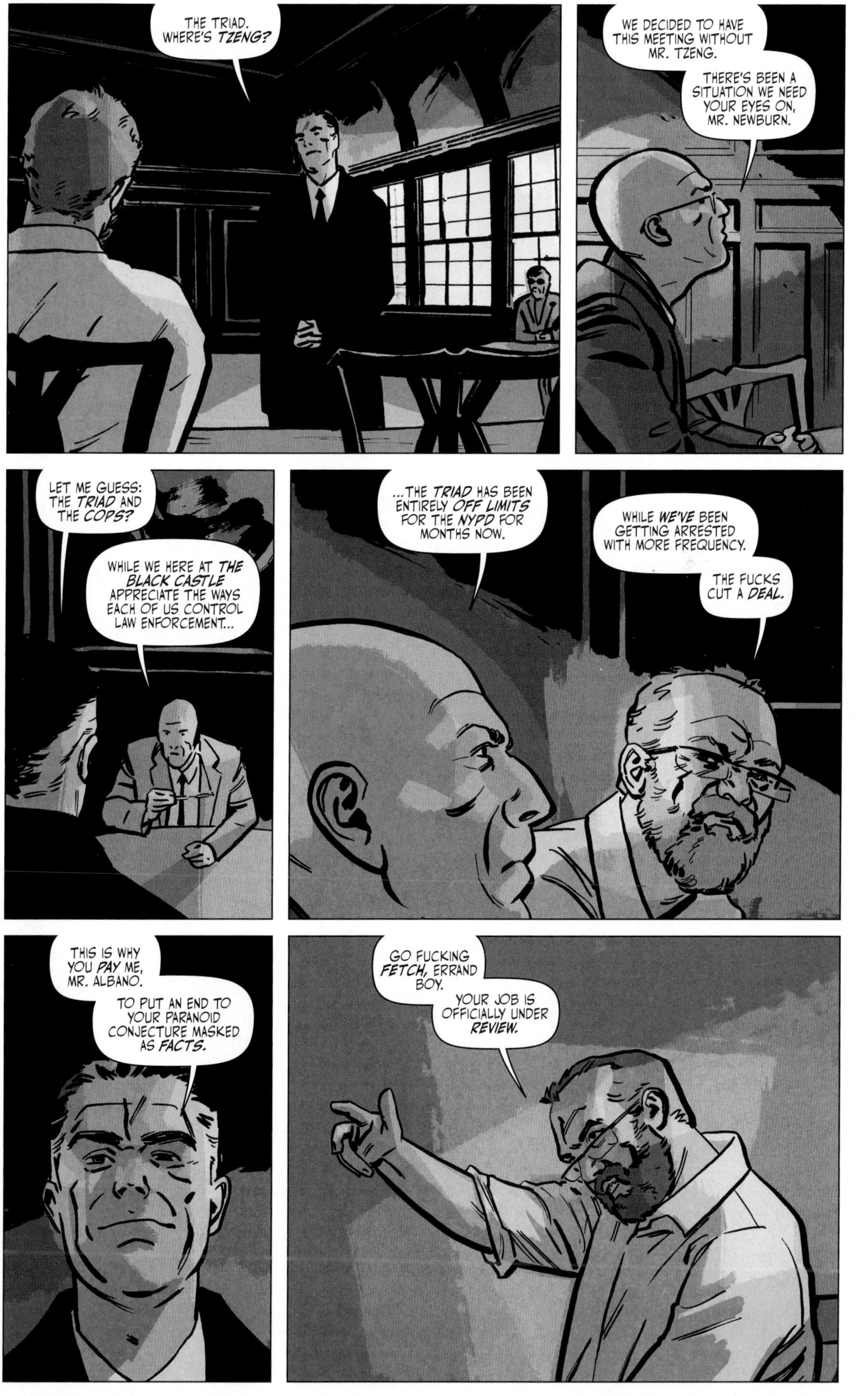
THE TRIAD. WHERE'S TZENG?
WE DECIDED TO HAVE THIS MEETING WITHOUT MR. TZENG.
THERE'S BEEN A SITUATION WE NEED YOUR EYES ON, MR. NEWBURN.
LET ME GUESS: THE TRIAD AND THE COPS?
WHILE WE HERE AT THE BLACK CASTLE APPRECIATE THE WAYS EACH OF US CONTROL LAW ENFORCEMENT...
...THE TRIAD HAS BEEN ENTIRELY OFF LIMITS FOR THE NYPD FOR MONTHS NOW.
WHILE WE'VE BEEN GETTING ARRESTED WITH MORE FREQUENCY.
THE FUCKS CUT A DEAL.
THIS IS WHY YOU PAY ME, MR. ALBANO.
TO PUT AN END TO YOUR PARANOID CONJECTURE MASKED AS FACTS.
GO FUCKING FETCH, ERRAND BOY.
YOUR JOB IS OFFICIALLY UNDER REVIEW.

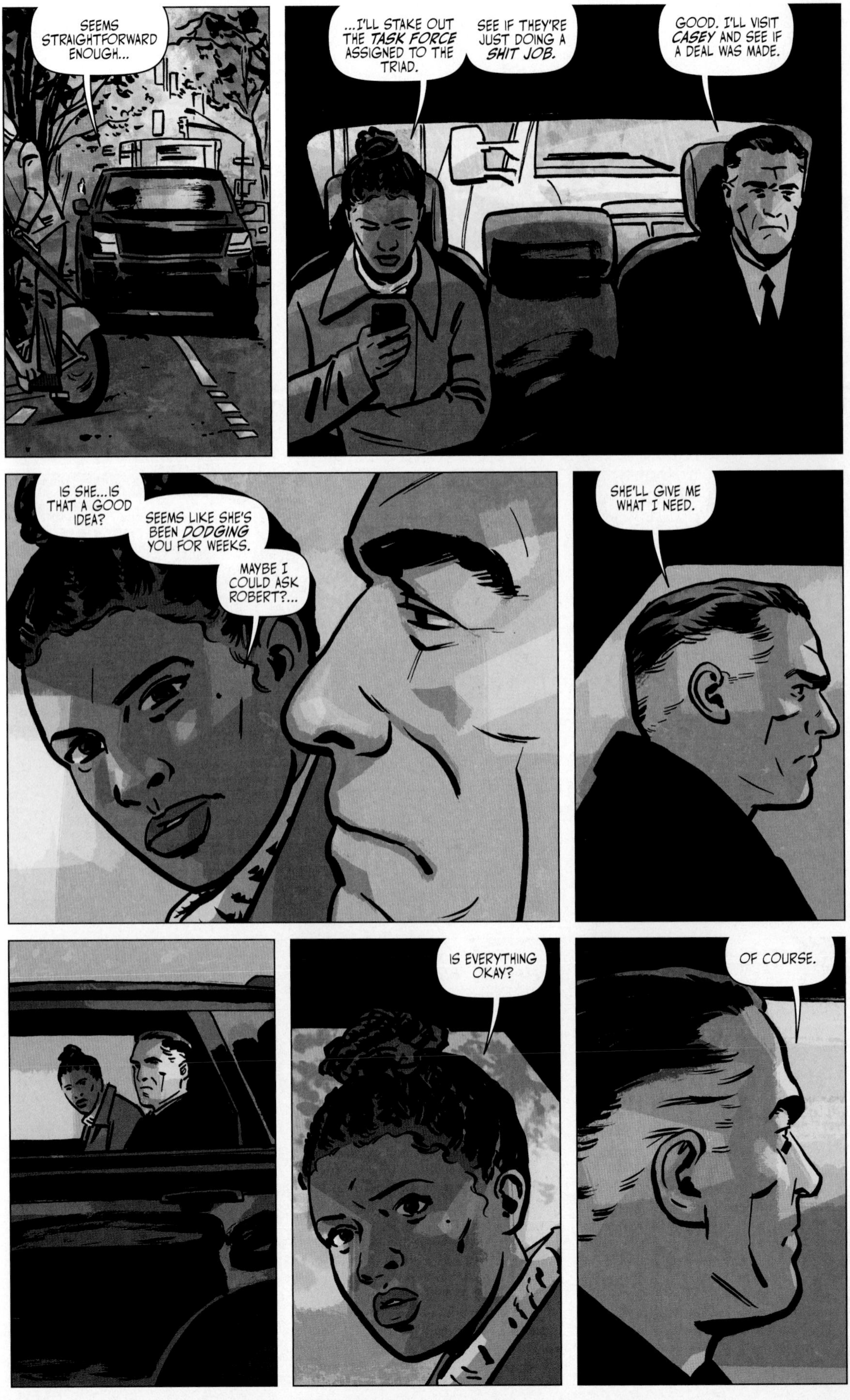
SEEMS STRAIGHTFORWARD ENOUGH...
...I'LL STAKE OUT THE TASK FORCE ASSIGNED TO THE TRIAD.
SEE IF THEY'RE JUST DOING A SHIT JOB.
GOOD. I'LL VISIT CASEY AND SEE IF A DEAL WAS MADE.
IS SHE...IS THAT A GOOD IDEA?
SEEMS LIKE SHE'S BEEN DODGING YOU FOR WEEKS.
MAYBE I COULD ASK ROBERT?...
SHE'LL GIVE ME WHAT I NEED.
IS EVERYTHING OKAY?
OF COURSE.

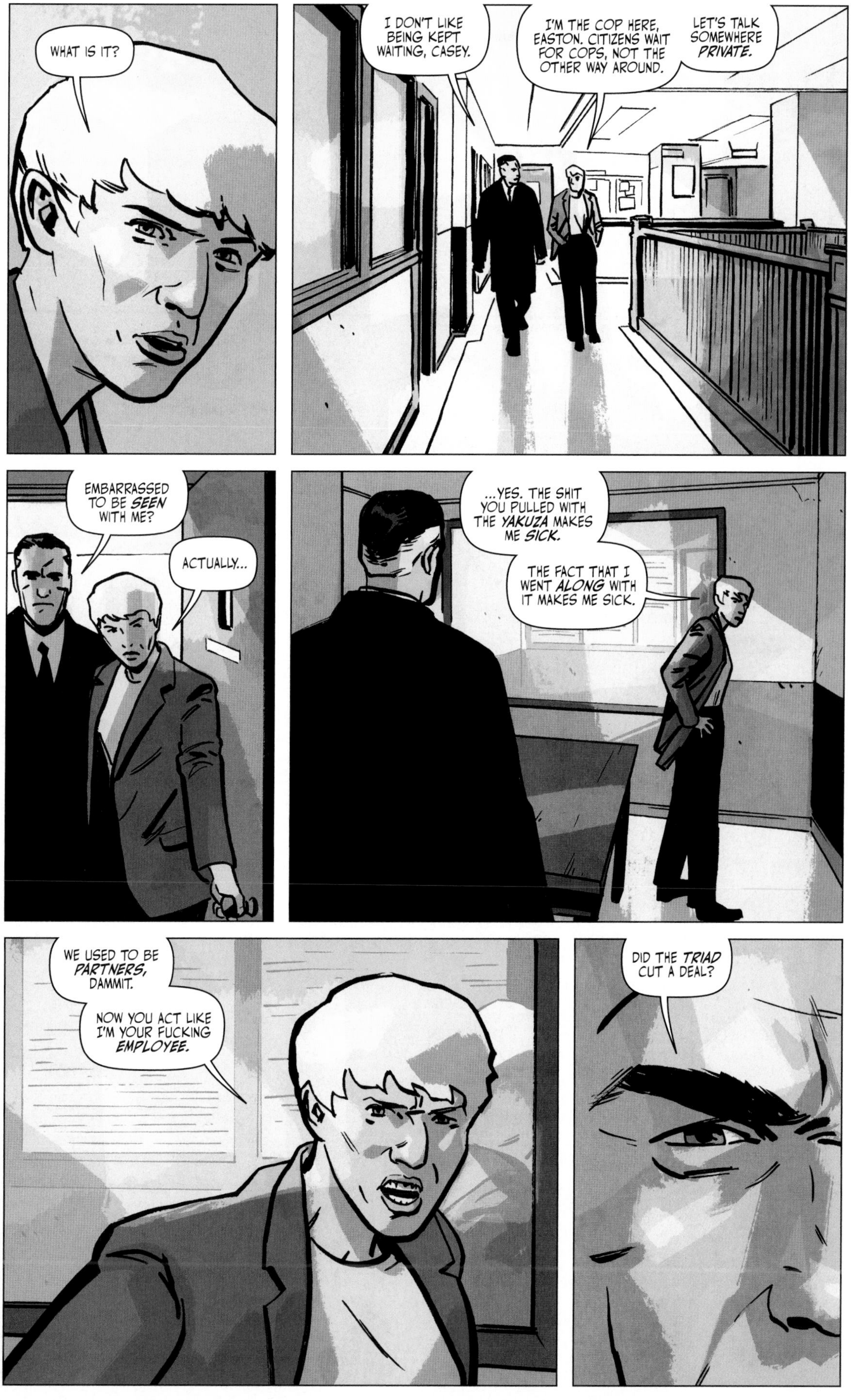
WHAT IS IT?
I DON'T LIKE BEING KEPT WAITING, CASEY.
I'M THE COP HERE, EASTON. CITIZENS WAIT FOR COPS, NOT THE OTHER WAY AROUND.
LET'S TALK SOMEWHERE *PRIVATE.*
EMBARRASSED TO BE *SEEN* WITH ME?
ACTUALLY...
...YES. THE SHIT YOU PULLED WITH THE *YAKUZA* MAKES ME *SICK.*
THE FACT THAT I WENT *ALONG* WITH IT MAKES ME SICK.
WE USED TO BE *PARTNERS,* DAMMIT.
NOW YOU ACT LIKE I'M YOUR FUCKING *EMPLOYEE.*
DID THE *TRIAD* CUT A DEAL?

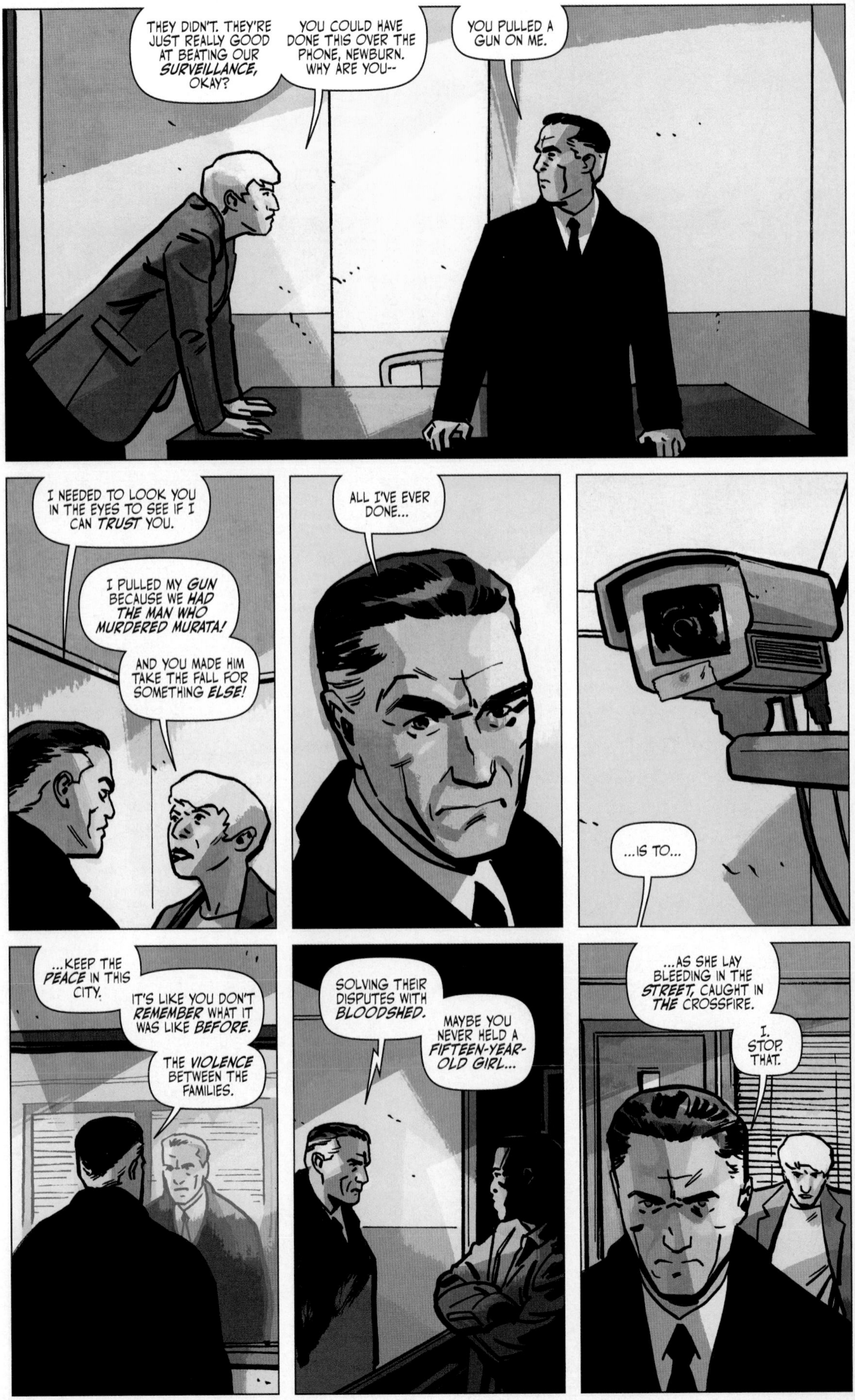
THEY DIDN'T. THEY'RE JUST REALLY GOOD AT BEATING OUR *SURVEILLANCE,* OKAY?
YOU COULD HAVE DONE THIS OVER THE PHONE, NEWBURN. WHY ARE YOU--
YOU PULLED A GUN ON ME.
I NEEDED TO LOOK YOU IN THE EYES TO SEE IF I CAN *TRUST* YOU.
I PULLED MY *GUN* BECAUSE WE *HAD THE MAN WHO MURDERED MURATA!*
AND YOU MADE HIM TAKE THE FALL FOR SOMETHING *ELSE!*
ALL I'VE EVER DONE...
...IS TO...
...KEEP THE *PEACE* IN THIS CITY.
IT'S LIKE YOU DON'T *REMEMBER* WHAT IT WAS LIKE *BEFORE.*
THE *VIOLENCE* BETWEEN THE FAMILIES.
SOLVING THEIR DISPUTES WITH *BLOODSHED.*
MAYBE YOU NEVER HELD A *FIFTEEN-YEAR-OLD GIRL...*
...AS SHE LAY BLEEDING IN THE *STREET,* CAUGHT IN *THE* CROSSFIRE.
I. STOP. THAT.

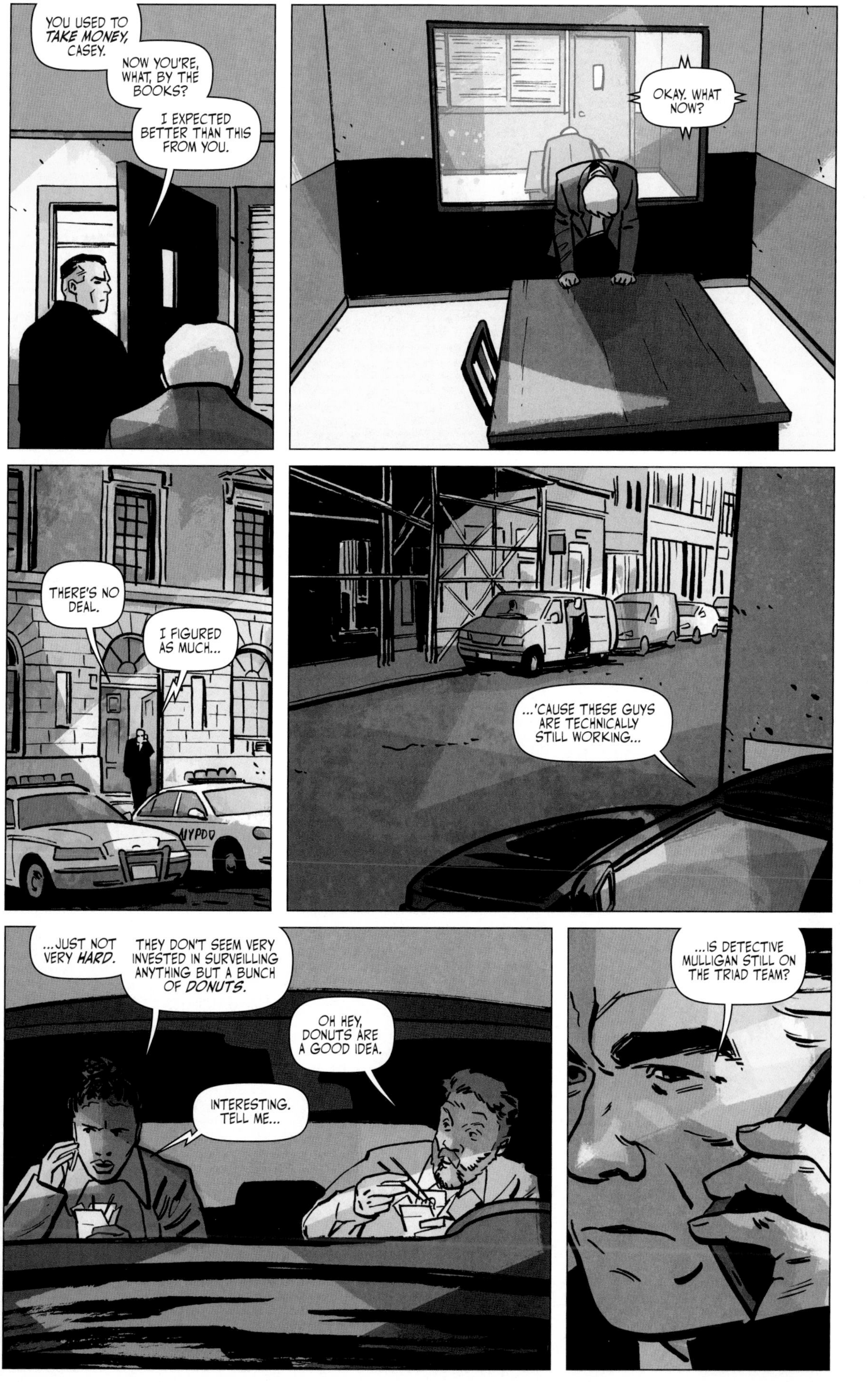
YOU USED TO TAKE MONEY, CASEY.
NOW YOU'RE, WHAT, BY THE BOOKS?
I EXPECTED BETTER THAN THIS FROM YOU.
OKAY. WHAT NOW?
THERE'S NO DEAL.
I FIGURED AS MUCH...
NYPD
...'CAUSE THESE GUYS ARE TECHNICALLY STILL WORKING...
...JUST NOT VERY HARD.
THEY DON'T SEEM VERY INVESTED IN SURVEILLING ANYTHING BUT A BUNCH OF DONUTS.
OH HEY, DONUTS ARE A GOOD IDEA.
INTERESTING. TELL ME...
...IS DETECTIVE MULLIGAN STILL ON THE TRIAD TEAM?

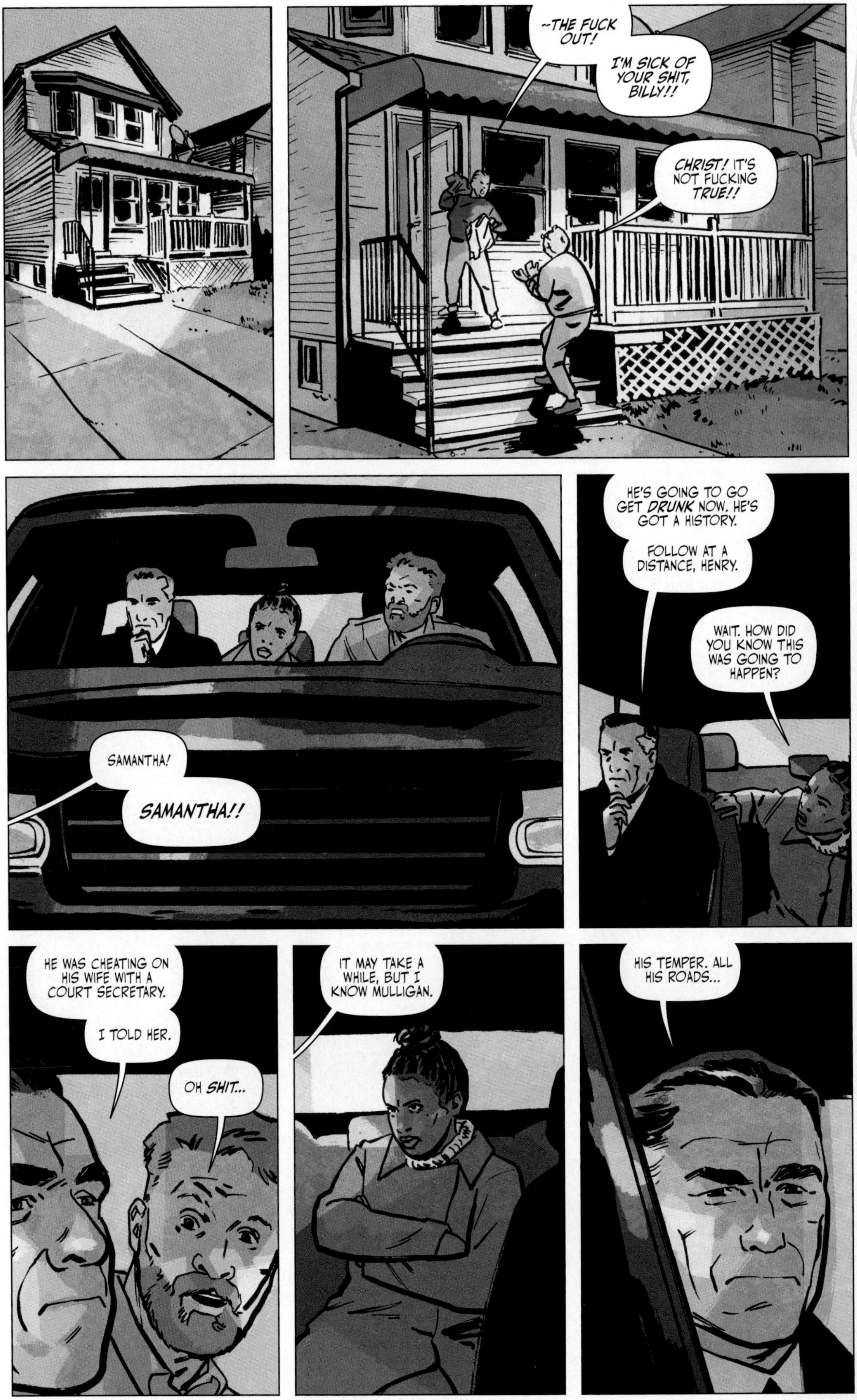
--THE FUCK OUT!
I'M SICK OF YOUR SHIT, BILLY!!
CHRIST! IT'S NOT FUCKING TRUE!!
SAMANTHA!
SAMANTHA!!
HE'S GOING TO GO GET DRUNK NOW. HE'S GOT A HISTORY.
FOLLOW AT A DISTANCE, HENRY.
WAIT. HOW DID YOU KNOW THIS WAS GOING TO HAPPEN?
HE WAS CHEATING ON HIS WIFE WITH A COURT SECRETARY.
I TOLD HER.
OH SHIT...
IT MAY TAKE A WHILE, BUT I KNOW MULLIGAN.
HIS TEMPER. ALL HIS ROADS...

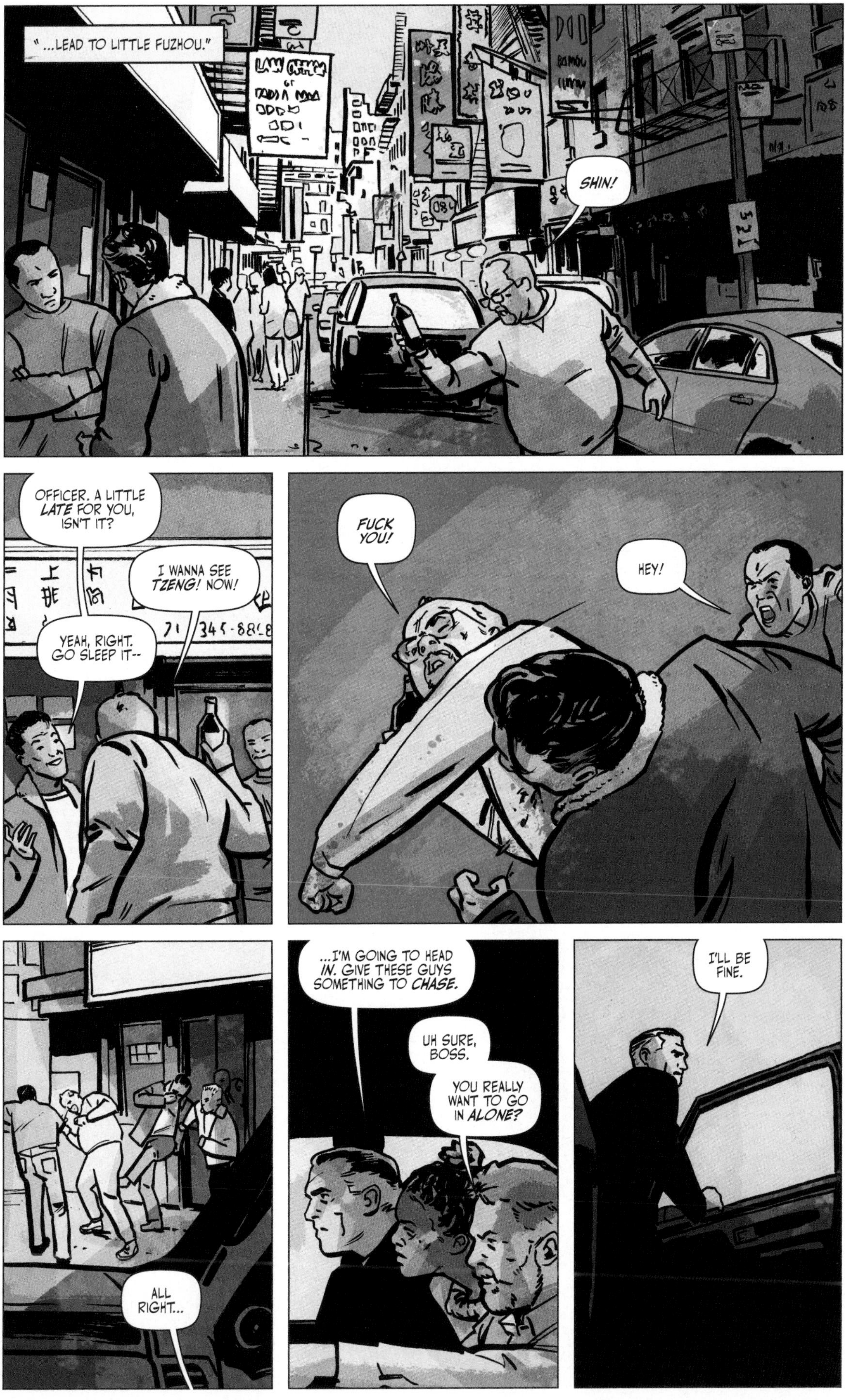

"...LEAD TO LITTLE FUZHOU."
SHIN!
OFFICER. A LITTLE LATE FOR YOU, ISN'T IT?
I WANNA SEE TZENG! NOW!
YEAH, RIGHT. GO SLEEP IT--
FUCK YOU!
HEY!
ALL RIGHT...
...I'M GOING TO HEAD IN. GIVE THESE GUYS SOMETHING TO CHASE.
UH SURE, BOSS.
YOU REALLY WANT TO GO IN ALONE?
I'LL BE FINE.

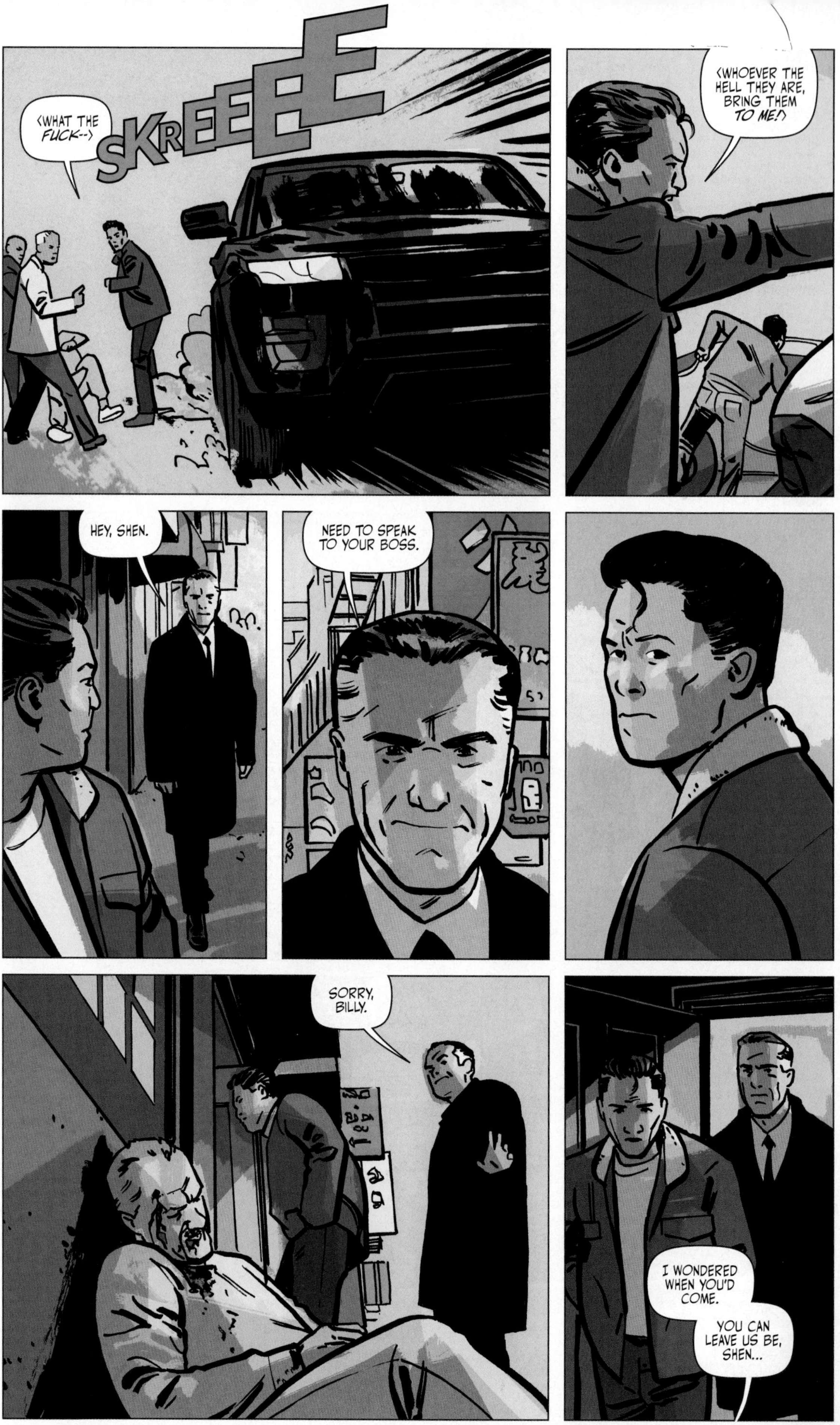

‹WHAT THE FUCK--›
SKREEEEE
‹WHOEVER THE HELL THEY ARE, BRING THEM TO ME!›
HEY, SHEN.
NEED TO SPEAK TO YOUR BOSS.
SORRY, BILLY.
I WONDERED WHEN YOU'D COME.
YOU CAN LEAVE US BE, SHEN...

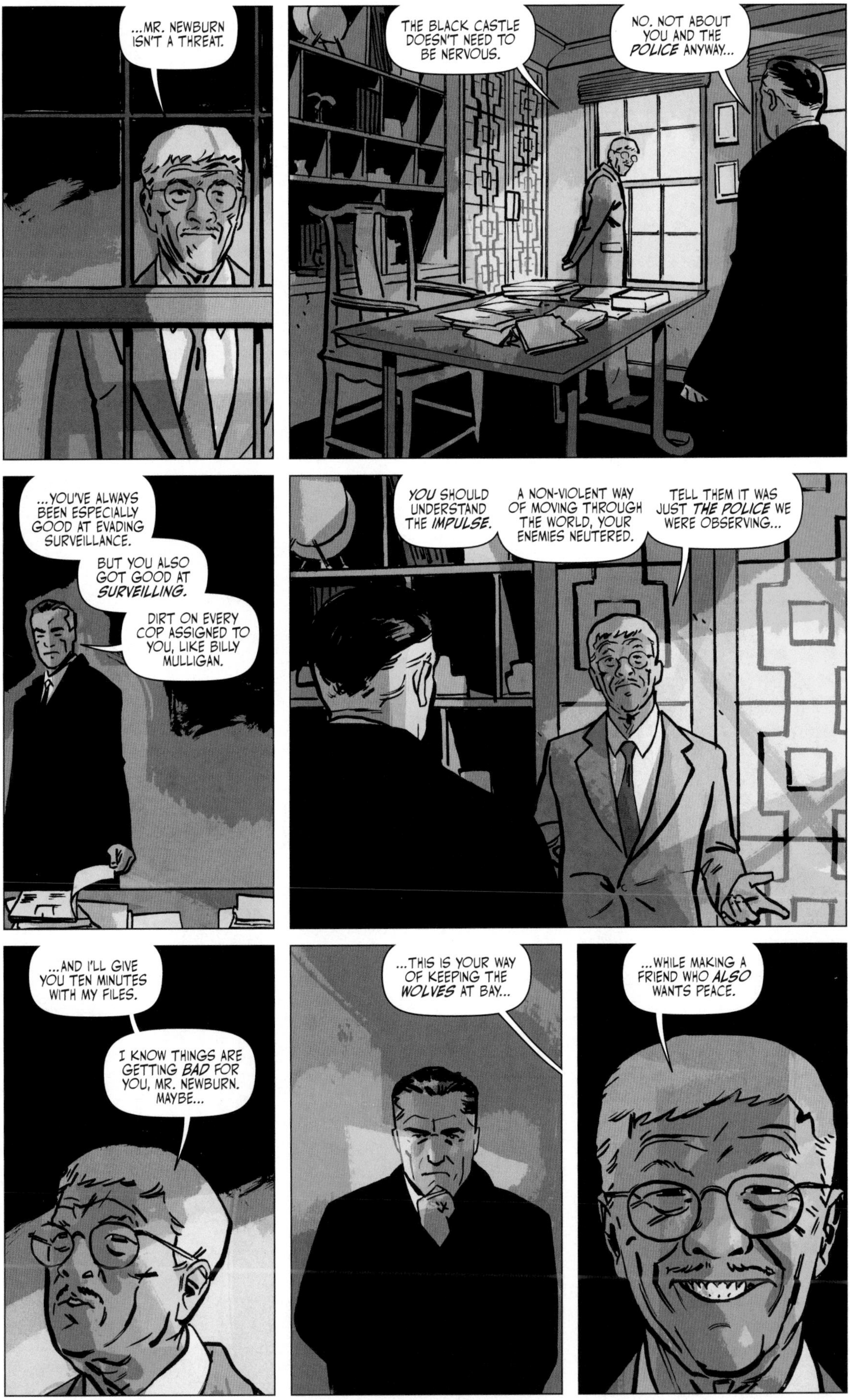
...MR. NEWBURN ISN'T A THREAT.
THE BLACK CASTLE DOESN'T NEED TO BE NERVOUS.
NO. NOT ABOUT YOU AND THE POLICE ANYWAY...
...YOU'VE ALWAYS BEEN ESPECIALLY GOOD AT EVADING SURVEILLANCE.
BUT YOU ALSO GOT GOOD AT SURVEILLING.
DIRT ON EVERY COP ASSIGNED TO YOU, LIKE BILLY MULLIGAN.
YOU SHOULD UNDERSTAND THE IMPULSE.
A NON-VIOLENT WAY OF MOVING THROUGH THE WORLD, YOUR ENEMIES NEUTERED.
TELL THEM IT WAS JUST THE POLICE WE WERE OBSERVING...
...AND I'LL GIVE YOU TEN MINUTES WITH MY FILES.
I KNOW THINGS ARE GETTING BAD FOR YOU, MR. NEWBURN. MAYBE...
...THIS IS YOUR WAY OF KEEPING THE WOLVES AT BAY...
...WHILE MAKING A FRIEND WHO ALSO WANTS PEACE.

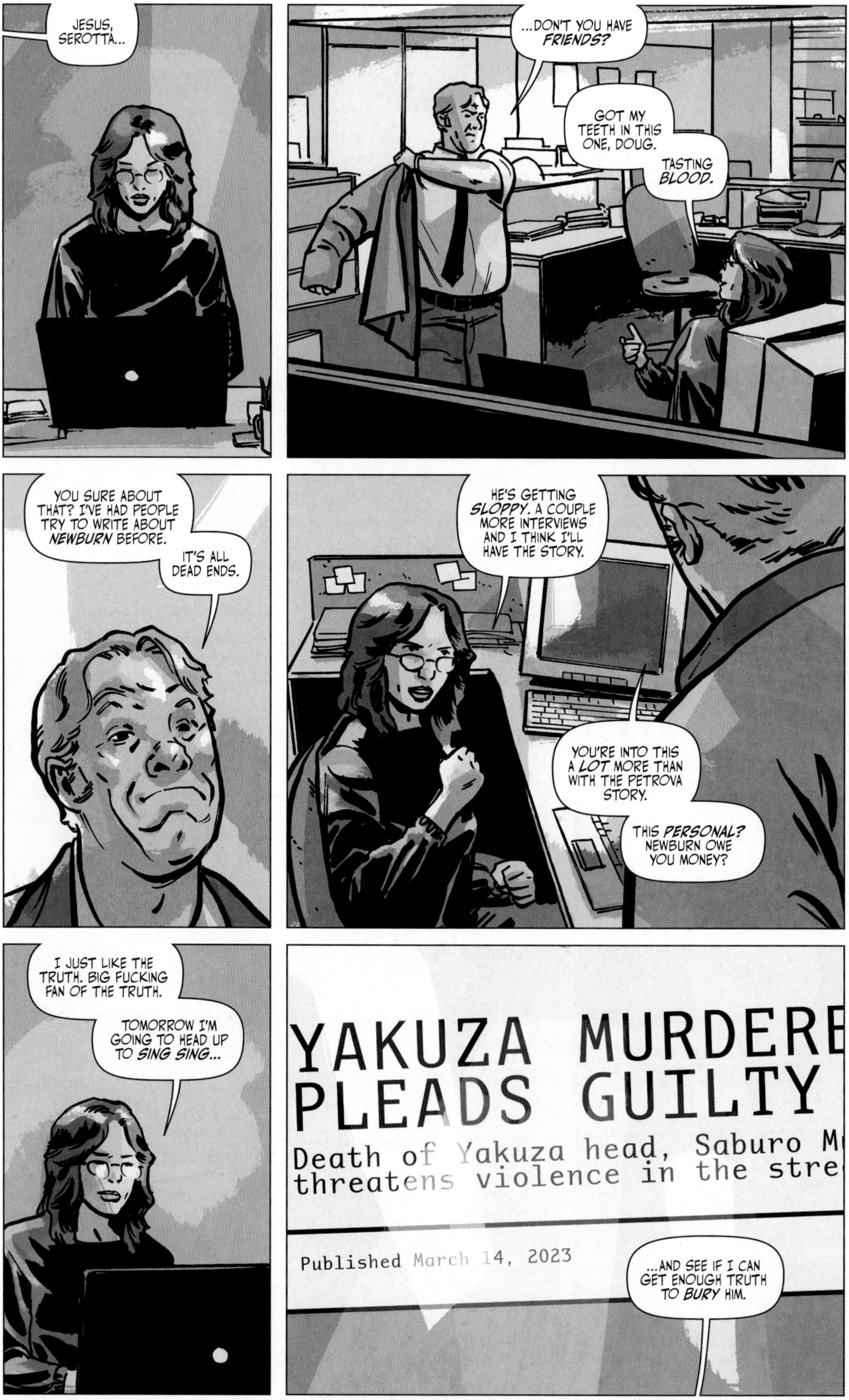

JESUS, SEROTTA...
...DON'T YOU HAVE FRIENDS?
GOT MY TEETH IN THIS ONE, DOUG.
TASTING BLOOD.
YOU SURE ABOUT THAT? I'VE HAD PEOPLE TRY TO WRITE ABOUT NEWBURN BEFORE.
IT'S ALL DEAD ENDS.
HE'S GETTING SLOPPY. A COUPLE MORE INTERVIEWS AND I THINK I'LL HAVE THE STORY.
YOU'RE INTO THIS A LOT MORE THAN WITH THE PETROVA STORY.
THIS PERSONAL? NEWBURN OWE YOU MONEY?
I JUST LIKE THE TRUTH. BIG FUCKING FAN OF THE TRUTH.
TOMORROW I'M GOING TO HEAD UP TO SING SING...
YAKUZA MURDERE
PLEADS GUILTY
Death of Yakuza head, Saburo M
threatens violence in the stre
Published March 14, 2023
...AND SEE IF I CAN GET ENOUGH TRUTH TO BURY HIM.

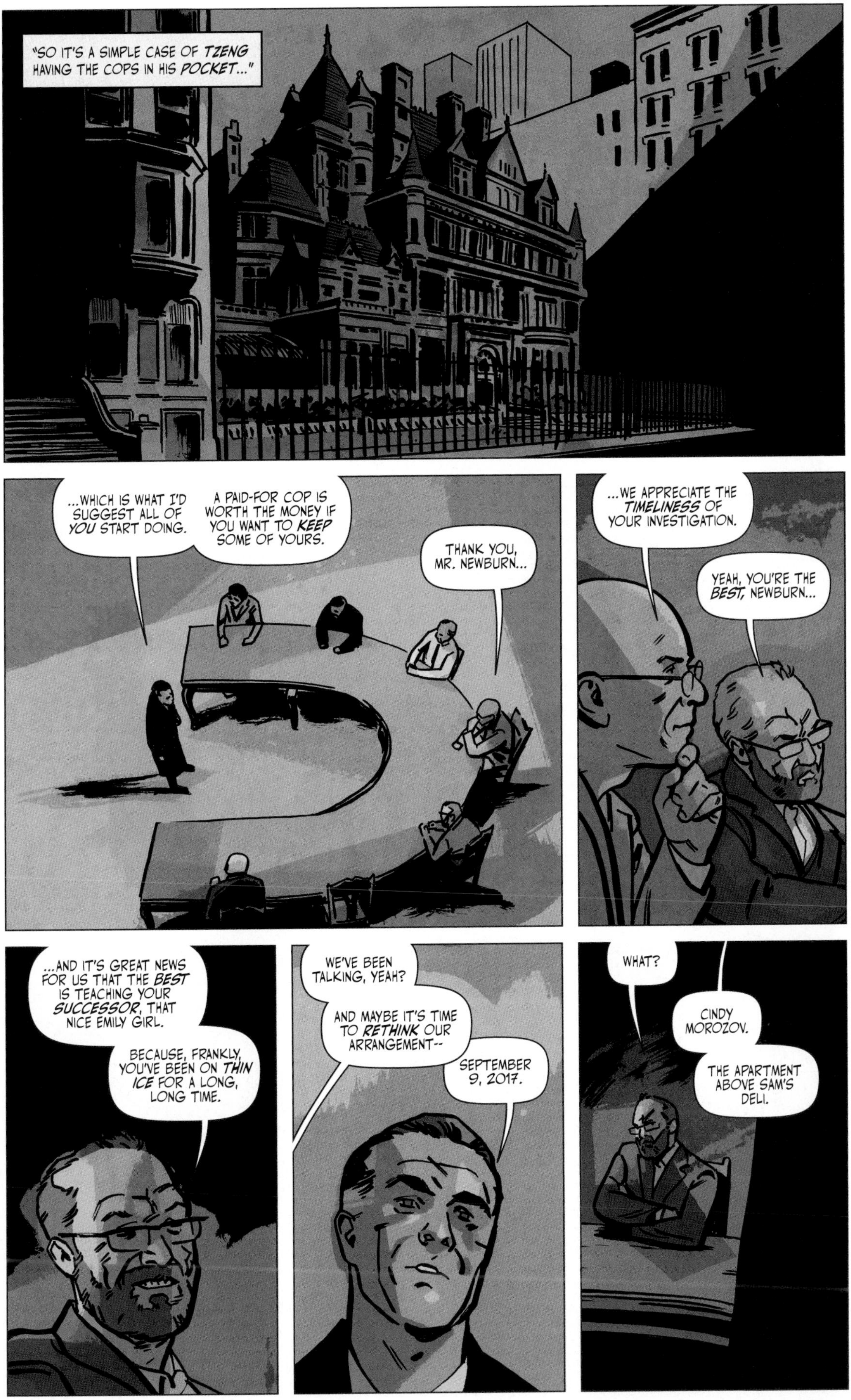
"SO IT'S A SIMPLE CASE OF TZENG HAVING THE COPS IN HIS POCKET..."
...WHICH IS WHAT I'D SUGGEST ALL OF YOU START DOING.
A PAID-FOR COP IS WORTH THE MONEY IF YOU WANT TO KEEP SOME OF YOURS.
THANK YOU, MR. NEWBURN...
...WE APPRECIATE THE TIMELINESS OF YOUR INVESTIGATION.
YEAH, YOU'RE THE BEST, NEWBURN...
...AND IT'S GREAT NEWS FOR US THAT THE BEST IS TEACHING YOUR SUCCESSOR, THAT NICE EMILY GIRL.
BECAUSE, FRANKLY, YOU'VE BEEN ON THIN ICE FOR A LONG, LONG TIME.
WE'VE BEEN TALKING, YEAH?
AND MAYBE IT'S TIME TO RETHINK OUR ARRANGEMENT--
SEPTEMBER 9, 2017.
WHAT?
CINDY MOROZOV.
THE APARTMENT ABOVE SAM'S DELI.

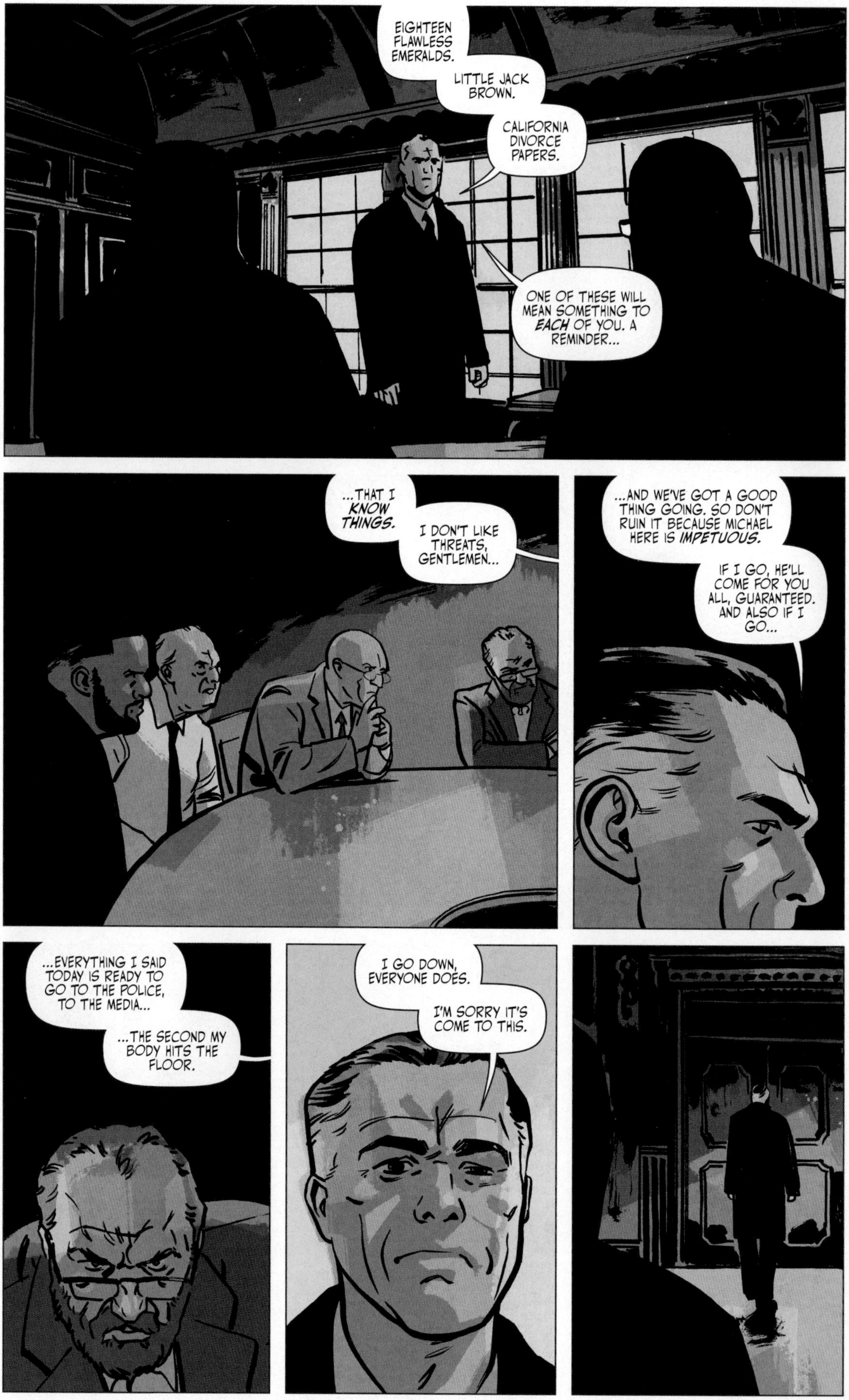
EIGHTEEN FLAWLESS EMERALDS.
LITTLE JACK BROWN.
CALIFORNIA DIVORCE PAPERS.
ONE OF THESE WILL MEAN SOMETHING TO *EACH* OF YOU. A REMINDER...
...THAT I *KNOW THINGS.*
I DON'T LIKE THREATS, GENTLEMEN...
...AND WE'VE GOT A GOOD THING GOING. SO DON'T RUIN IT BECAUSE MICHAEL HERE IS *IMPETUOUS.*
IF I GO, HE'LL COME FOR YOU ALL, GUARANTEED. AND ALSO IF I GO...
...EVERYTHING I SAID TODAY IS READY TO GO TO THE POLICE, TO THE MEDIA...
...THE SECOND MY BODY HITS THE FLOOR.
I GO DOWN, EVERYONE DOES.
I'M SORRY IT'S COME TO THIS.

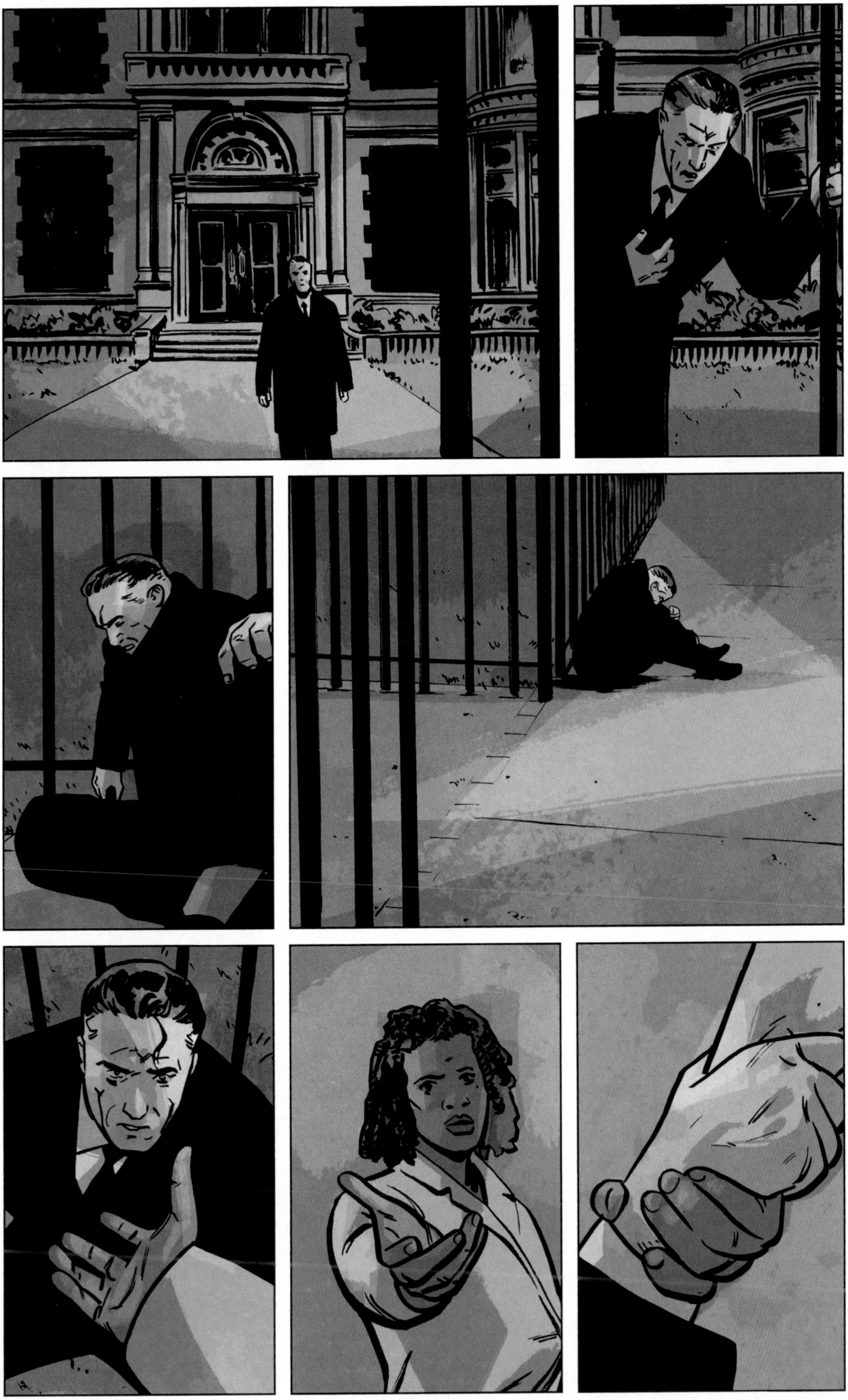

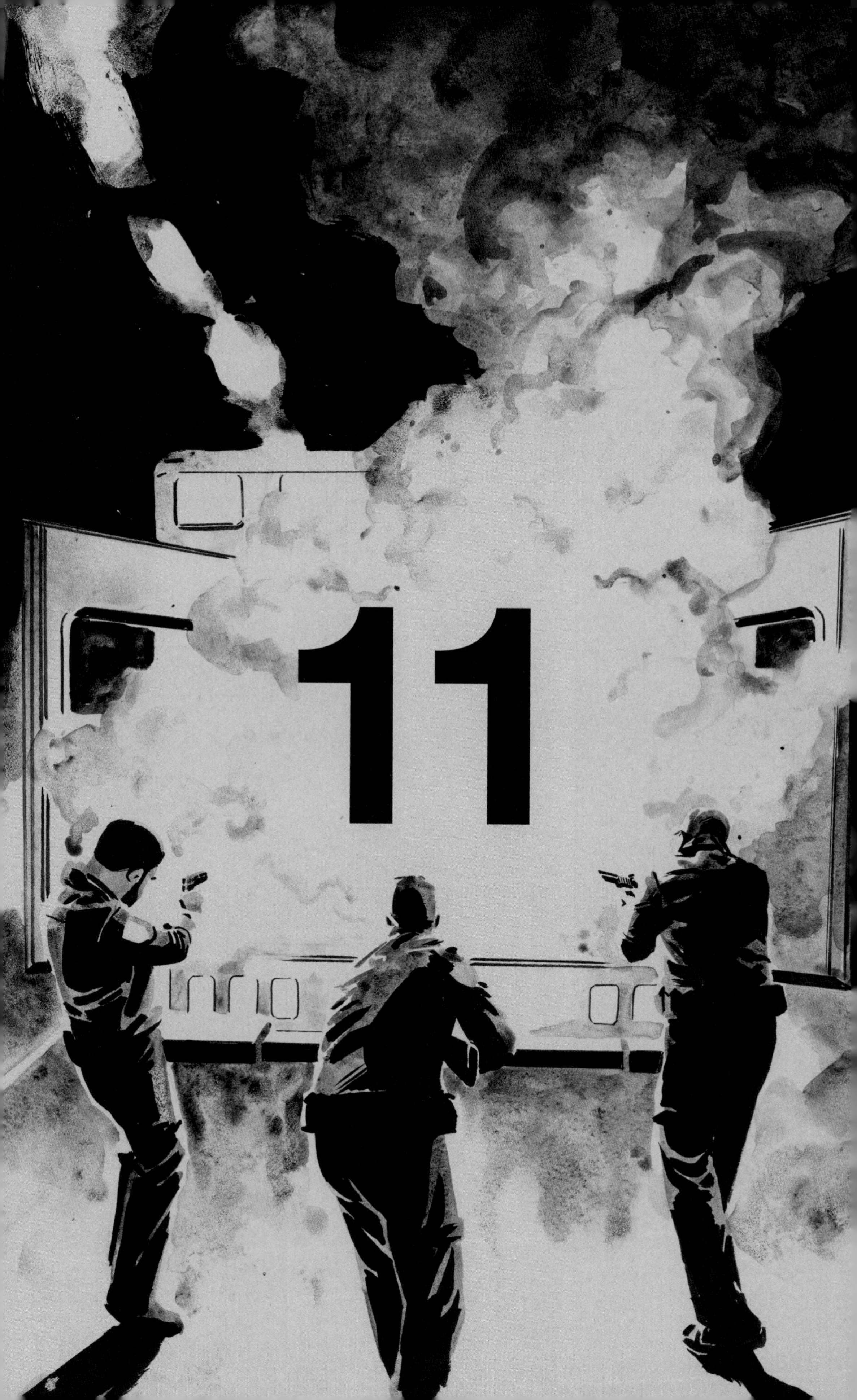
11

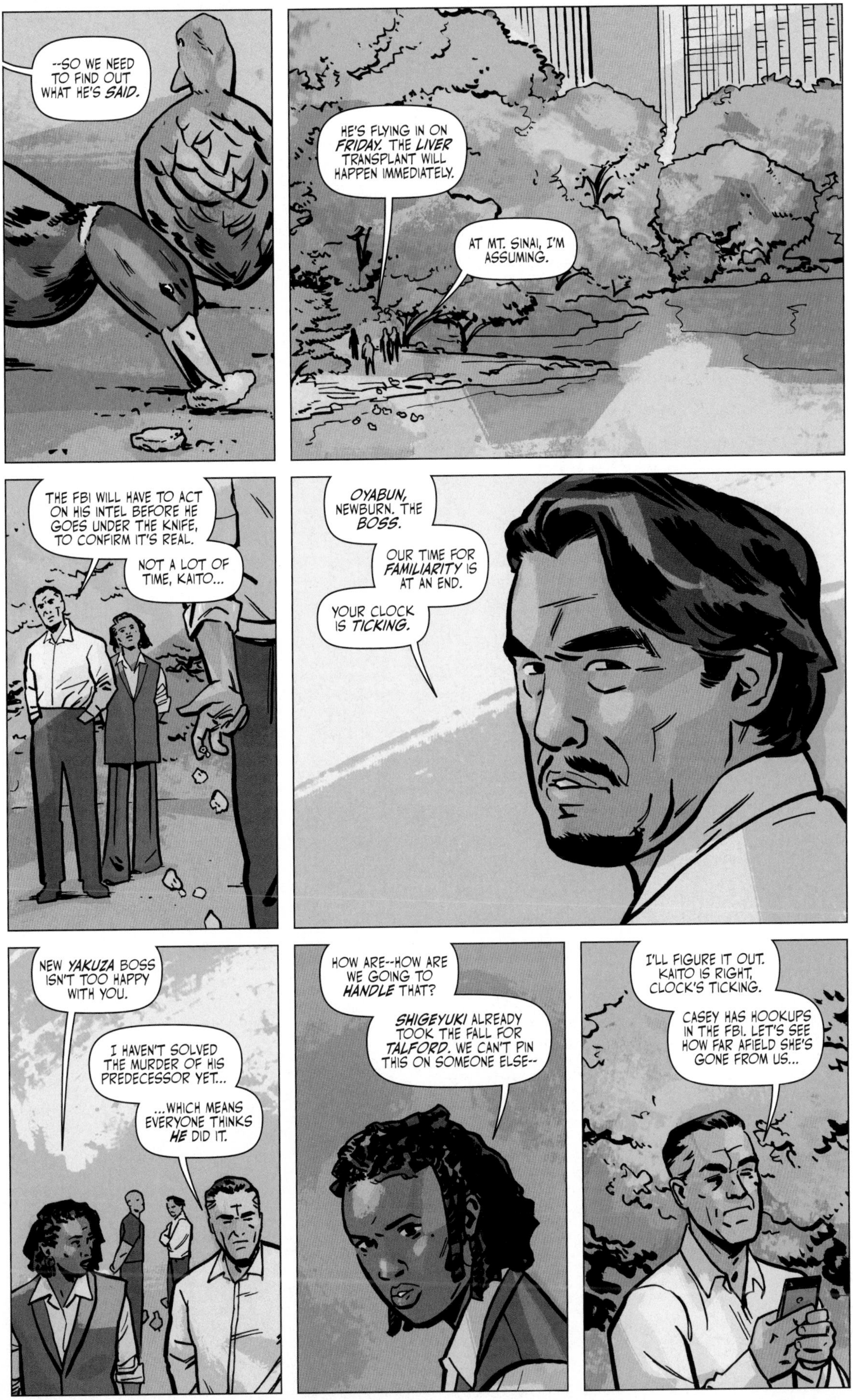
--SO WE NEED TO FIND OUT WHAT HE'S SAID.
HE'S FLYING IN ON FRIDAY. THE LIVER TRANSPLANT WILL HAPPEN IMMEDIATELY.
AT MT. SINAI, I'M ASSUMING.
THE FBI WILL HAVE TO ACT ON HIS INTEL BEFORE HE GOES UNDER THE KNIFE, TO CONFIRM IT'S REAL.
NOT A LOT OF TIME, KAITO...
OYABUN, NEWBURN. THE BOSS.
OUR TIME FOR FAMILIARITY IS AT AN END.
YOUR CLOCK IS TICKING.
NEW YAKUZA BOSS ISN'T TOO HAPPY WITH YOU.
I HAVEN'T SOLVED THE MURDER OF HIS PREDECESSOR YET...
...WHICH MEANS EVERYONE THINKS HE DID IT.
HOW ARE--HOW ARE WE GOING TO HANDLE THAT?
SHIGEYUKI ALREADY TOOK THE FALL FOR TALFORD. WE CAN'T PIN THIS ON SOMEONE ELSE--
I'LL FIGURE IT OUT. KAITO IS RIGHT, CLOCK'S TICKING.
CASEY HAS HOOKUPS IN THE FBI. LET'S SEE HOW FAR AFIELD SHE'S GONE FROM US...

EMILY'S JOURNAL
09/12/22

It's a new day for the New York Yakuza: Kaito Watanabe is the boss. But how can you be boss when your predecessor's murder hasn't been solved yet? How do you lead your people when they all suspect you?

We're supposed to be solving it, but we already know who did it: Shigeyuki Shiroo, who we sent down the river for the murder of Mario Albano.

Newburn is supposed to be the best. How long can he go without solving this murder before Kaito comes for us?

Maybe we can buy some time with this case.

Kiyoshi Kajiyama is an important member of the Tokyo Yakuza and his liver is failing. He's coming to America to receive a new one, but the only way that could happen is if he talked to the Feds to get a special visa deal. Which means he traded information, more than likely on the Yakuza's U.S. operations.

We need to find out what he's traded before the operation.

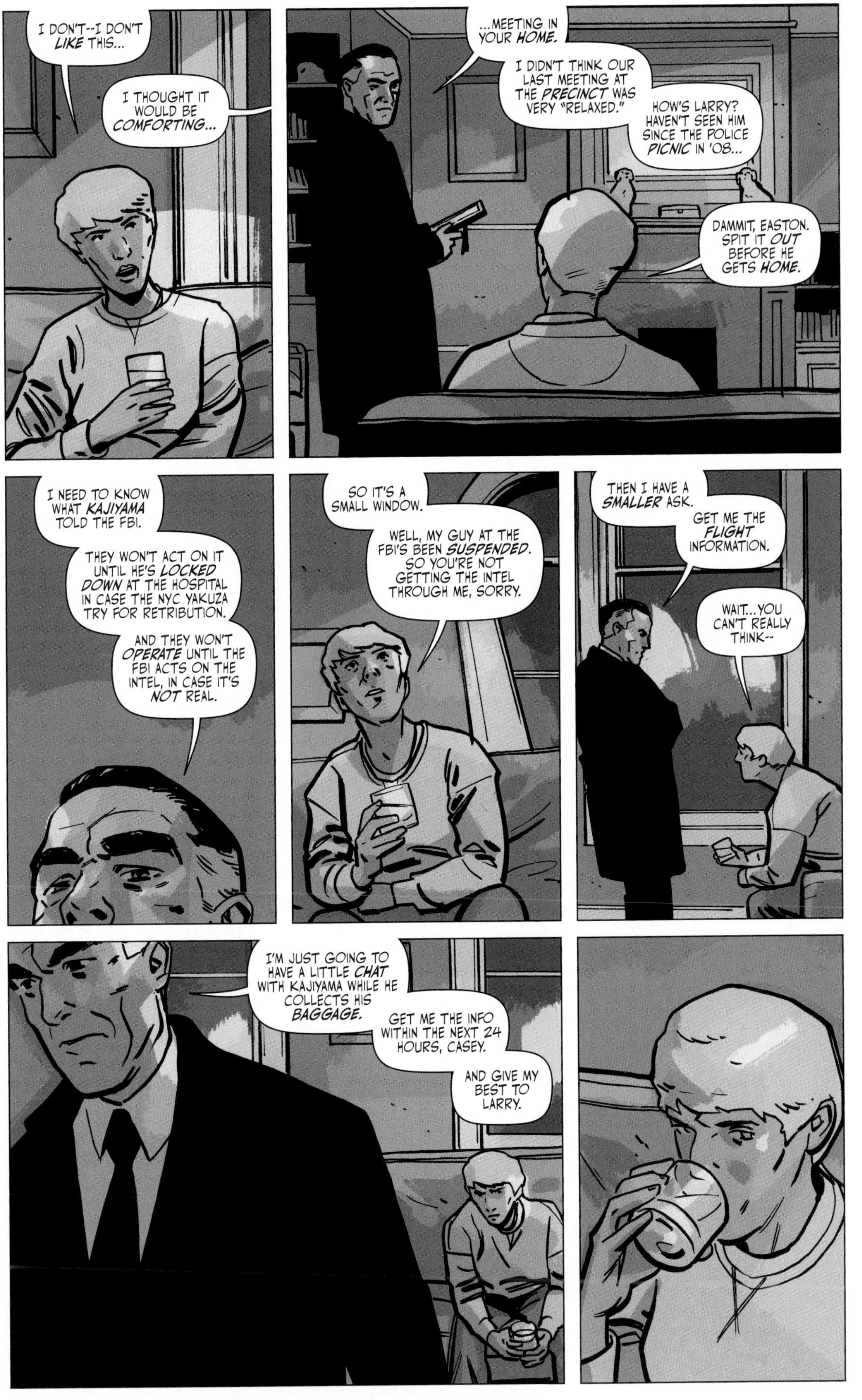

I DON'T--I DON'T LIKE THIS...
...MEETING IN YOUR HOME.
I THOUGHT IT WOULD BE COMFORTING...
I DIDN'T THINK OUR LAST MEETING AT THE PRECINCT WAS VERY "RELAXED."
HOW'S LARRY? HAVEN'T SEEN HIM SINCE THE POLICE PICNIC IN '08...
DAMMIT, EASTON. SPIT IT OUT BEFORE HE GETS HOME.
I NEED TO KNOW WHAT KAJIYAMA TOLD THE FBI.
THEY WON'T ACT ON IT UNTIL HE'S LOCKED DOWN AT THE HOSPITAL IN CASE THE NYC YAKUZA TRY FOR RETRIBUTION.
AND THEY WON'T OPERATE UNTIL THE FBI ACTS ON THE INTEL, IN CASE IT'S NOT REAL.
SO IT'S A SMALL WINDOW.
WELL, MY GUY AT THE FBI'S BEEN SUSPENDED. SO YOU'RE NOT GETTING THE INTEL THROUGH ME, SORRY.
THEN I HAVE A SMALLER ASK.
GET ME THE FLIGHT INFORMATION.
WAIT...YOU CAN'T REALLY THINK--
I'M JUST GOING TO HAVE A LITTLE CHAT WITH KAJIYAMA WHILE HE COLLECTS HIS BAGGAGE.
GET ME THE INFO WITHIN THE NEXT 24 HOURS, CASEY.
AND GIVE MY BEST TO LARRY.

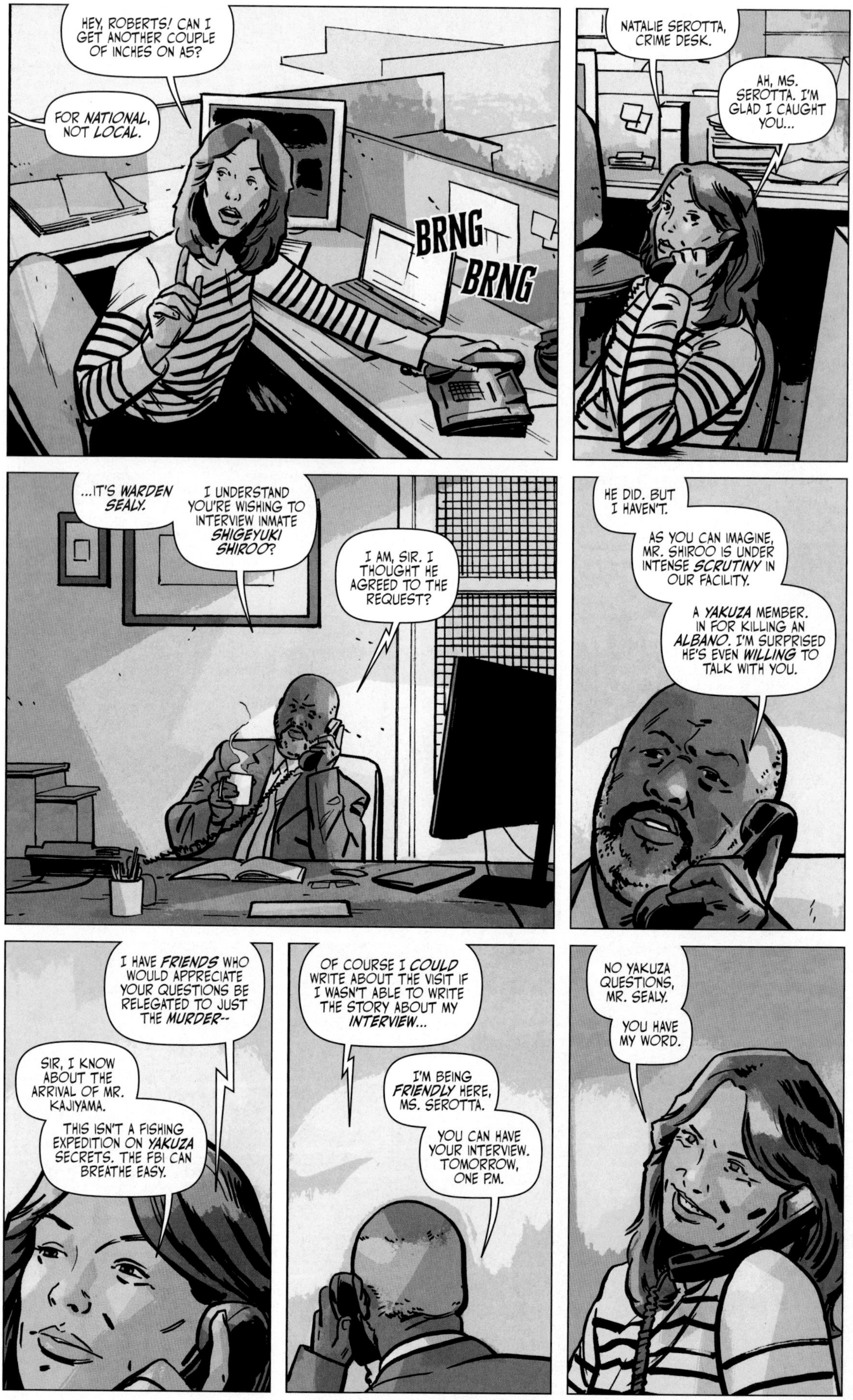
HEY, ROBERTS! CAN I GET ANOTHER COUPLE OF INCHES ON A5?
FOR NATIONAL, NOT LOCAL.
BRNG
BRNG
NATALIE SEROTTA, CRIME DESK.
AH, MS. SEROTTA. I'M GLAD I CAUGHT YOU...
...IT'S WARDEN SEALY.
I UNDERSTAND YOU'RE WISHING TO INTERVIEW INMATE SHIGEYUKI SHIROO?
I AM, SIR. I THOUGHT HE AGREED TO THE REQUEST?
HE DID. BUT I HAVEN'T.
AS YOU CAN IMAGINE, MR. SHIROO IS UNDER INTENSE SCRUTINY IN OUR FACILITY.
A YAKUZA MEMBER. IN FOR KILLING AN ALBANO. I'M SURPRISED HE'S EVEN WILLING TO TALK WITH YOU.
I HAVE FRIENDS WHO WOULD APPRECIATE YOUR QUESTIONS BE RELEGATED TO JUST THE MURDER--
SIR, I KNOW ABOUT THE ARRIVAL OF MR. KAJIYAMA.
THIS ISN'T A FISHING EXPEDITION ON YAKUZA SECRETS. THE FBI CAN BREATHE EASY.
OF COURSE I COULD WRITE ABOUT THE VISIT IF I WASN'T ABLE TO WRITE THE STORY ABOUT MY INTERVIEW...
I'M BEING FRIENDLY HERE, MS. SEROTTA.
YOU CAN HAVE YOUR INTERVIEW. TOMORROW, ONE P.M.
NO YAKUZA QUESTIONS, MR. SEALY.
YOU HAVE MY WORD.

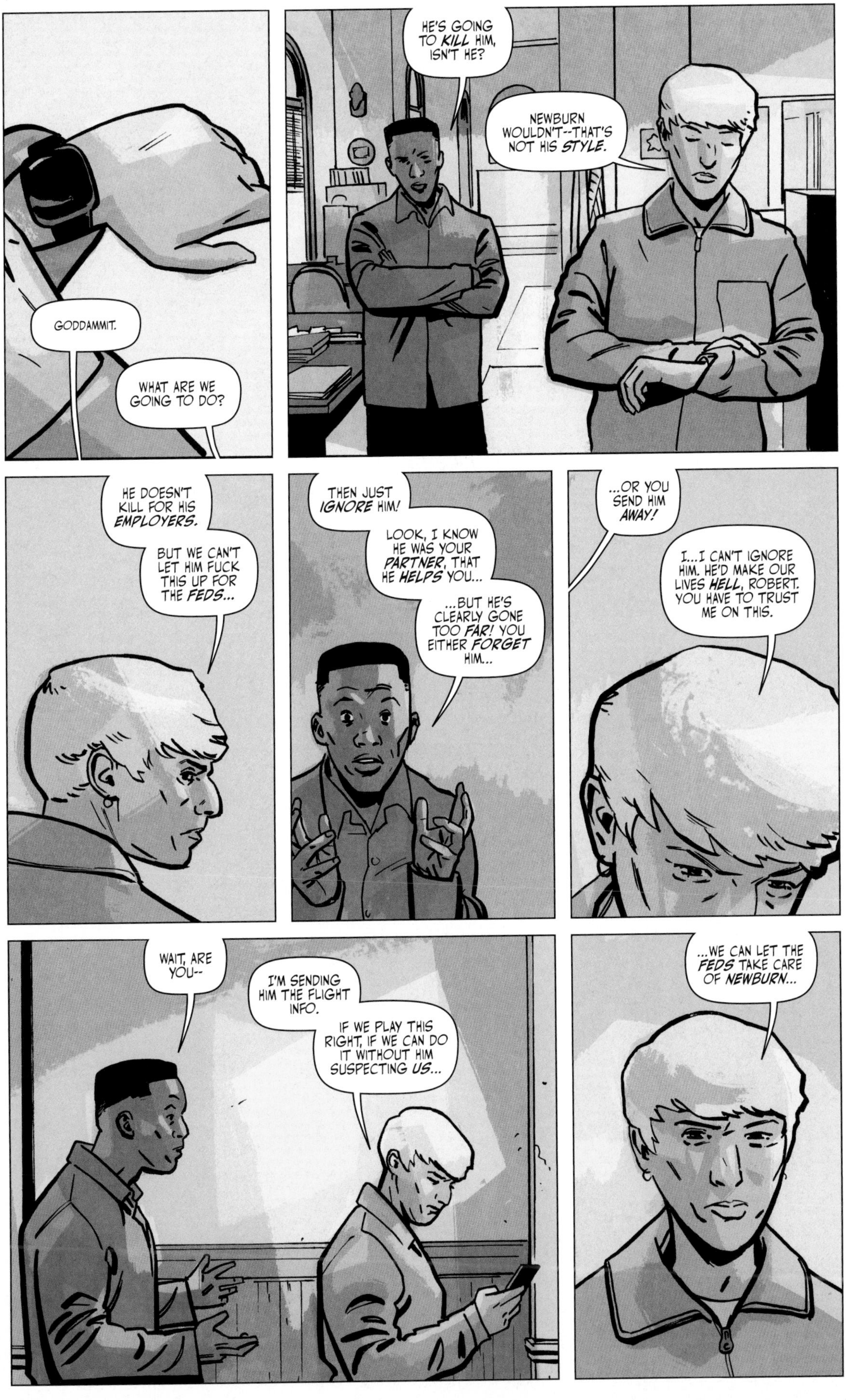
GODDAMMIT.
WHAT ARE WE GOING TO DO?
HE'S GOING TO KILL HIM, ISN'T HE?
NEWBURN WOULDN'T--THAT'S NOT HIS STYLE.
HE DOESN'T KILL FOR HIS EMPLOYERS.
BUT WE CAN'T LET HIM FUCK THIS UP FOR THE FEDS...
THEN JUST IGNORE HIM!
LOOK, I KNOW HE WAS YOUR PARTNER, THAT HE HELPS YOU...
...BUT HE'S CLEARLY GONE TOO FAR! YOU EITHER FORGET HIM...
...OR YOU SEND HIM AWAY!
I...I CAN'T IGNORE HIM. HE'D MAKE OUR LIVES HELL, ROBERT. YOU HAVE TO TRUST ME ON THIS.
WAIT, ARE YOU--
I'M SENDING HIM THE FLIGHT INFO.
IF WE PLAY THIS RIGHT, IF WE CAN DO IT WITHOUT HIM SUSPECTING US...
...WE CAN LET THE FEDS TAKE CARE OF NEWBURN...

EMILY'S JOURNAL
09/14/22

We need friends more than ever.

Newburn and his former police partner, Casey, are on the outs. I'm still piecing it together, but there was a confrontation over what to do about the Yakuza murder. And it seems like Newburn put Casey in her place over it.

It's a quid pro quo relationship. She helps us, we help her. But I'm starting to suspect that she's not willing to pay that price anymore just for some career-boosting busts that we throw her.

I feel like we can deal with the Yakuza, with the Albanos. But if Casey turns on us and we have the full NYPD on our ass, it'll just be a matter of time before we're of little use to the crime families.

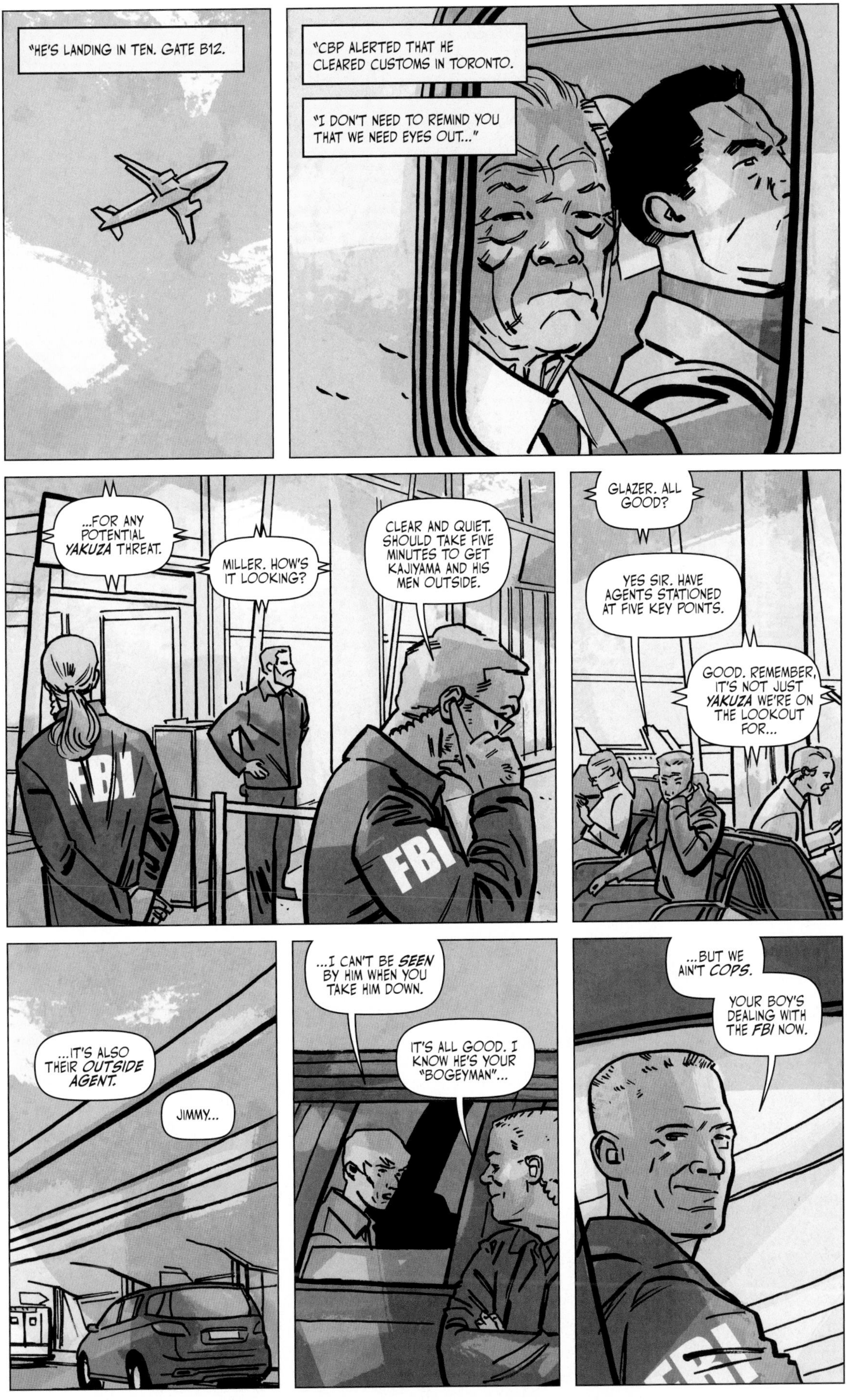
"HE'S LANDING IN TEN. GATE B12.
"CBP ALERTED THAT HE CLEARED CUSTOMS IN TORONTO.
"I DON'T NEED TO REMIND YOU THAT WE NEED EYES OUT..."
...FOR ANY POTENTIAL YAKUZA THREAT.
MILLER. HOW'S IT LOOKING?
CLEAR AND QUIET. SHOULD TAKE FIVE MINUTES TO GET KAJIYAMA AND HIS MEN OUTSIDE.
FBI
FBI
FBI
GLAZER. ALL GOOD?
YES SIR. HAVE AGENTS STATIONED AT FIVE KEY POINTS.
GOOD. REMEMBER, IT'S NOT JUST YAKUZA WE'RE ON THE LOOKOUT FOR...
...IT'S ALSO THEIR OUTSIDE AGENT.
JIMMY...
...I CAN'T BE SEEN BY HIM WHEN YOU TAKE HIM DOWN.
IT'S ALL GOOD. I KNOW HE'S YOUR "BOGEYMAN"...
...BUT WE AIN'T COPS.
YOUR BOY'S DEALING WITH THE FBI NOW.

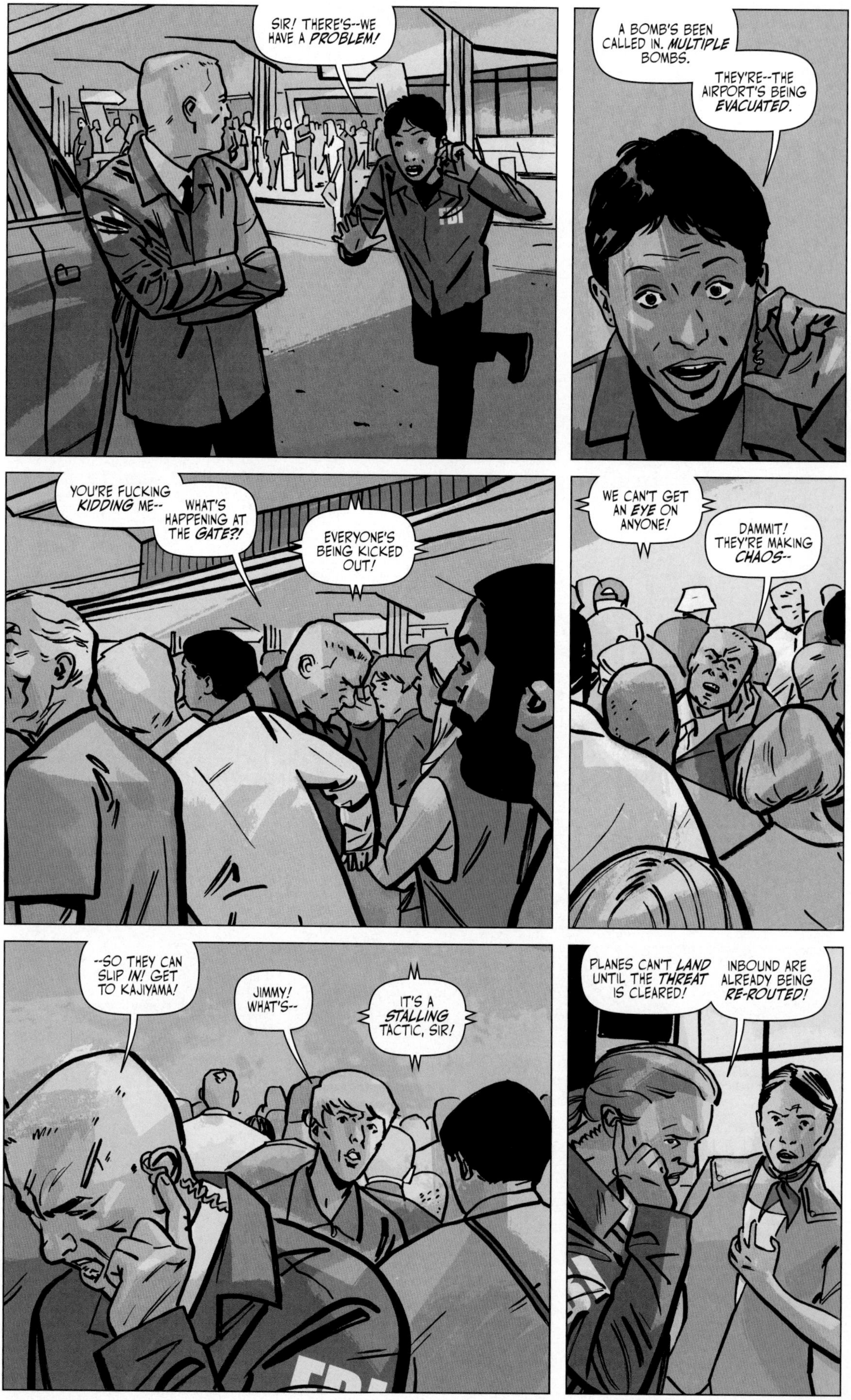
SIR! THERE'S--WE HAVE A PROBLEM!
FBI
A BOMB'S BEEN CALLED IN. MULTIPLE BOMBS.
THEY'RE--THE AIRPORT'S BEING EVACUATED.
YOU'RE FUCKING KIDDING ME--
WHAT'S HAPPENING AT THE GATE?!
EVERYONE'S BEING KICKED OUT!
WE CAN'T GET AN EYE ON ANYONE!
DAMMIT! THEY'RE MAKING CHAOS--
--SO THEY CAN SLIP IN! GET TO KAJIYAMA!
JIMMY! WHAT'S--
IT'S A STALLING TACTIC, SIR!
PLANES CAN'T LAND UNTIL THE THREAT IS CLEARED!
INBOUND ARE ALREADY BEING RE-ROUTED!

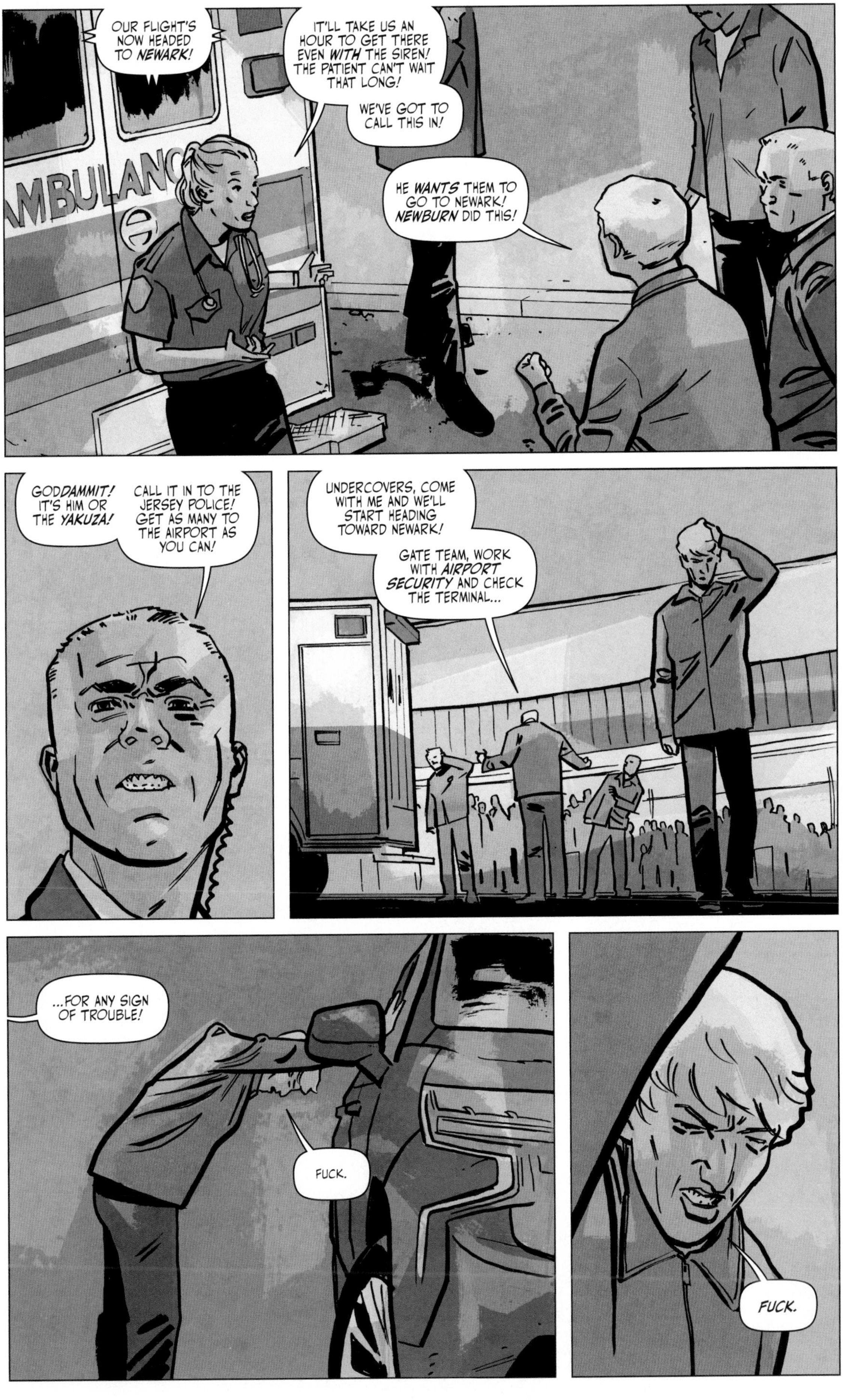
OUR FLIGHT'S NOW HEADED TO *NEWARK!*
IT'LL TAKE US AN HOUR TO GET THERE EVEN *WITH* THE SIREN! THE PATIENT CAN'T WAIT THAT LONG!
WE'VE GOT TO CALL THIS IN!
HE *WANTS* THEM TO GO TO NEWARK! *NEWBURN* DID THIS!
GOD*DAMMIT!* IT'S HIM OR THE *YAKUZA!*
CALL IT IN TO THE JERSEY POLICE! GET AS MANY TO THE AIRPORT AS YOU CAN!
UNDERCOVERS, COME WITH ME AND WE'LL START HEADING TOWARD NEWARK!
GATE TEAM, WORK WITH *AIRPORT SECURITY* AND CHECK THE TERMINAL...
...FOR ANY SIGN OF TROUBLE!
FUCK.
FUCK.

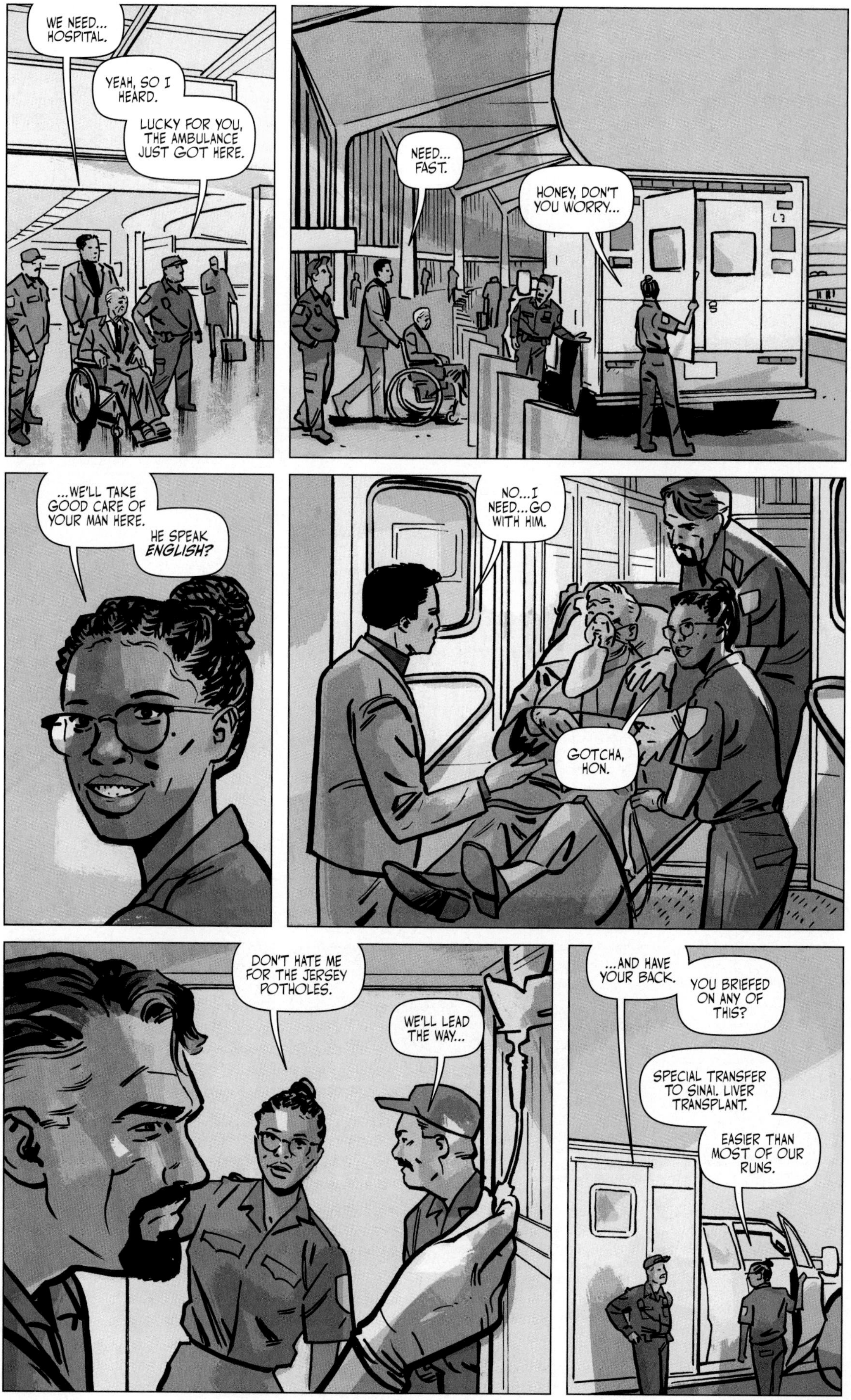
WE NEED... HOSPITAL.
YEAH, SO I HEARD.
LUCKY FOR YOU, THE AMBULANCE JUST GOT HERE.
NEED... FAST.
HONEY, DON'T YOU WORRY...
...WE'LL TAKE GOOD CARE OF YOUR MAN HERE.
HE SPEAK *ENGLISH?*
NO...I NEED...GO WITH HIM.
GOTCHA, HON.
DON'T HATE ME FOR THE JERSEY POTHOLES.
WE'LL LEAD THE WAY...
...AND HAVE YOUR BACK.
YOU BRIEFED ON ANY OF THIS?
SPECIAL TRANSFER TO SINAI. LIVER TRANSPLANT.
EASIER THAN MOST OF OUR RUNS.

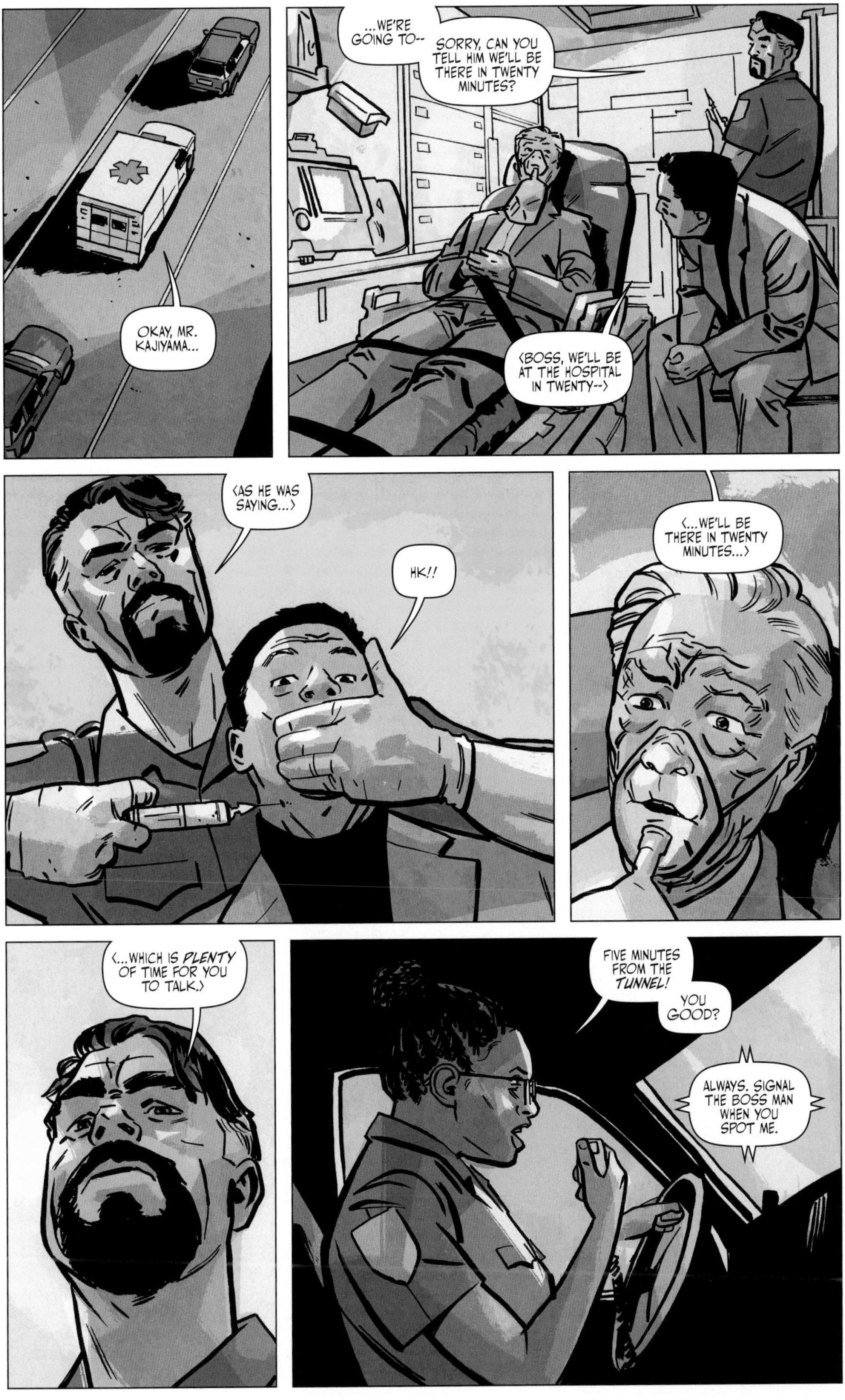
OKAY, MR. KAJIYAMA...
...WE'RE GOING TO--
SORRY, CAN YOU TELL HIM WE'LL BE THERE IN TWENTY MINUTES?
<BOSS, WE'LL BE AT THE HOSPITAL IN TWENTY-->
<AS HE WAS SAYING...>
HK!!
<...WE'LL BE THERE IN TWENTY MINUTES...>
<...WHICH IS PLENTY OF TIME FOR YOU TO TALK.>
FIVE MINUTES FROM THE TUNNEL!
YOU GOOD?
ALWAYS. SIGNAL THE BOSS MAN WHEN YOU SPOT ME.

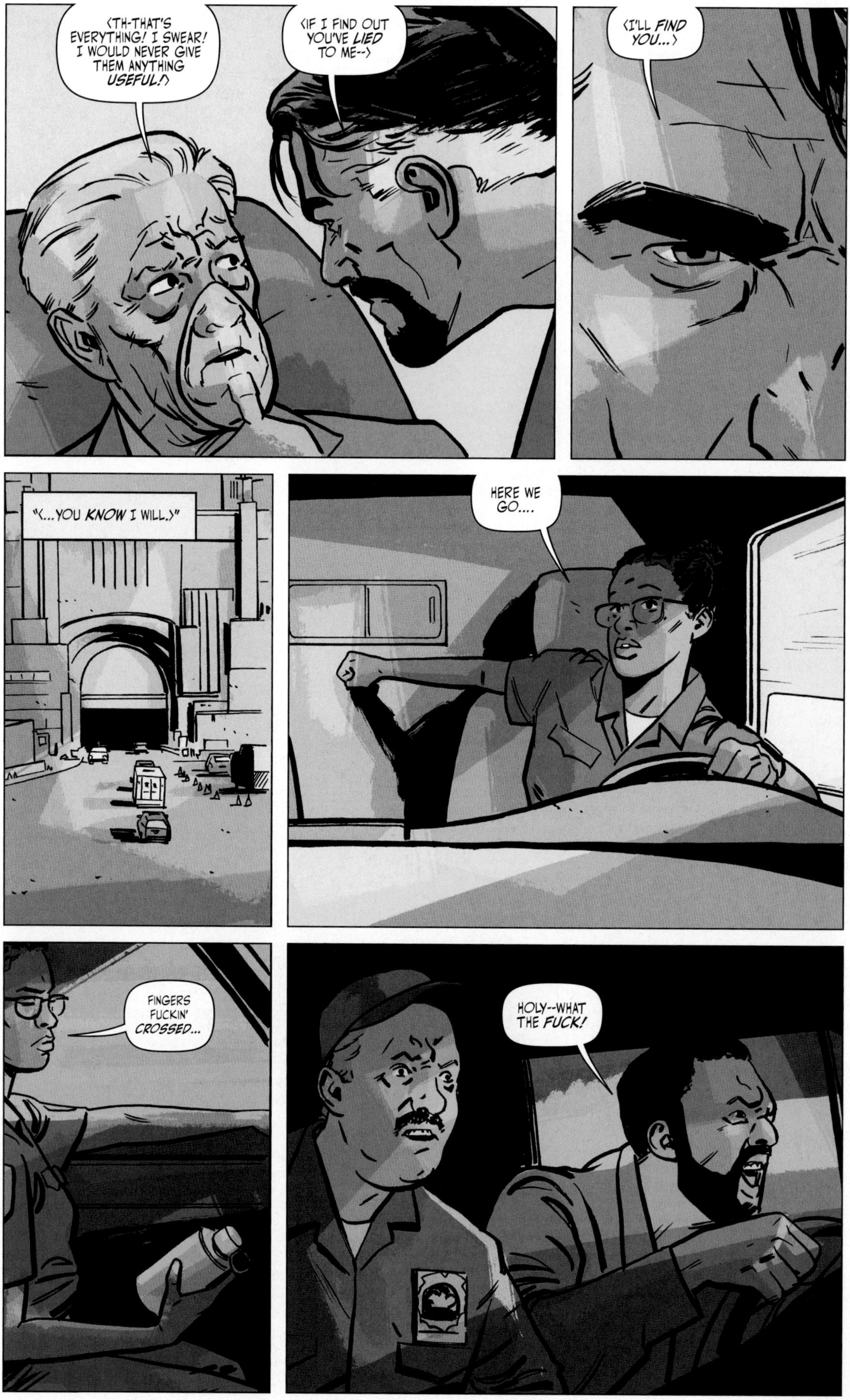
‹TH-THAT'S EVERYTHING! I SWEAR! I WOULD NEVER GIVE THEM ANYTHING USEFUL!›
‹IF I FIND OUT YOU'VE LIED TO ME--›
‹I'LL FIND YOU...›
"‹...YOU KNOW I WILL.›"
HERE WE GO....
FINGERS FUCKIN' CROSSED...
HOLY--WHAT THE FUCK!

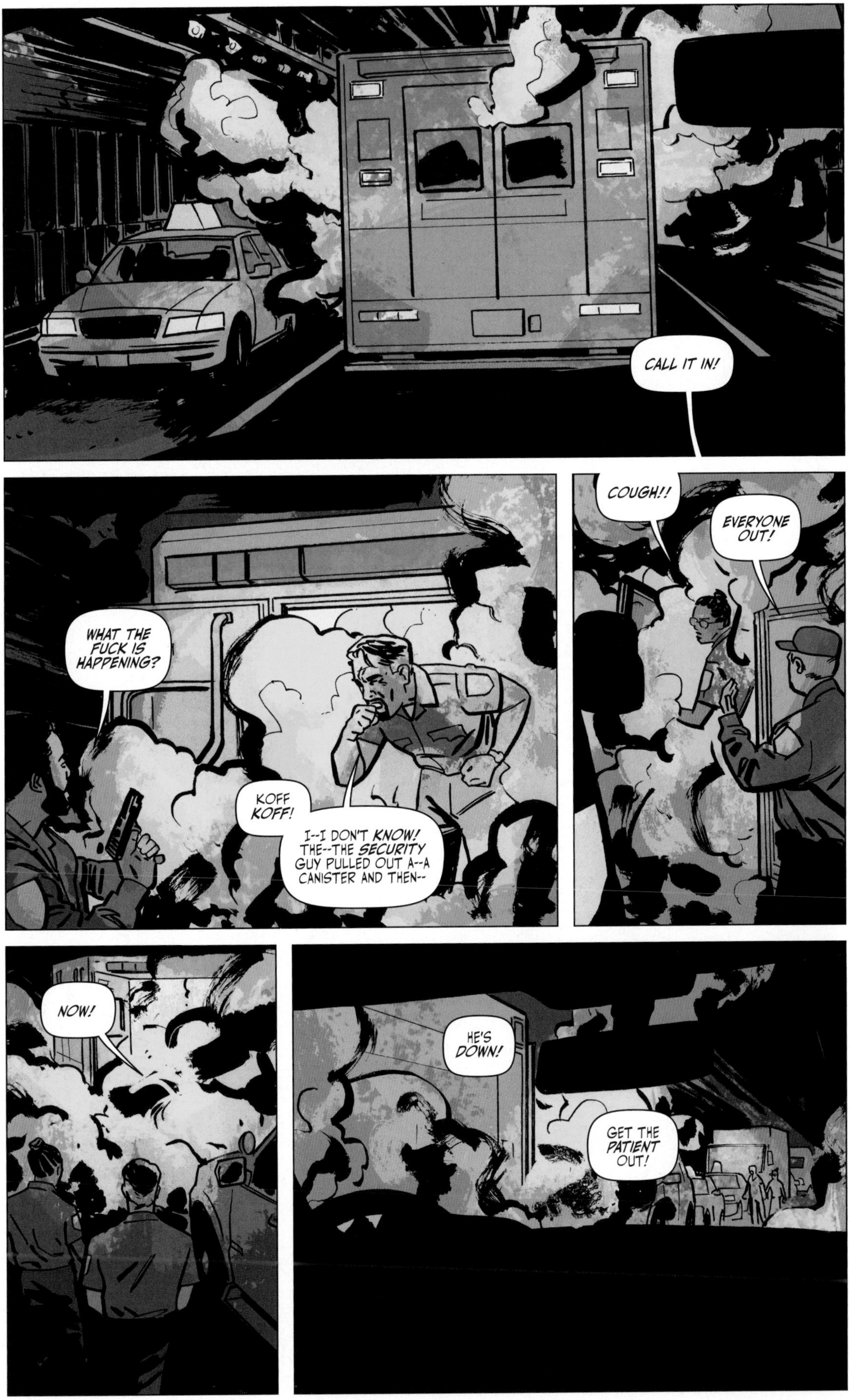
CALL IT IN!
WHAT THE FUCK IS HAPPENING?
KOFF KOFF!
I--I DON'T KNOW! THE--THE SECURITY GUY PULLED OUT A--A CANISTER AND THEN--
COUGH!!
EVERYONE OUT!
NOW!
HE'S DOWN!
GET THE PATIENT OUT!

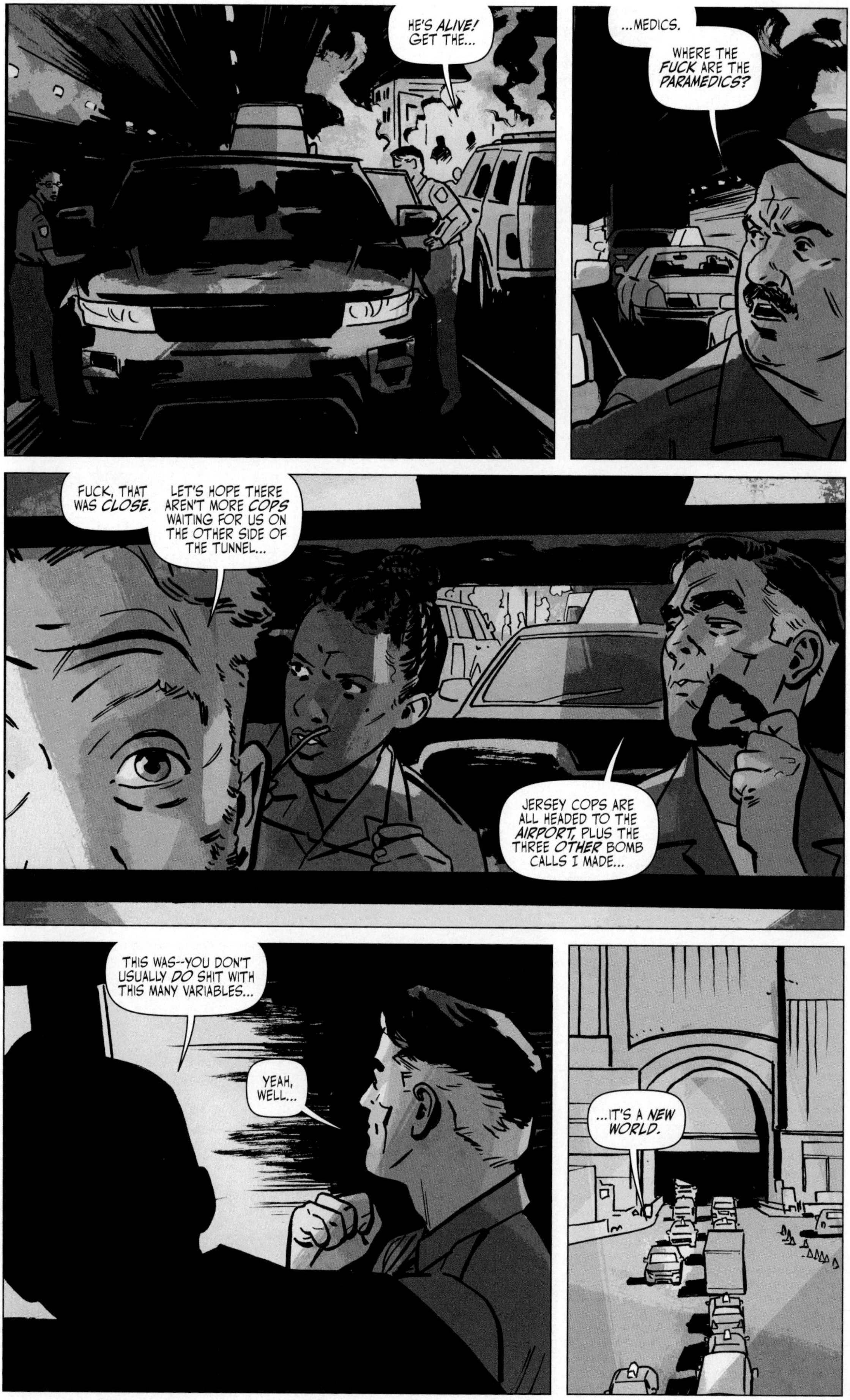
HE'S ALIVE! GET THE...
...MEDICS.
WHERE THE FUCK ARE THE PARAMEDICS?
FUCK, THAT WAS CLOSE.
LET'S HOPE THERE AREN'T MORE COPS WAITING FOR US ON THE OTHER SIDE OF THE TUNNEL...
JERSEY COPS ARE ALL HEADED TO THE AIRPORT, PLUS THE THREE OTHER BOMB CALLS I MADE...
THIS WAS--YOU DON'T USUALLY DO SHIT WITH THIS MANY VARIABLES...
YEAH, WELL...
...IT'S A NEW WORLD.

THANKS FOR AGREEING TO TALK, MR. SHIROO--

JUST-- SHIGEYUKI IS FINE...

I KNOW YOU WERE *TOLD* TO TALK WITH ME, BUT I STILL APPRECIATE IT.

I HAVE SOME QUESTIONS ABOUT *MARIO ALBANO*...

I...I DON'T KNOW WHAT I CAN *SAY*...

WELL, YOU'RE HERE FOR HIS *MURDER*...

...SO YOU MUST HAVE *SOMETHING* TO SAY.

THE STORY YOU TOLD WAS ABOUT SOME *GAMBLING GRIEVANCE* BACK IN THE DAY?

THAT YOU DIDN'T KNOW HE WAS AN *ALBANO*?

THAT'S RIGHT.

WELL, YOU KNOW WHAT I THINK?

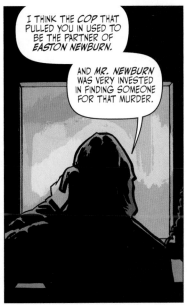

I THINK THE *COP* THAT PULLED YOU IN USED TO BE THE PARTNER OF *EASTON NEWBURN*.

AND *MR. NEWBURN* WAS VERY INVESTED IN FINDING SOMEONE FOR THAT MURDER.

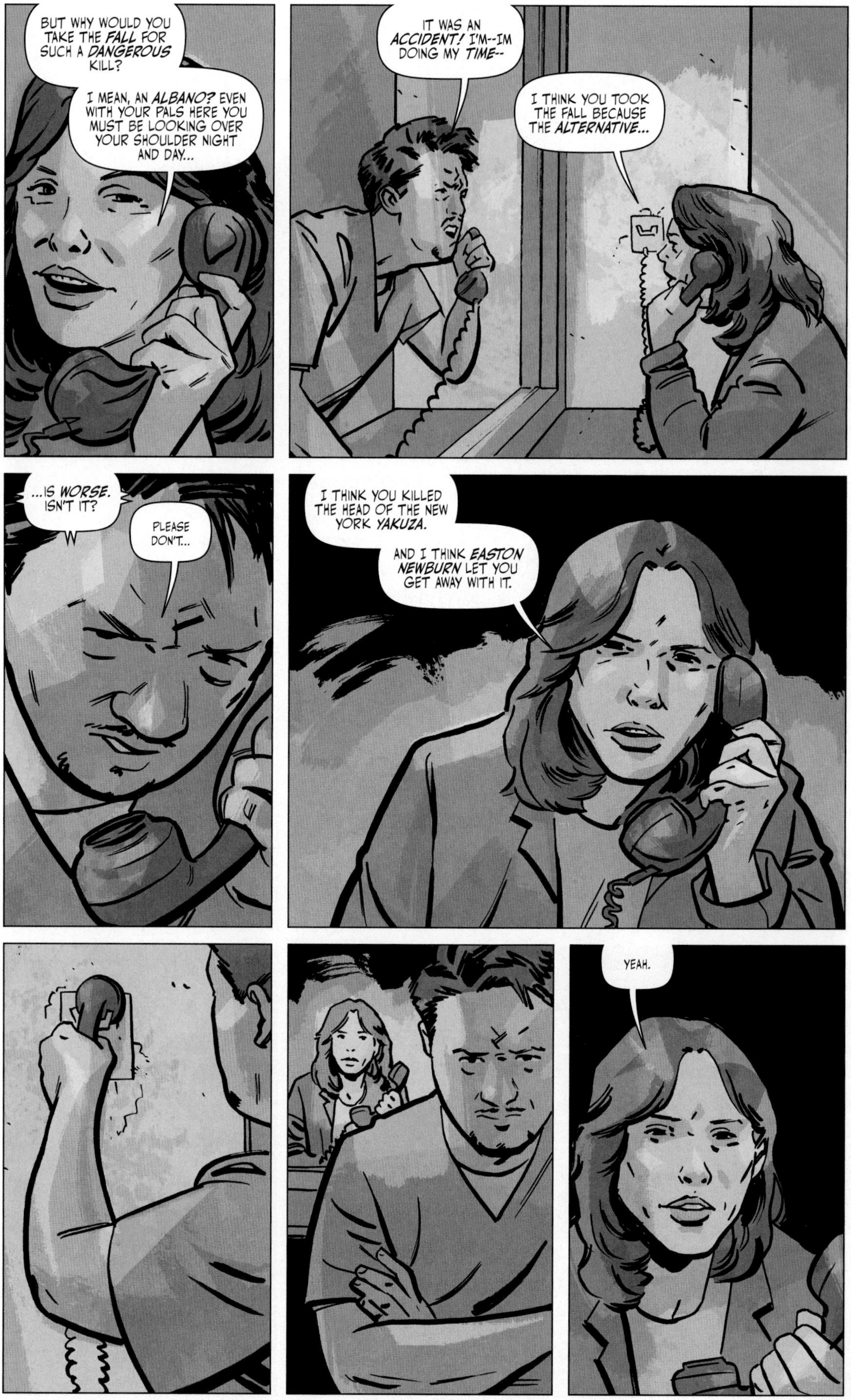
BUT WHY WOULD YOU TAKE THE FALL FOR SUCH A DANGEROUS KILL?
I MEAN, AN ALBANO? EVEN WITH YOUR PALS HERE YOU MUST BE LOOKING OVER YOUR SHOULDER NIGHT AND DAY...
IT WAS AN ACCIDENT! I'M--IM DOING MY TIME--
I THINK YOU TOOK THE FALL BECAUSE THE ALTERNATIVE...
...IS WORSE. ISN'T IT?
PLEASE DON'T...
I THINK YOU KILLED THE HEAD OF THE NEW YORK YAKUZA.
AND I THINK EASTON NEWBURN LET YOU GET AWAY WITH IT.
YEAH.

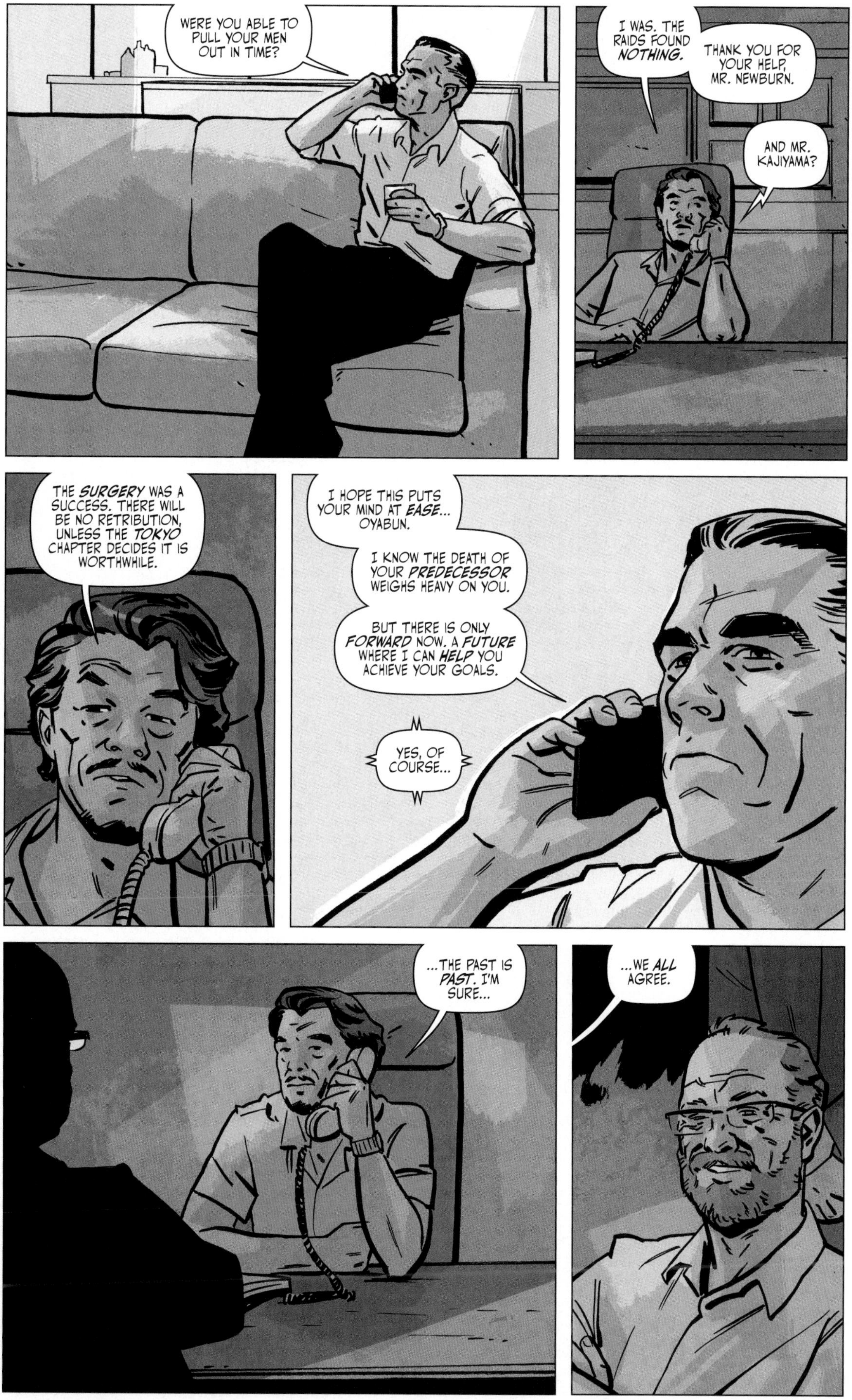
WERE YOU ABLE TO PULL YOUR MEN OUT IN TIME?
I WAS. THE RAIDS FOUND NOTHING.
THANK YOU FOR YOUR HELP, MR. NEWBURN.
AND MR. KAJIYAMA?
THE SURGERY WAS A SUCCESS. THERE WILL BE NO RETRIBUTION, UNLESS THE TOKYO CHAPTER DECIDES IT IS WORTHWHILE.
I HOPE THIS PUTS YOUR MIND AT EASE... OYABUN.
I KNOW THE DEATH OF YOUR PREDECESSOR WEIGHS HEAVY ON YOU.
BUT THERE IS ONLY FORWARD NOW. A FUTURE WHERE I CAN HELP YOU ACHIEVE YOUR GOALS.
YES, OF COURSE...
...THE PAST IS PAST. I'M SURE...
...WE ALL AGREE.

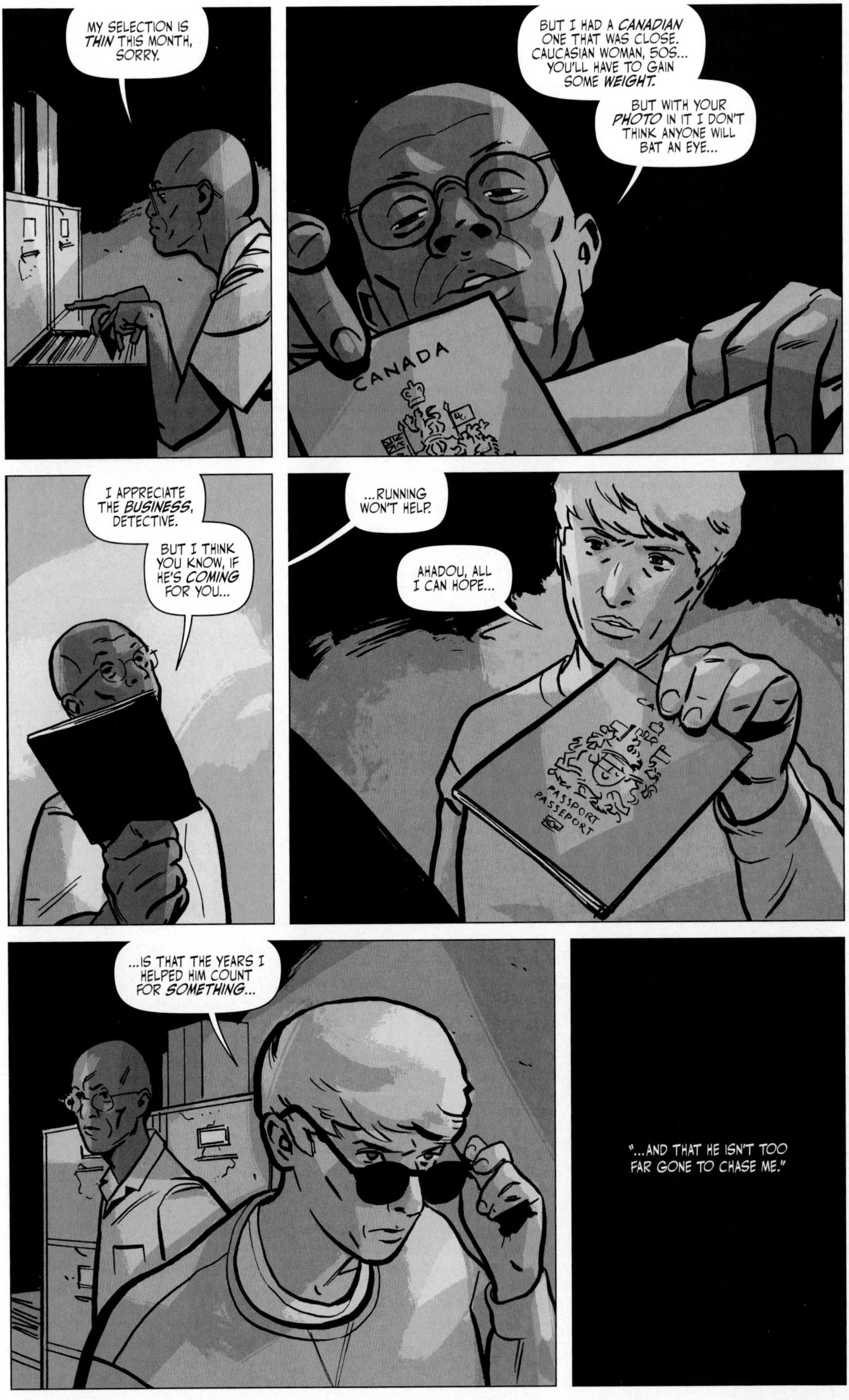
MY SELECTION IS THIN THIS MONTH, SORRY.
BUT I HAD A CANADIAN ONE THAT WAS CLOSE. CAUCASIAN WOMAN, 50S... YOU'LL HAVE TO GAIN SOME WEIGHT.
BUT WITH YOUR PHOTO IN IT I DON'T THINK ANYONE WILL BAT AN EYE...
CANADA
I APPRECIATE THE BUSINESS, DETECTIVE.
BUT I THINK YOU KNOW, IF HE'S COMING FOR YOU...
...RUNNING WON'T HELP.
AHADOU, ALL I CAN HOPE...
PASSPORT
PASSEPORT
...IS THAT THE YEARS I HELPED HIM COUNT FOR SOMETHING...
"...AND THAT HE ISN'T TOO FAR GONE TO CHASE ME."

12

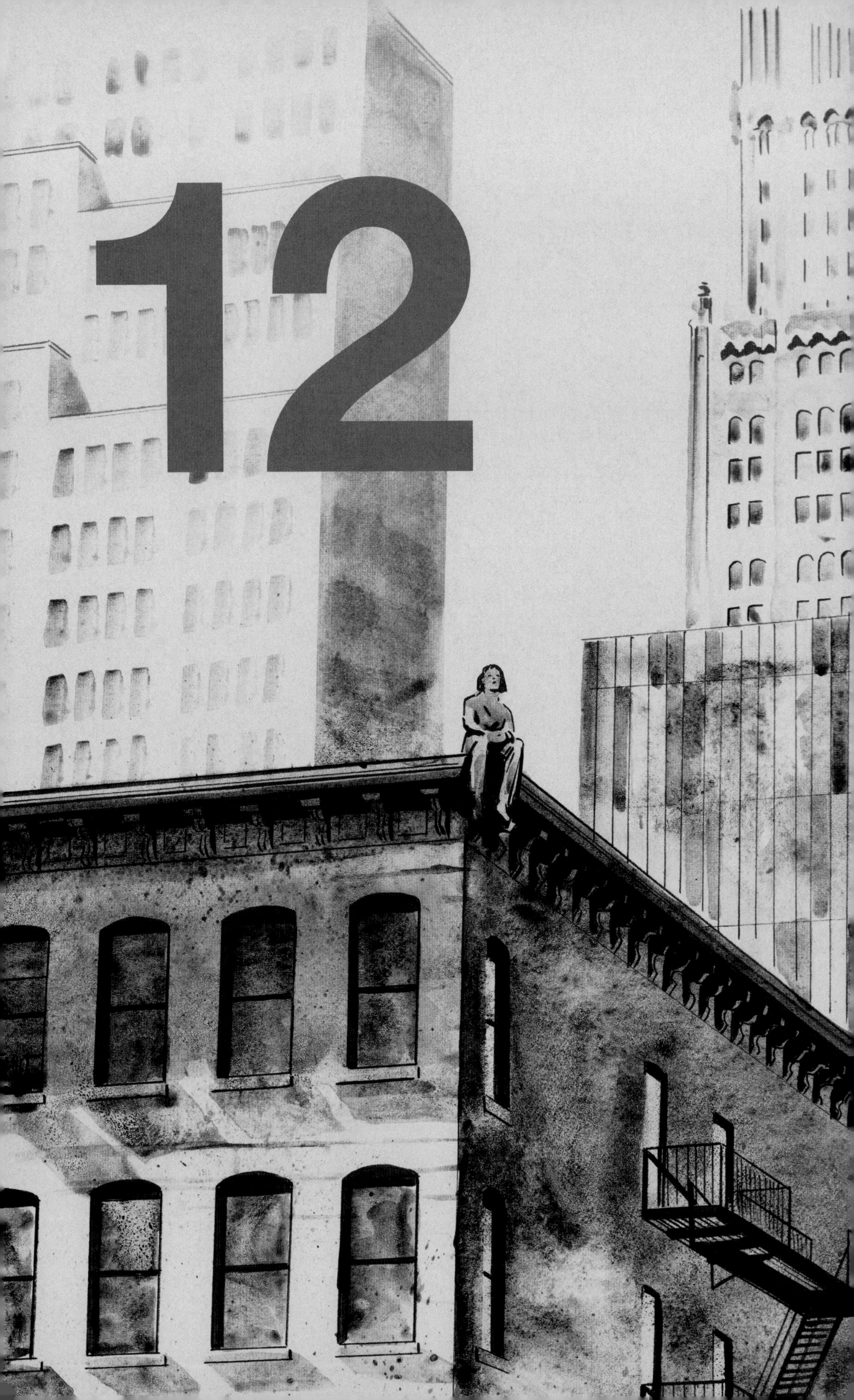

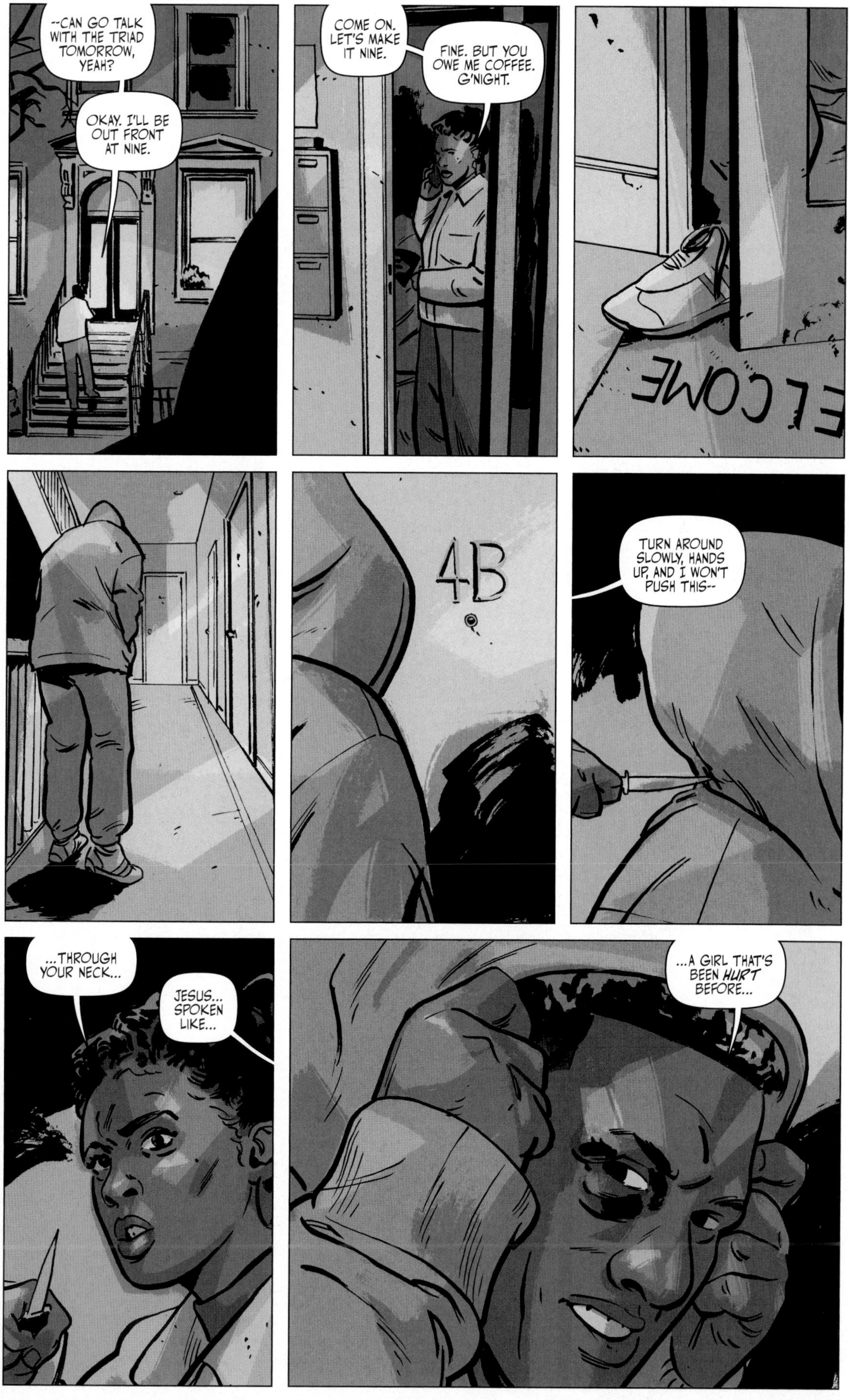
--CAN GO TALK WITH THE TRIAD TOMORROW, YEAH?
OKAY. I'LL BE OUT FRONT AT NINE.
COME ON. LET'S MAKE IT NINE.
FINE. BUT YOU OWE ME COFFEE. G'NIGHT.
ELCOME
4B
TURN AROUND SLOWLY, HANDS UP, AND I WON'T PUSH THIS--
...THROUGH YOUR NECK...
JESUS... SPOKEN LIKE...
...A GIRL THAT'S BEEN *HURT* BEFORE...

EMILY'S JOURNAL
12/03/22

Armand.

He was a small-time thief, bouncing around from job to job and was ecstatic when I dropped out of the police academy. In his mind, we were the next "Bonnie & Clyde." But really, we were a reluctant Bonnie doing all the work and a Clyde who spent all our proceeds.

There were fights, there was love, but when he almost got us pinched—and worse, didn't care—I moved on.

I'd hear stories from time to time. That he'd run afoul of one gang or another. In the back of my mind I always knew this day would come.

The day I had to bail him out.

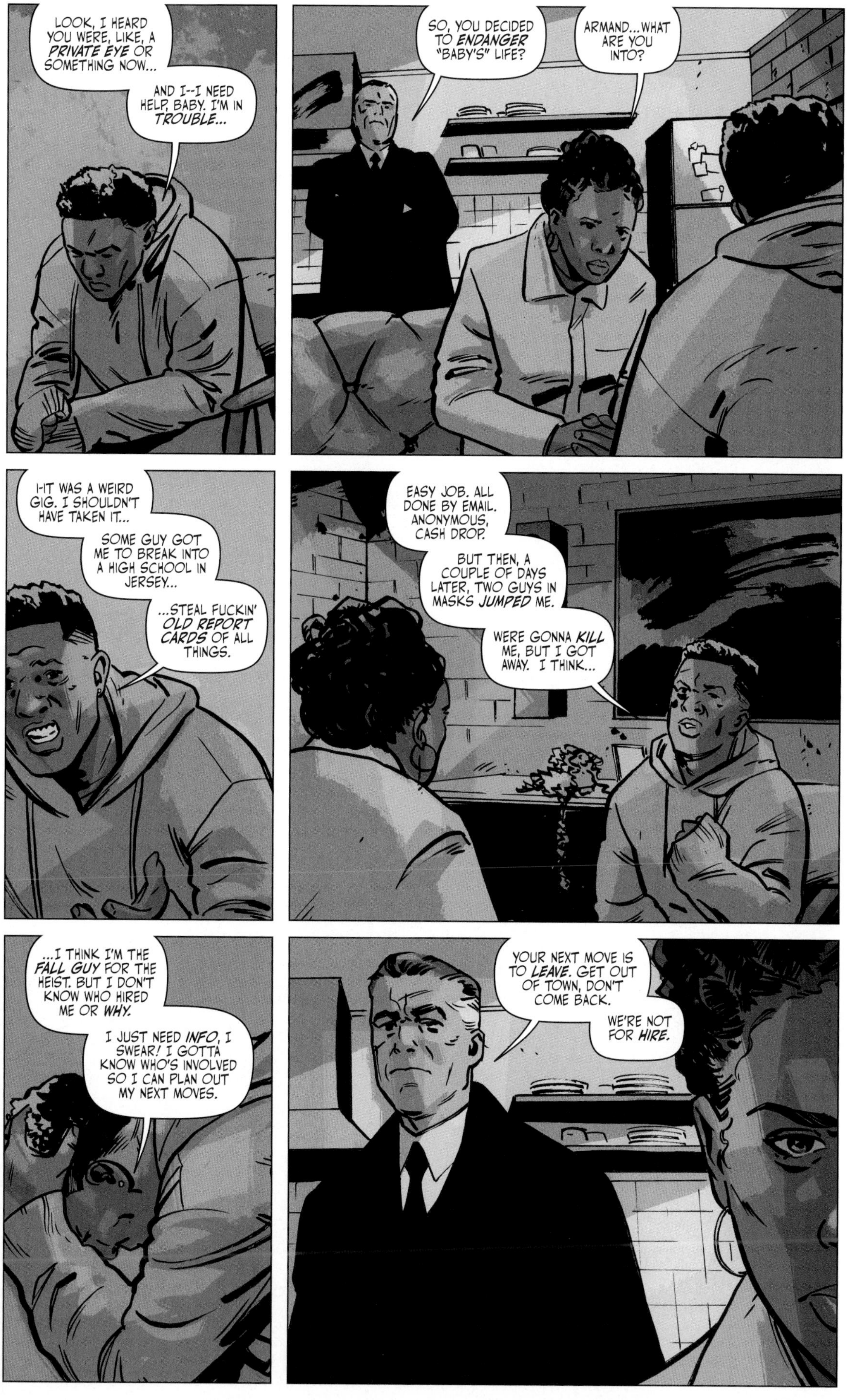

LOOK, I HEARD YOU WERE, LIKE, A PRIVATE EYE OR SOMETHING NOW...
AND I--I NEED HELP, BABY. I'M IN TROUBLE...
SO, YOU DECIDED TO ENDANGER "BABY'S" LIFE?
ARMAND...WHAT ARE YOU INTO?
I-IT WAS A WEIRD GIG. I SHOULDN'T HAVE TAKEN IT...
SOME GUY GOT ME TO BREAK INTO A HIGH SCHOOL IN JERSEY...
...STEAL FUCKIN' OLD REPORT CARDS OF ALL THINGS.
EASY JOB. ALL DONE BY EMAIL. ANONYMOUS, CASH DROP.
BUT THEN, A COUPLE OF DAYS LATER, TWO GUYS IN MASKS JUMPED ME.
WERE GONNA KILL ME, BUT I GOT AWAY. I THINK...
...I THINK I'M THE FALL GUY FOR THE HEIST. BUT I DON'T KNOW WHO HIRED ME OR WHY.
I JUST NEED INFO, I SWEAR! I GOTTA KNOW WHO'S INVOLVED SO I CAN PLAN OUT MY NEXT MOVES.
YOUR NEXT MOVE IS TO LEAVE. GET OUT OF TOWN, DON'T COME BACK.
WE'RE NOT FOR HIRE.

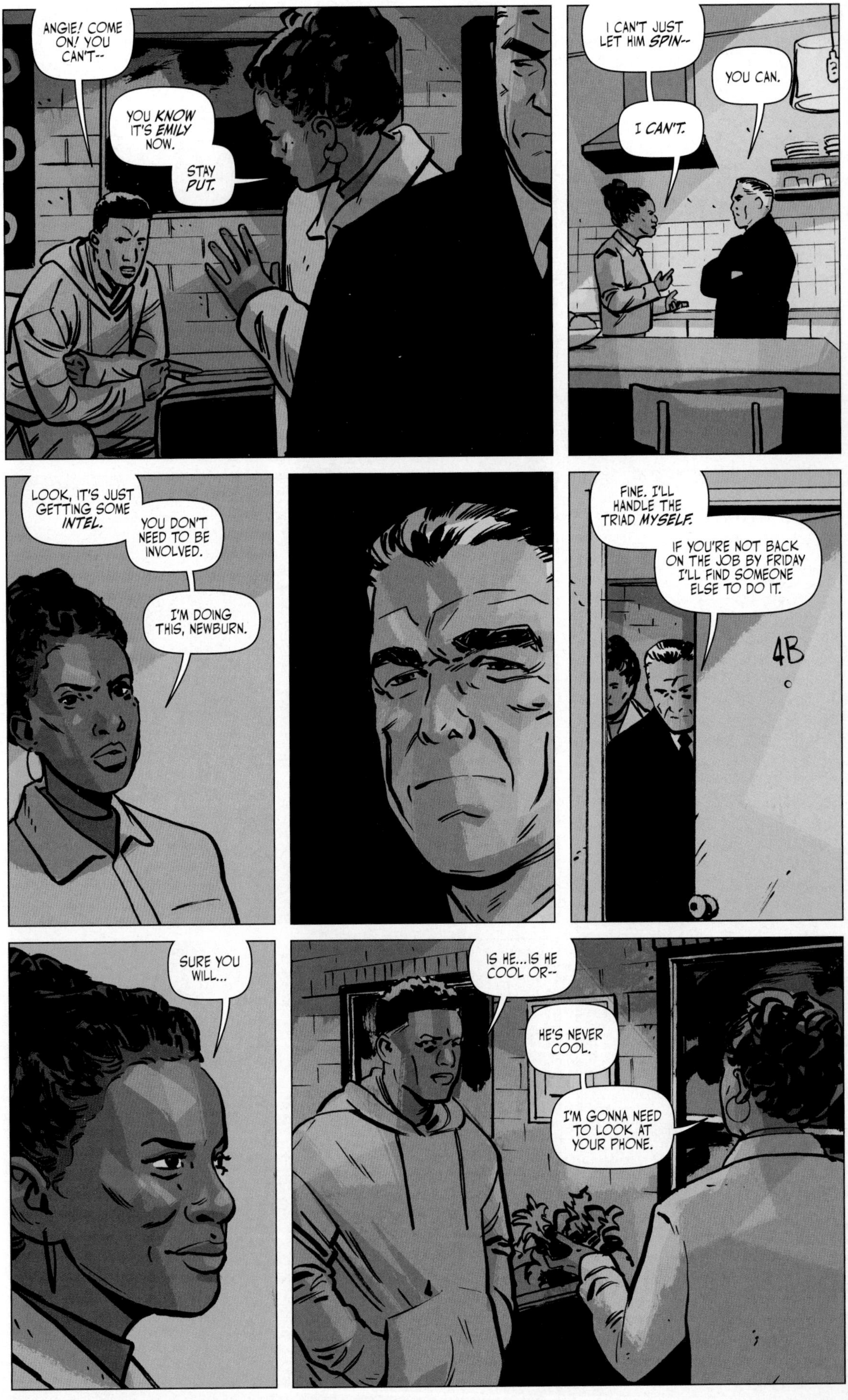
ANGIE! COME ON! YOU CAN'T--
YOU KNOW IT'S EMILY NOW.
STAY PUT.
I CAN'T JUST LET HIM SPIN--
YOU CAN.
I CAN'T.
LOOK, IT'S JUST GETTING SOME INTEL.
YOU DON'T NEED TO BE INVOLVED.
I'M DOING THIS, NEWBURN.
FINE. I'LL HANDLE THE TRIAD MYSELF.
IF YOU'RE NOT BACK ON THE JOB BY FRIDAY I'LL FIND SOMEONE ELSE TO DO IT.
4B
SURE YOU WILL...
IS HE...IS HE COOL OR--
HE'S NEVER COOL.
I'M GONNA NEED TO LOOK AT YOUR PHONE.

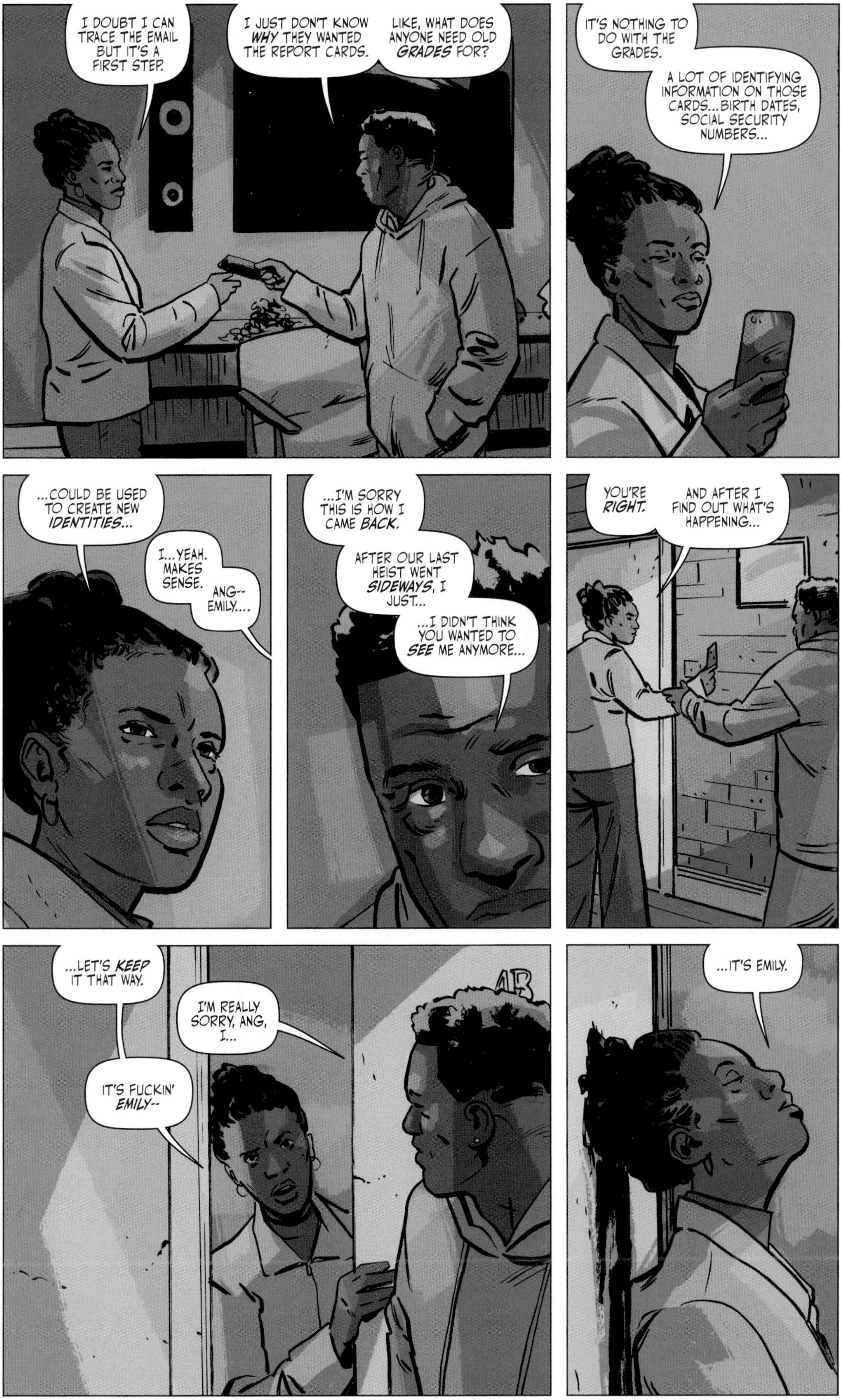
I DOUBT I CAN TRACE THE EMAIL BUT IT'S A FIRST STEP.
I JUST DON'T KNOW WHY THEY WANTED THE REPORT CARDS.
LIKE, WHAT DOES ANYONE NEED OLD GRADES FOR?
IT'S NOTHING TO DO WITH THE GRADES.
A LOT OF IDENTIFYING INFORMATION ON THOSE CARDS...BIRTH DATES, SOCIAL SECURITY NUMBERS...
...COULD BE USED TO CREATE NEW IDENTITIES...
I...YEAH. MAKES SENSE.
ANG-- EMILY....
...I'M SORRY THIS IS HOW I CAME BACK.
AFTER OUR LAST HEIST WENT SIDEWAYS, I JUST...
...I DIDN'T THINK YOU WANTED TO SEE ME ANYMORE...
YOU'RE RIGHT.
AND AFTER I FIND OUT WHAT'S HAPPENING...
...LET'S KEEP IT THAT WAY.
I'M REALLY SORRY, ANG, I...
IT'S FUCKIN' EMILY--
...IT'S EMILY.

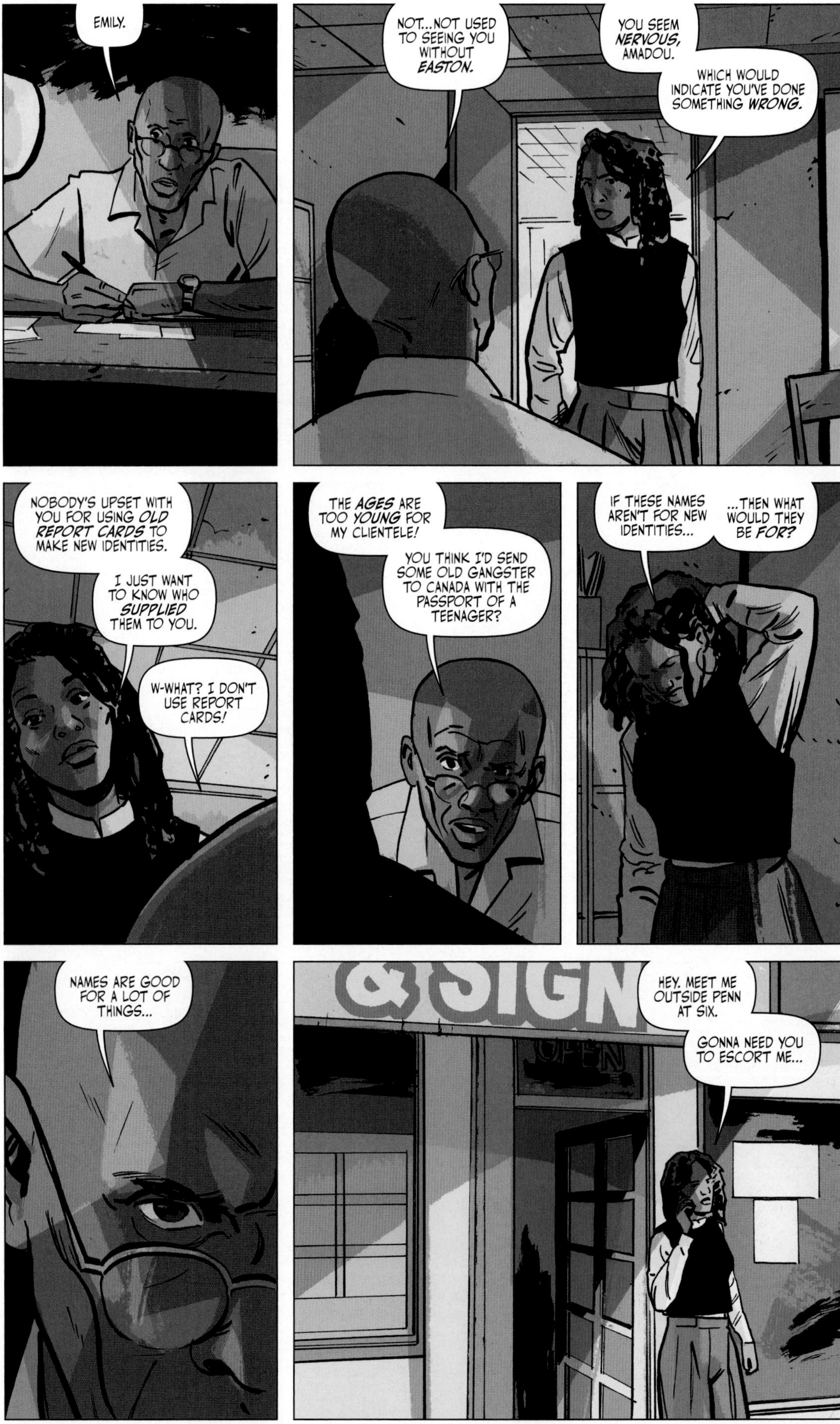
EMILY.
NOT...NOT USED TO SEEING YOU WITHOUT EASTON.
YOU SEEM NERVOUS, AMADOU.
WHICH WOULD INDICATE YOU'VE DONE SOMETHING WRONG.
NOBODY'S UPSET WITH YOU FOR USING OLD REPORT CARDS TO MAKE NEW IDENTITIES.
I JUST WANT TO KNOW WHO SUPPLIED THEM TO YOU.
W-WHAT? I DON'T USE REPORT CARDS!
THE AGES ARE TOO YOUNG FOR MY CLIENTELE!
YOU THINK I'D SEND SOME OLD GANGSTER TO CANADA WITH THE PASSPORT OF A TEENAGER?
IF THESE NAMES AREN'T FOR NEW IDENTITIES...
...THEN WHAT WOULD THEY BE FOR?
NAMES ARE GOOD FOR A LOT OF THINGS...
& SIGN
HEY. MEET ME OUTSIDE PENN AT SIX.
GONNA NEED YOU TO ESCORT ME...

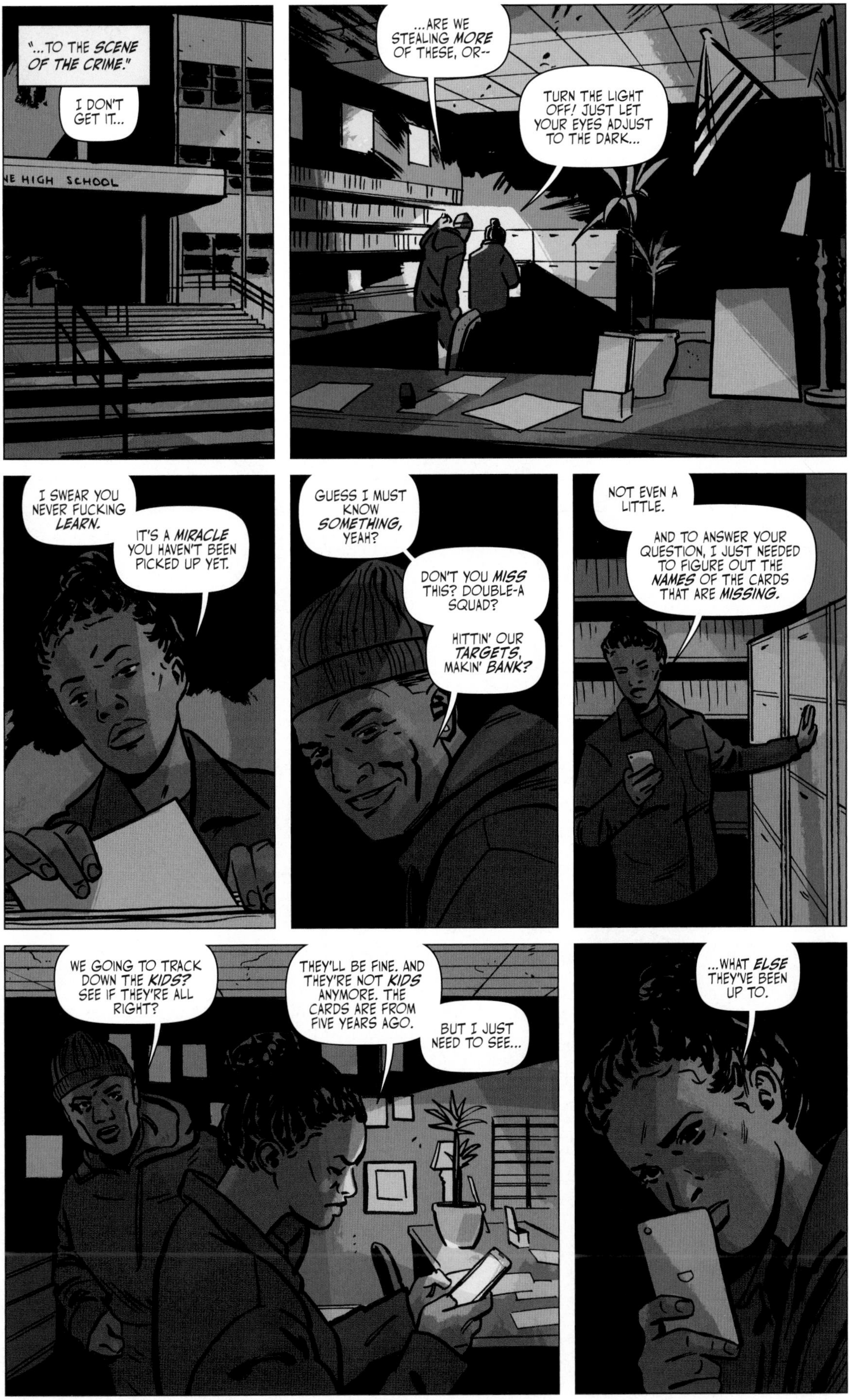
"...TO THE SCENE OF THE CRIME."
I DON'T GET IT...
NE HIGH SCHOOL
...ARE WE STEALING MORE OF THESE, OR--
TURN THE LIGHT OFF! JUST LET YOUR EYES ADJUST TO THE DARK...
I SWEAR YOU NEVER FUCKING LEARN.
IT'S A MIRACLE YOU HAVEN'T BEEN PICKED UP YET.
GUESS I MUST KNOW SOMETHING, YEAH?
DON'T YOU MISS THIS? DOUBLE-A SQUAD?
HITTIN' OUR TARGETS, MAKIN' BANK?
NOT EVEN A LITTLE.
AND TO ANSWER YOUR QUESTION, I JUST NEEDED TO FIGURE OUT THE NAMES OF THE CARDS THAT ARE MISSING.
WE GOING TO TRACK DOWN THE KIDS? SEE IF THEY'RE ALL RIGHT?
THEY'LL BE FINE. AND THEY'RE NOT KIDS ANYMORE. THE CARDS ARE FROM FIVE YEARS AGO.
BUT I JUST NEED TO SEE...
...WHAT ELSE THEY'VE BEEN UP TO.

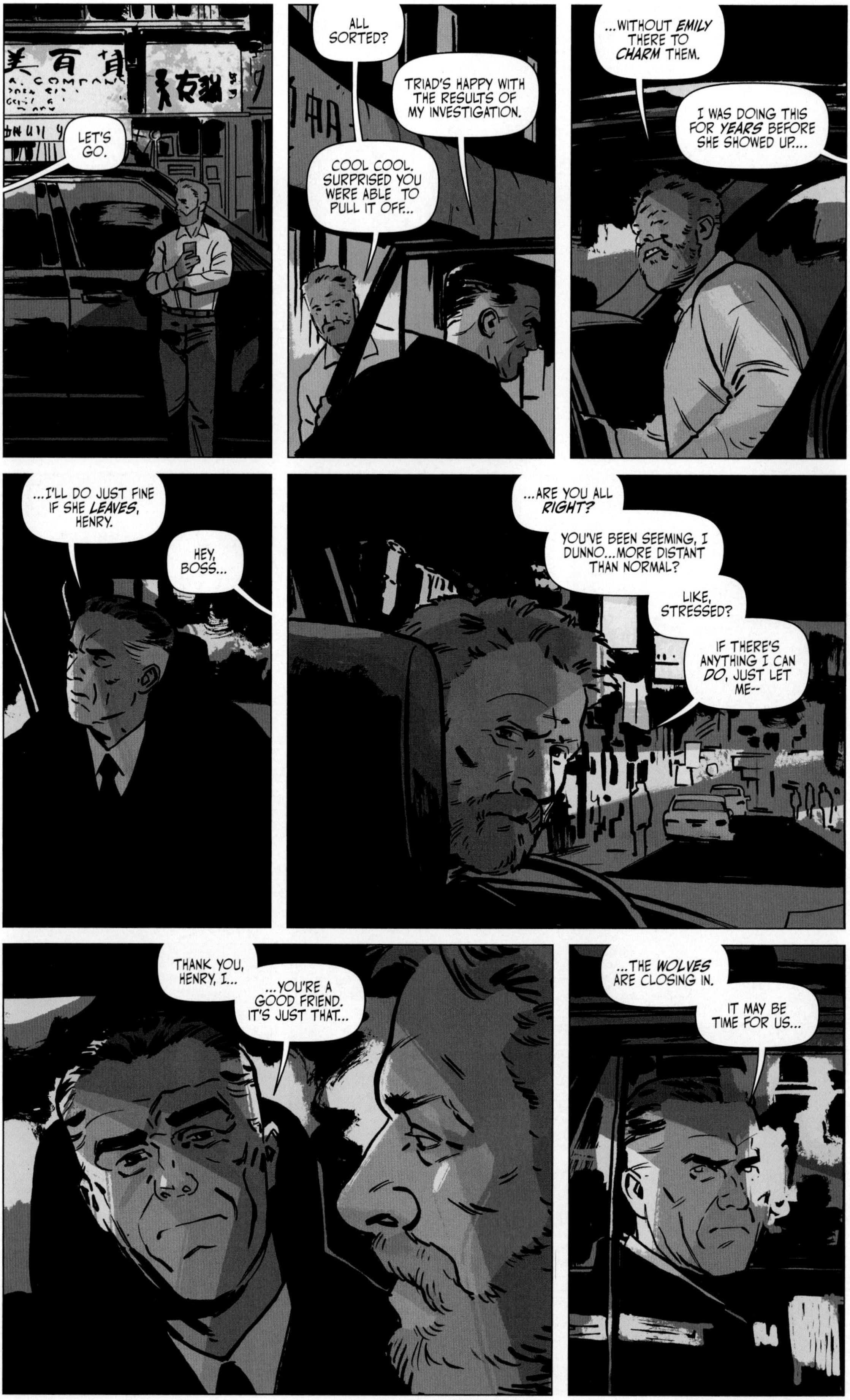
LET'S GO.
ALL SORTED?
TRIAD'S HAPPY WITH THE RESULTS OF MY INVESTIGATION.
COOL COOL. SURPRISED YOU WERE ABLE TO PULL IT OFF...
...WITHOUT EMILY THERE TO CHARM THEM.
I WAS DOING THIS FOR YEARS BEFORE SHE SHOWED UP....
...I'LL DO JUST FINE IF SHE LEAVES, HENRY.
HEY, BOSS...
...ARE YOU ALL RIGHT?
YOU'VE BEEN SEEMING, I DUNNO...MORE DISTANT THAN NORMAL?
LIKE, STRESSED?
IF THERE'S ANYTHING I CAN DO, JUST LET ME--
THANK YOU, HENRY, I...
...YOU'RE A GOOD FRIEND. IT'S JUST THAT...
...THE WOLVES ARE CLOSING IN.
IT MAY BE TIME FOR US...

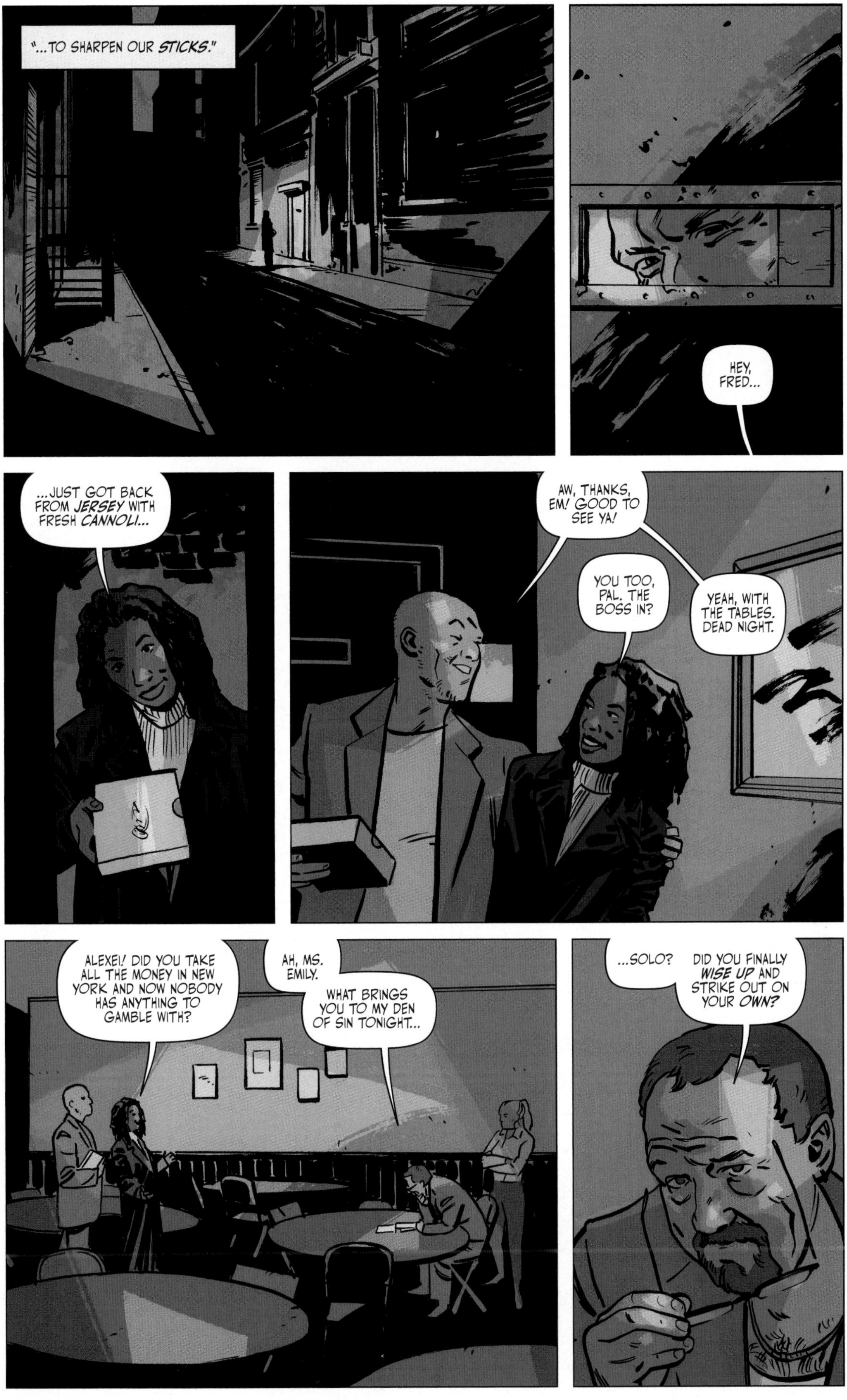
"...TO SHARPEN OUR STICKS."
HEY, FRED...
...JUST GOT BACK FROM JERSEY WITH FRESH CANNOLI...
AW, THANKS, EM! GOOD TO SEE YA!
YOU TOO, PAL. THE BOSS IN?
YEAH, WITH THE TABLES. DEAD NIGHT.
ALEXEI! DID YOU TAKE ALL THE MONEY IN NEW YORK AND NOW NOBODY HAS ANYTHING TO GAMBLE WITH?
AH, MS. EMILY.
WHAT BRINGS YOU TO MY DEN OF SIN TONIGHT...
...SOLO?
DID YOU FINALLY WISE UP AND STRIKE OUT ON YOUR OWN?

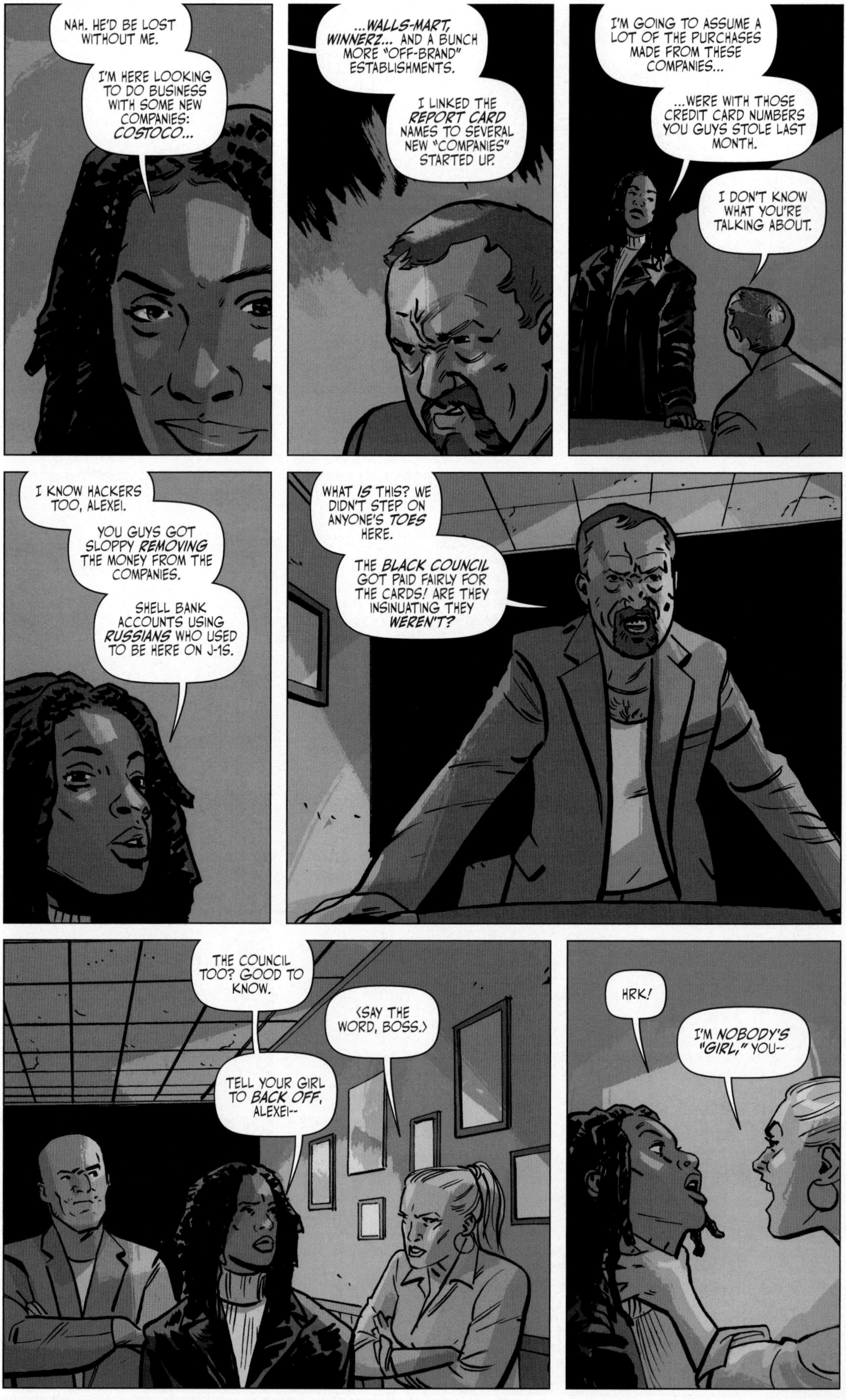
NAH. HE'D BE LOST WITHOUT ME.
I'M HERE LOOKING TO DO BUSINESS WITH SOME NEW COMPANIES: COSTOCO...
...WALLS-MART, WINNERZ... AND A BUNCH MORE "OFF-BRAND" ESTABLISHMENTS.
I LINKED THE REPORT CARD NAMES TO SEVERAL NEW "COMPANIES" STARTED UP.
I'M GOING TO ASSUME A LOT OF THE PURCHASES MADE FROM THESE COMPANIES...
...WERE WITH THOSE CREDIT CARD NUMBERS YOU GUYS STOLE LAST MONTH.
I DON'T KNOW WHAT YOU'RE TALKING ABOUT.
I KNOW HACKERS TOO, ALEXEI.
YOU GUYS GOT SLOPPY REMOVING THE MONEY FROM THE COMPANIES.
SHELL BANK ACCOUNTS USING RUSSIANS WHO USED TO BE HERE ON J-1S.
WHAT IS THIS? WE DIDN'T STEP ON ANYONE'S TOES HERE.
THE BLACK COUNCIL GOT PAID FAIRLY FOR THE CARDS! ARE THEY INSINUATING THEY WEREN'T?
THE COUNCIL TOO? GOOD TO KNOW.
TELL YOUR GIRL TO BACK OFF, ALEXEI--
<SAY THE WORD, BOSS.>
HRK!
I'M NOBODY'S "GIRL," YOU--

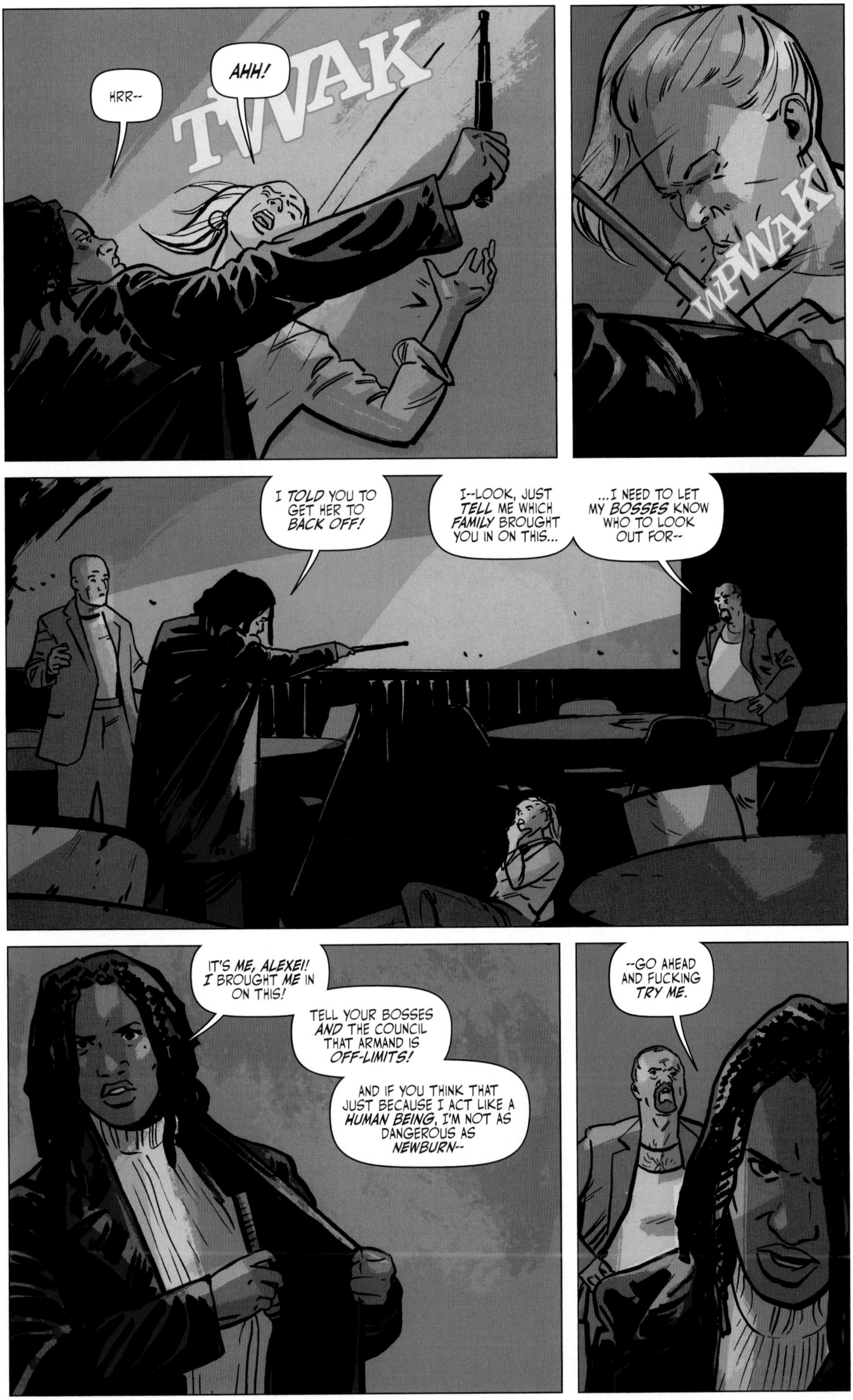

HRR--
AHH!
TWAK
WPWAK
I TOLD YOU TO GET HER TO BACK OFF!
I--LOOK, JUST TELL ME WHICH FAMILY BROUGHT YOU IN ON THIS...
...I NEED TO LET MY BOSSES KNOW WHO TO LOOK OUT FOR--
IT'S ME, ALEXEI! I BROUGHT ME IN ON THIS!
TELL YOUR BOSSES AND THE COUNCIL THAT ARMAND IS OFF-LIMITS!
AND IF YOU THINK THAT JUST BECAUSE I ACT LIKE A HUMAN BEING, I'M NOT AS DANGEROUS AS NEWBURN--
--GO AHEAD AND FUCKING TRY ME.

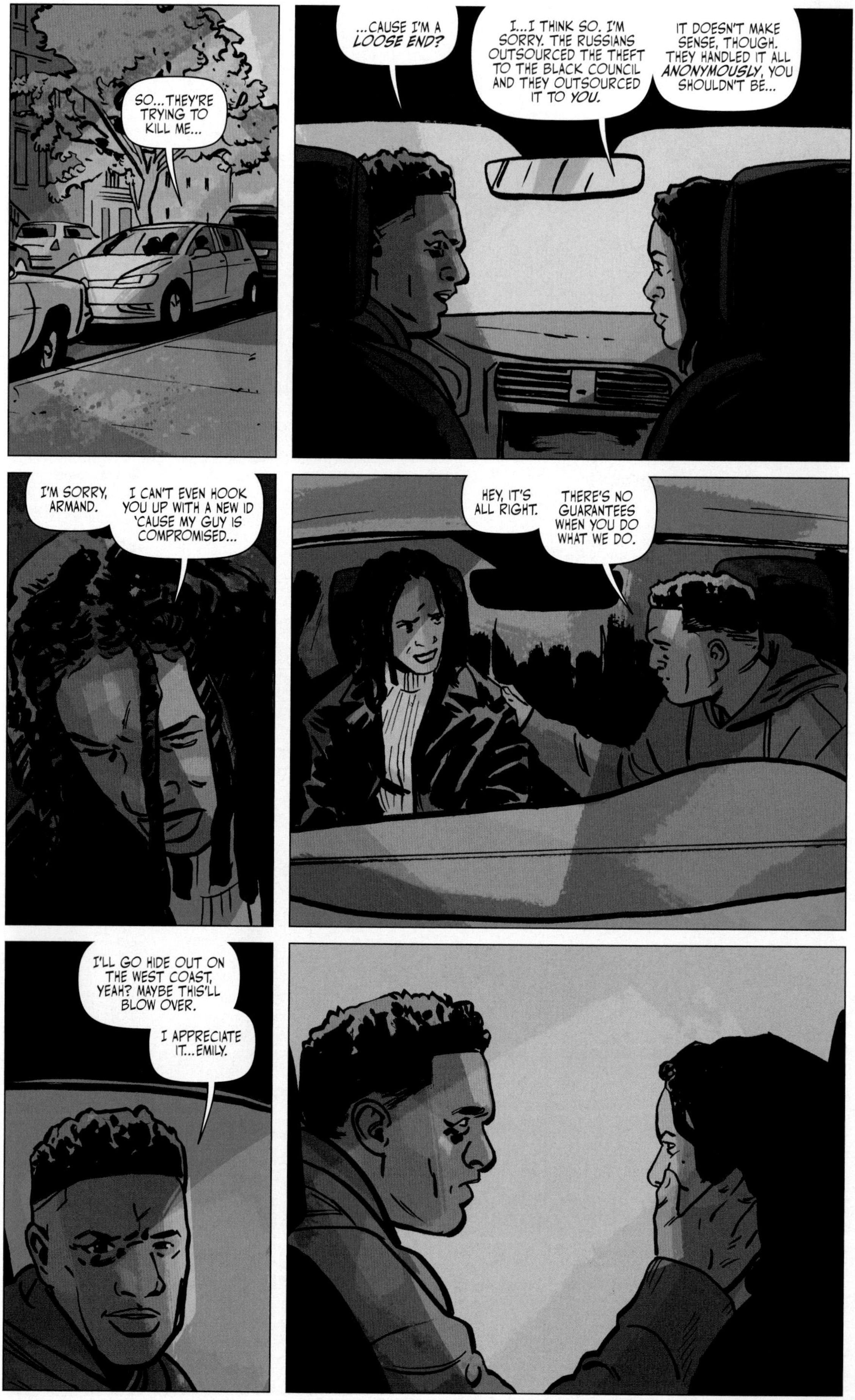
SO...THEY'RE TRYING TO KILL ME...
...CAUSE I'M A LOOSE END?
I...I THINK SO. I'M SORRY. THE RUSSIANS OUTSOURCED THE THEFT TO THE BLACK COUNCIL AND THEY OUTSOURCED IT TO YOU.
IT DOESN'T MAKE SENSE, THOUGH. THEY HANDLED IT ALL ANONYMOUSLY, YOU SHOULDN'T BE...
I'M SORRY, ARMAND.
I CAN'T EVEN HOOK YOU UP WITH A NEW ID 'CAUSE MY GUY IS COMPROMISED...
HEY, IT'S ALL RIGHT.
THERE'S NO GUARANTEES WHEN YOU DO WHAT WE DO.
I'LL GO HIDE OUT ON THE WEST COAST, YEAH? MAYBE THIS'LL BLOW OVER.
I APPRECIATE IT...EMILY.

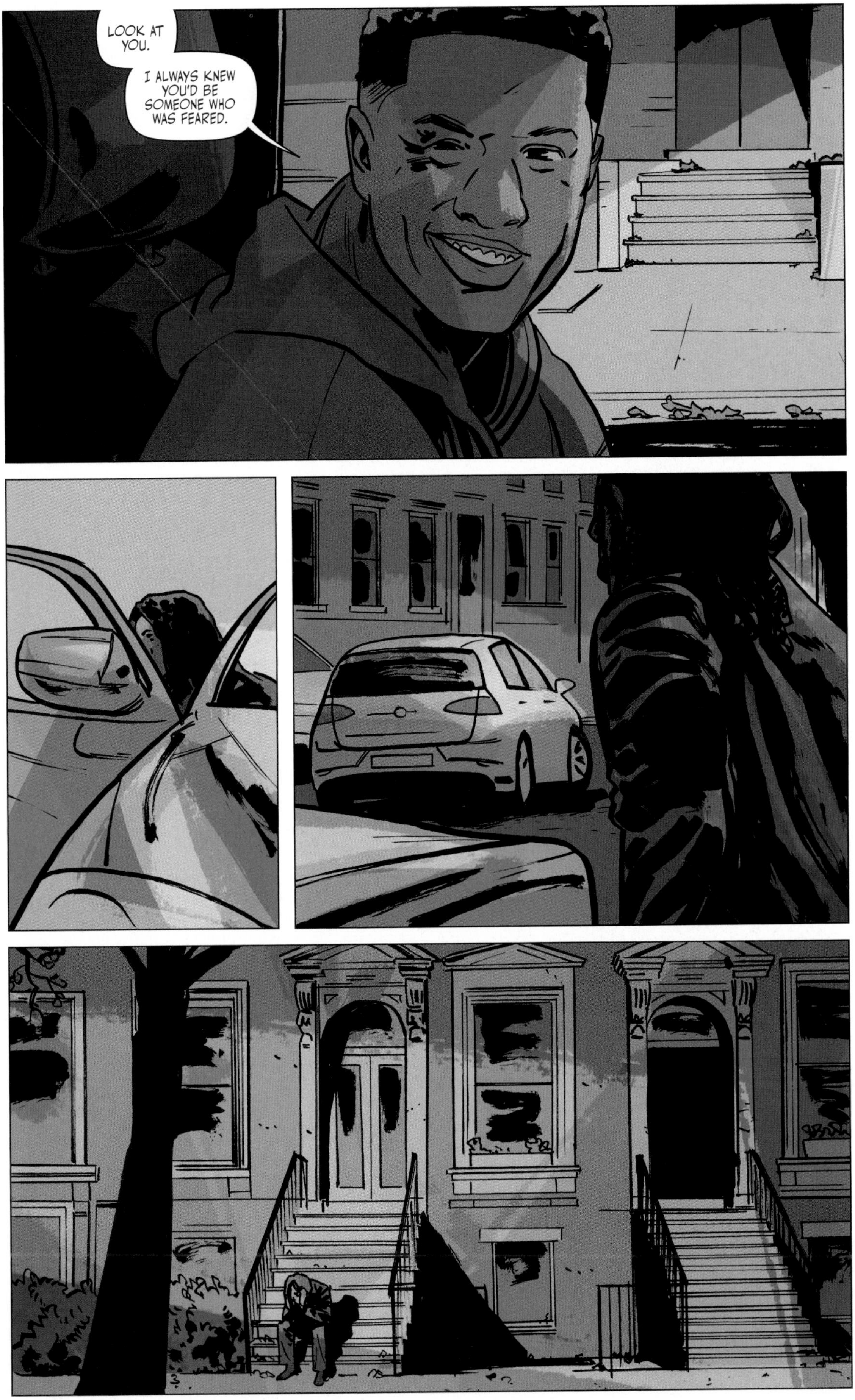
LOOK AT YOU.
I ALWAYS KNEW YOU'D BE SOMEONE WHO WAS FEARED.

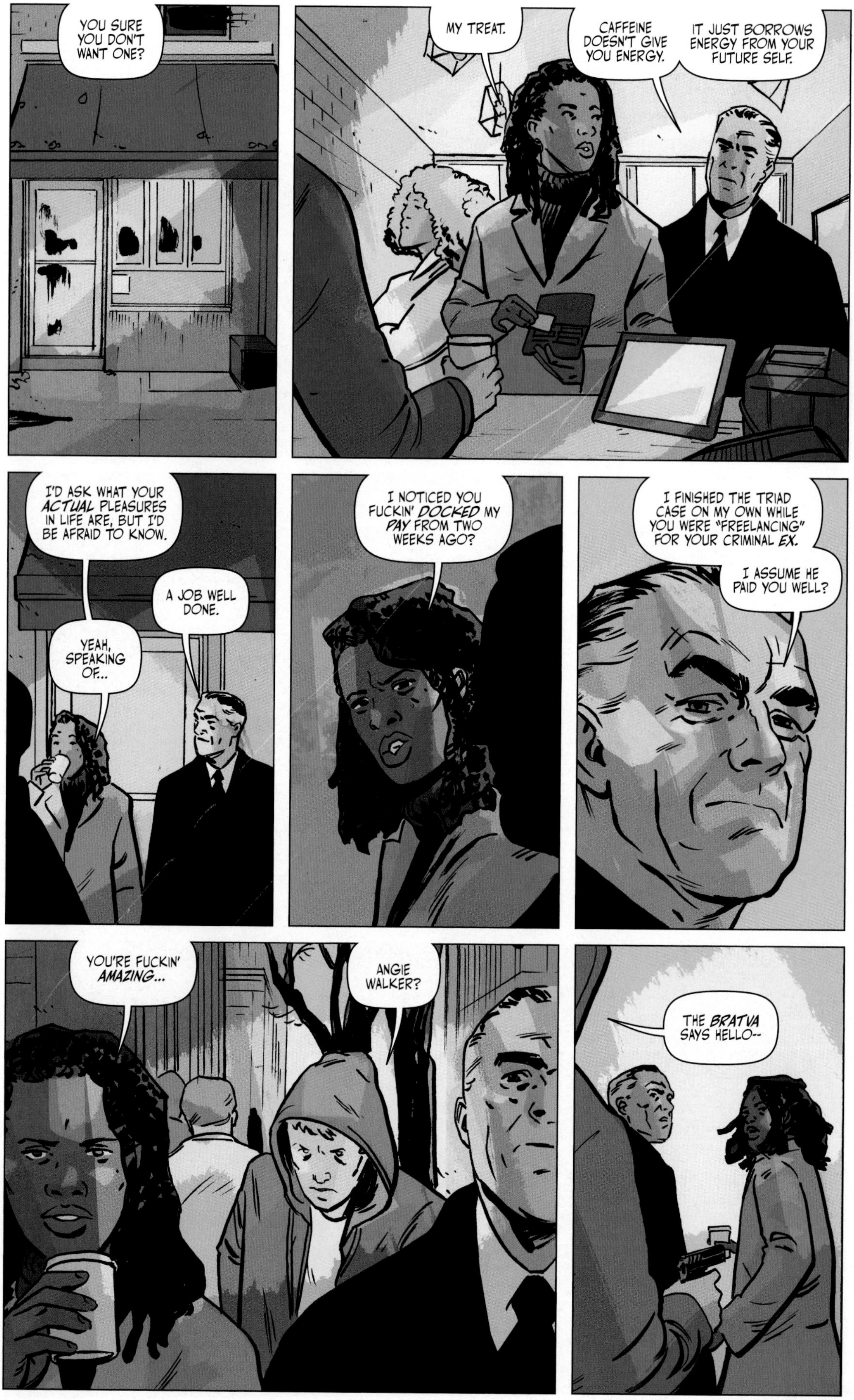
YOU SURE YOU DON'T WANT ONE?
MY TREAT.
CAFFEINE DOESN'T GIVE YOU ENERGY.
IT JUST BORROWS ENERGY FROM YOUR FUTURE SELF.
I'D ASK WHAT YOUR ACTUAL PLEASURES IN LIFE ARE, BUT I'D BE AFRAID TO KNOW.
A JOB WELL DONE.
YEAH, SPEAKING OF...
I NOTICED YOU FUCKIN' DOCKED MY PAY FROM TWO WEEKS AGO?
I FINISHED THE TRIAD CASE ON MY OWN WHILE YOU WERE "FREELANCING" FOR YOUR CRIMINAL EX.
I ASSUME HE PAID YOU WELL?
YOU'RE FUCKIN' AMAZING...
ANGIE WALKER?
THE BRATVA SAYS HELLO--

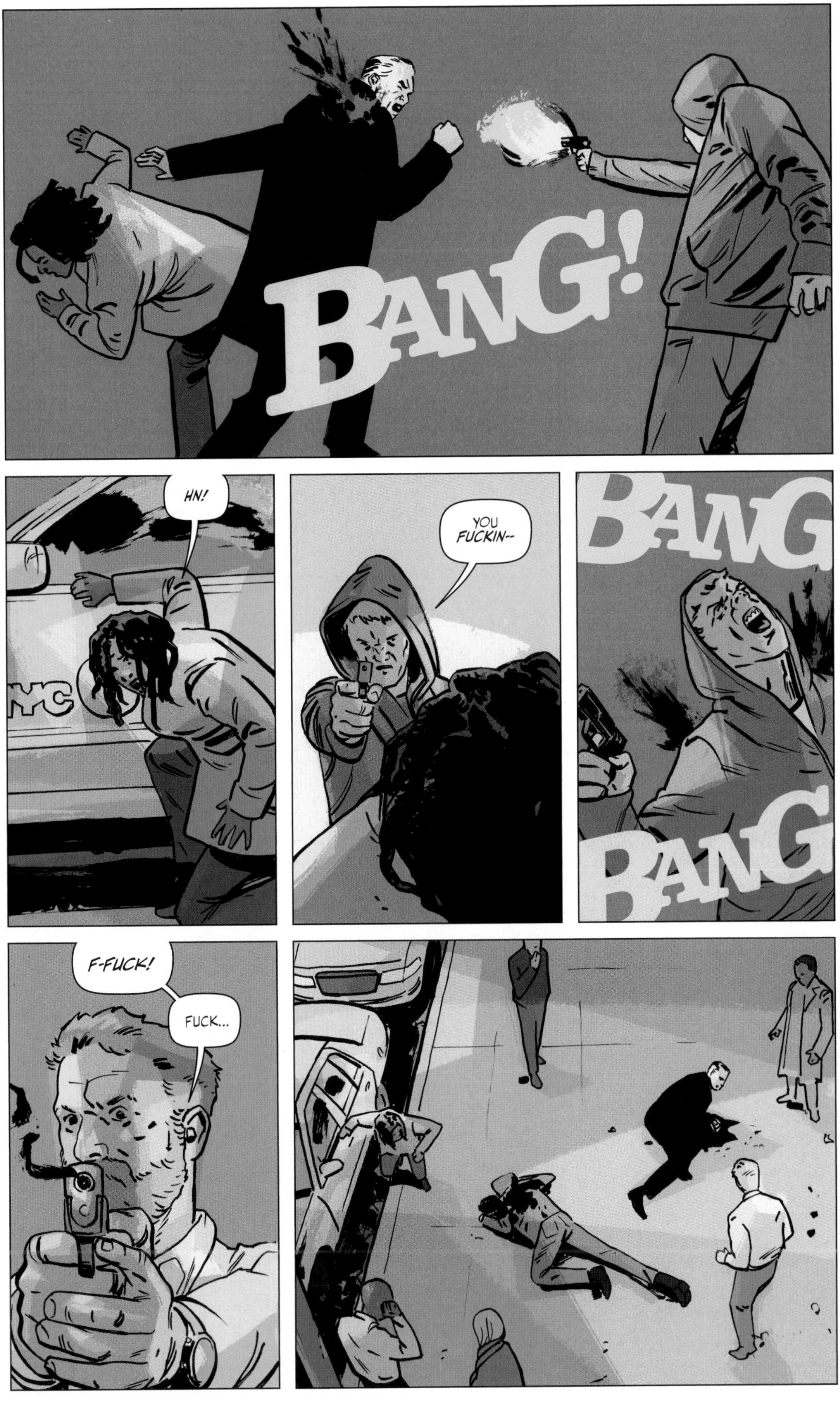
BANG!
HN!
YOU FUCKIN--
BANG
BANG
F-FUCK!
FUCK...

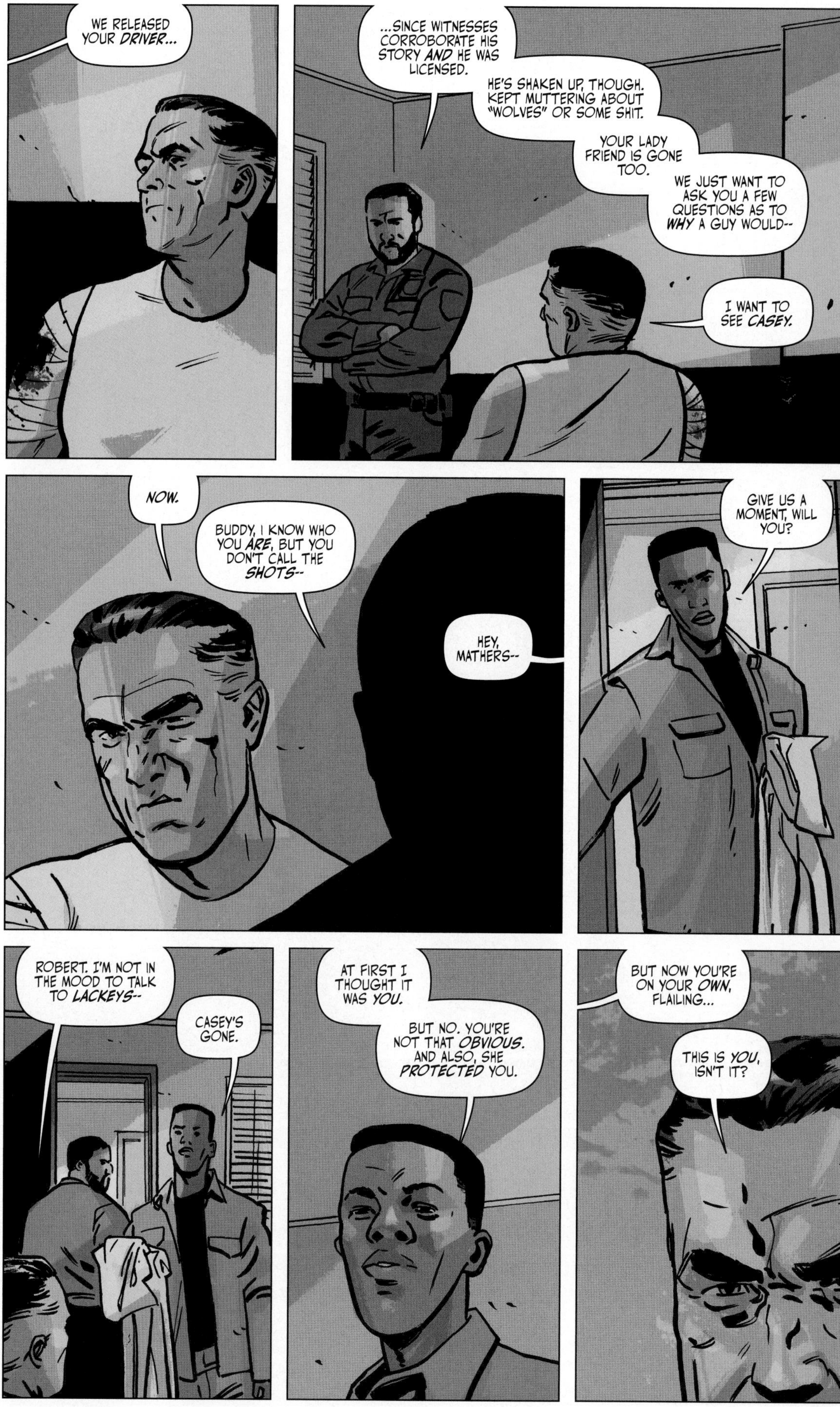
WE RELEASED YOUR DRIVER...
...SINCE WITNESSES CORROBORATE HIS STORY AND HE WAS LICENSED.
HE'S SHAKEN UP, THOUGH. KEPT MUTTERING ABOUT "WOLVES" OR SOME SHIT.
YOUR LADY FRIEND IS GONE TOO.
WE JUST WANT TO ASK YOU A FEW QUESTIONS AS TO WHY A GUY WOULD--
I WANT TO SEE CASEY.
NOW.
BUDDY, I KNOW WHO YOU ARE, BUT YOU DON'T CALL THE SHOTS--
HEY, MATHERS--
GIVE US A MOMENT, WILL YOU?
ROBERT. I'M NOT IN THE MOOD TO TALK TO LACKEYS--
CASEY'S GONE.
AT FIRST I THOUGHT IT WAS YOU.
BUT NO. YOU'RE NOT THAT OBVIOUS. AND ALSO, SHE PROTECTED YOU.
BUT NOW YOU'RE ON YOUR OWN, FLAILING...
THIS IS YOU, ISN'T IT?

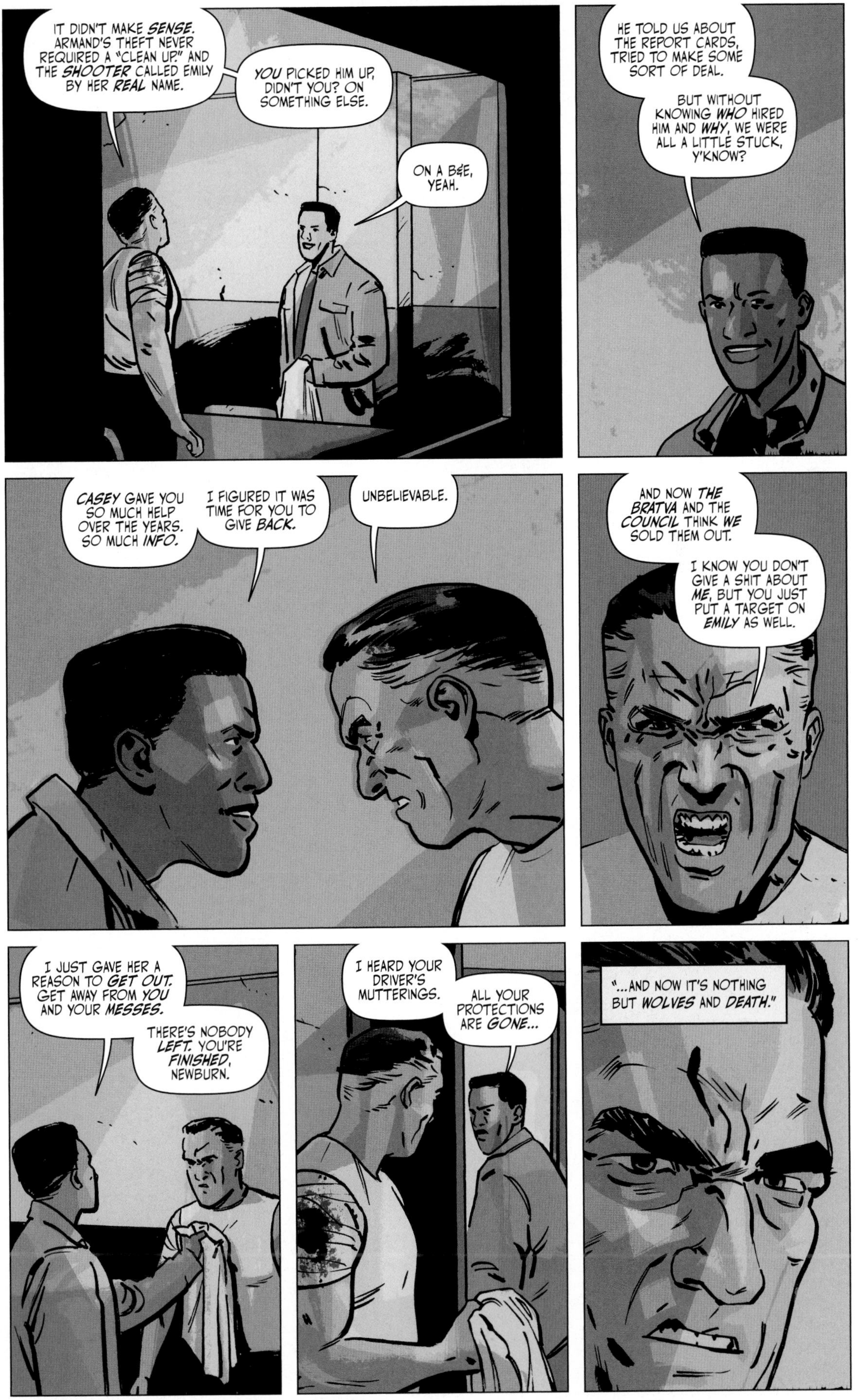
IT DIDN'T MAKE SENSE. ARMAND'S THEFT NEVER REQUIRED A "CLEAN UP." AND THE SHOOTER CALLED EMILY BY HER REAL NAME.
YOU PICKED HIM UP, DIDN'T YOU? ON SOMETHING ELSE.
ON A B&E, YEAH.
HE TOLD US ABOUT THE REPORT CARDS, TRIED TO MAKE SOME SORT OF DEAL.
BUT WITHOUT KNOWING WHO HIRED HIM AND WHY, WE WERE ALL A LITTLE STUCK, Y'KNOW?
CASEY GAVE YOU SO MUCH HELP OVER THE YEARS. SO MUCH INFO.
I FIGURED IT WAS TIME FOR YOU TO GIVE BACK.
UNBELIEVABLE.
AND NOW THE BRATVA AND THE COUNCIL THINK WE SOLD THEM OUT.
I KNOW YOU DON'T GIVE A SHIT ABOUT ME, BUT YOU JUST PUT A TARGET ON EMILY AS WELL.
I JUST GAVE HER A REASON TO GET OUT. GET AWAY FROM YOU AND YOUR MESSES.
THERE'S NOBODY LEFT. YOU'RE FINISHED, NEWBURN.
I HEARD YOUR DRIVER'S MUTTERINGS.
ALL YOUR PROTECTIONS ARE GONE...
"...AND NOW IT'S NOTHING BUT WOLVES AND DEATH."

13

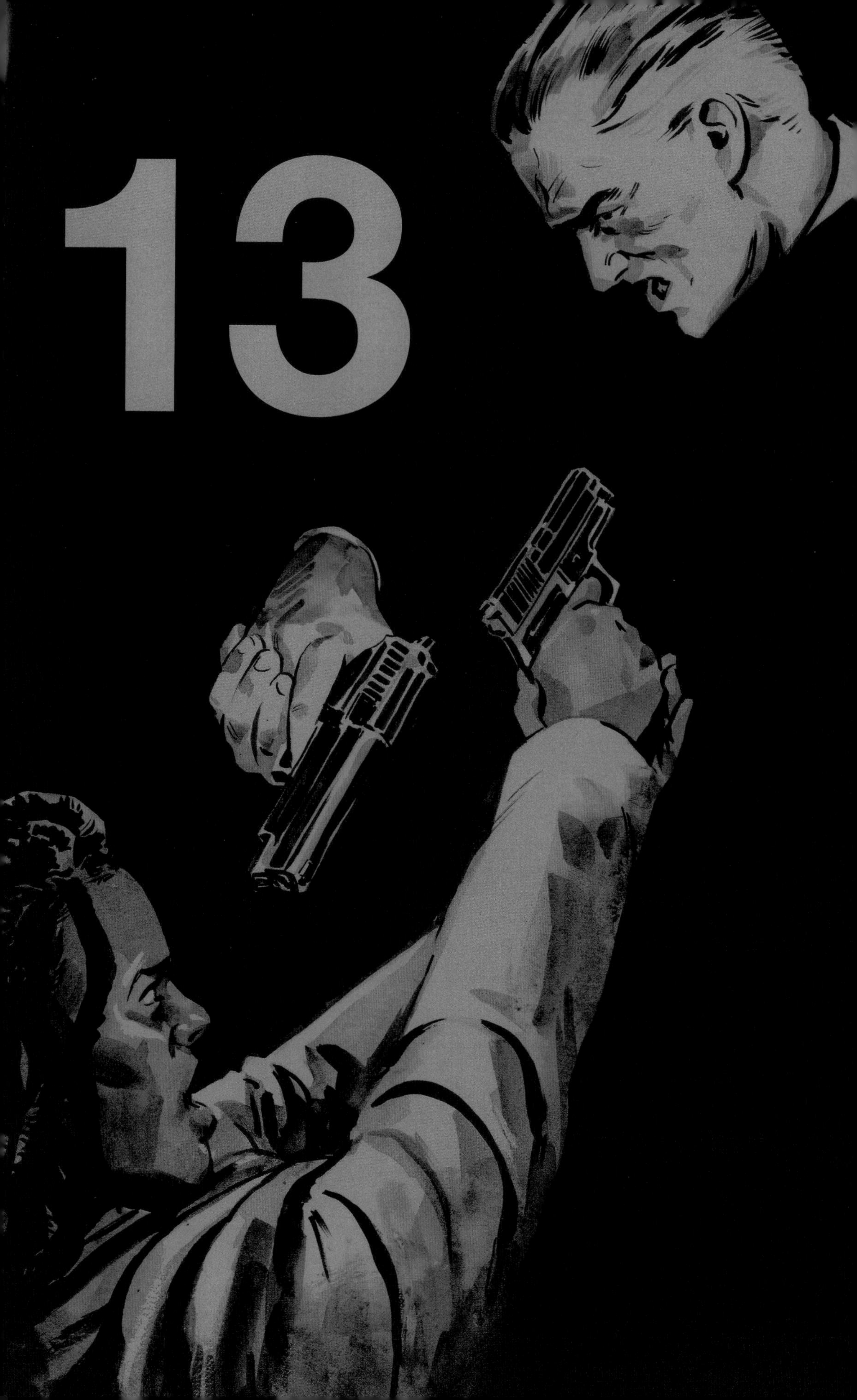

YOU CAN'T KEEP DOING THIS, NATALIE.

IT'S NOT READY.

IT'S NOT GOING TO *BE* READY IF YOU DON'T LOOP IN YOUR EDITOR!

I JUST DON'T WANT TO GET YOUR HOPES UP.

I NEED TO CORROBORATE A COUPLE MORE SOURCES.

FIRST DRAFT ON YOUR DESK WEDNESDAY, I SWEAR.

IT BETTER BE.

WE JUST LET STU AND KELLY GO.

I'M GOING TO NEED YOU TO START COVERING MORE OF THE DAY-TO-DAY BEGINNING NEXT WEEK.

I'M NOT JOKING AROUND, NAT.

I GET IT. DON'T WORRY...

...THIS STORY'S WORTH IT.

IT JUST NEEDS...

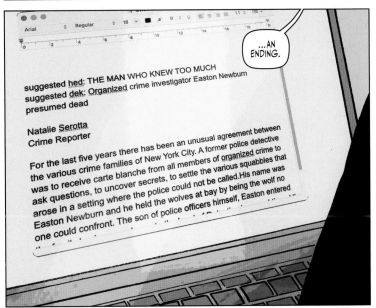

...AN ENDING.

Arial   Regular   18

suggested hed: THE MAN WHO KNEW TOO MUCH
suggested dek: Organized crime investigator Easton Newburn presumed dead

Natalie Serotta
Crime Reporter

For the last five years there has been an unusual agreement between the various crime families of New York City. A former police detective was to receive carte blanche from all members of organized crime to ask questions, to uncover secrets, to settle the various squabbles that arose in a setting where the police could not be called. His name was Easton Newburn and he held the wolves at bay by being the wolf no one could confront. The son of police officers himself, Easton entered

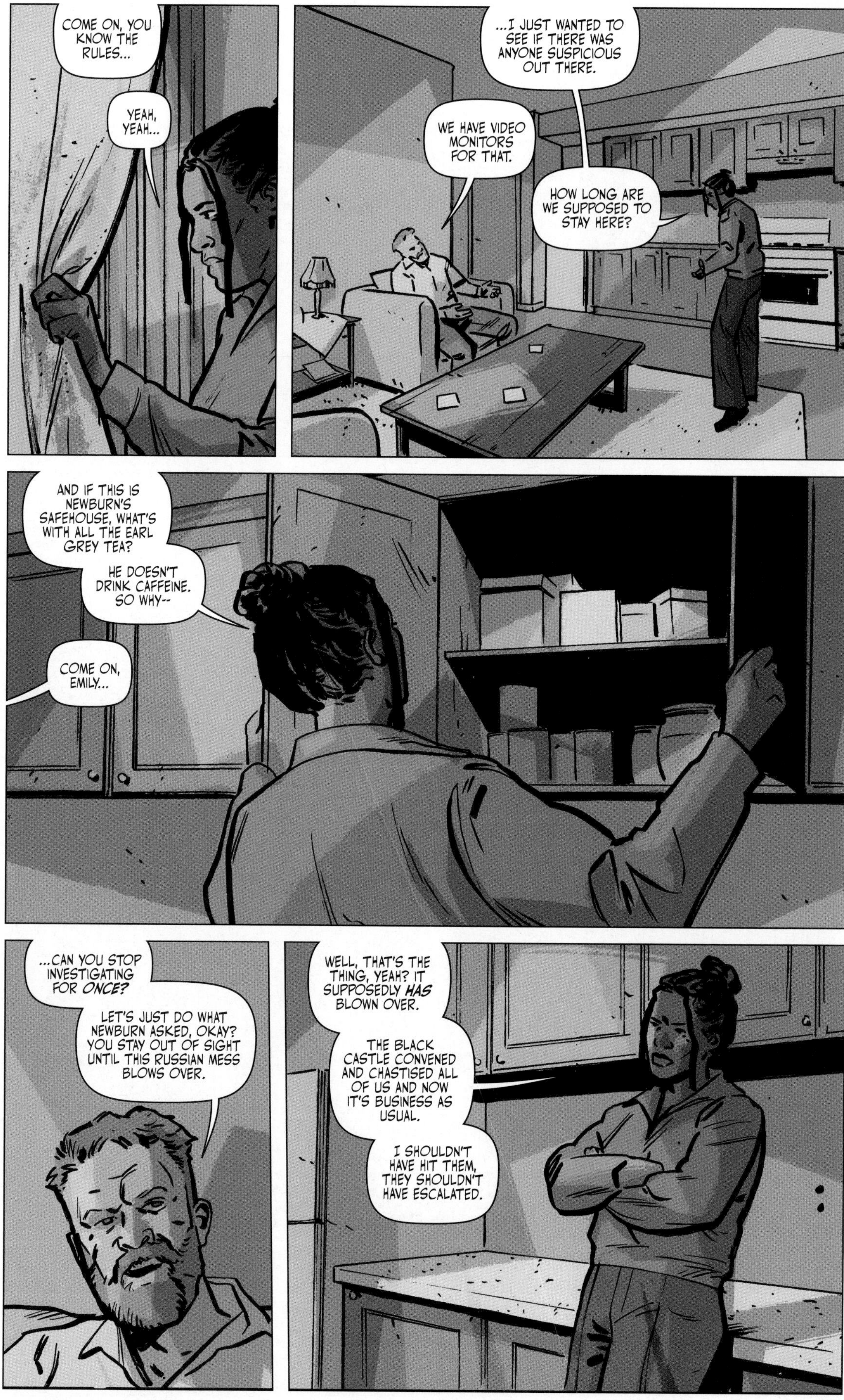
COME ON, YOU KNOW THE RULES...
YEAH, YEAH...
...I JUST WANTED TO SEE IF THERE WAS ANYONE SUSPICIOUS OUT THERE.
WE HAVE VIDEO MONITORS FOR THAT.
HOW LONG ARE WE SUPPOSED TO STAY HERE?
AND IF THIS IS NEWBURN'S SAFEHOUSE, WHAT'S WITH ALL THE EARL GREY TEA?
HE DOESN'T DRINK CAFFEINE. SO WHY--
COME ON, EMILY...
...CAN YOU STOP INVESTIGATING FOR *ONCE?*
LET'S JUST DO WHAT NEWBURN ASKED, OKAY? YOU STAY OUT OF SIGHT UNTIL THIS RUSSIAN MESS BLOWS OVER.
WELL, THAT'S THE THING, YEAH? IT SUPPOSEDLY *HAS* BLOWN OVER.
THE BLACK CASTLE CONVENED AND CHASTISED ALL OF US AND NOW IT'S BUSINESS AS USUAL.
I SHOULDN'T HAVE HIT THEM, THEY SHOULDN'T HAVE ESCALATED.

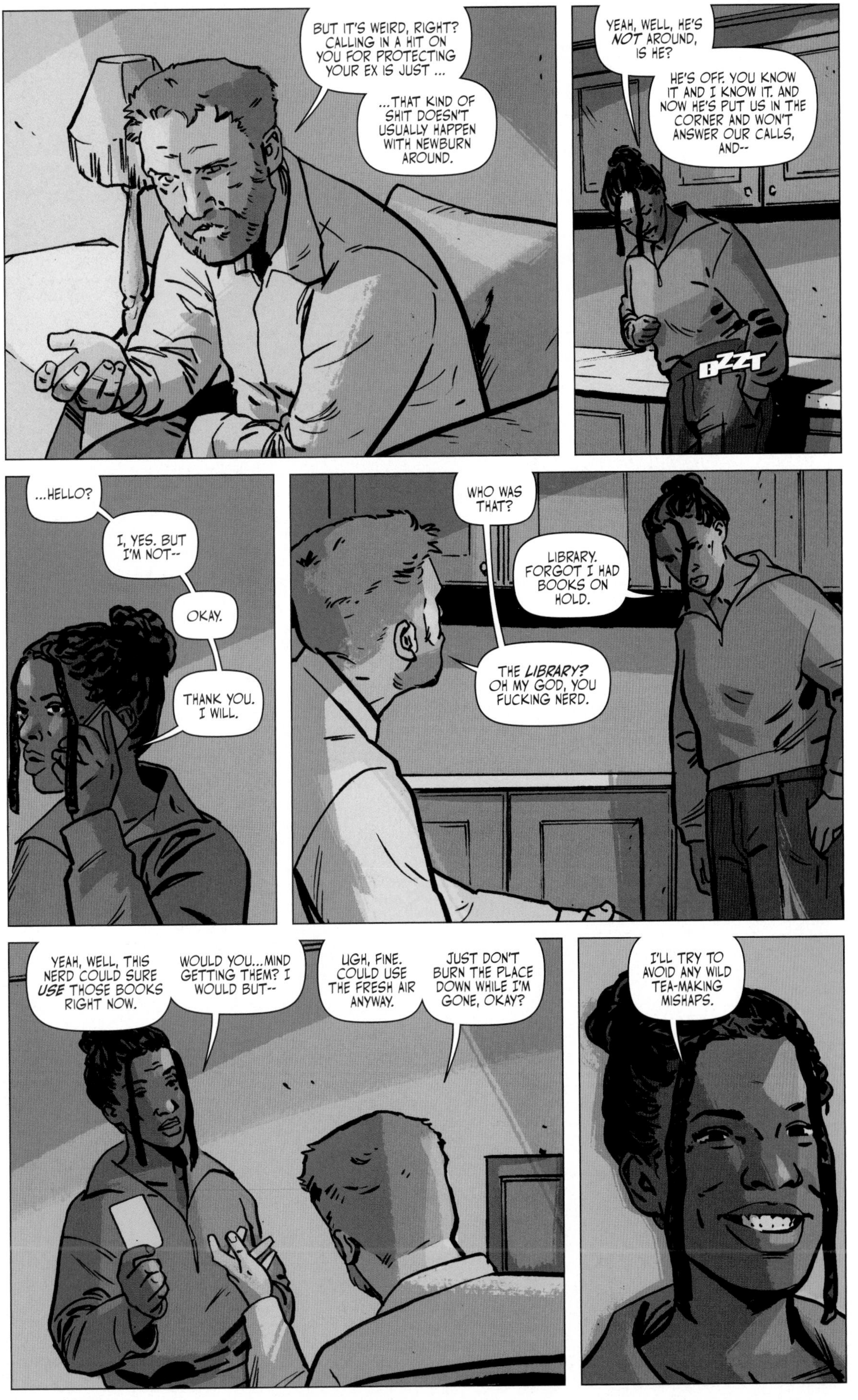
BUT IT'S WEIRD, RIGHT? CALLING IN A HIT ON YOU FOR PROTECTING YOUR EX IS JUST ...
...THAT KIND OF SHIT DOESN'T USUALLY HAPPEN WITH NEWBURN AROUND.
YEAH, WELL, HE'S *NOT* AROUND, IS HE?
HE'S OFF. YOU KNOW IT AND I KNOW IT. AND NOW HE'S PUT US IN THE CORNER AND WON'T ANSWER OUR CALLS, AND--
BZZT
...HELLO?
I, YES. BUT I'M NOT--
OKAY.
THANK YOU. I WILL.
WHO WAS THAT?
LIBRARY. FORGOT I HAD BOOKS ON HOLD.
THE *LIBRARY?* OH MY GOD, YOU FUCKING NERD.
YEAH, WELL, THIS NERD COULD SURE *USE* THOSE BOOKS RIGHT NOW.
WOULD YOU...MIND GETTING THEM? I WOULD BUT--
UGH, FINE. COULD USE THE FRESH AIR ANYWAY.
JUST DON'T BURN THE PLACE DOWN WHILE I'M GONE, OKAY?
I'LL TRY TO AVOID ANY WILD TEA-MAKING MISHAPS.

EMILY'S JOURNAL
01/16/23

I can't figure out a next move. Frankly, that's always been Newburn's thing.

Armand tricked me into taking on the Bratva on behalf of the cops. But even though things are smoothed over, I'm still here in the safehouse. Is it Newburn just being overly cautious?

I killed a cousin in the Albano crime family. And the man who killed the head of the Yakuza is rotting in prison for my crime. Nice and simple, except for the fact that we don't have anyone to hand over for the Yakuza murder.

And the new head wants answers.

Am I being hidden away until Newburn figures out how to handle that? Everything feels like it's unravelling.

All I know is: I need to do something.

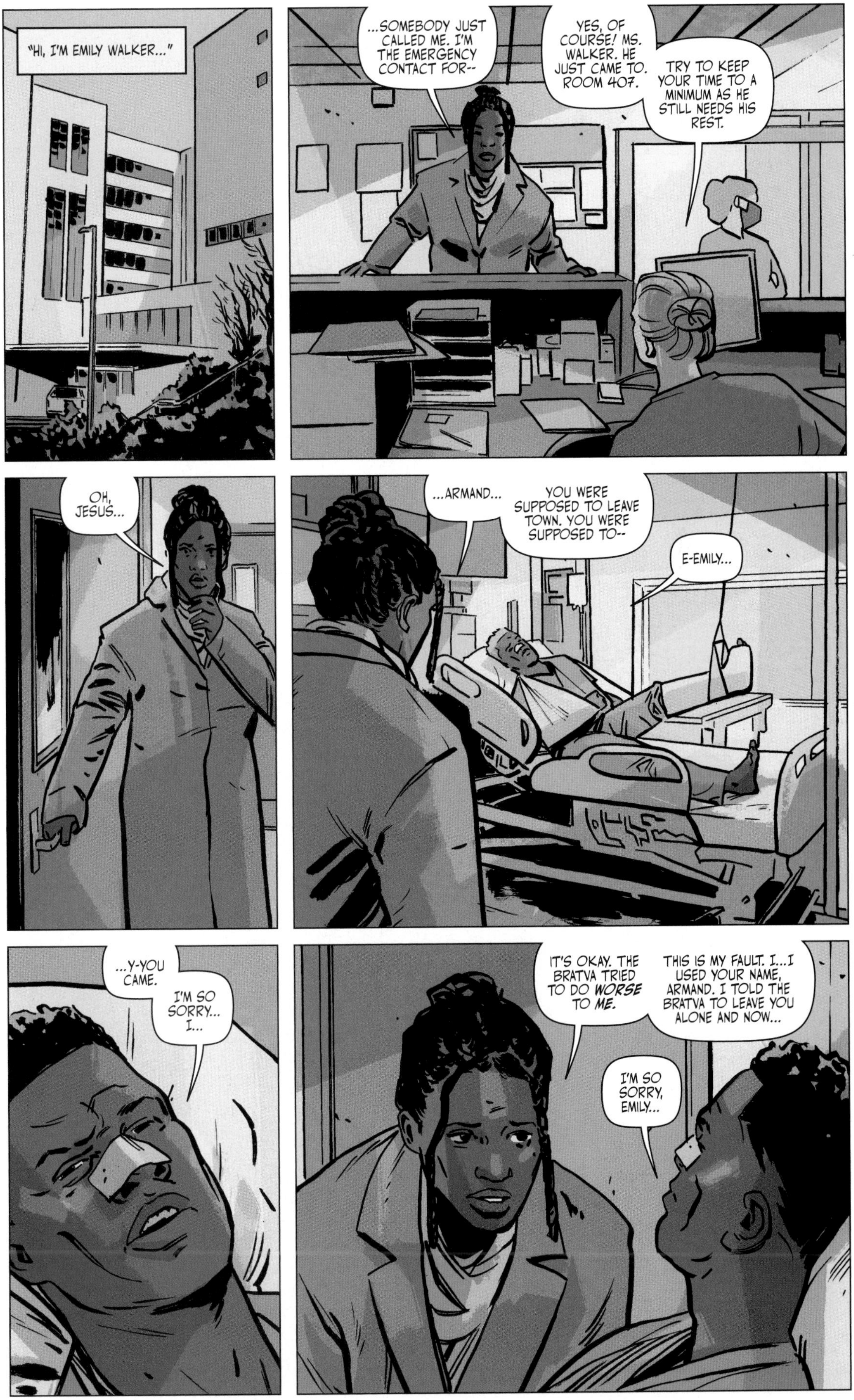
"HI, I'M EMILY WALKER..."
...SOMEBODY JUST CALLED ME. I'M THE EMERGENCY CONTACT FOR--
YES, OF COURSE! MS. WALKER. HE JUST CAME TO. ROOM 407.
TRY TO KEEP YOUR TIME TO A MINIMUM AS HE STILL NEEDS HIS REST.
OH, JESUS...
...ARMAND...
YOU WERE SUPPOSED TO LEAVE TOWN. YOU WERE SUPPOSED TO--
E-EMILY...
...Y-YOU CAME.
I'M SO SORRY... I...
IT'S OKAY. THE BRATVA TRIED TO DO WORSE TO ME.
THIS IS MY FAULT. I...I USED YOUR NAME, ARMAND. I TOLD THE BRATVA TO LEAVE YOU ALONE AND NOW...
I'M SO SORRY, EMILY...

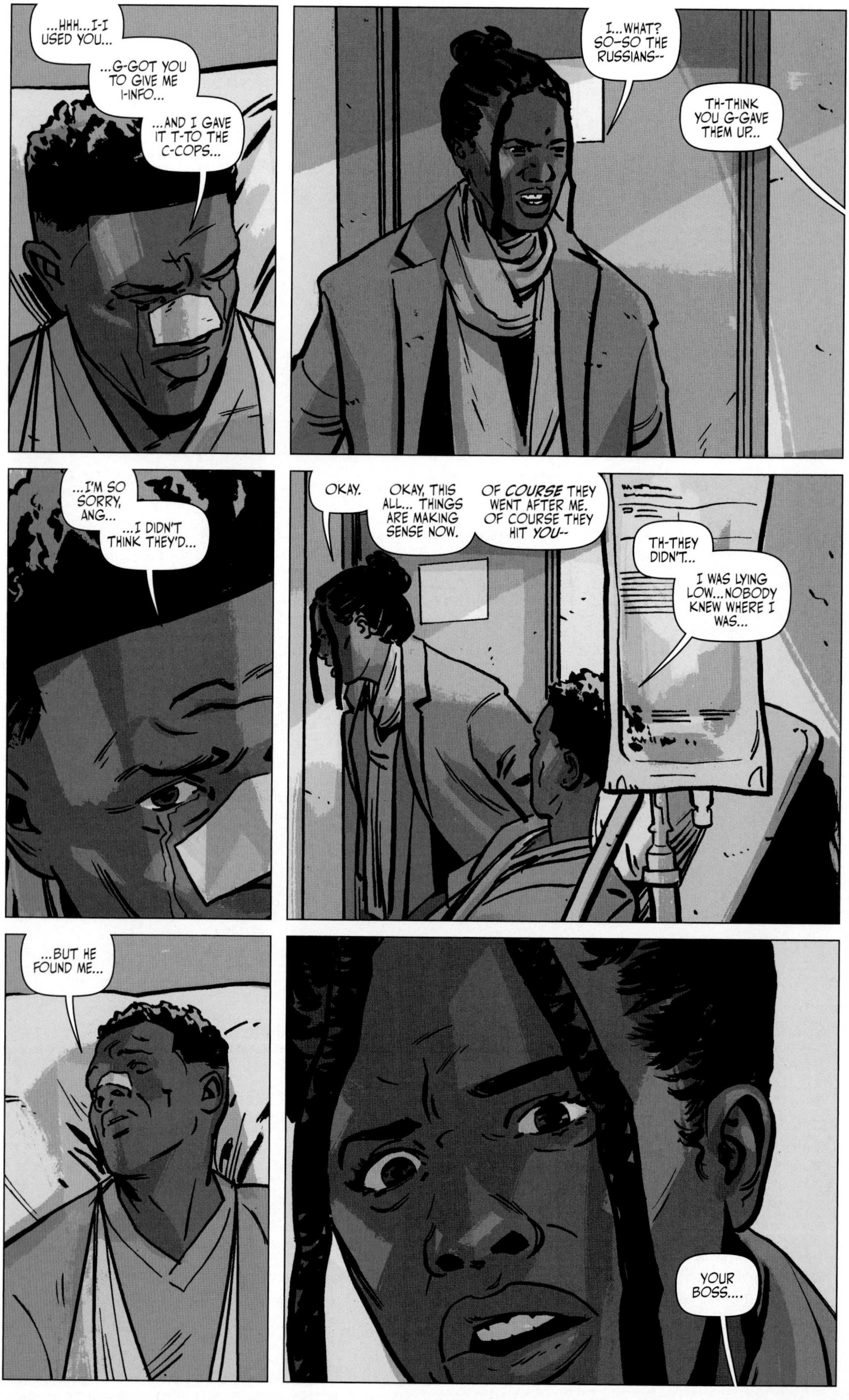
...HHH...I-I USED YOU...
...G-GOT YOU TO GIVE ME I-INFO...
...AND I GAVE IT T-TO THE C-COPS...
I...WHAT? SO-SO THE RUSSIANS--
TH-THINK YOU G-GAVE THEM UP...
...I'M SO SORRY, ANG...
...I DIDN'T THINK THEY'D...
OKAY.
OKAY, THIS ALL... THINGS ARE MAKING SENSE NOW.
OF COURSE THEY WENT AFTER ME. OF COURSE THEY HIT YOU--
TH-THEY DIDN'T...
I WAS LYING LOW...NOBODY KNEW WHERE I WAS...
...BUT HE FOUND ME...
YOUR BOSS....

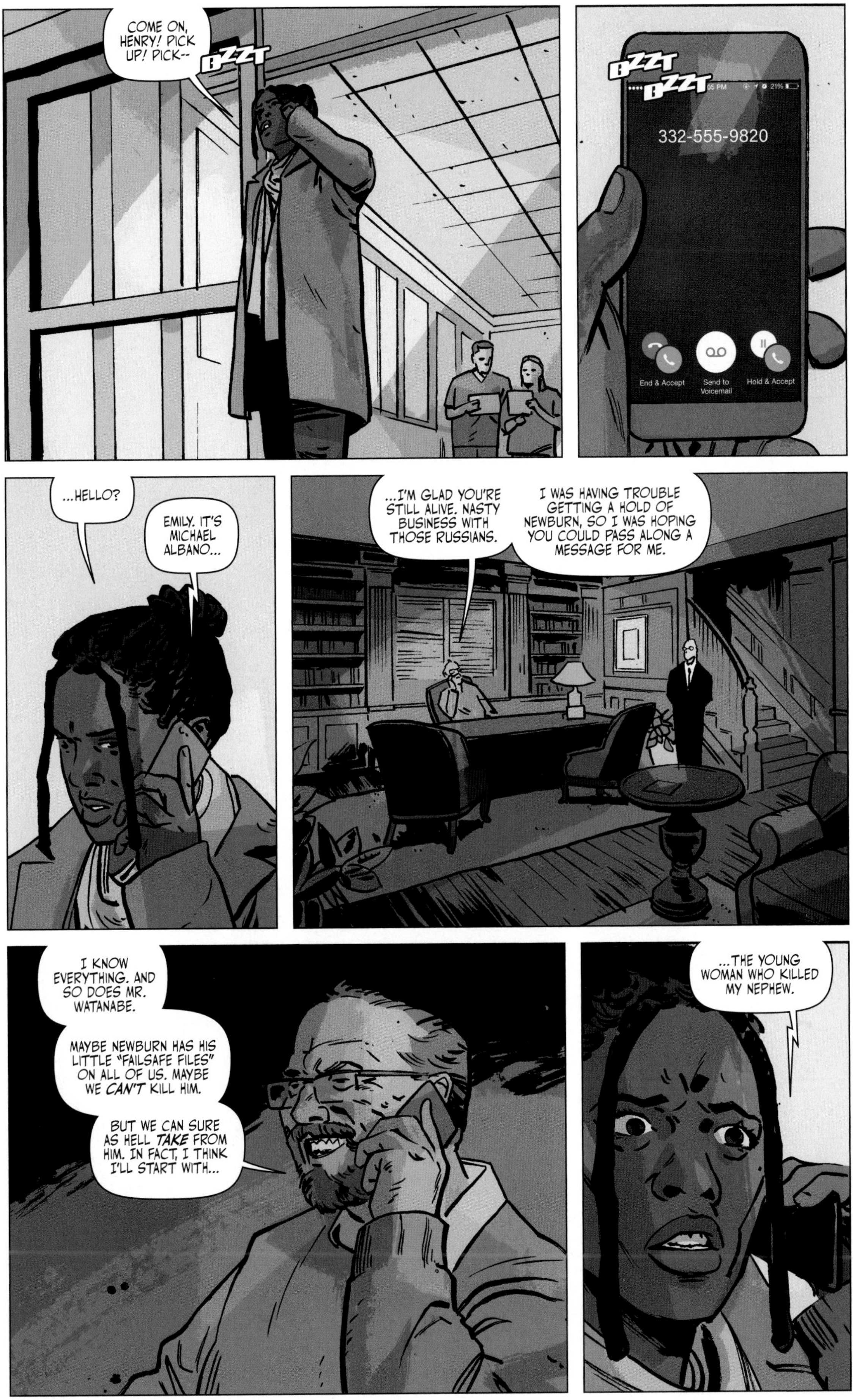
COME ON, HENRY! PICK UP! PICK--
BZZT
BZZT BZZT
05 PM
21%
332-555-9820
End & Accept
Send to Voicemail
Hold & Accept
...HELLO?
EMILY. IT'S MICHAEL ALBANO...
...I'M GLAD YOU'RE STILL ALIVE. NASTY BUSINESS WITH THOSE RUSSIANS.
I WAS HAVING TROUBLE GETTING A HOLD OF NEWBURN, SO I WAS HOPING YOU COULD PASS ALONG A MESSAGE FOR ME.
I KNOW EVERYTHING. AND SO DOES MR. WATANABE.
MAYBE NEWBURN HAS HIS LITTLE "FAILSAFE FILES" ON ALL OF US. MAYBE WE *CAN'T* KILL HIM.
BUT WE CAN SURE AS HELL *TAKE* FROM HIM. IN FACT, I THINK I'LL START WITH...
...THE YOUNG WOMAN WHO KILLED MY NEPHEW.

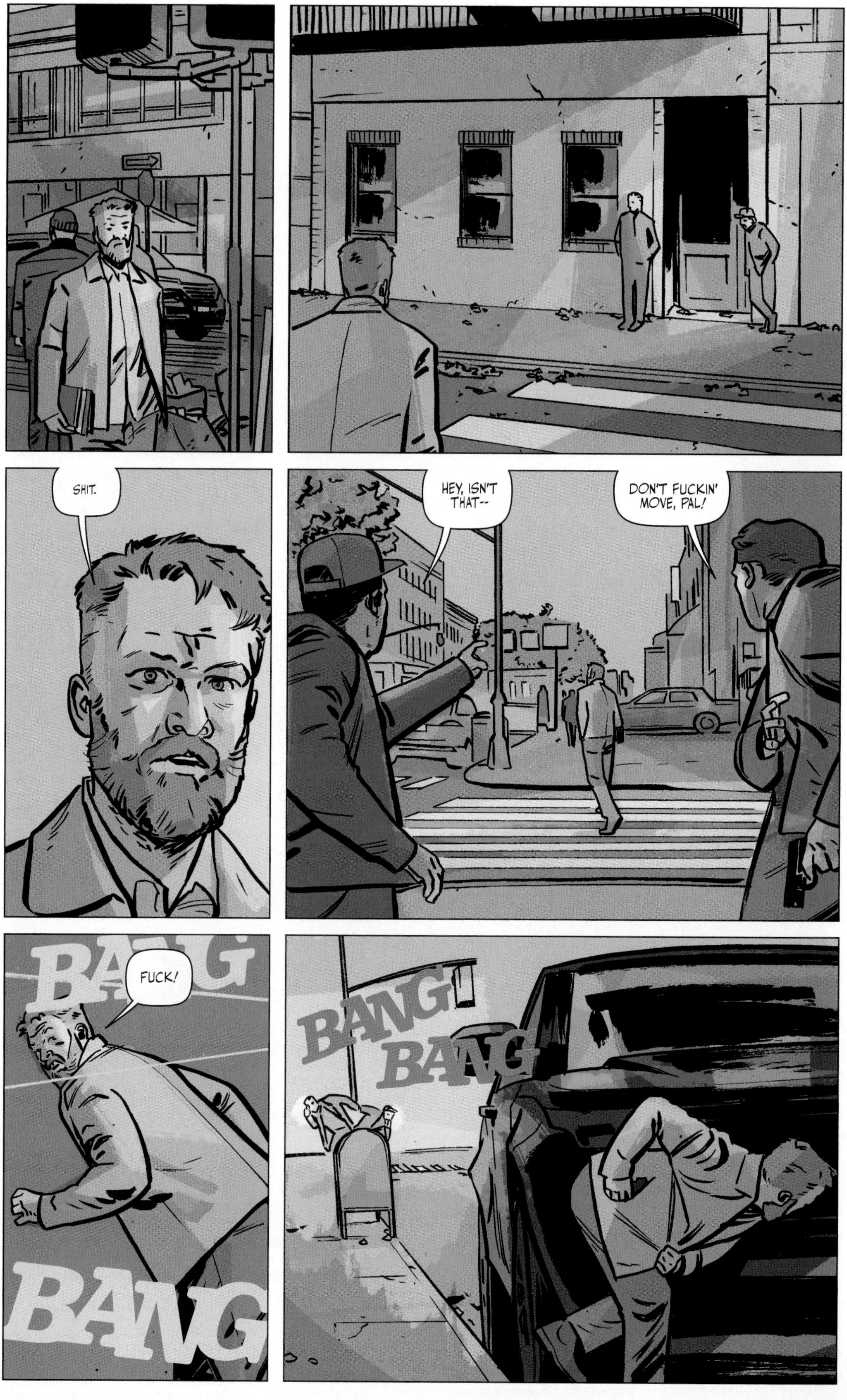
SHIT.
HEY, ISN'T THAT--
DON'T FUCKIN' MOVE, PAL!
BANG
FUCK!
BANG
BANG
BANG

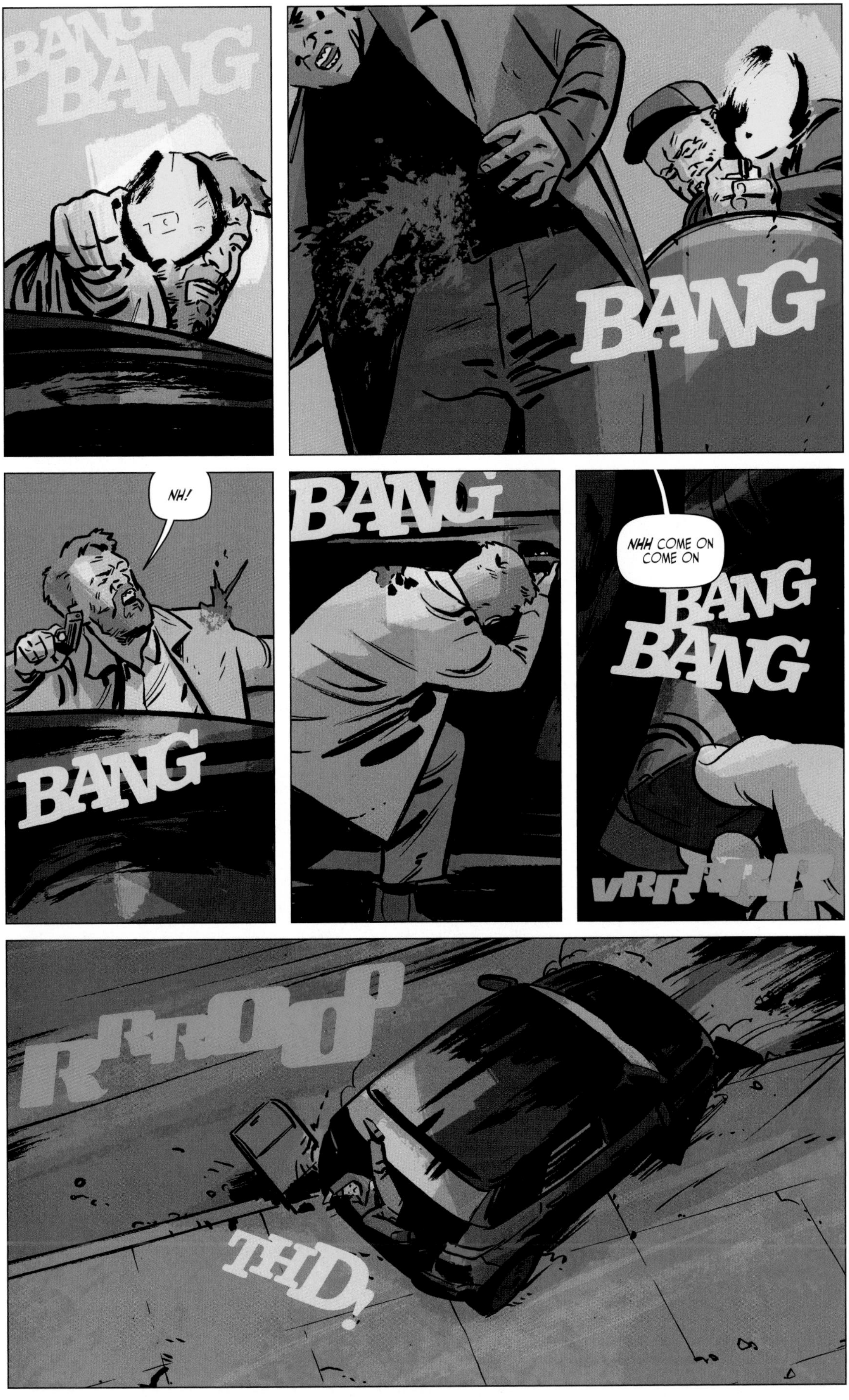
BANG
BANG
BANG
NH!
BANG
BANG
NHH COME ON COME ON
BANG
BANG
VRRRRR
RRROOP
THD!

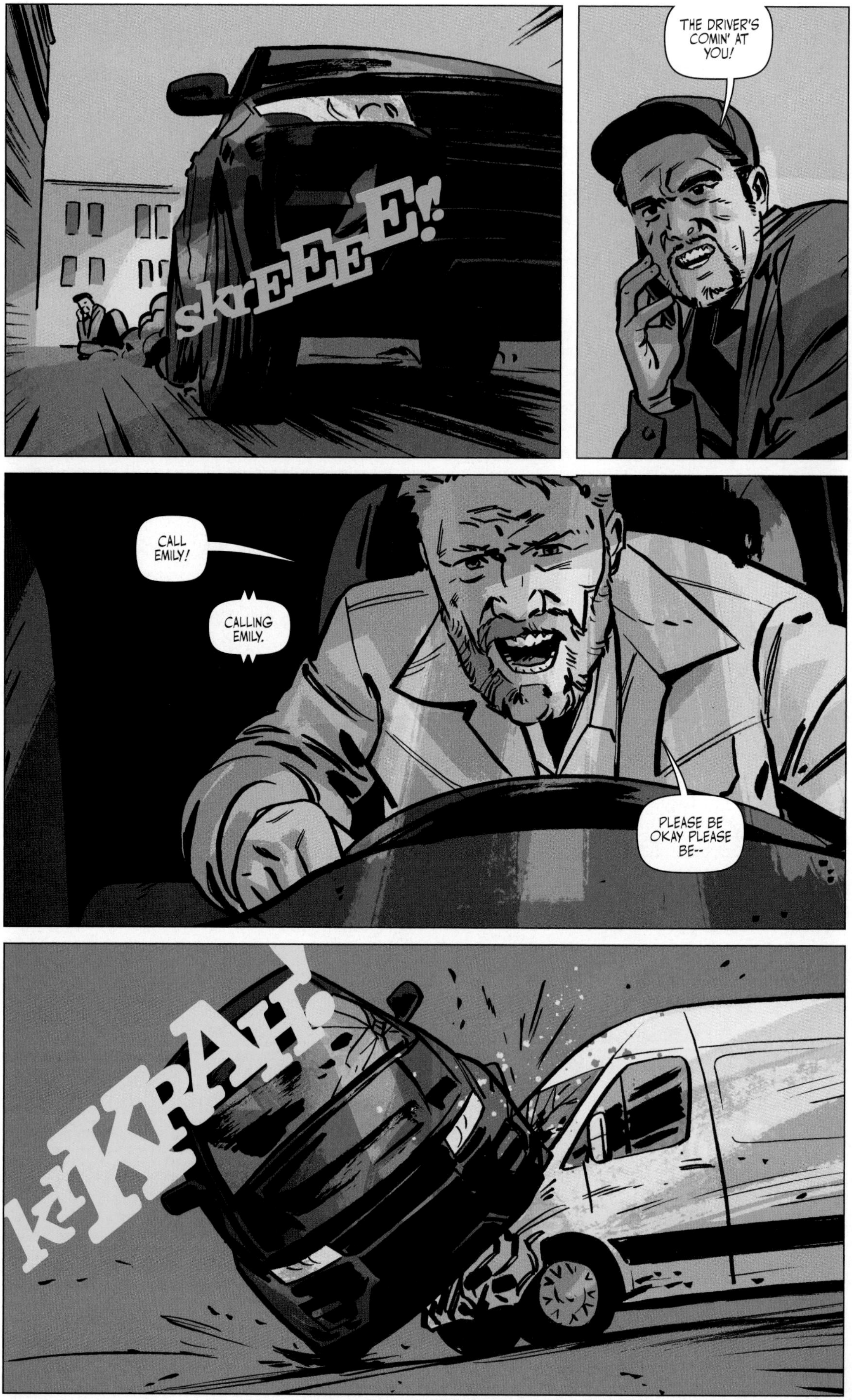
skrEEEE!
THE DRIVER'S COMIN' AT YOU!
CALL EMILY!
CALLING EMILY.
PLEASE BE OKAY PLEASE BE--
krKRAH!

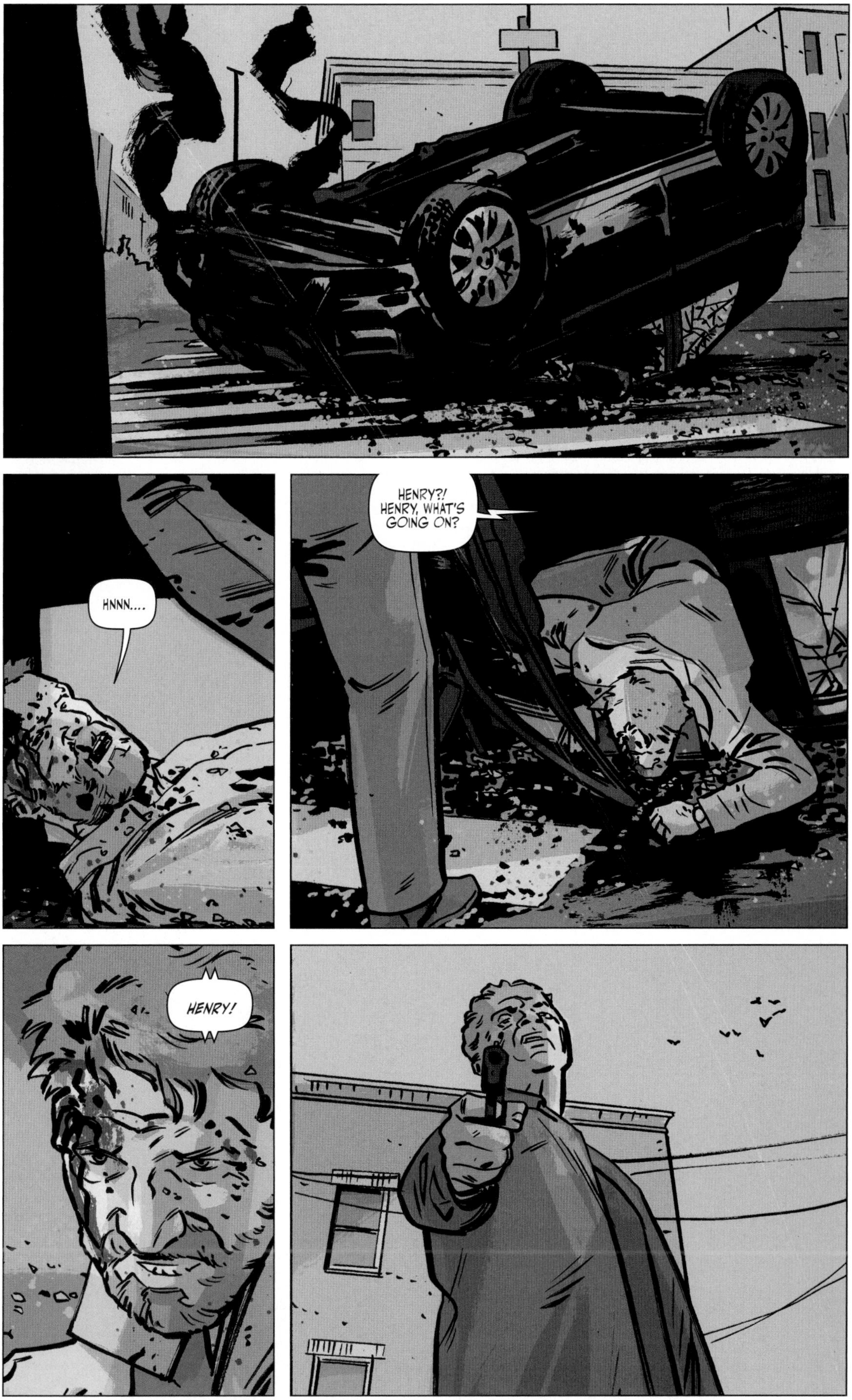
HNNN....
HENRY?! HENRY, WHAT'S GOING ON?
HENRY!

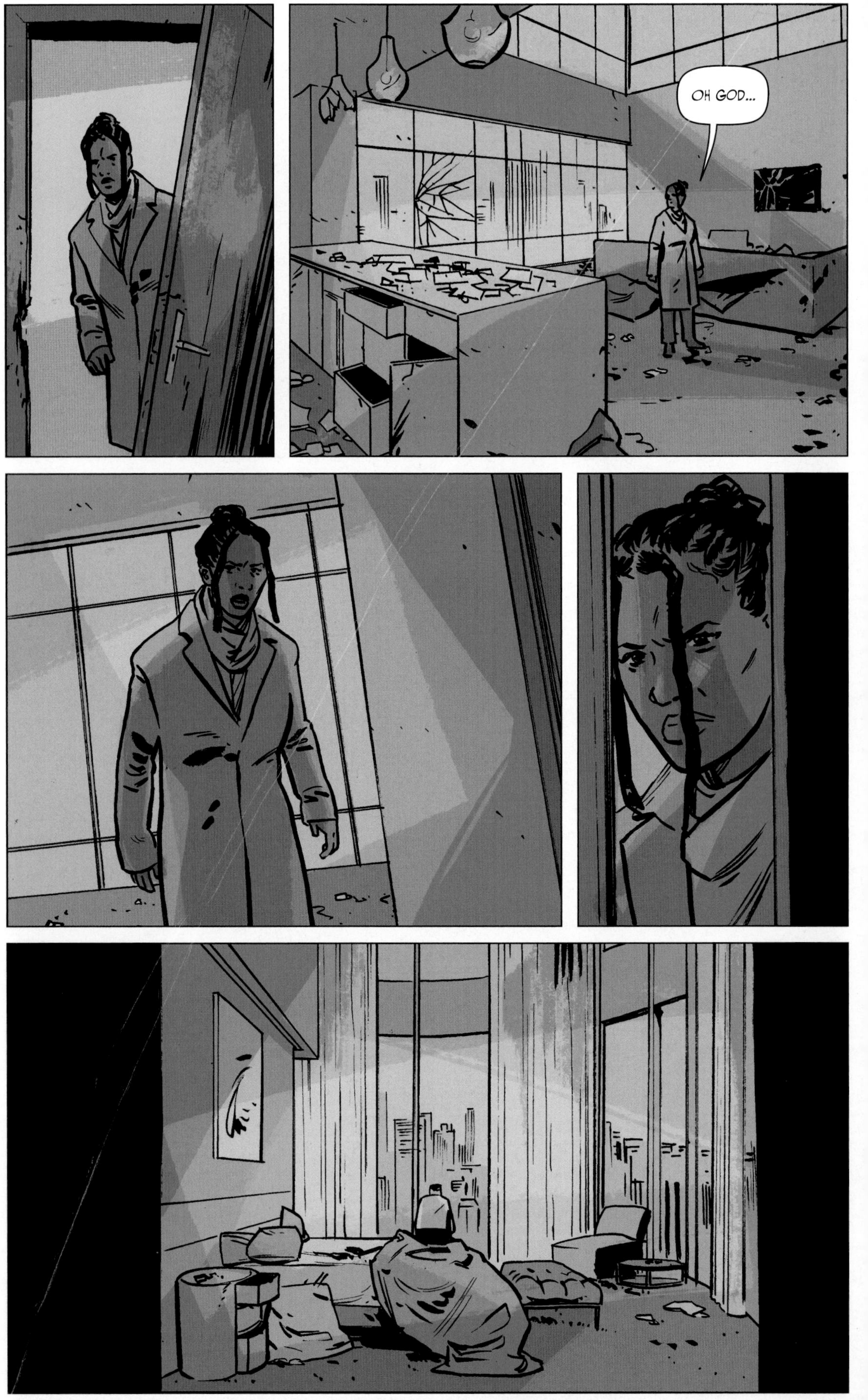
OH GOD...

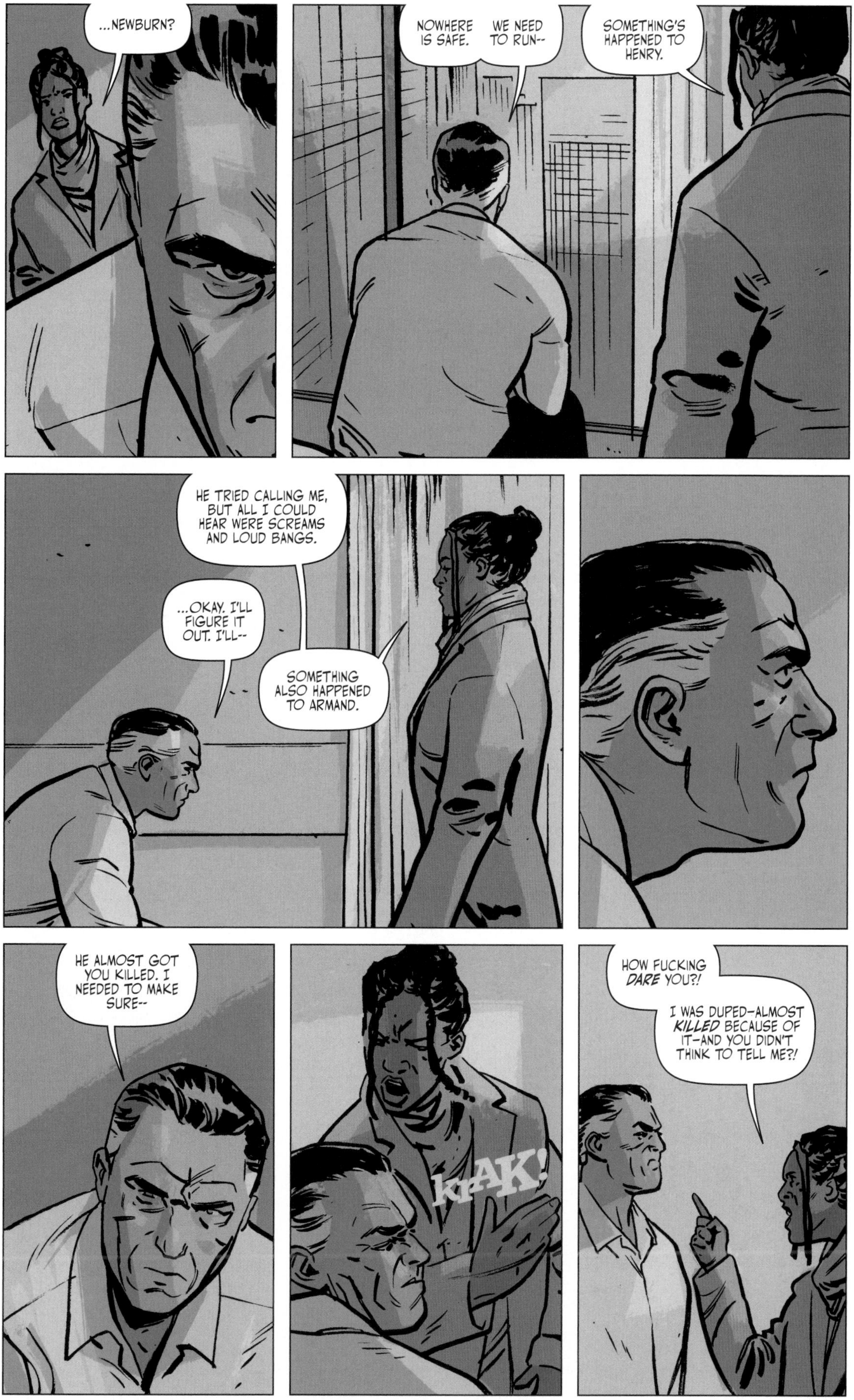
...NEWBURN?
NOWHERE IS SAFE.
WE NEED TO RUN--
SOMETHING'S HAPPENED TO HENRY.
HE TRIED CALLING ME, BUT ALL I COULD HEAR WERE SCREAMS AND LOUD BANGS.
...OKAY. I'LL FIGURE IT OUT. I'LL--
SOMETHING ALSO HAPPENED TO ARMAND.
HE ALMOST GOT YOU KILLED. I NEEDED TO MAKE SURE--
KRAK!
HOW FUCKING *DARE* YOU?!
I WAS DUPED--ALMOST *KILLED* BECAUSE OF IT--AND YOU DIDN'T THINK TO TELL ME?!

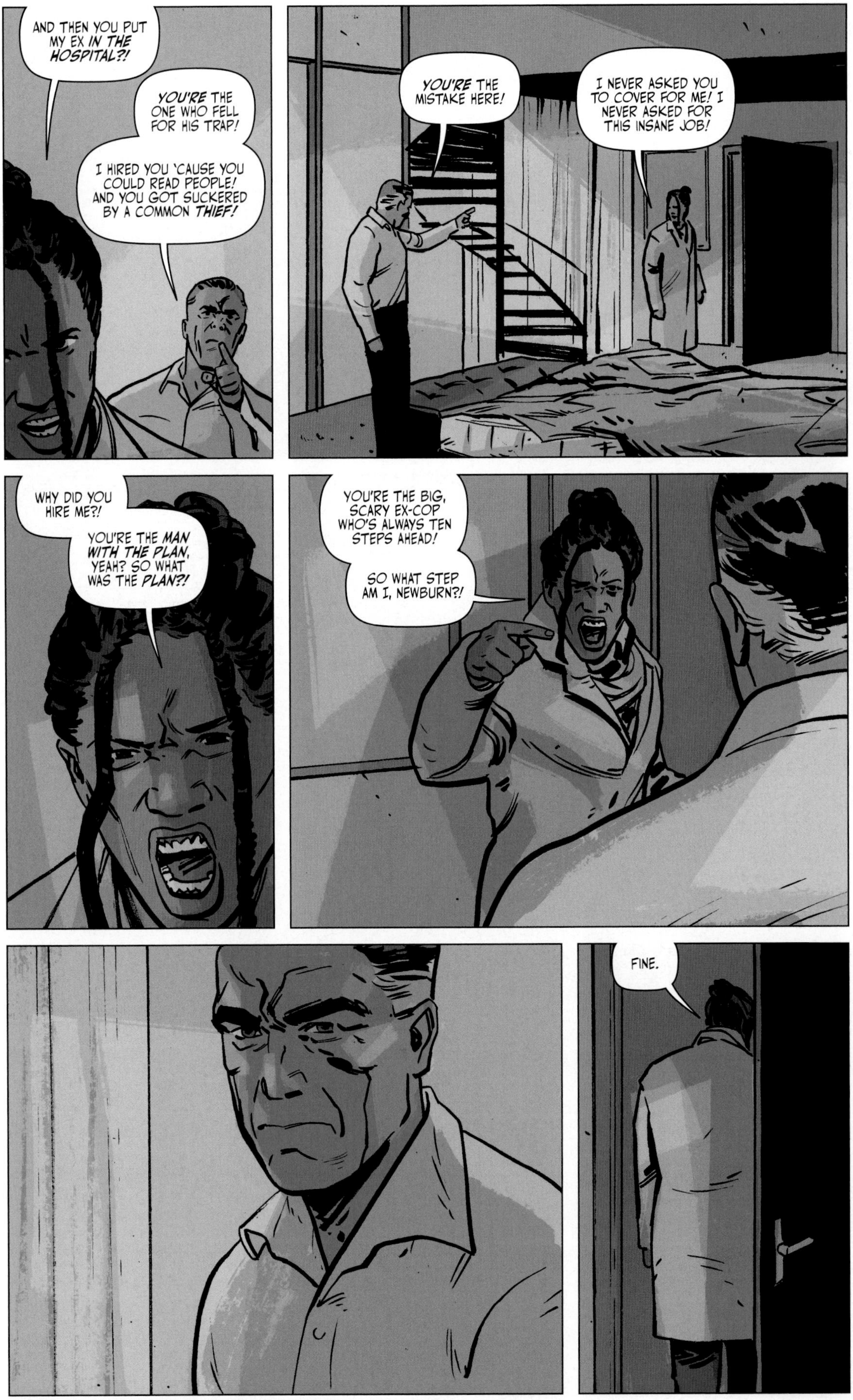
AND THEN YOU PUT MY EX IN THE HOSPITAL?!
YOU'RE THE ONE WHO FELL FOR HIS TRAP!
I HIRED YOU 'CAUSE YOU COULD READ PEOPLE! AND YOU GOT SUCKERED BY A COMMON THIEF!
YOU'RE THE MISTAKE HERE!
I NEVER ASKED YOU TO COVER FOR ME! I NEVER ASKED FOR THIS INSANE JOB!
WHY DID YOU HIRE ME?!
YOU'RE THE MAN WITH THE PLAN, YEAH? SO WHAT WAS THE PLAN?!
YOU'RE THE BIG, SCARY EX-COP WHO'S ALWAYS TEN STEPS AHEAD!
SO WHAT STEP AM I, NEWBURN?!
FINE.

EMILY. WE CAN GET THROUGH THIS. I--

IF HE'S STILL ALIVE, I'M GOING TO FIND HENRY AND GET HIM AN AMOUD PASSPORT.

BZZT

BZZT

MR. WATANABE.

MR. NEWBURN. I'M AFRAID I HAVE AN ISSUE I NEED TO DISCUSS WITH YOU.

AS YOU KNOW, I'VE BEEN DISPLEASED WITH YOUR LACK OF PROGRESS IN SOLVING MY PREDECESSOR'S MURDER.

SO, I DECIDED TO START MY OWN INVESTIGATION.

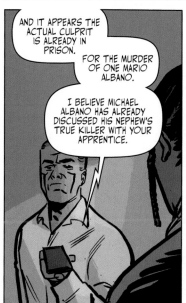

AND IT APPEARS THE ACTUAL CULPRIT IS ALREADY IN PRISON.

FOR THE MURDER OF ONE MARIO ALBANO.

I BELIEVE MICHAEL ALBANO HAS ALREADY DISCUSSED HIS NEPHEW'S TRUE KILLER WITH YOUR APPRENTICE.

YOUR CHAUFFEUR IS ALIVE.

I WILL HAVE SHIGEYUKI SHIROO KILLED IN HIS CELL FOR THE MURDER OF SABURO MURATA.

MR. ALBANO WILL ELIMINATE MS. WALKER FOR THE MURDER OF HIS NEPHEW.

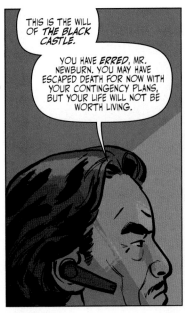

THIS IS THE WILL OF *THE BLACK CASTLE.*

YOU HAVE *ERRED*, MR. NEWBURN. YOU MAY HAVE ESCAPED DEATH FOR NOW WITH YOUR CONTINGENCY PLANS, BUT YOUR LIFE WILL NOT BE WORTH LIVING.

clk

A TEXT. THE BLACK CASTLE HAS REQUESTED OUR PRESENCE.

OKAY. THEY WANT US TO WALK INTO THE SLAUGHTERHOUSE APPARENTLY.

WE NEED A PLAN. AND THE ONLY WAY WE CAN *MAKE* A PLAN...

...IS IF WE HAVE ALL THE INFORMATION.

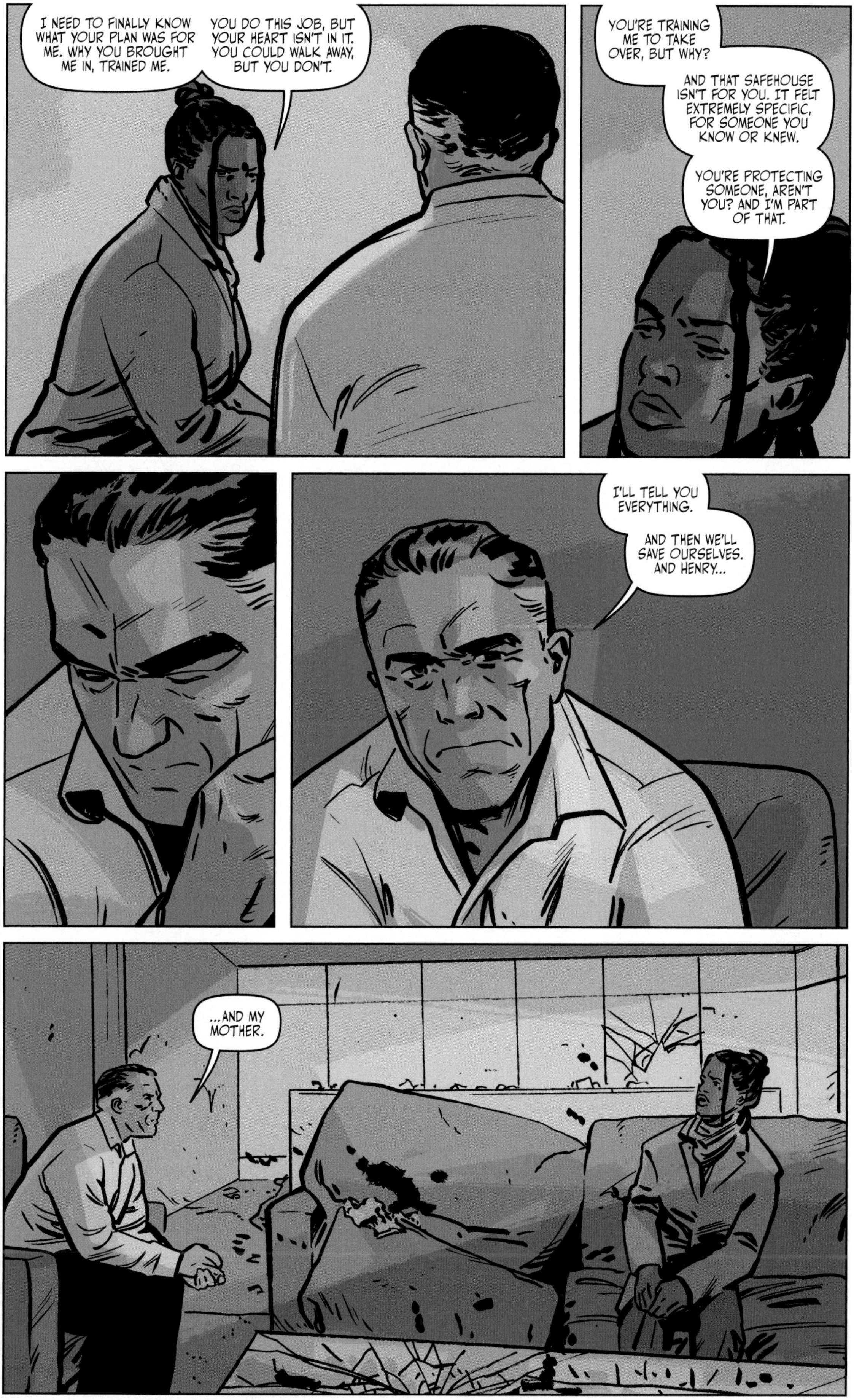
I NEED TO FINALLY KNOW WHAT YOUR PLAN WAS FOR ME. WHY YOU BROUGHT ME IN, TRAINED ME.
YOU DO THIS JOB, BUT YOUR HEART ISN'T IN IT. YOU COULD WALK AWAY, BUT YOU DON'T.
YOU'RE TRAINING ME TO TAKE OVER, BUT WHY?
AND THAT SAFEHOUSE ISN'T FOR YOU. IT FELT EXTREMELY SPECIFIC, FOR SOMEONE YOU KNOW OR KNEW.
YOU'RE PROTECTING SOMEONE, AREN'T YOU? AND I'M PART OF THAT.
I'LL TELL YOU EVERYTHING.
AND THEN WE'LL SAVE OURSELVES. AND HENRY...
...AND MY MOTHER.

14

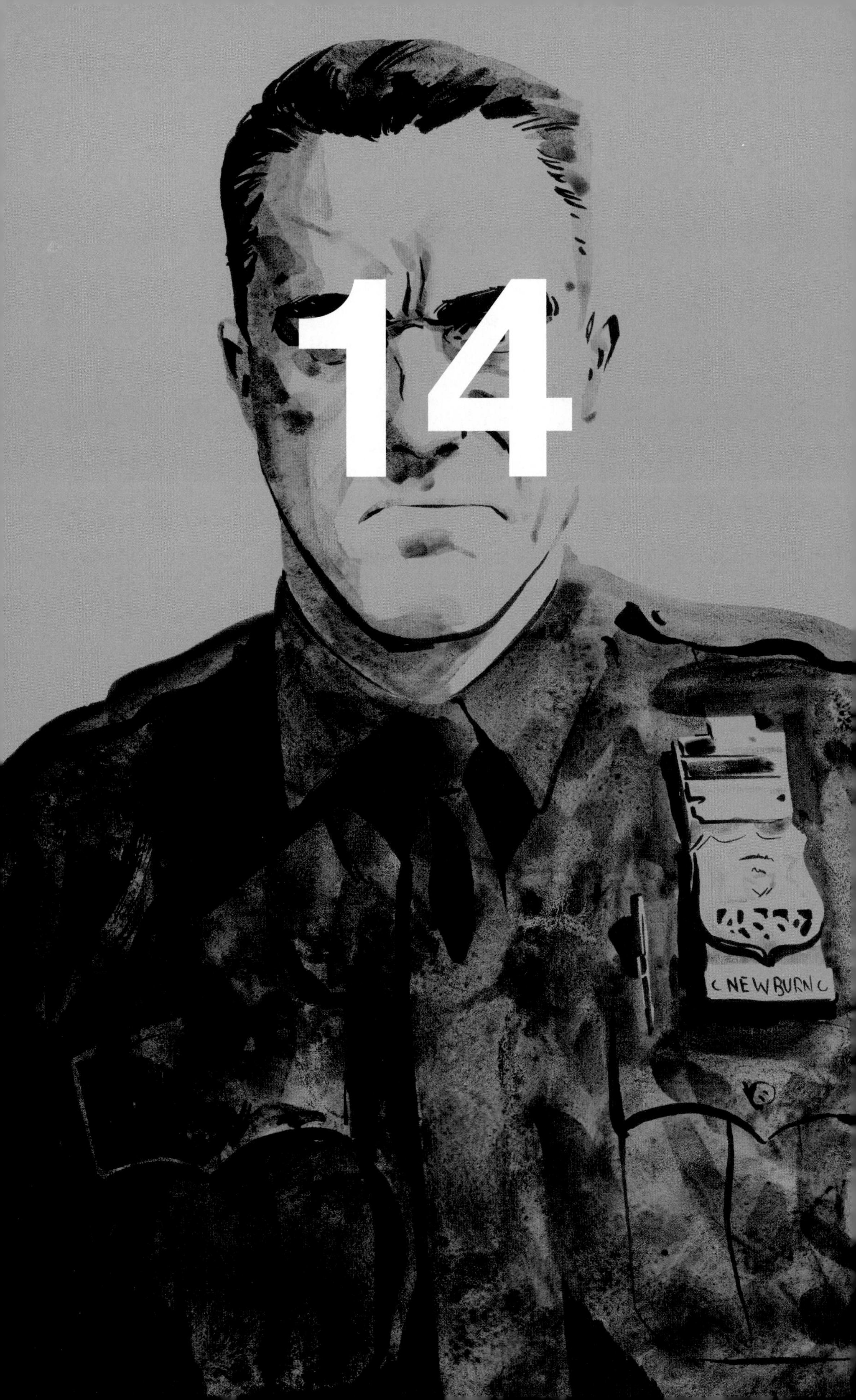
NEWBURN

You deserve the world but all I can give you is the truth, as I see it.

Of course you taught me how important "as I see it" is. That there is objective, provable truth, but there's also the subjective memories and feelings of suspects and victims. Words and tics where we need to read between the lines to work out as much reality as we can manage as we piece together accurate stories.

So, with that caveat, here is what I can offer.

I'm the son of cops. In a household where the job, the duty, was all that mattered until I was old enough to see another layer: the puzzles. You may have espoused ideas of justice and helping, but the reality for you was the same for me: solving the puzzles that people shatter into millions of pieces and spread throughout the city.

I inherited that illness. The itch.

Did I ever stand a chance?

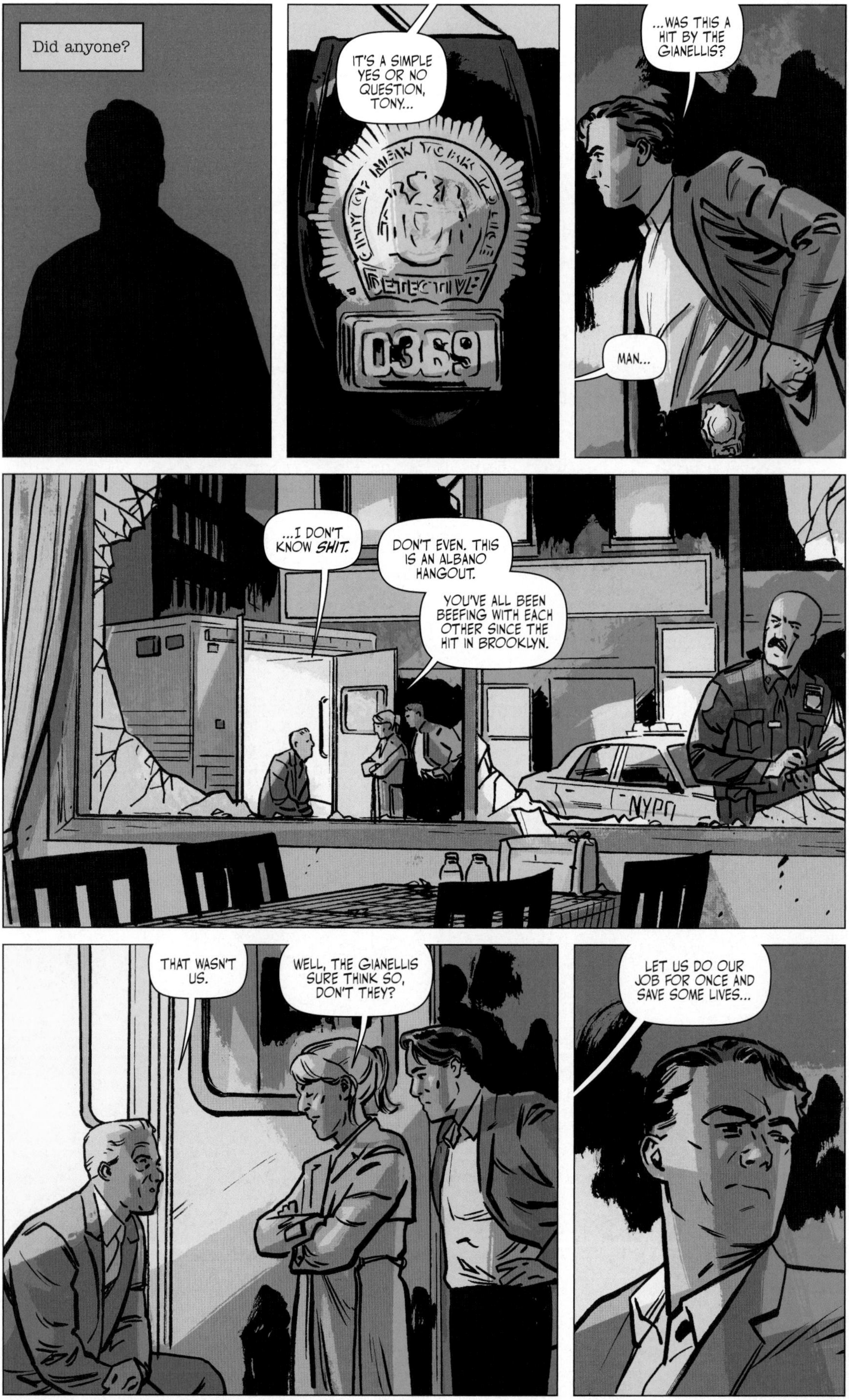

Did anyone?
IT'S A SIMPLE YES OR NO QUESTION, TONY...
DETECTIVE
0369
...WAS THIS A HIT BY THE GIANELLIS?
MAN...
...I DON'T KNOW SHIT.
DON'T EVEN. THIS IS AN ALBANO HANGOUT.
YOU'VE ALL BEEN BEEFING WITH EACH OTHER SINCE THE HIT IN BROOKLYN.
NYPD
THAT WASN'T US.
WELL, THE GIANELLIS SURE THINK SO, DON'T THEY?
LET US DO OUR JOB FOR ONCE AND SAVE SOME LIVES...

EVEN *SHITBAG* LIVES.

HEY!

WHO THE FUCK LET YOU INTO MY CRIME SCENE?

JESUS, NEWBURN. COOL YOUR JETS.

JUST DOING MY STRAIGHT EIGHT, PAL.

I had that righteous anger.

GK!

FOR US OR THE GIANELLIS, YOU DIRTY PIECE OF--

That could explode into violence.

But maybe it wasn't that righteous after all.

JESUS, EASTON! CALM DOWN!

FINE! JUST GET HIM THE HELL OUT OF HERE!

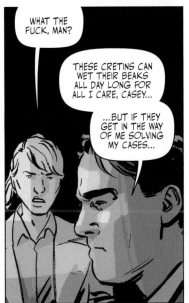

WHAT THE FUCK, MAN?

THESE CRETINS CAN WET THEIR BEAKS ALL DAY LONG FOR ALL I CARE, CASEY...

...BUT IF THEY GET IN THE WAY OF ME SOLVING MY CASES...

...I'LL FINISH THEM.

No, it wasn't righteous.

I didn't care about the cops on the take. I was never a
believer in the system, not really. I just enjoyed the challenge.
Every night a new puzzle was laid out before me and I had to
piece it together. Some other cops liked that part, sure. But
most of them were in it for the power. They spent a lifetime
being abused by authority figures, being embarrassed by the
prom queen, being picked on, and they wanted the feel of a
gun on their hip. They wanted the fake respect that came
with being an officer, where people say "yes sir" and "no
ma'am" not because they think you deserve it, but because
they're scared of what will happen if they don't.

Cops took bribes, cash handouts from crime families. I didn't
begrudge them that. Take what you can get, the NYPD was
just another crime family. It wasn't for me. It just muddied
up my cases, took puzzle pieces away from me.

It might seem strange, where I ended up. But nobody has
power over me or my cases anymore. I'm not beholden to a
police chief in the Bratva's pocket. I'm not supposed to turn a
blind eye because the Yakuza line my pockets. I have freedom
because I keep balance in the city.

I'm no longer a cop, but I can finally be a cop.

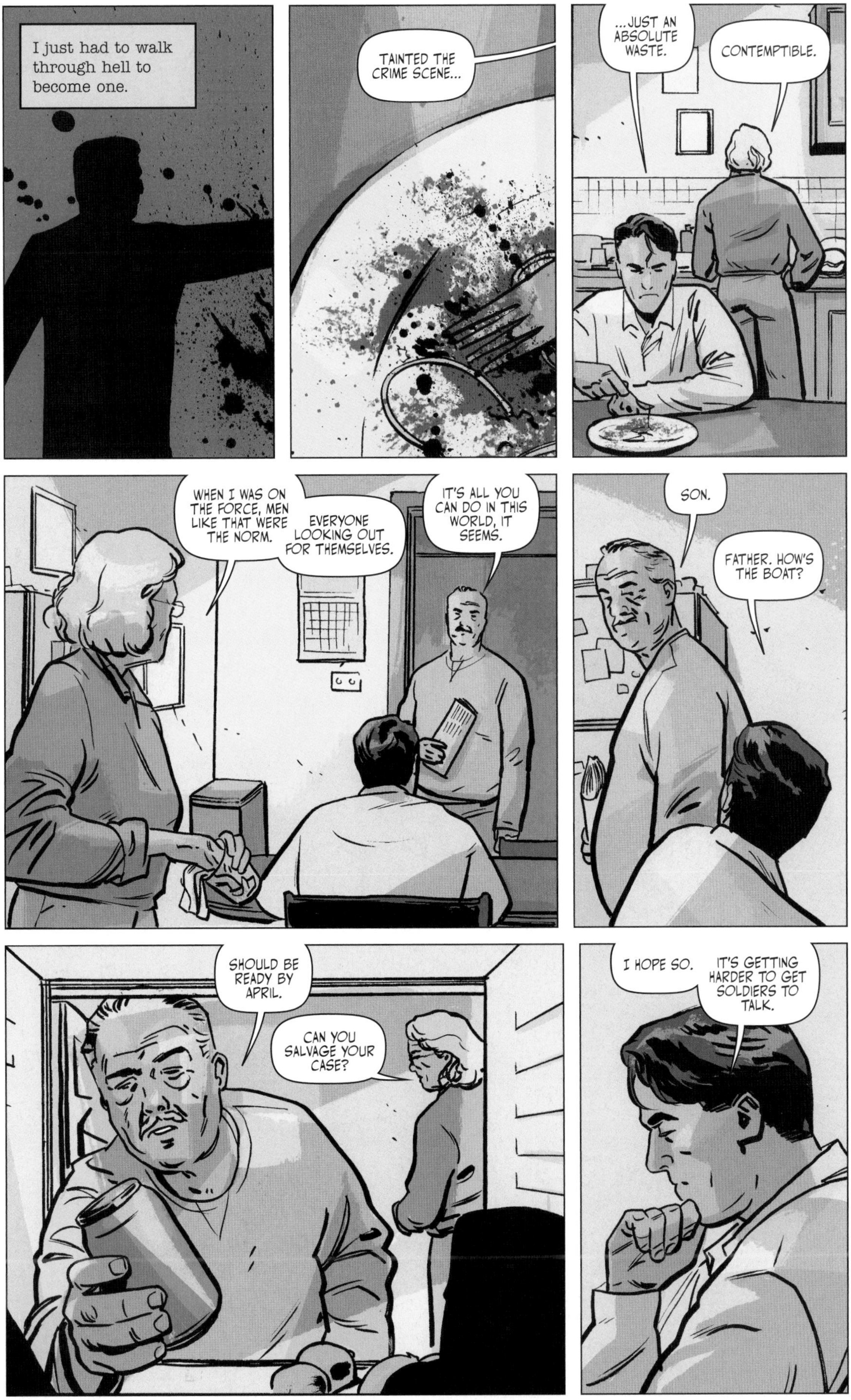
I just had to walk through hell to become one.
TAINTED THE CRIME SCENE...
...JUST AN ABSOLUTE WASTE.
CONTEMPTIBLE.
WHEN I WAS ON THE FORCE, MEN LIKE THAT WERE THE NORM.
EVERYONE LOOKING OUT FOR THEMSELVES.
IT'S ALL YOU CAN DO IN THIS WORLD, IT SEEMS.
SON.
FATHER. HOW'S THE BOAT?
SHOULD BE READY BY APRIL.
CAN YOU SALVAGE YOUR CASE?
I HOPE SO.
IT'S GETTING HARDER TO GET SOLDIERS TO TALK.

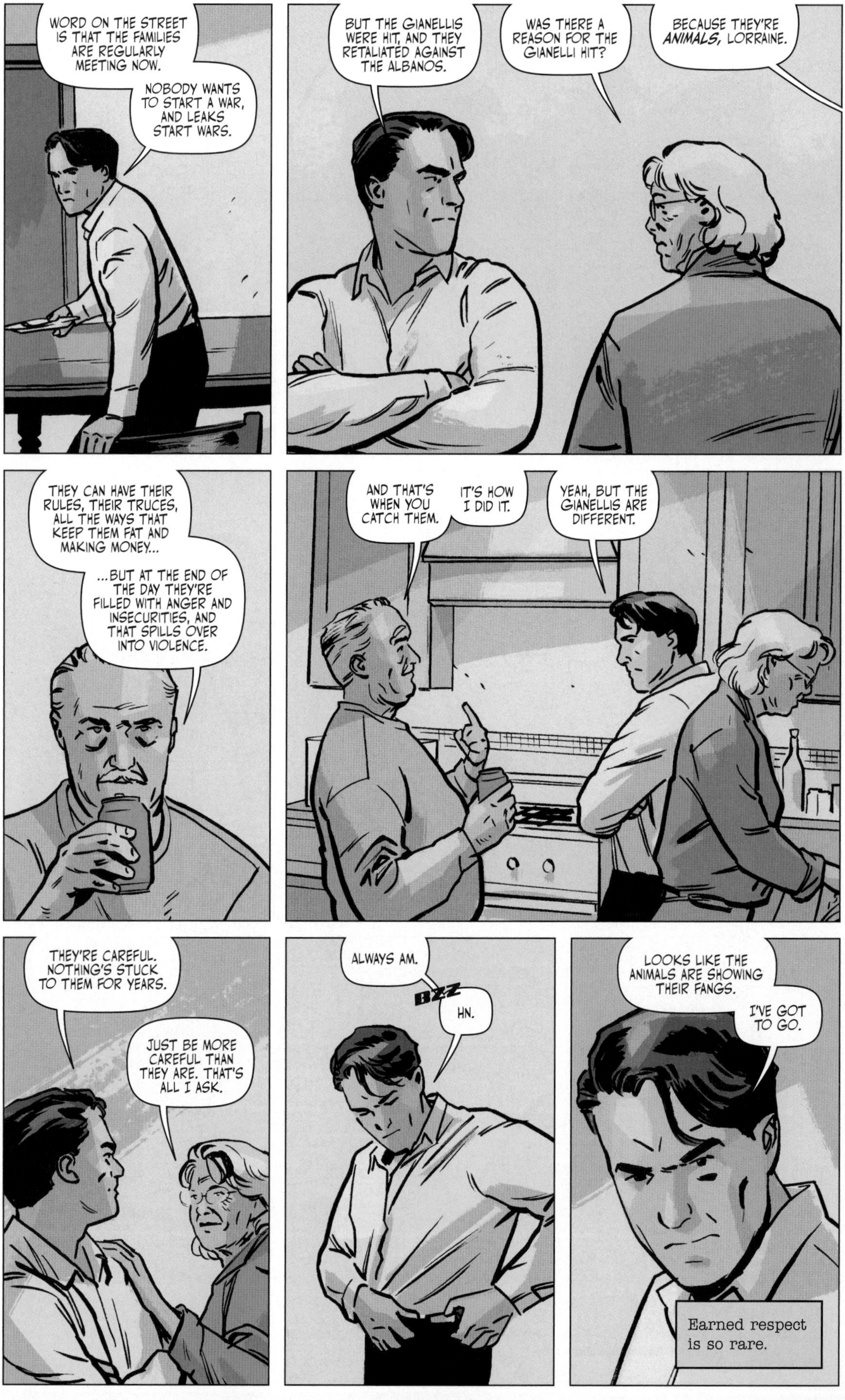
WORD ON THE STREET IS THAT THE FAMILIES ARE REGULARLY MEETING NOW.
NOBODY WANTS TO START A WAR, AND LEAKS START WARS.
BUT THE GIANELLIS WERE HIT, AND THEY RETALIATED AGAINST THE ALBANOS.
WAS THERE A REASON FOR THE GIANELLI HIT?
BECAUSE THEY'RE *ANIMALS,* LORRAINE.
THEY CAN HAVE THEIR RULES, THEIR TRUCES, ALL THE WAYS THAT KEEP THEM FAT AND MAKING MONEY...
...BUT AT THE END OF THE DAY THEY'RE FILLED WITH ANGER AND INSECURITIES, AND THAT SPILLS OVER INTO VIOLENCE.
AND THAT'S WHEN YOU CATCH THEM.
IT'S HOW I DID IT.
YEAH, BUT THE GIANELLIS ARE DIFFERENT.
THEY'RE CAREFUL. NOTHING'S STUCK TO THEM FOR YEARS.
JUST BE MORE CAREFUL THAN THEY ARE. THAT'S ALL I ASK.
ALWAYS AM.
BZZ
HN.
LOOKS LIKE THE ANIMALS ARE SHOWING THEIR FANGS.
I'VE GOT TO GO.
Earned respect is so rare.

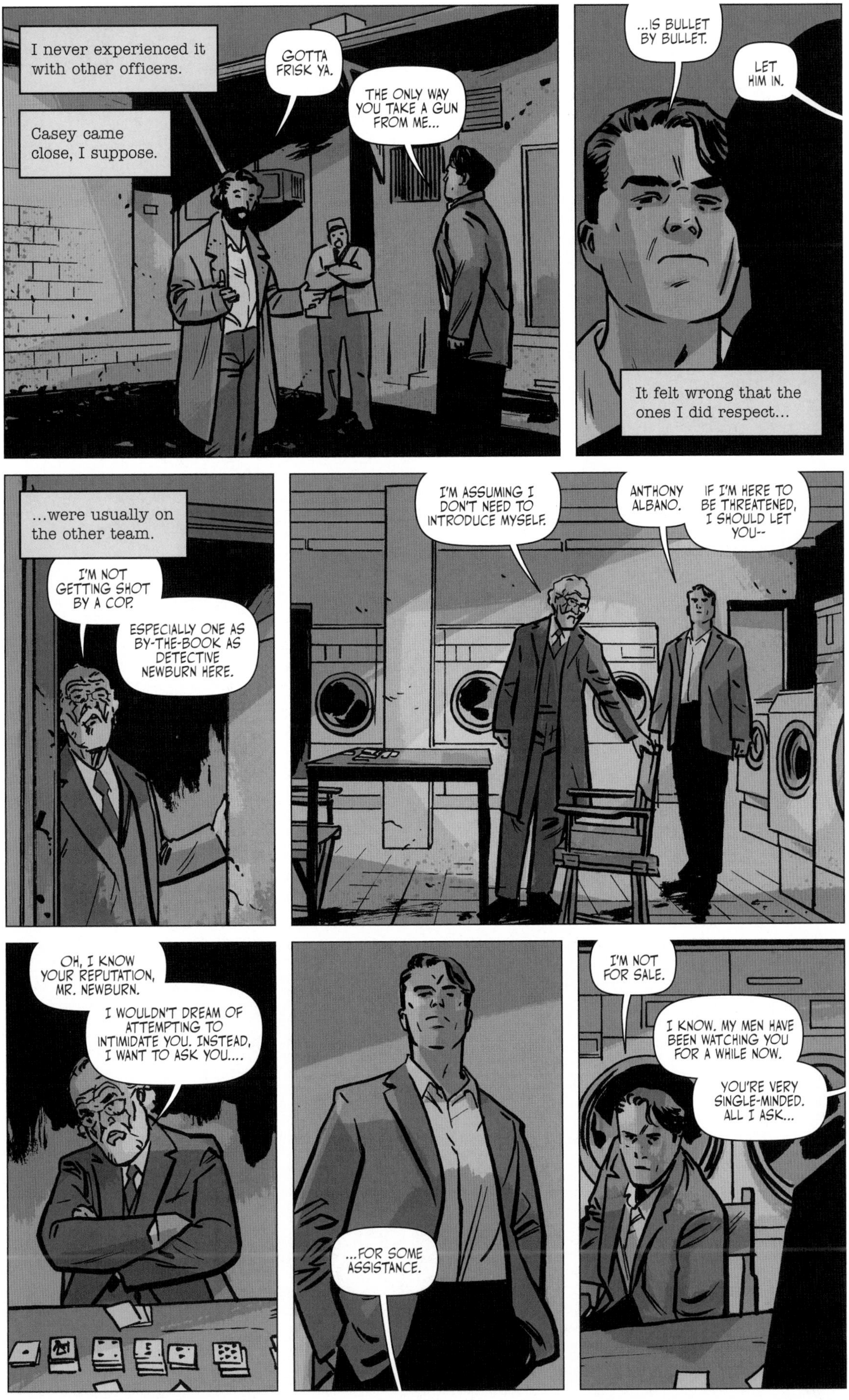

I never experienced it with other officers.
Casey came close, I suppose.
GOTTA FRISK YA.
THE ONLY WAY YOU TAKE A GUN FROM ME...
...IS BULLET BY BULLET.
LET HIM IN.
It felt wrong that the ones I did respect...
...were usually on the other team.
I'M NOT GETTING SHOT BY A COP.
ESPECIALLY ONE AS BY-THE-BOOK AS DETECTIVE NEWBURN HERE.
I'M ASSUMING I DON'T NEED TO INTRODUCE MYSELF.
ANTHONY ALBANO.
IF I'M HERE TO BE THREATENED, I SHOULD LET YOU--
OH, I KNOW YOUR REPUTATION, MR. NEWBURN.
I WOULDN'T DREAM OF ATTEMPTING TO INTIMIDATE YOU. INSTEAD, I WANT TO ASK YOU....
...FOR SOME ASSISTANCE.
I'M NOT FOR SALE.
I KNOW. MY MEN HAVE BEEN WATCHING YOU FOR A WHILE NOW.
YOU'RE VERY SINGLE-MINDED. ALL I ASK...

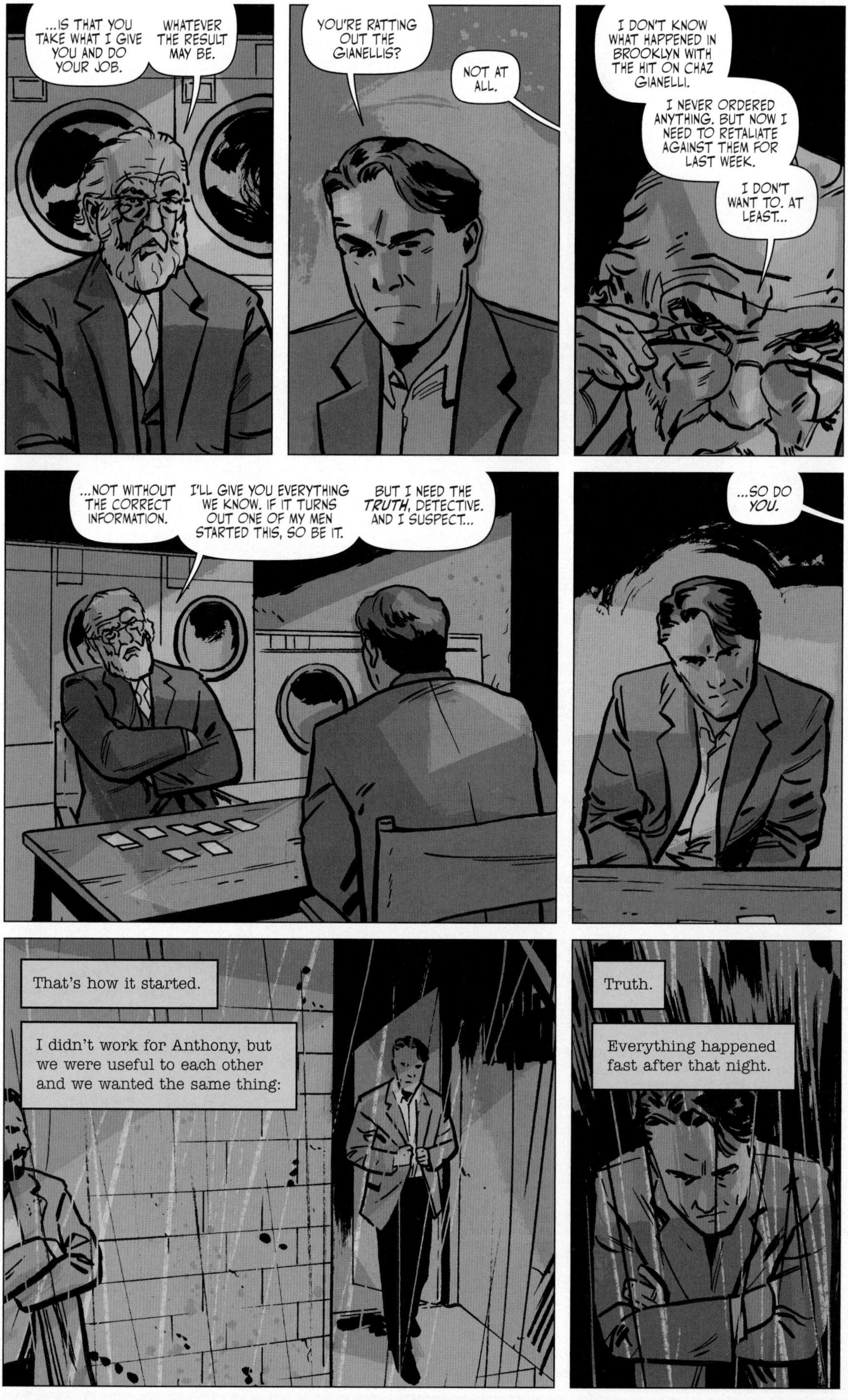
...IS THAT YOU TAKE WHAT I GIVE YOU AND DO YOUR JOB.
WHATEVER THE RESULT MAY BE.
YOU'RE RATTING OUT THE GIANELLIS?
NOT AT ALL.
I DON'T KNOW WHAT HAPPENED IN BROOKLYN WITH THE HIT ON CHAZ GIANELLI.
I NEVER ORDERED ANYTHING. BUT NOW I NEED TO RETALIATE AGAINST THEM FOR LAST WEEK.
I DON'T WANT TO. AT LEAST...
...NOT WITHOUT THE CORRECT INFORMATION.
I'LL GIVE YOU EVERYTHING WE KNOW. IF IT TURNS OUT ONE OF MY MEN STARTED THIS, SO BE IT.
BUT I NEED THE *TRUTH*, DETECTIVE. AND I SUSPECT...
...SO DO *YOU*.
That's how it started.
I didn't work for Anthony, but we were useful to each other and we wanted the same thing:
Truth.
Everything happened fast after that night.

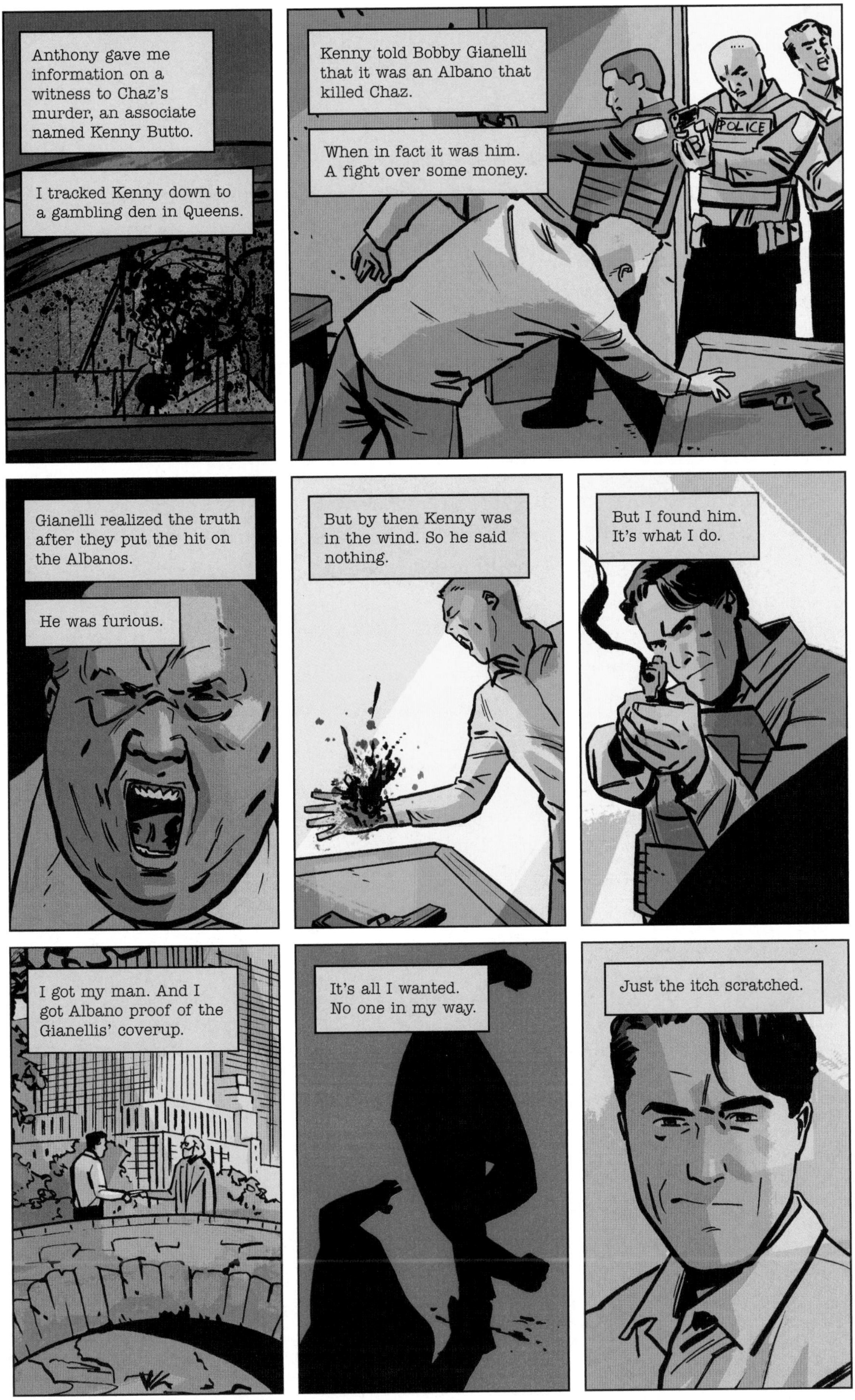

Anthony gave me information on a witness to Chaz's murder, an associate named Kenny Butto.
I tracked Kenny down to a gambling den in Queens.
Kenny told Bobby Gianelli that it was an Albano that killed Chaz.
When in fact it was him. A fight over some money.
POLICE
Gianelli realized the truth after they put the hit on the Albanos.
He was furious.
But by then Kenny was in the wind. So he said nothing.
But I found him. It's what I do.
I got my man. And I got Albano proof of the Gianellis' coverup.
It's all I wanted. No one in my way.
Just the itch scratched.

But my scratched itch meant that The Gianellis were in deep trouble. Their mistake was almost understandable and forgivable. What else could they do except get payback when they thought an Albano was involved? Lives were lost, but a handshake could end things.

Unfortunately, they lied. They made the mistake and tried to cover it up. Word spread quickly. All the families convened and they put a tax on them for betraying the truce and almost starting a war. Bobby Gianelli, the head of the family, had to give up his deed to a prime piece of real estate in Manhattan, of which every family now had equal ownership.A place to solidify the bond between criminal organizations, where they could meet to sort out their issues.

Bobby was furious, but kneecapped. And I had my head held high, like I'd figured it all out. Anthony Albano was a criminal, but he was a smart one. He had my respect and I had his.

All was calm in the city. And I thought it was because of me.

But I didn't have any power. Didn't have any failsafes.
Not like now.

And so they came.

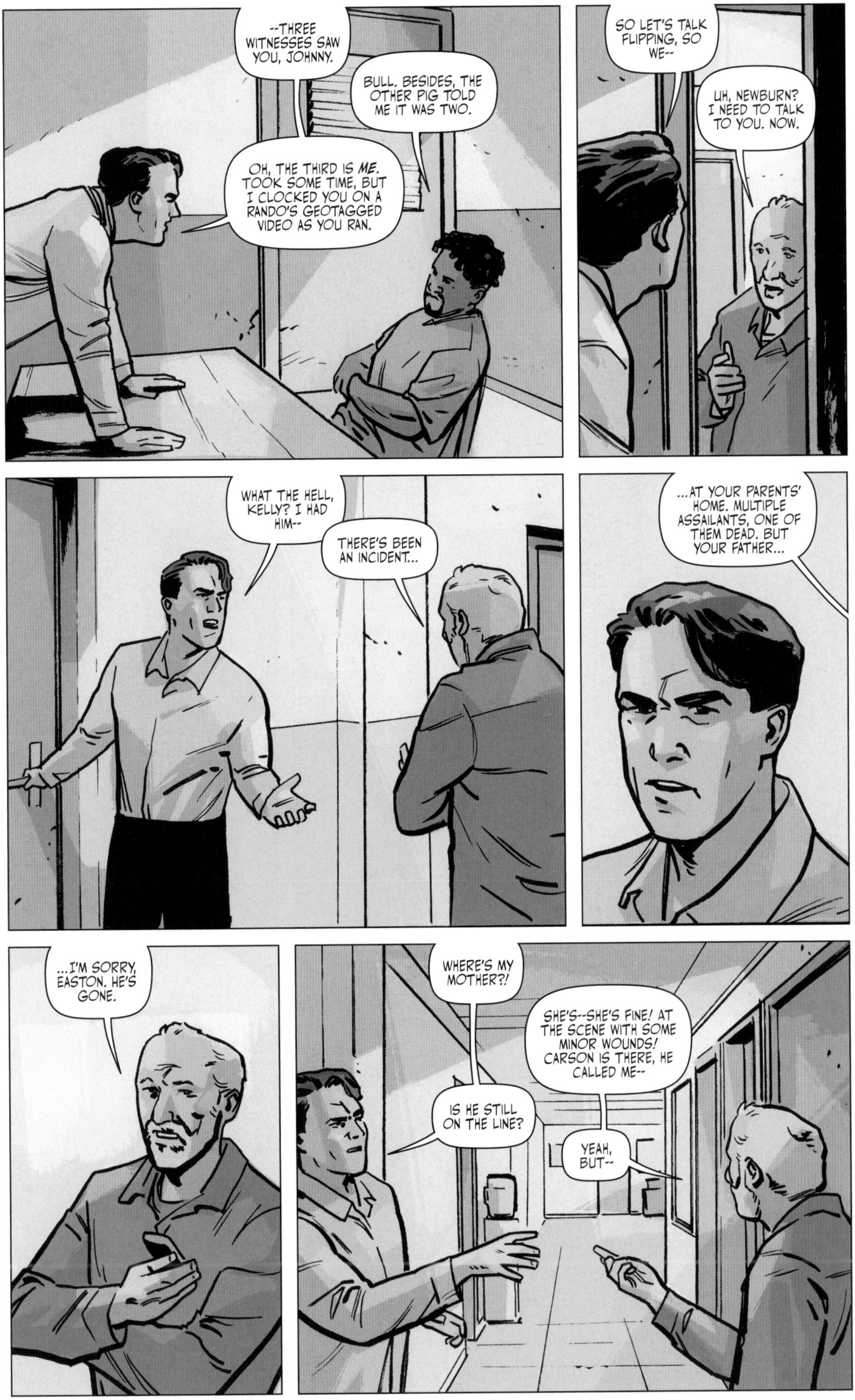
--THREE WITNESSES SAW YOU, JOHNNY.
BULL. BESIDES, THE OTHER PIG TOLD ME IT WAS TWO.
OH, THE THIRD IS *ME*. TOOK SOME TIME, BUT I CLOCKED YOU ON A RANDO'S GEOTAGGED VIDEO AS YOU RAN.
SO LET'S TALK FLIPPING, SO WE--
UH, NEWBURN? I NEED TO TALK TO YOU. NOW.
WHAT THE HELL, KELLY? I HAD HIM--
THERE'S BEEN AN INCIDENT...
...AT YOUR PARENTS' HOME. MULTIPLE ASSAILANTS, ONE OF THEM DEAD. BUT YOUR FATHER...
...I'M SORRY, EASTON. HE'S GONE.
WHERE'S MY MOTHER?!
SHE'S--SHE'S FINE! AT THE SCENE WITH SOME MINOR WOUNDS! CARSON IS THERE, HE CALLED ME--
IS HE STILL ON THE LINE?
YEAH, BUT--

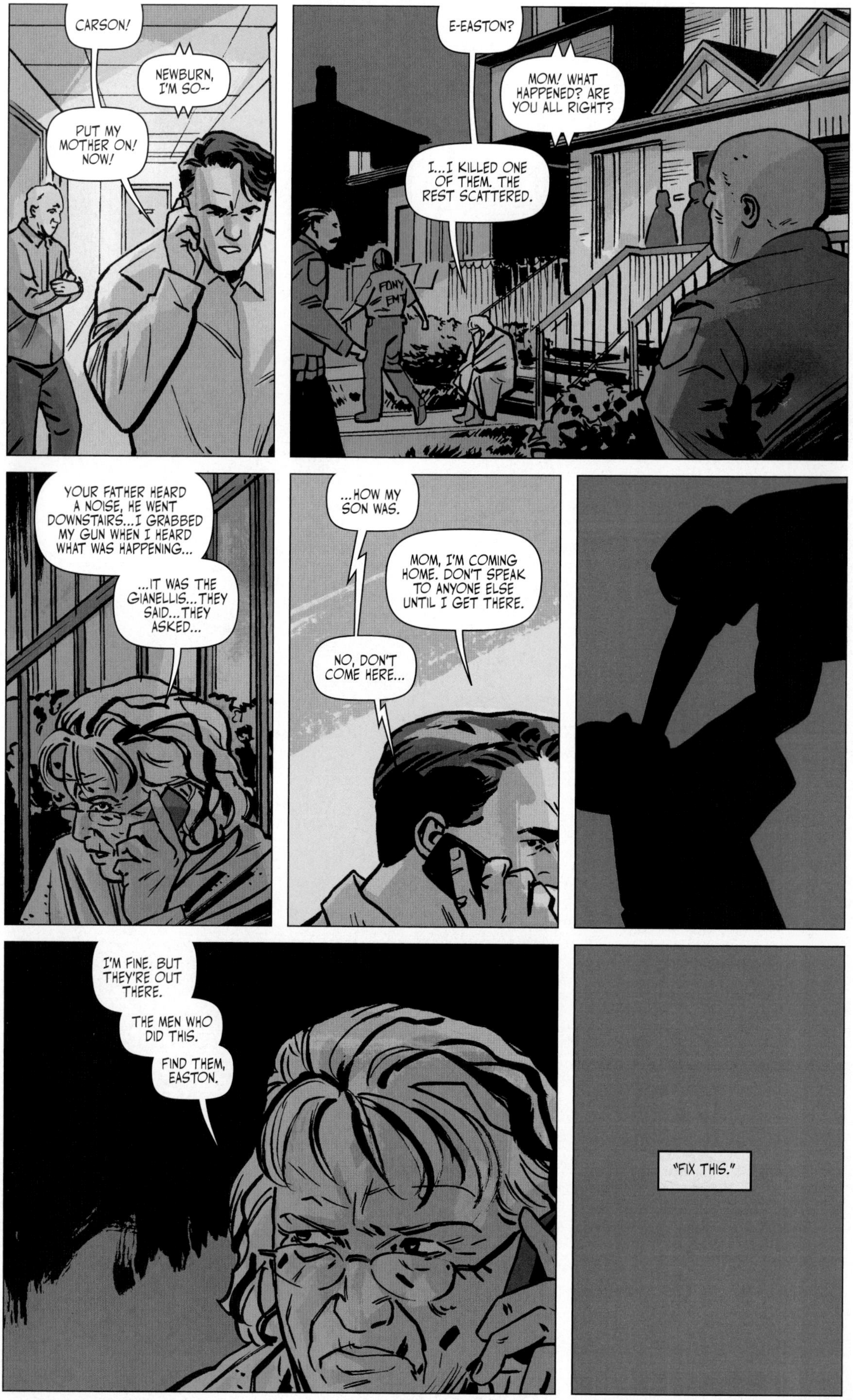
CARSON!
NEWBURN, I'M SO--
PUT MY MOTHER ON! NOW!
E-EASTON?
MOM! WHAT HAPPENED? ARE YOU ALL RIGHT?
I...I KILLED ONE OF THEM. THE REST SCATTERED.
FDNY EMT
YOUR FATHER HEARD A NOISE, HE WENT DOWNSTAIRS...I GRABBED MY GUN WHEN I HEARD WHAT WAS HAPPENING...
...IT WAS THE GIANELLIS...THEY SAID...THEY ASKED...
...HOW MY SON WAS.
MOM, I'M COMING HOME. DON'T SPEAK TO ANYONE ELSE UNTIL I GET THERE.
NO, DON'T COME HERE...
I'M FINE. BUT THEY'RE OUT THERE.
THE MEN WHO DID THIS.
FIND THEM, EASTON.
"FIX THIS."

Those were your words: "Fix this."

Dad was dead because of me. How do I fix that? Charge into heaven? Into hell? You were right, but to put those words into my head and heart, I often wonder what you thought I'd do. Put the sirens on? Beat the streets looking for answers? For justice on the other end of handcuffs?

Was that who you'd raised? Was that what you wanted when you said those words, sharp and cold?

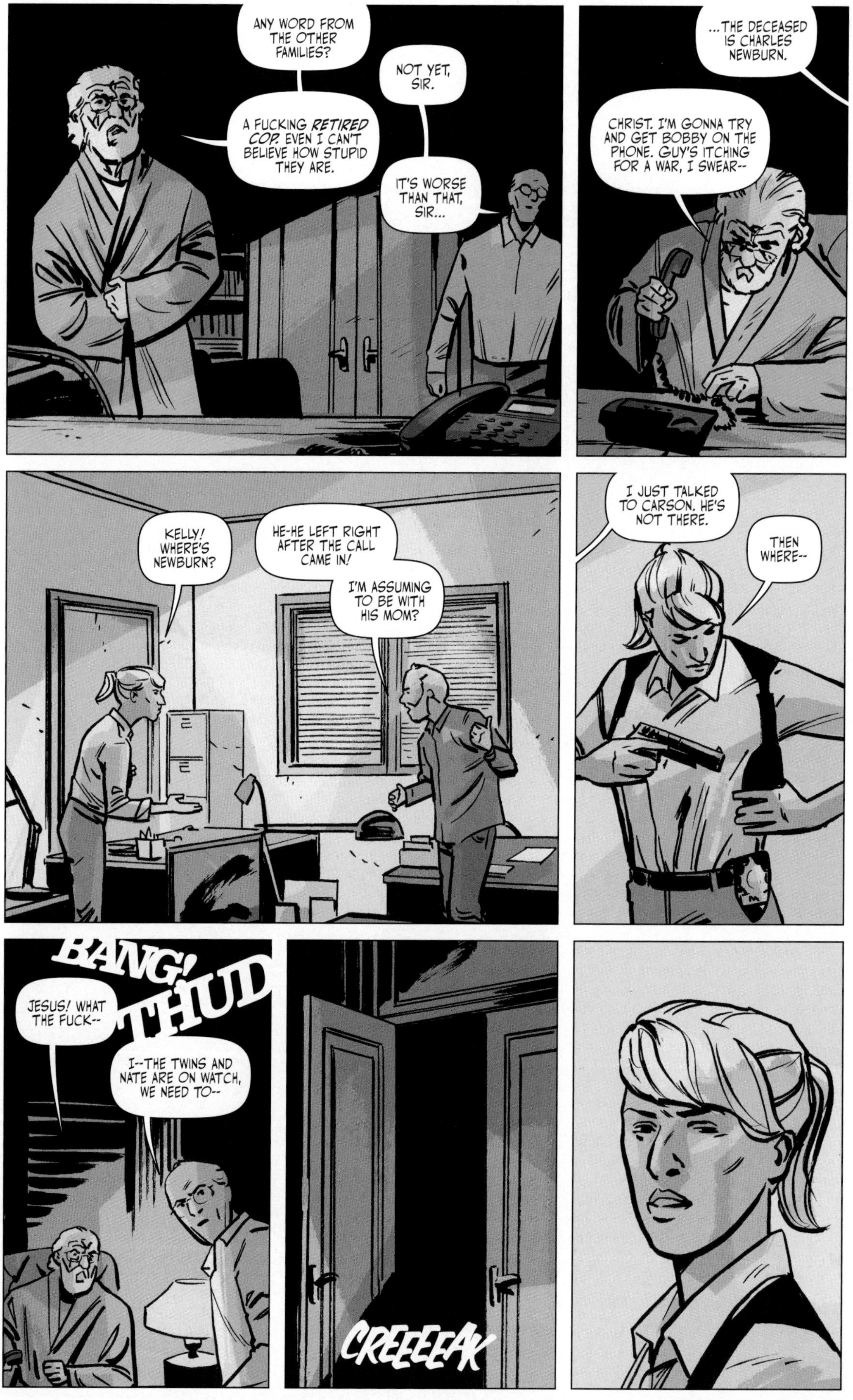
ANY WORD FROM THE OTHER FAMILIES?
NOT YET, SIR.
A FUCKING RETIRED COP. EVEN I CAN'T BELIEVE HOW STUPID THEY ARE.
IT'S WORSE THAN THAT, SIR...
...THE DECEASED IS CHARLES NEWBURN.
CHRIST. I'M GONNA TRY AND GET BOBBY ON THE PHONE. GUY'S ITCHING FOR A WAR, I SWEAR--
KELLY! WHERE'S NEWBURN?
HE-HE LEFT RIGHT AFTER THE CALL CAME IN!
I'M ASSUMING TO BE WITH HIS MOM?
I JUST TALKED TO CARSON. HE'S NOT THERE.
THEN WHERE--
BANG!
THUD
JESUS! WHAT THE FUCK--
I--THE TWINS AND NATE ARE ON WATCH, WE NEED TO--
CREEEEAK

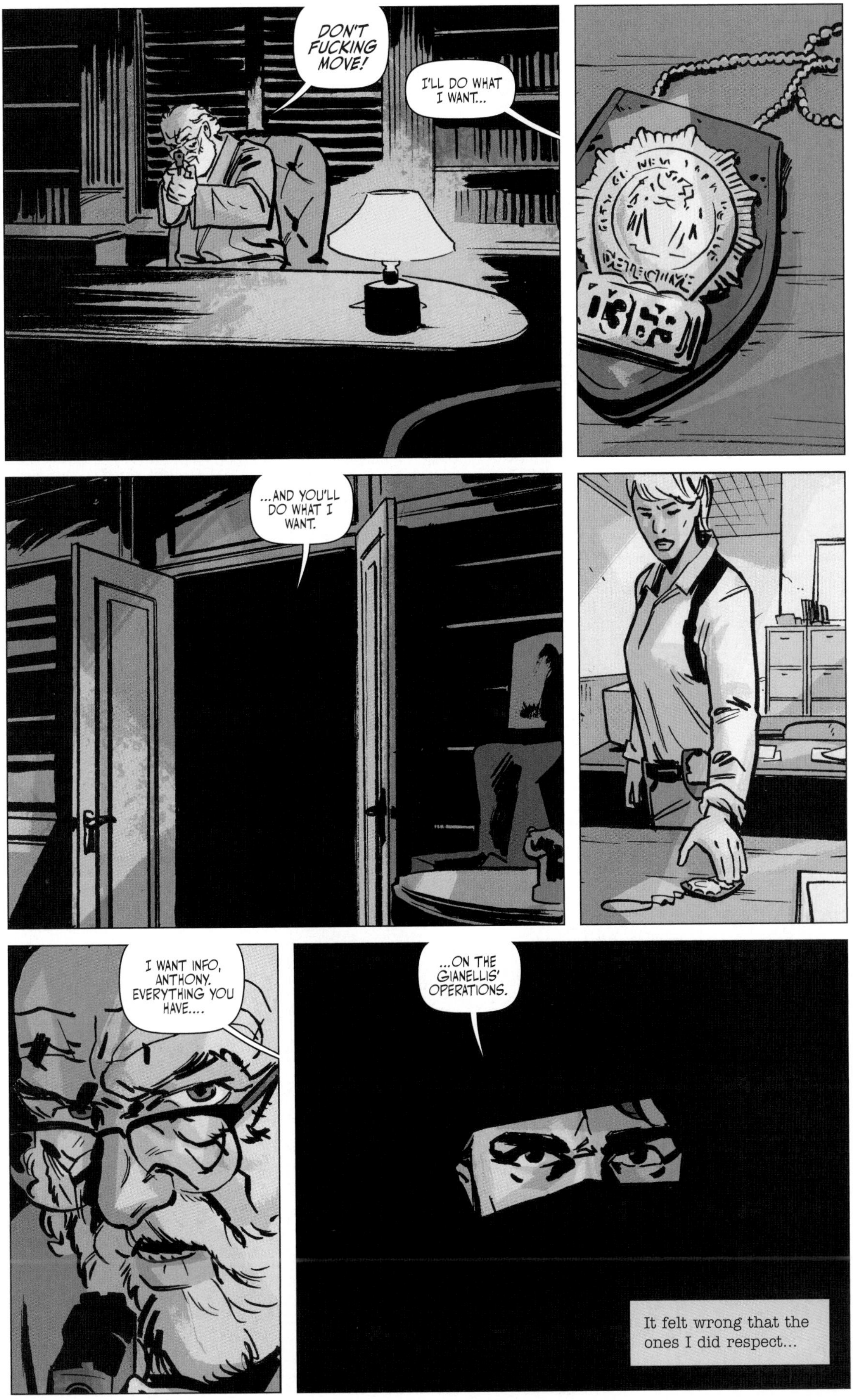
DON'T FUCKING MOVE!
I'LL DO WHAT I WANT...
...AND YOU'LL DO WHAT I WANT.
I WANT INFO, ANTHONY. EVERYTHING YOU HAVE....
...ON THE GIANELLIS' OPERATIONS.
It felt wrong that the ones I did respect...

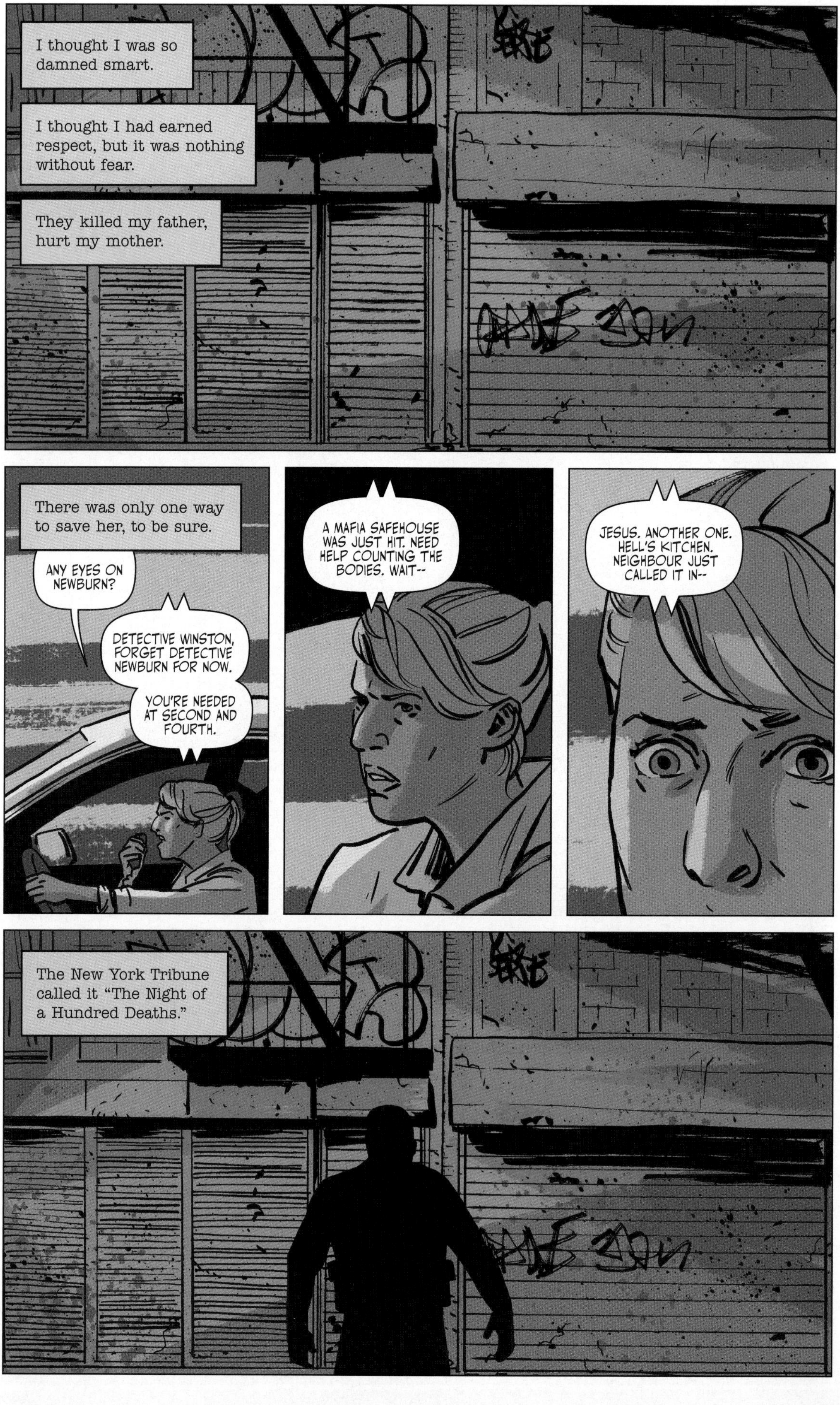
I thought I was so damned smart.
I thought I had earned respect, but it was nothing without fear.
They killed my father, hurt my mother.
There was only one way to save her, to be sure.
ANY EYES ON NEWBURN?
DETECTIVE WINSTON, FORGET DETECTIVE NEWBURN FOR NOW.
YOU'RE NEEDED AT SECOND AND FOURTH.
A MAFIA SAFEHOUSE WAS JUST HIT. NEED HELP COUNTING THE BODIES. WAIT--
JESUS. ANOTHER ONE. HELL'S KITCHEN. NEIGHBOUR JUST CALLED IT IN--
The New York Tribune called it "The Night of a Hundred Deaths."

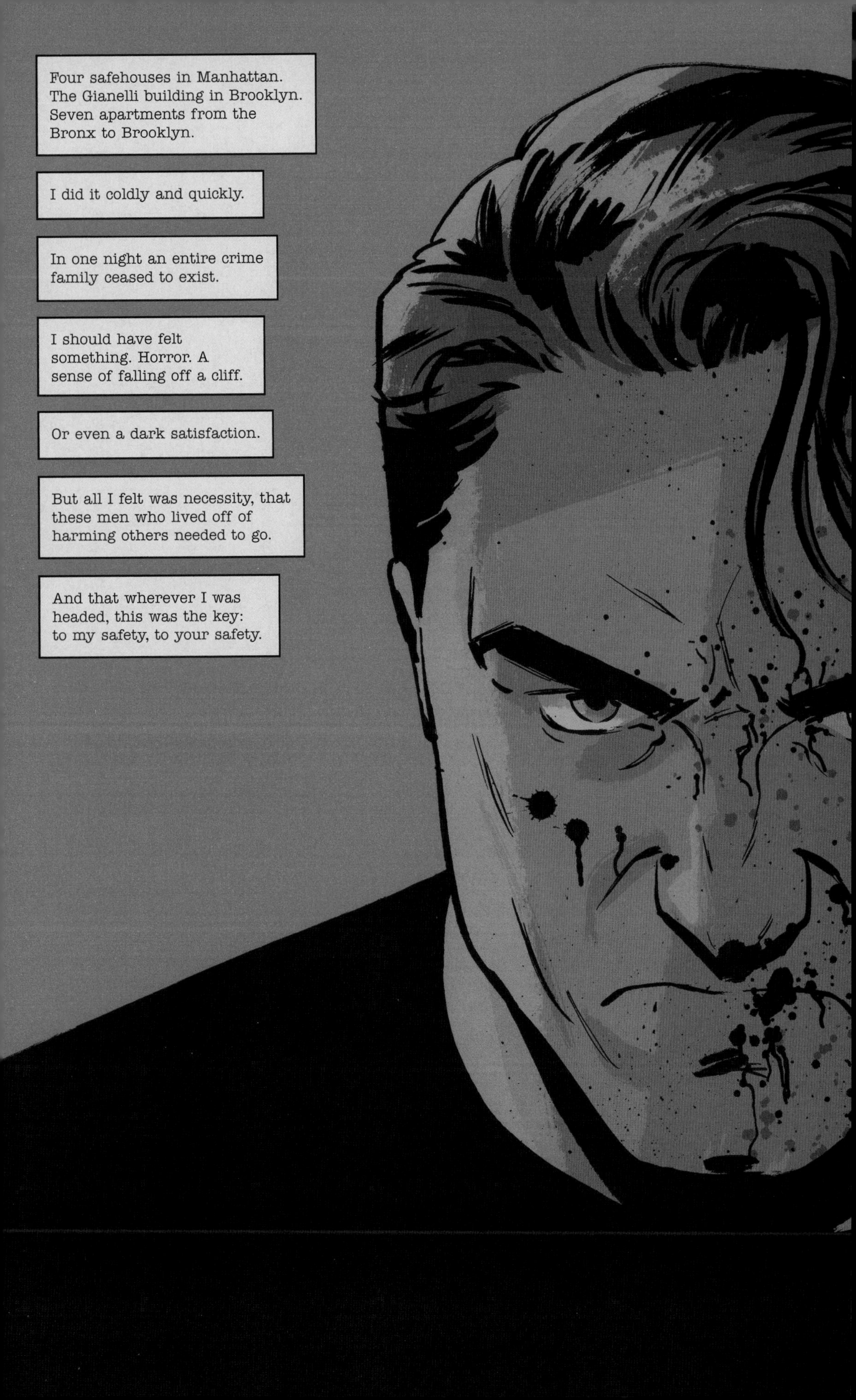
Four safehouses in Manhattan. The Gianelli building in Brooklyn. Seven apartments from the Bronx to Brooklyn.
I did it coldly and quickly.
In one night an entire crime family ceased to exist.
I should have felt something. Horror. A sense of falling off a cliff.
Or even a dark satisfaction.
But all I felt was necessity, that these men who lived off of harming others needed to go.
And that wherever I was headed, this was the key: to my safety, to your safety.

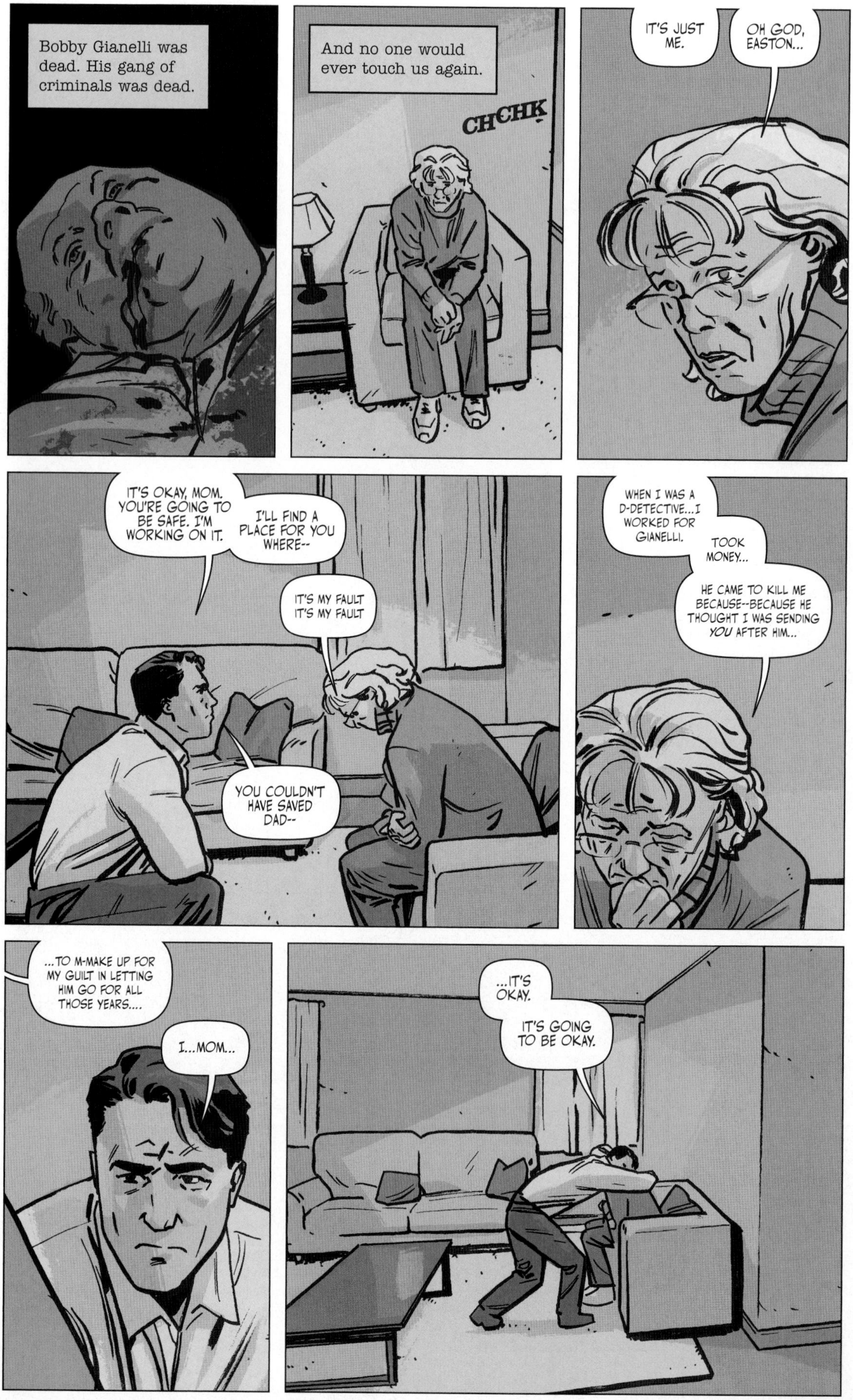
Bobby Gianelli was dead. His gang of criminals was dead.
And no one would ever touch us again.
CHCHK
IT'S JUST ME.
OH GOD, EASTON...
IT'S OKAY, MOM. YOU'RE GOING TO BE SAFE. I'M WORKING ON IT.
I'LL FIND A PLACE FOR YOU WHERE--
IT'S MY FAULT IT'S MY FAULT
YOU COULDN'T HAVE SAVED DAD--
WHEN I WAS A D-DETECTIVE...I WORKED FOR GIANELLI.
TOOK MONEY...
HE CAME TO KILL ME BECAUSE--BECAUSE HE THOUGHT I WAS SENDING YOU AFTER HIM...
...TO M-MAKE UP FOR MY GUILT IN LETTING HIM GO FOR ALL THOSE YEARS....
I...MOM...
...IT'S OKAY.
IT'S GOING TO BE OKAY.

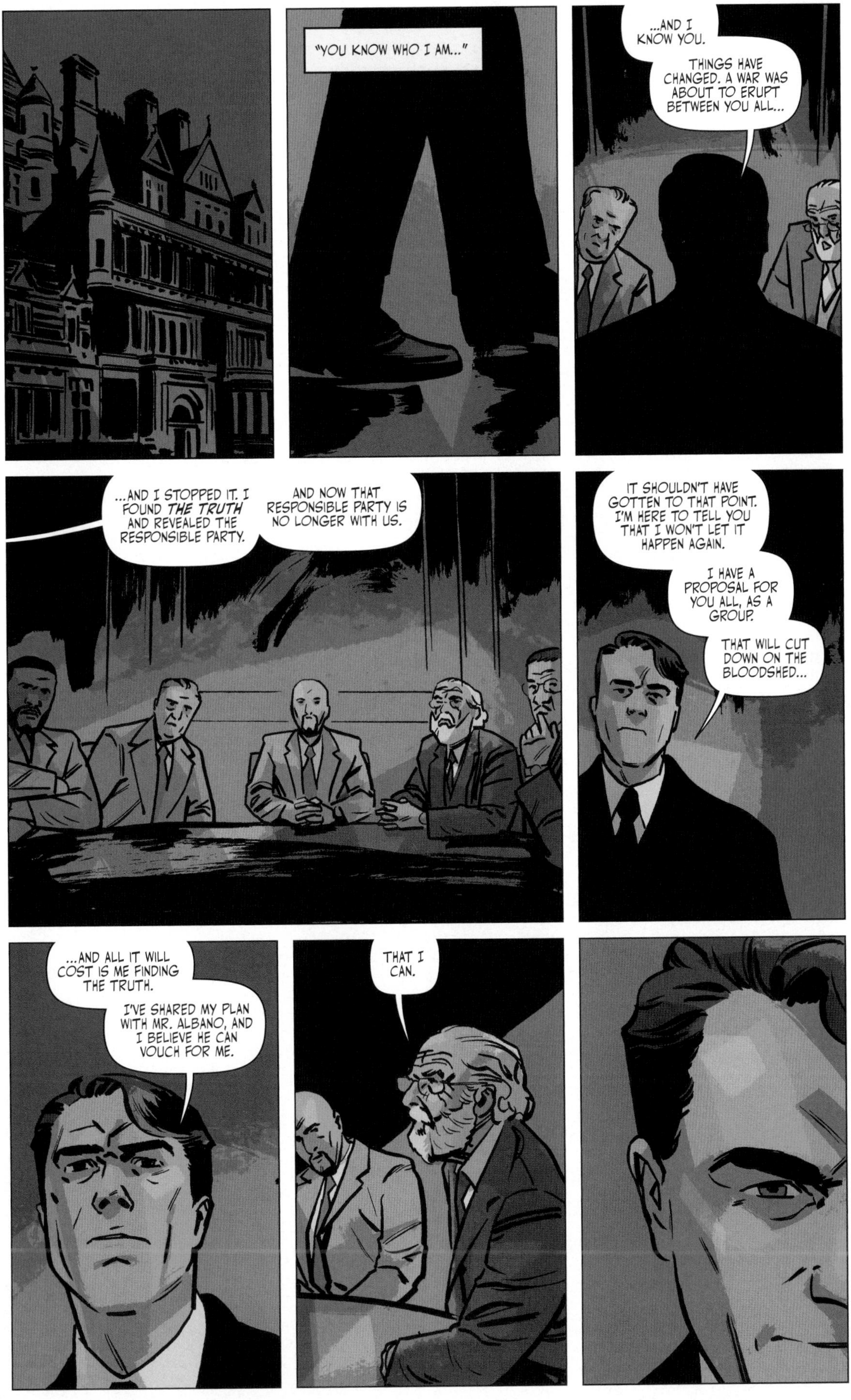
"YOU KNOW WHO I AM..."
...AND I KNOW YOU.
THINGS HAVE CHANGED. A WAR WAS ABOUT TO ERUPT BETWEEN YOU ALL...
...AND I STOPPED IT. I FOUND *THE TRUTH* AND REVEALED THE RESPONSIBLE PARTY.
AND NOW THAT RESPONSIBLE PARTY IS NO LONGER WITH US.
IT SHOULDN'T HAVE GOTTEN TO THAT POINT. I'M HERE TO TELL YOU THAT I WON'T LET IT HAPPEN AGAIN.
I HAVE A PROPOSAL FOR YOU ALL, AS A GROUP.
THAT WILL CUT DOWN ON THE BLOODSHED...
...AND ALL IT WILL COST IS ME FINDING THE TRUTH.
I'VE SHARED MY PLAN WITH MR. ALBANO, AND I BELIEVE HE CAN VOUCH FOR ME.
THAT I CAN.

They agreed to my deal. It helped that I spent months prior gaining dirt on each of them in case anyone decided to make a move on me. I was untouchable and would work for them all, solving the grievances between them. And they'd pay. Enough to hide you, to secure a future for both of us in case an errant Gianelli decided to avenge the New York deaths.

I know you blame yourself for Dad. But it was all of us. I played my part, naively thinking I could float through such a dangerous world without protection. And Dad happily looked the other way as you lined both of your pockets. We were all cops who thought the job gave us power, but it just gave us the illusion of power.

It's been too long since I've seen you. The job fills a void, but I think of you often, Mother. I'm making plans for how I can finally join you, but it's hard. My value to the families keeps us alive and I need to keep proving myself. But maybe I can find someone else of value who can keep the wolves at bay.

As always, burn this letter.

I love you, Mother. Remember: be more careful than they are.

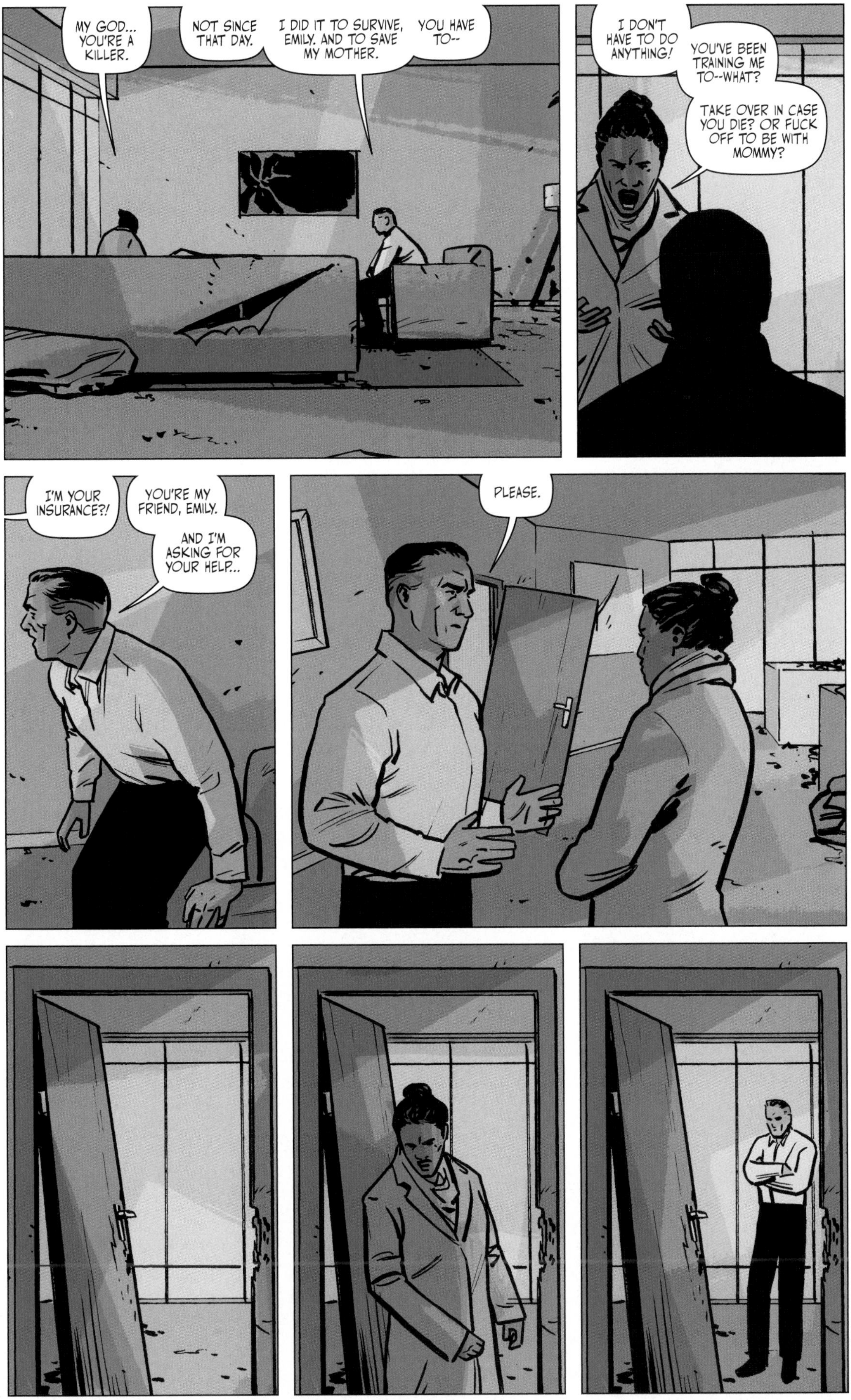
MY GOD... YOU'RE A KILLER.
NOT SINCE THAT DAY.
I DID IT TO SURVIVE, EMILY. AND TO SAVE MY MOTHER.
YOU HAVE TO--
I DON'T HAVE TO DO ANYTHING!
YOU'VE BEEN TRAINING ME TO--WHAT?
TAKE OVER IN CASE YOU DIE? OR FUCK OFF TO BE WITH MOMMY?
I'M YOUR INSURANCE?!
YOU'RE MY FRIEND, EMILY.
AND I'M ASKING FOR YOUR HELP...
PLEASE.

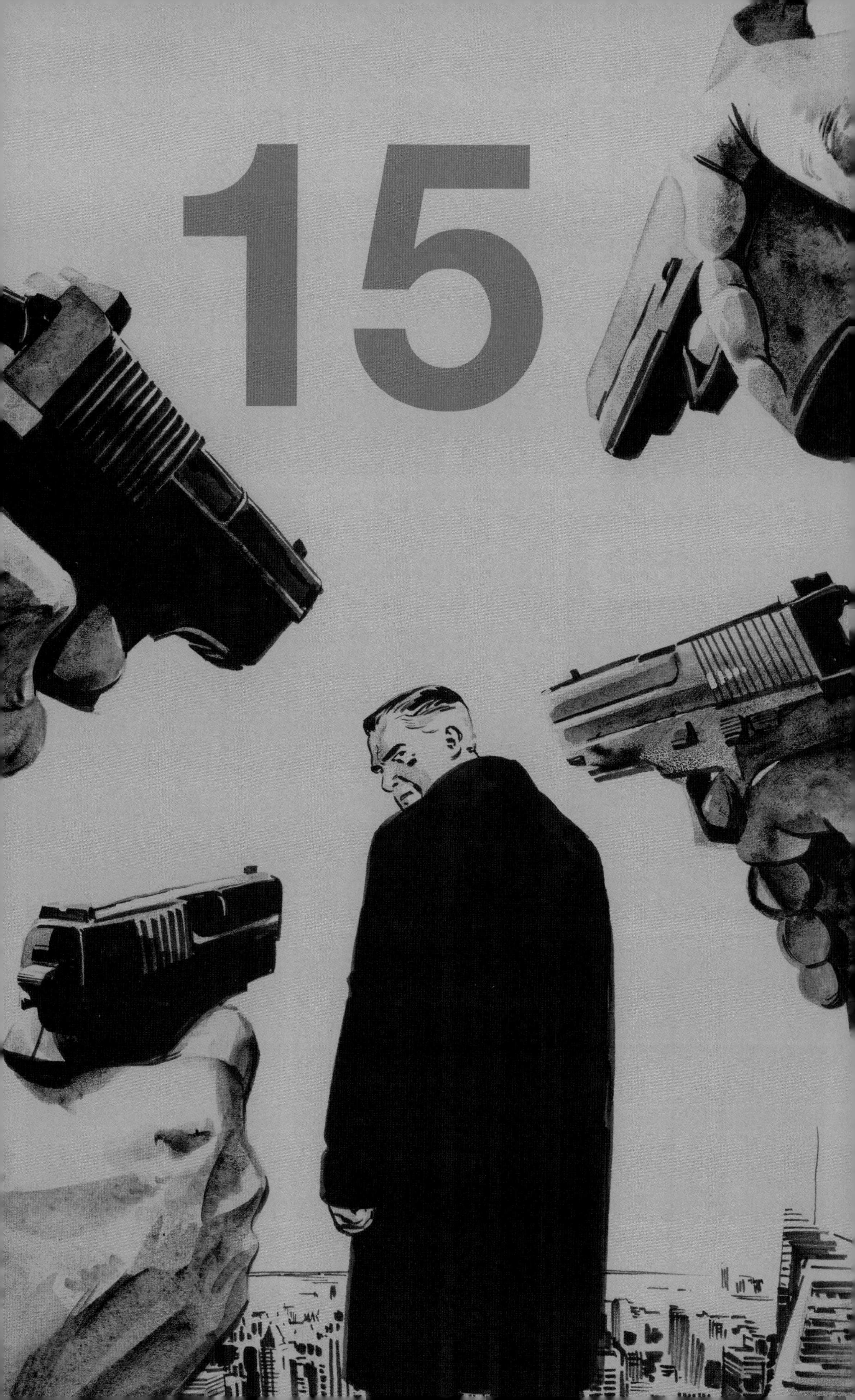
15

EMILY'S JOURNAL
01/17/23

Here we go.

GOD DAMN
YOU.

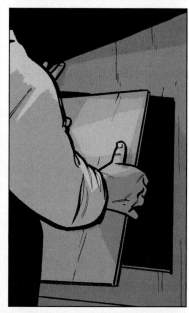

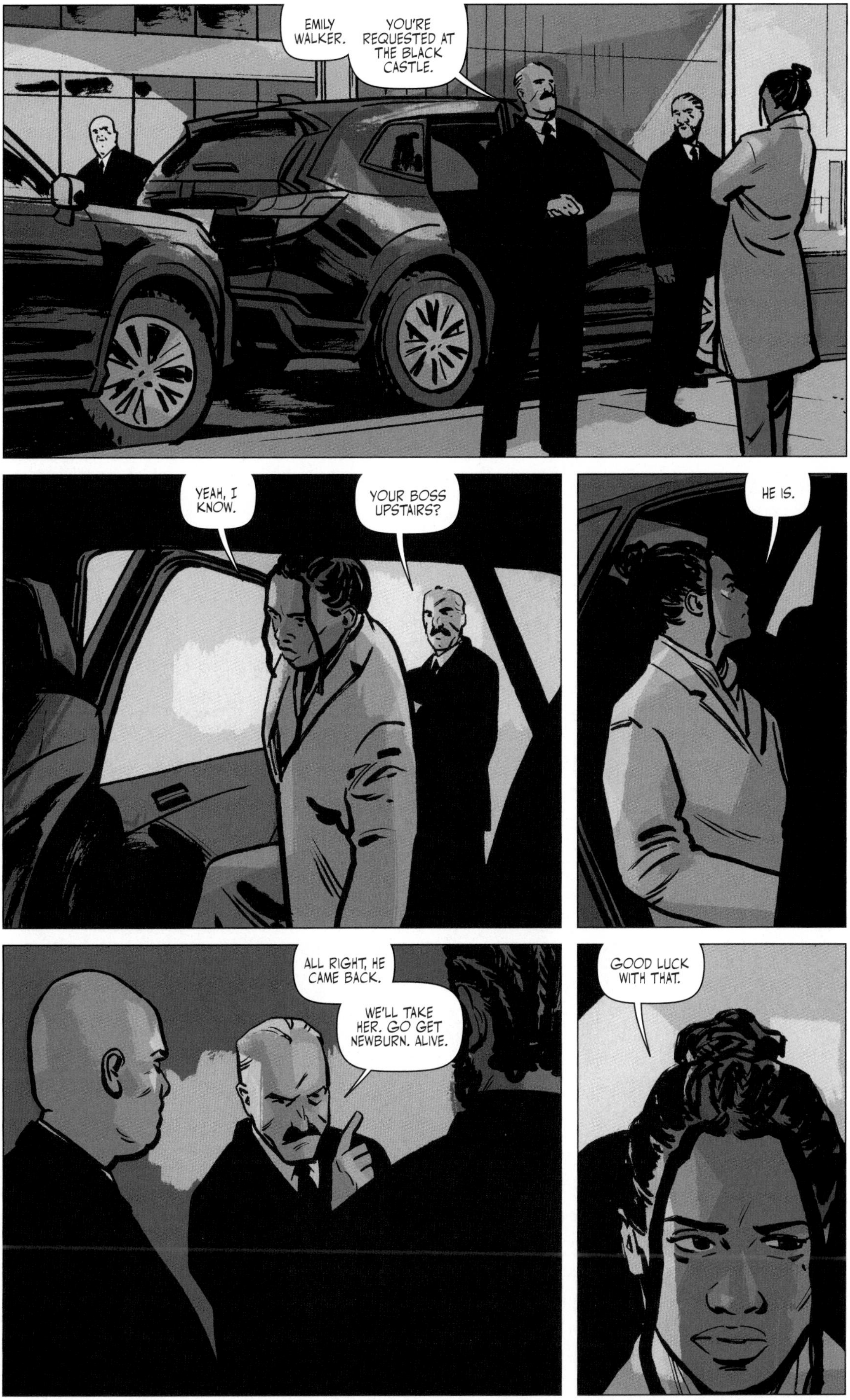
EMILY WALKER.
YOU'RE REQUESTED AT THE BLACK CASTLE.
YEAH, I KNOW.
YOUR BOSS UPSTAIRS?
HE IS.
ALL RIGHT, HE CAME BACK.
WE'LL TAKE HER. GO GET NEWBURN. ALIVE.
GOOD LUCK WITH THAT.

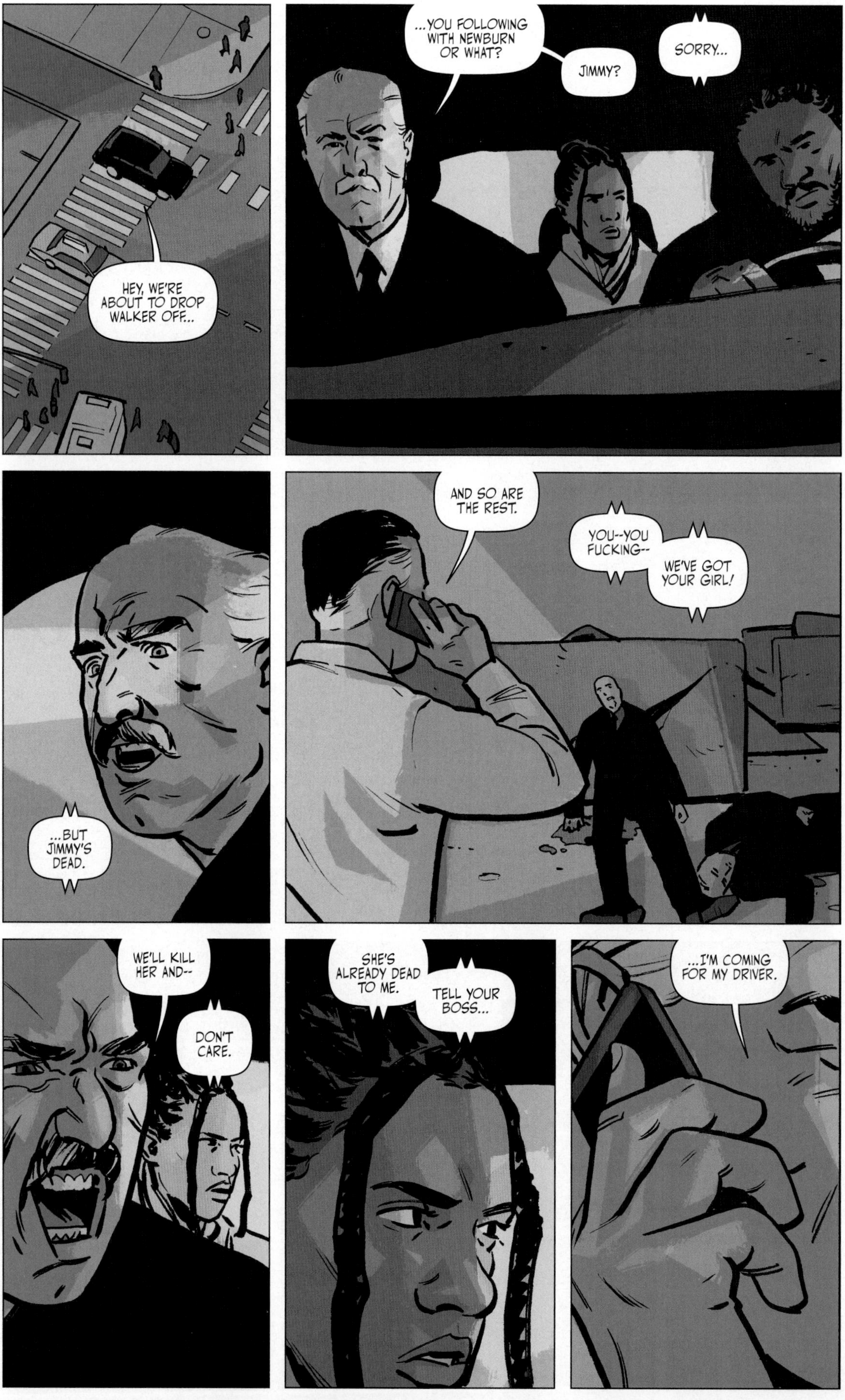
HEY, WE'RE ABOUT TO DROP WALKER OFF...
...YOU FOLLOWING WITH NEWBURN OR WHAT?
JIMMY?
SORRY...
...BUT JIMMY'S DEAD.
AND SO ARE THE REST.
YOU--YOU FUCKING--
WE'VE GOT YOUR GIRL!
WE'LL KILL HER AND--
DON'T CARE.
SHE'S ALREADY DEAD TO ME.
TELL YOUR BOSS...
...I'M COMING FOR MY DRIVER.

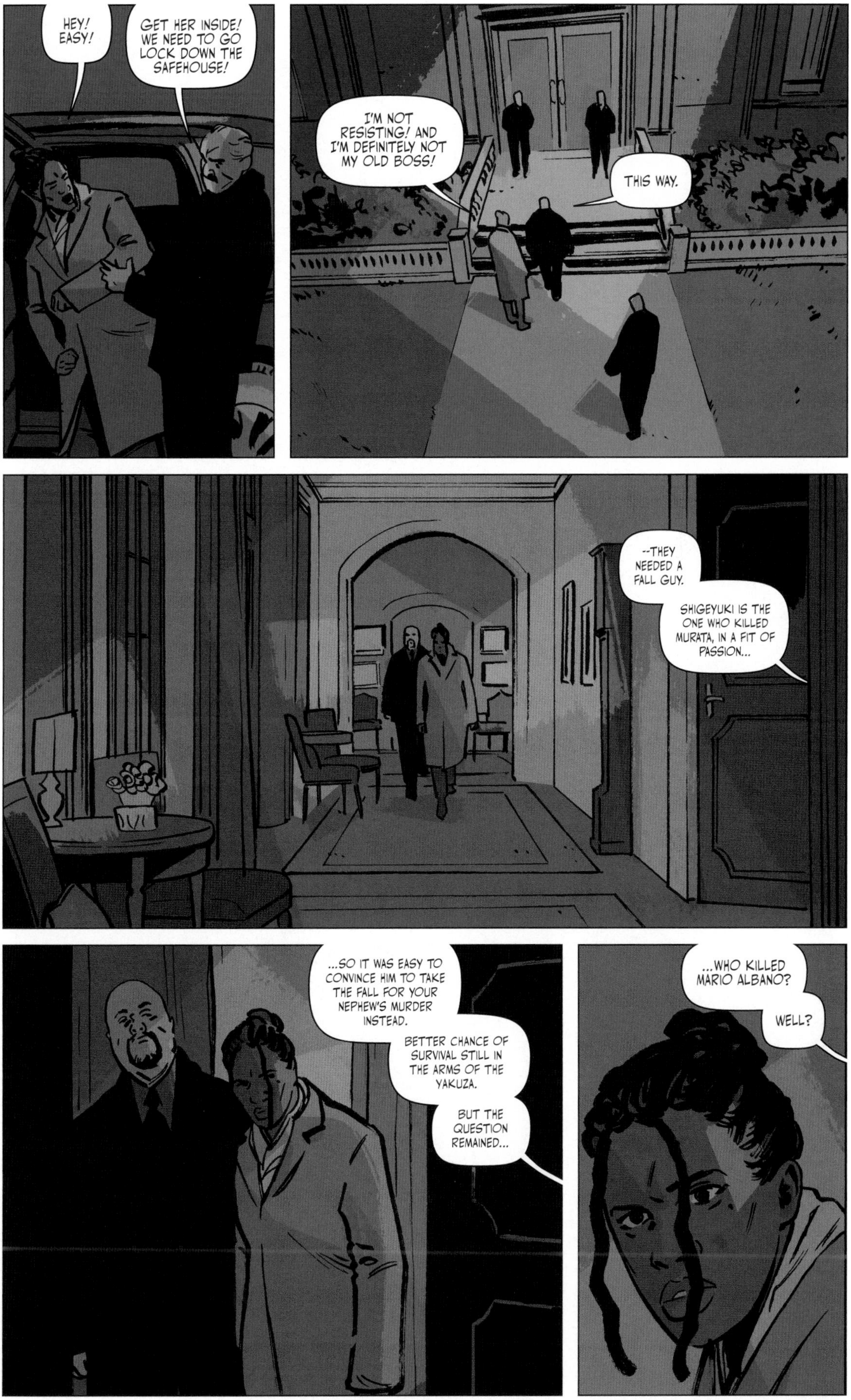
HEY! EASY!
GET HER INSIDE! WE NEED TO GO LOCK DOWN THE SAFEHOUSE!
I'M NOT RESISTING! AND I'M DEFINITELY NOT MY OLD BOSS!
THIS WAY.
--THEY NEEDED A FALL GUY.
SHIGEYUKI IS THE ONE WHO KILLED MURATA, IN A FIT OF PASSION...
...SO IT WAS EASY TO CONVINCE HIM TO TAKE THE FALL FOR YOUR NEPHEW'S MURDER INSTEAD.
BETTER CHANCE OF SURVIVAL STILL IN THE ARMS OF THE YAKUZA.
BUT THE QUESTION REMAINED...
...WHO KILLED MARIO ALBANO?
WELL?

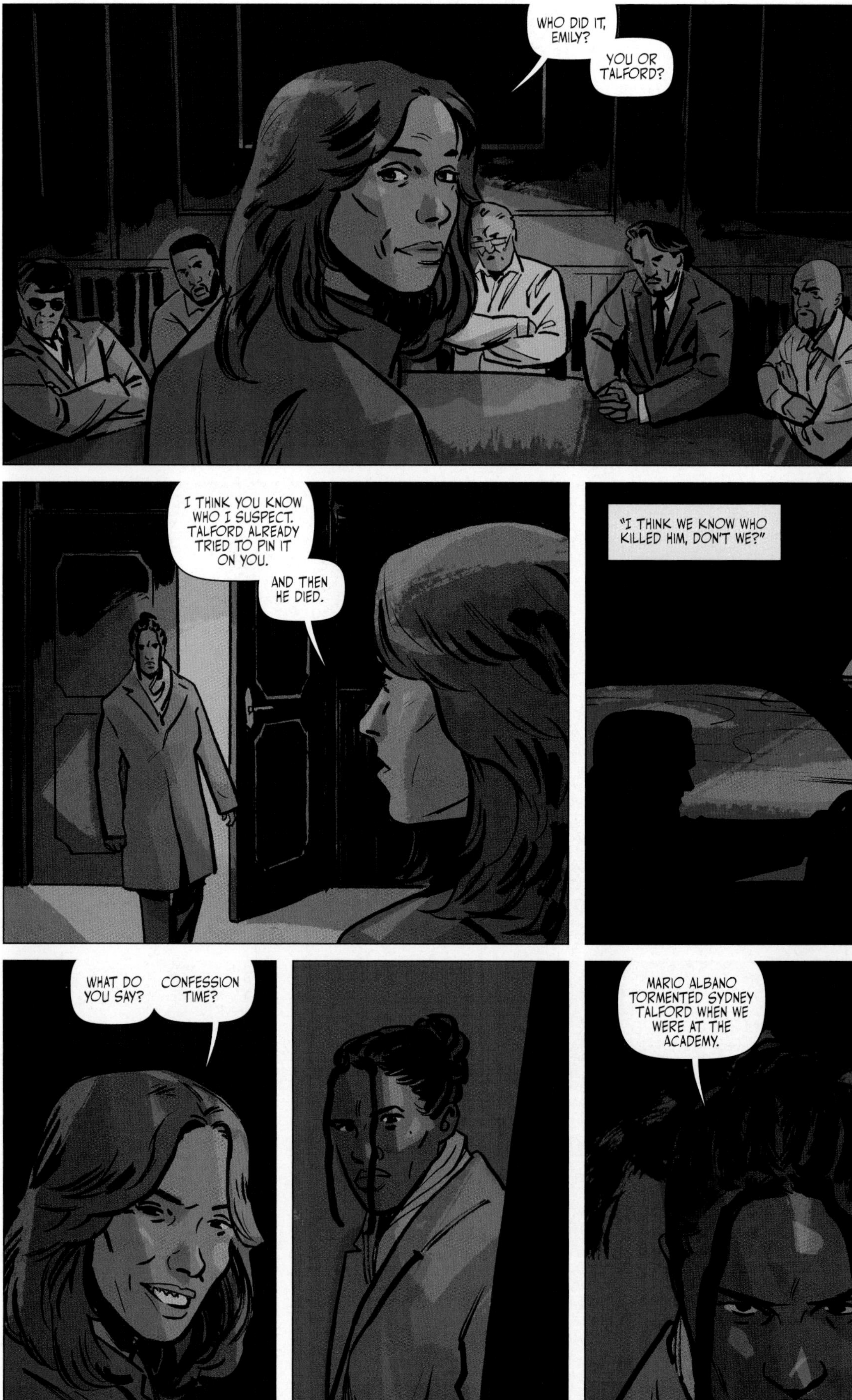
WHO DID IT, EMILY?
YOU OR TALFORD?
I THINK YOU KNOW WHO I SUSPECT. TALFORD ALREADY TRIED TO PIN IT ON YOU.
AND THEN HE DIED.
"I THINK WE KNOW WHO KILLED HIM, DON'T WE?"
WHAT DO YOU SAY?
CONFESSION TIME?
MARIO ALBANO TORMENTED SYDNEY TALFORD WHEN WE WERE AT THE ACADEMY.

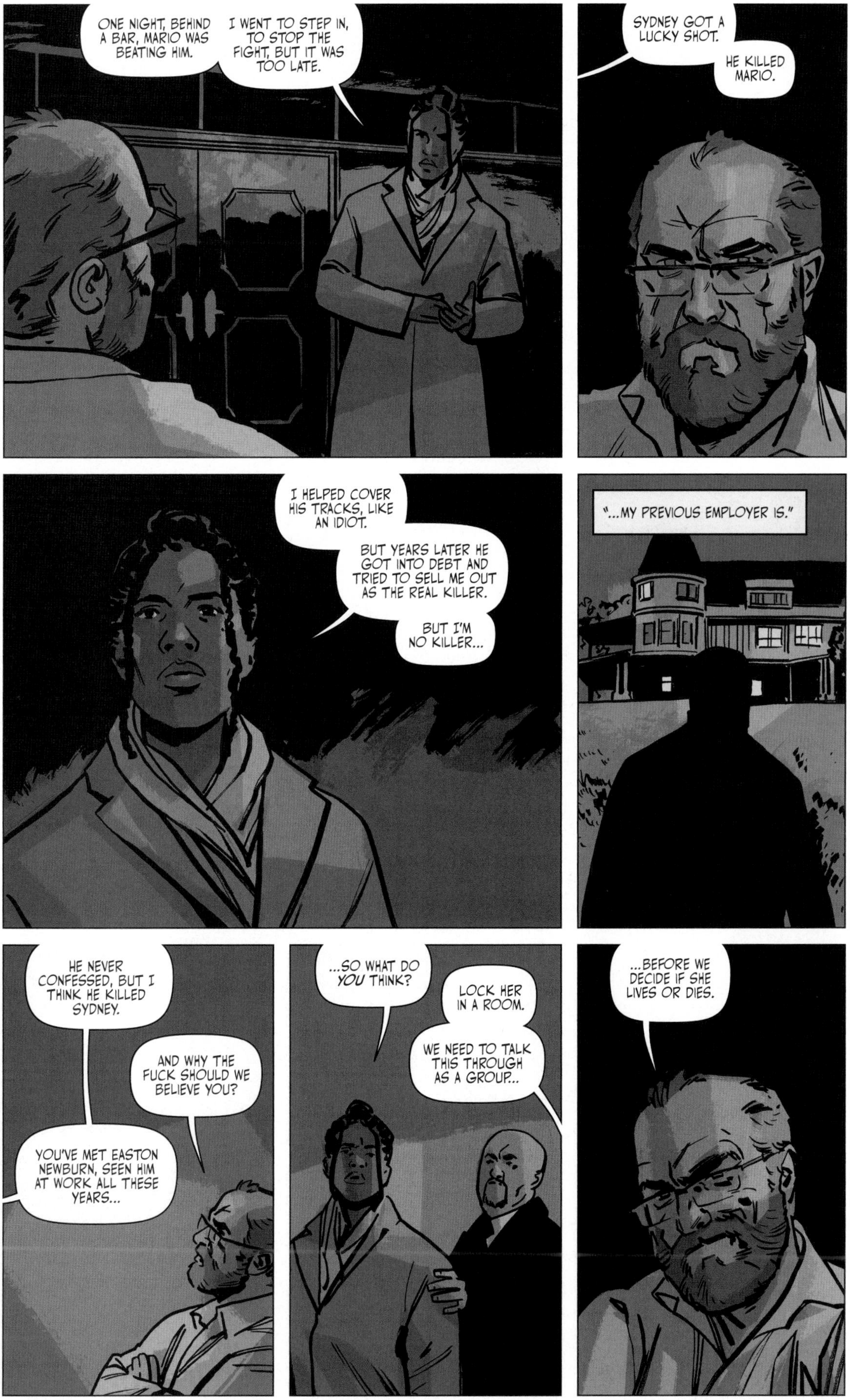
ONE NIGHT, BEHIND A BAR, MARIO WAS BEATING HIM.
I WENT TO STEP IN, TO STOP THE FIGHT, BUT IT WAS TOO LATE.
SYDNEY GOT A LUCKY SHOT.
HE KILLED MARIO.
I HELPED COVER HIS TRACKS, LIKE AN IDIOT.
BUT YEARS LATER HE GOT INTO DEBT AND TRIED TO SELL ME OUT AS THE REAL KILLER.
BUT I'M NO KILLER...
"...MY PREVIOUS EMPLOYER IS."
HE NEVER CONFESSED, BUT I THINK HE KILLED SYDNEY.
AND WHY THE FUCK SHOULD WE BELIEVE YOU?
YOU'VE MET EASTON NEWBURN, SEEN HIM AT WORK ALL THESE YEARS...
...SO WHAT DO *YOU* THINK?
LOCK HER IN A ROOM.
WE NEED TO TALK THIS THROUGH AS A GROUP...
...BEFORE WE DECIDE IF SHE LIVES OR DIES.

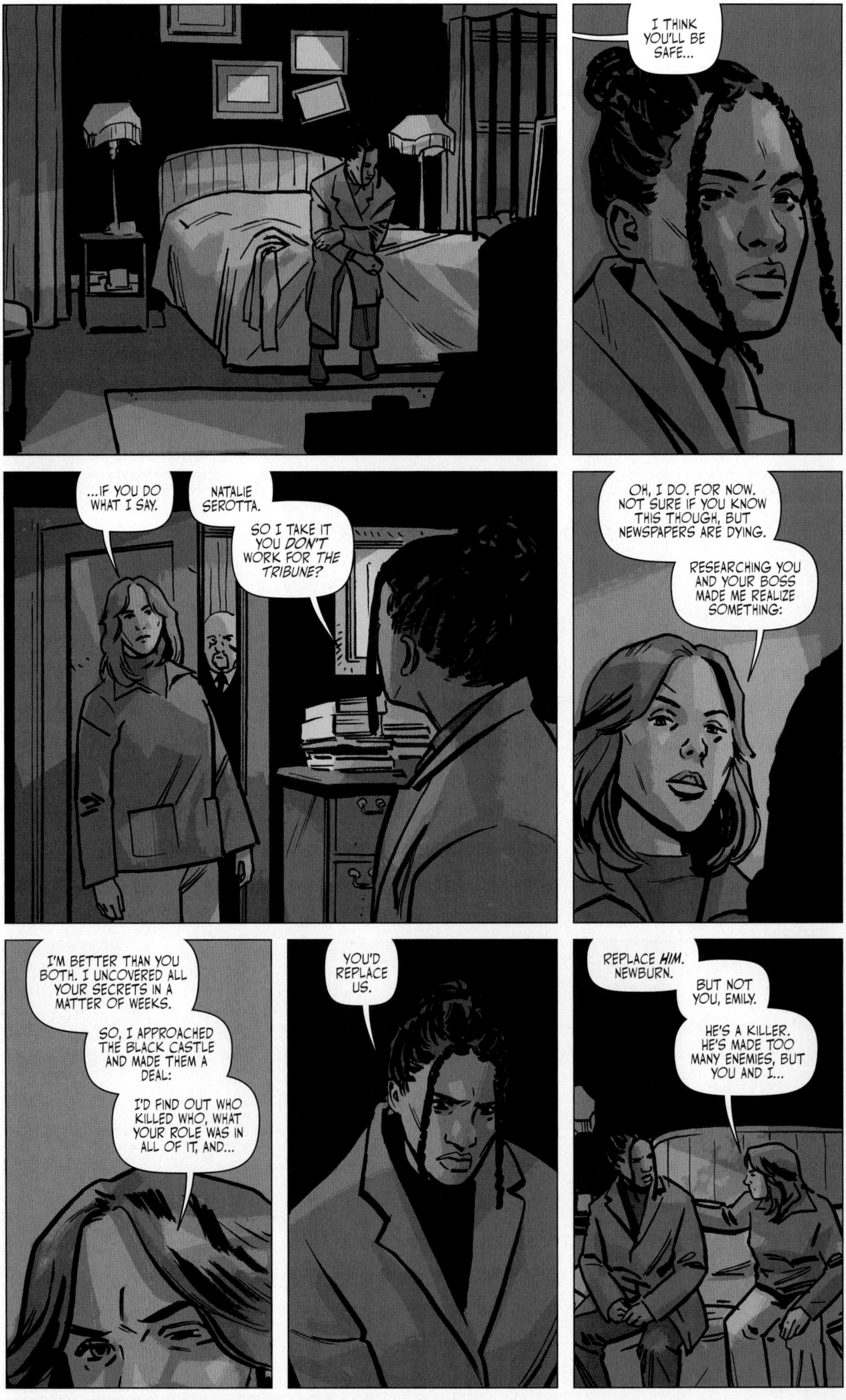
I THINK YOU'LL BE SAFE...
...IF YOU DO WHAT I SAY.
NATALIE SEROTTA.
SO I TAKE IT YOU *DON'T* WORK FOR THE *TRIBUNE*?
OH, I DO. FOR NOW. NOT SURE IF YOU KNOW THIS THOUGH, BUT NEWSPAPERS ARE DYING.
RESEARCHING YOU AND YOUR BOSS MADE ME REALIZE SOMETHING:
I'M BETTER THAN YOU BOTH. I UNCOVERED ALL YOUR SECRETS IN A MATTER OF WEEKS.
SO, I APPROACHED THE BLACK CASTLE AND MADE THEM A DEAL:
I'D FIND OUT WHO KILLED WHO, WHAT YOUR ROLE WAS IN ALL OF IT, AND...
YOU'D REPLACE US.
REPLACE ***HIM***. NEWBURN.
BUT NOT YOU, EMILY.
HE'S A KILLER. HE'S MADE TOO MANY ENEMIES, BUT YOU AND I...

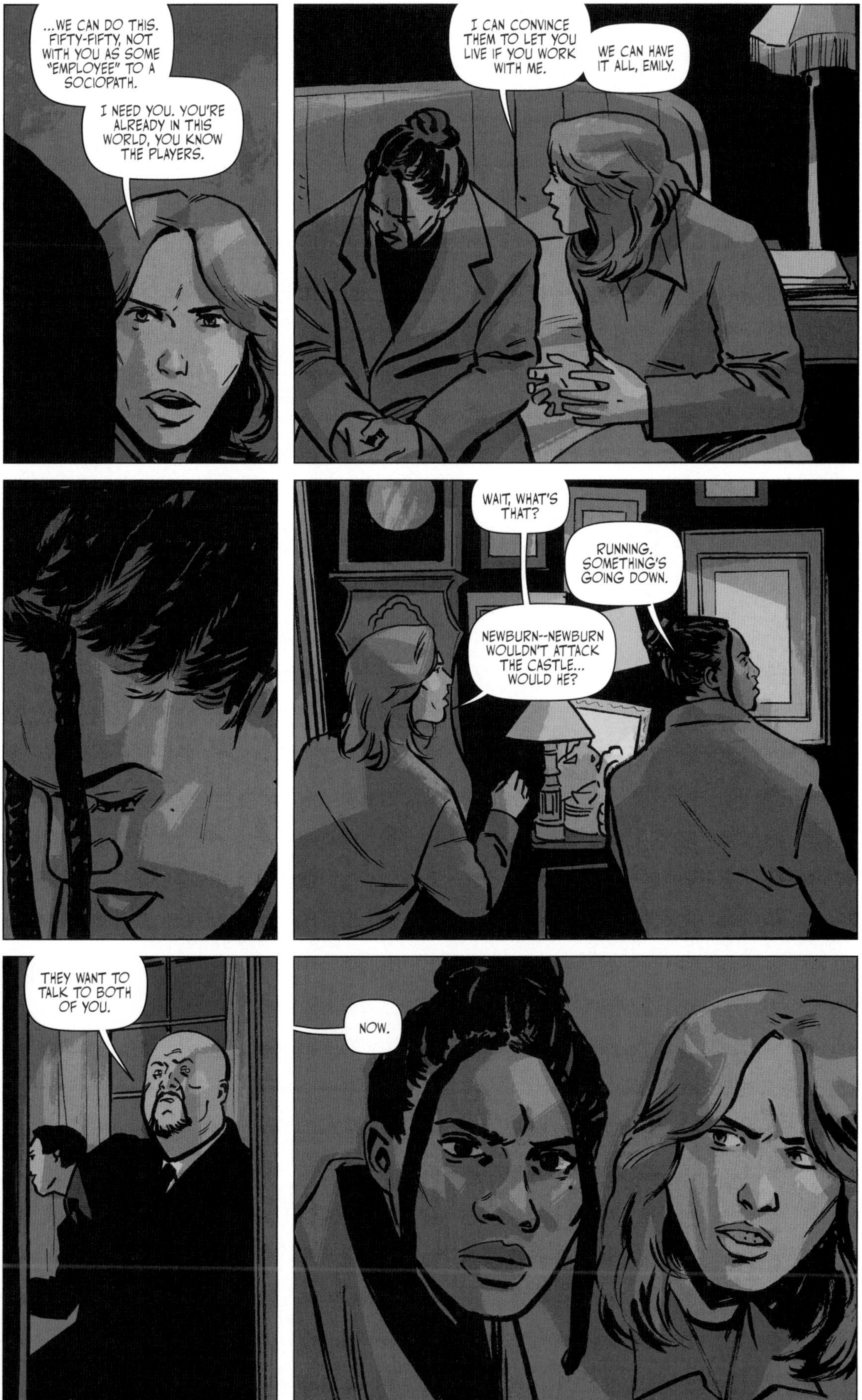
...WE CAN DO THIS. FIFTY-FIFTY, NOT WITH YOU AS SOME "EMPLOYEE" TO A SOCIOPATH.
I NEED YOU. YOU'RE ALREADY IN THIS WORLD, YOU KNOW THE PLAYERS.
I CAN CONVINCE THEM TO LET YOU LIVE IF YOU WORK WITH ME.
WE CAN HAVE IT ALL, EMILY.
WAIT, WHAT'S THAT?
RUNNING. SOMETHING'S GOING DOWN.
NEWBURN--NEWBURN WOULDN'T ATTACK THE CASTLE... WOULD HE?
THEY WANT TO TALK TO BOTH OF YOU.
NOW.

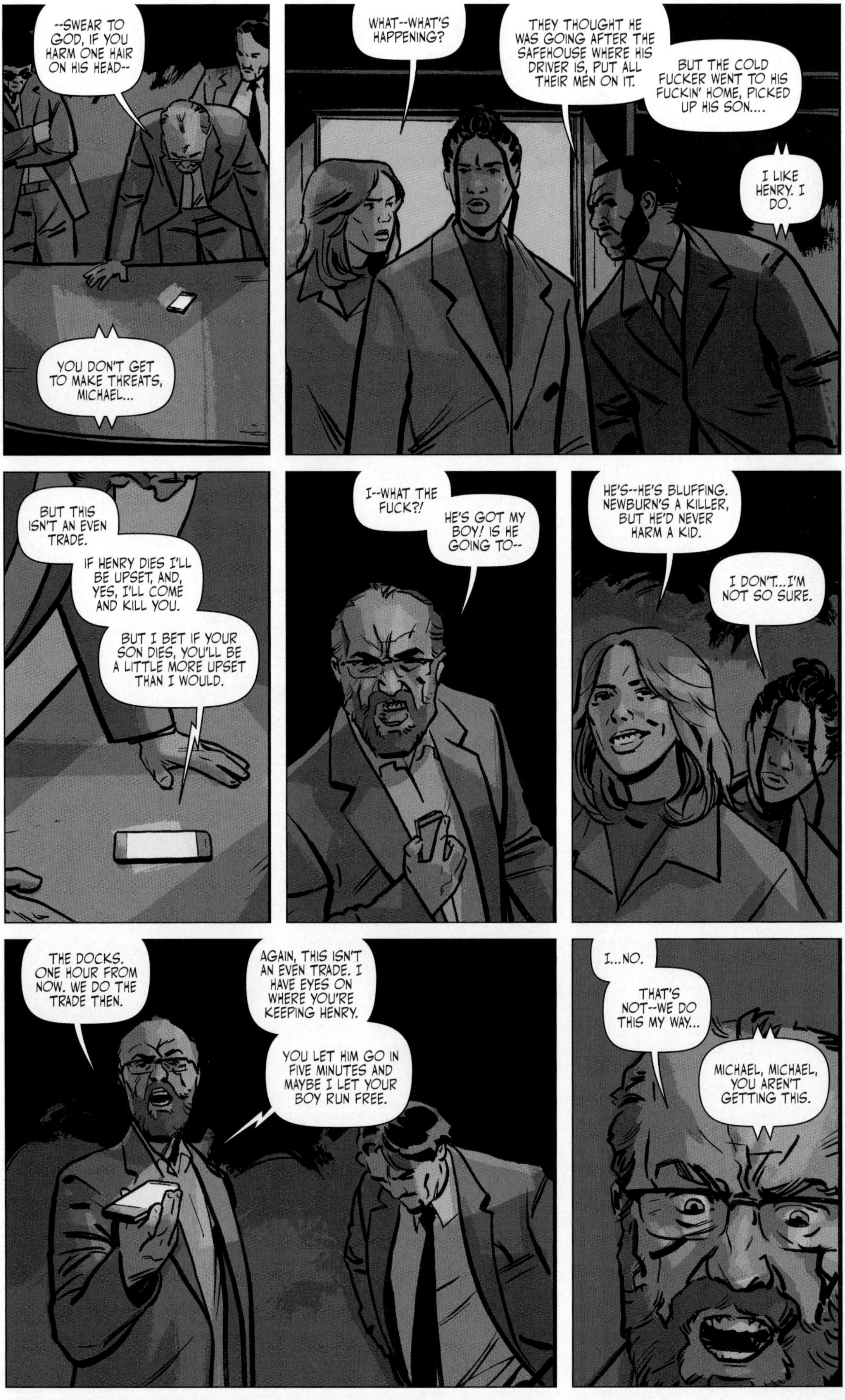
--SWEAR TO GOD, IF YOU HARM ONE HAIR ON HIS HEAD--
YOU DON'T GET TO MAKE THREATS, MICHAEL...
WHAT--WHAT'S HAPPENING?
THEY THOUGHT HE WAS GOING AFTER THE SAFEHOUSE WHERE HIS DRIVER IS, PUT ALL THEIR MEN ON IT.
BUT THE COLD FUCKER WENT TO HIS FUCKIN' HOME, PICKED UP HIS SON....
I LIKE HENRY. I DO.
BUT THIS ISN'T AN EVEN TRADE.
IF HENRY DIES I'LL BE UPSET, AND, YES, I'LL COME AND KILL YOU.
BUT I BET IF YOUR SON DIES, YOU'LL BE A LITTLE MORE UPSET THAN I WOULD.
I--WHAT THE FUCK?!
HE'S GOT MY BOY! IS HE GOING TO--
HE'S--HE'S BLUFFING. NEWBURN'S A KILLER, BUT HE'D NEVER HARM A KID.
I DON'T...I'M NOT SO SURE.
THE DOCKS. ONE HOUR FROM NOW. WE DO THE TRADE THEN.
AGAIN, THIS ISN'T AN EVEN TRADE. I HAVE EYES ON WHERE YOU'RE KEEPING HENRY.
YOU LET HIM GO IN FIVE MINUTES AND MAYBE I LET YOUR BOY RUN FREE.
I...NO.
THAT'S NOT--WE DO THIS MY WAY...
MICHAEL, MICHAEL, YOU AREN'T GETTING THIS.

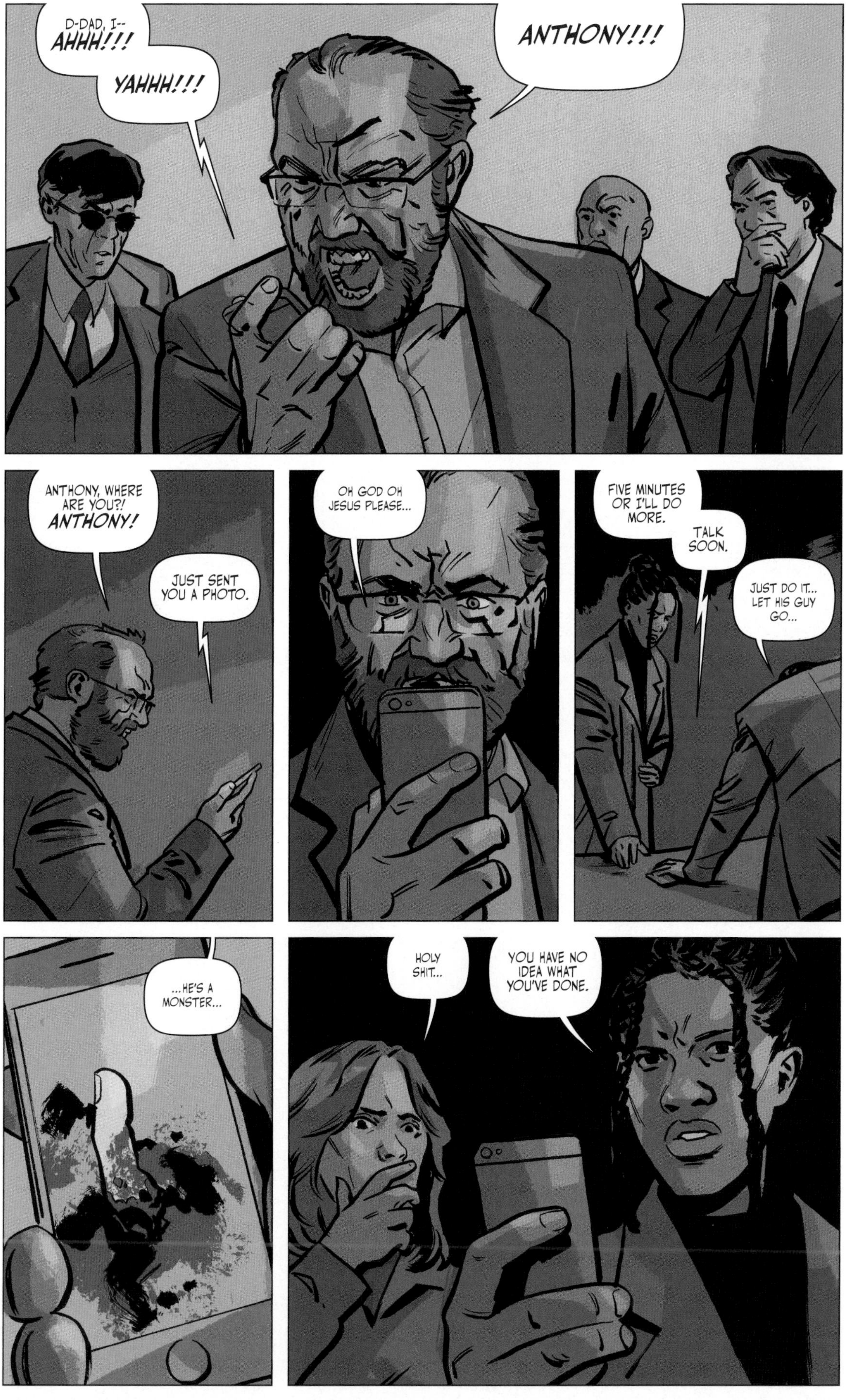
D-DAD, I-- AHHH!!!
YAHHH!!!
ANTHONY!!!
ANTHONY, WHERE ARE YOU?! ANTHONY!
JUST SENT YOU A PHOTO.
OH GOD OH JESUS PLEASE...
FIVE MINUTES OR I'LL DO MORE.
TALK SOON.
JUST DO IT... LET HIS GUY GO...
...HE'S A MONSTER...
HOLY SHIT...
YOU HAVE NO IDEA WHAT YOU'VE DONE.

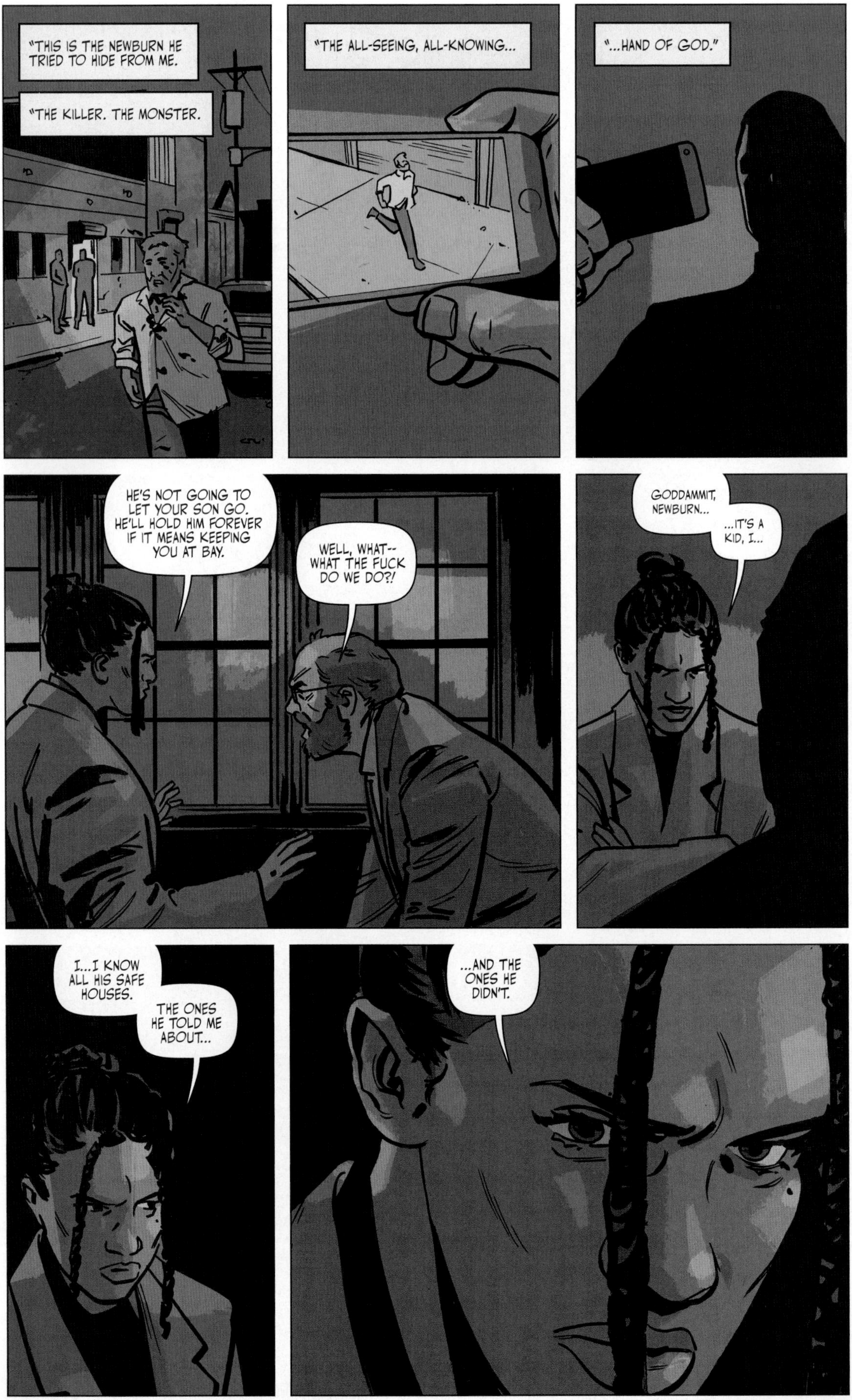
"THIS IS THE NEWBURN HE TRIED TO HIDE FROM ME.
"THE KILLER. THE MONSTER.
"THE ALL-SEEING, ALL-KNOWING...
"...HAND OF GOD."
HE'S NOT GOING TO LET YOUR SON GO. HE'LL HOLD HIM FOREVER IF IT MEANS KEEPING YOU AT BAY.
WELL, WHAT-- WHAT THE FUCK DO WE DO?!
GODDAMMIT, NEWBURN...
...IT'S A KID, I...
I...I KNOW ALL HIS SAFE HOUSES.
THE ONES HE TOLD ME ABOUT...
...AND THE ONES HE DIDN'T.

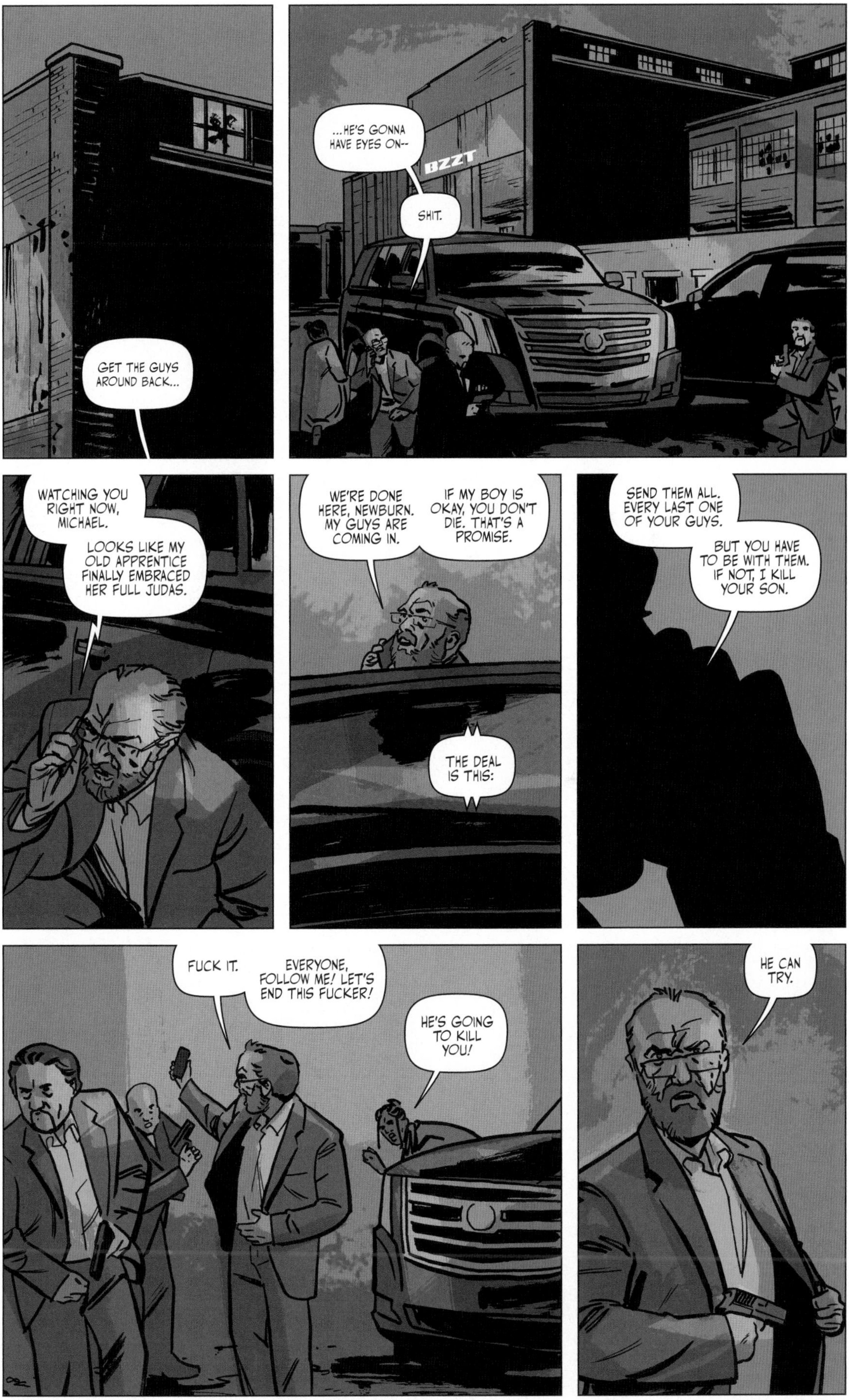
GET THE GUYS AROUND BACK...
...HE'S GONNA HAVE EYES ON--
BZZT
SHIT.
WATCHING YOU RIGHT NOW, MICHAEL.
LOOKS LIKE MY OLD APPRENTICE FINALLY EMBRACED HER FULL JUDAS.
WE'RE DONE HERE, NEWBURN. MY GUYS ARE COMING IN.
IF MY BOY IS OKAY, YOU DON'T DIE. THAT'S A PROMISE.
THE DEAL IS THIS:
SEND THEM ALL. EVERY LAST ONE OF YOUR GUYS.
BUT YOU HAVE TO BE WITH THEM. IF NOT, I KILL YOUR SON.
FUCK IT.
EVERYONE, FOLLOW ME! LET'S END THIS FUCKER!
HE'S GOING TO KILL YOU!
HE CAN TRY.

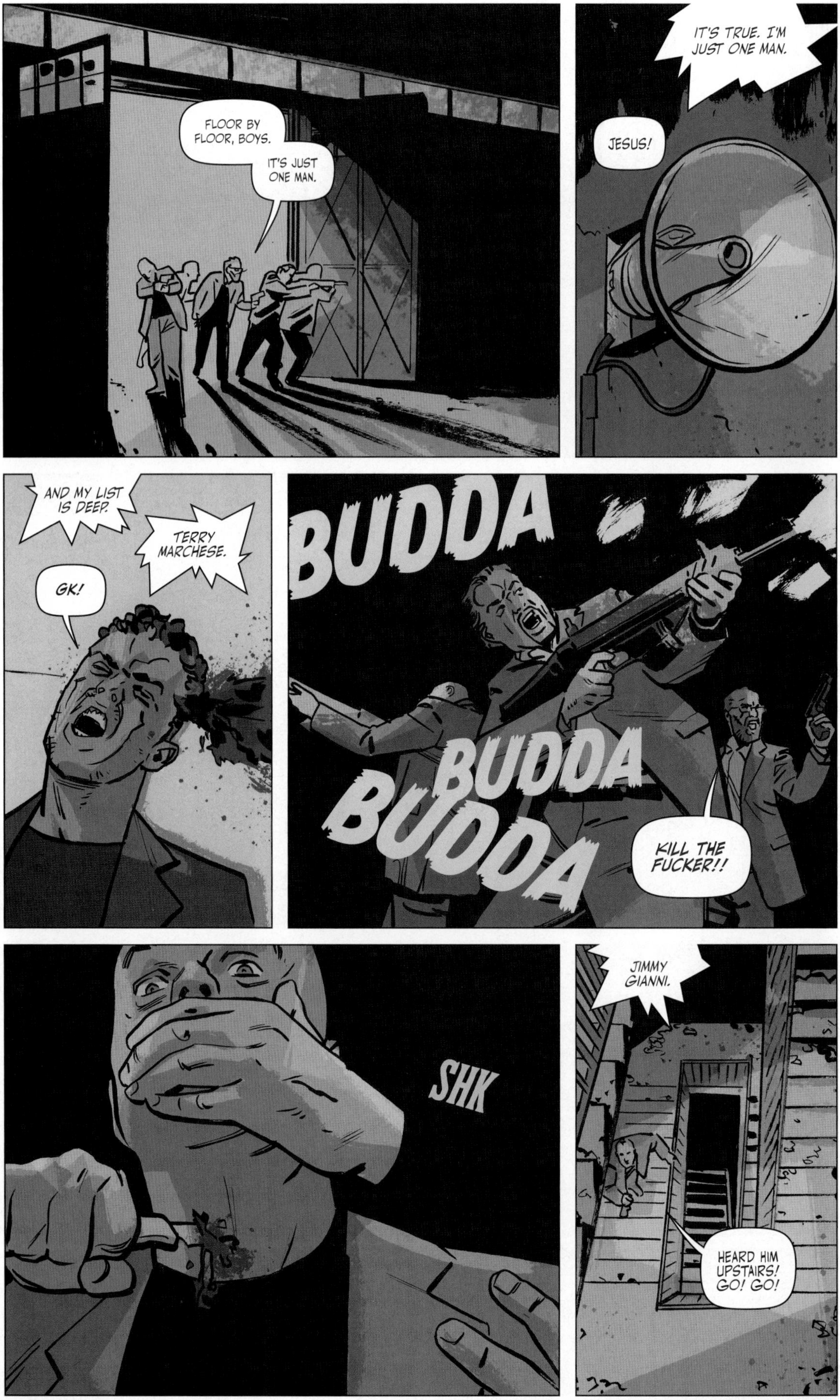
FLOOR BY FLOOR, BOYS.
IT'S JUST ONE MAN.
IT'S TRUE. I'M JUST ONE MAN.
JESUS!
AND MY LIST IS DEEP.
TERRY MARCHESE.
GK!
BUDDA
BUDDA
BUDDA
KILL THE FUCKER!!
SHK
JIMMY GIANNI.
HEARD HIM UPSTAIRS! GO! GO!

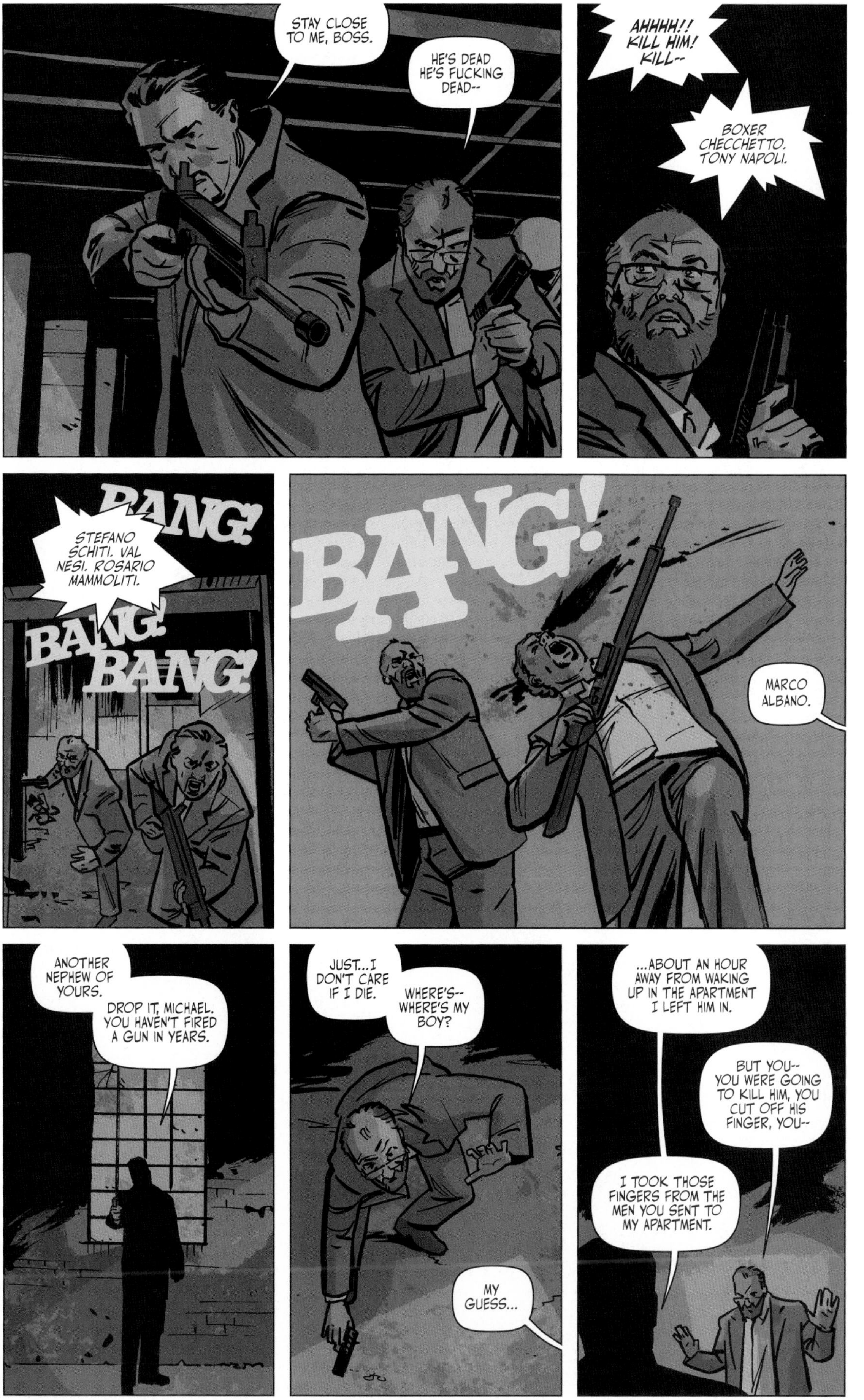

STAY CLOSE TO ME, BOSS.
HE'S DEAD HE'S FUCKING DEAD--
AHHHH!! KILL HIM! KILL--
BOXER CHECCHETTO. TONY NAPOLI.
BANG!
STEFANO SCHITI. VAL NESI. ROSARIO MAMMOLITI.
BANG!
BANG!
BANG!
MARCO ALBANO.
ANOTHER NEPHEW OF YOURS.
DROP IT, MICHAEL. YOU HAVEN'T FIRED A GUN IN YEARS.
JUST...I DON'T CARE IF I DIE.
WHERE'S-- WHERE'S MY BOY?
MY GUESS...
...ABOUT AN HOUR AWAY FROM WAKING UP IN THE APARTMENT I LEFT HIM IN.
BUT YOU-- YOU WERE GOING TO KILL HIM, YOU CUT OFF HIS FINGER, YOU--
I TOOK THOSE FINGERS FROM THE MEN YOU SENT TO MY APARTMENT.

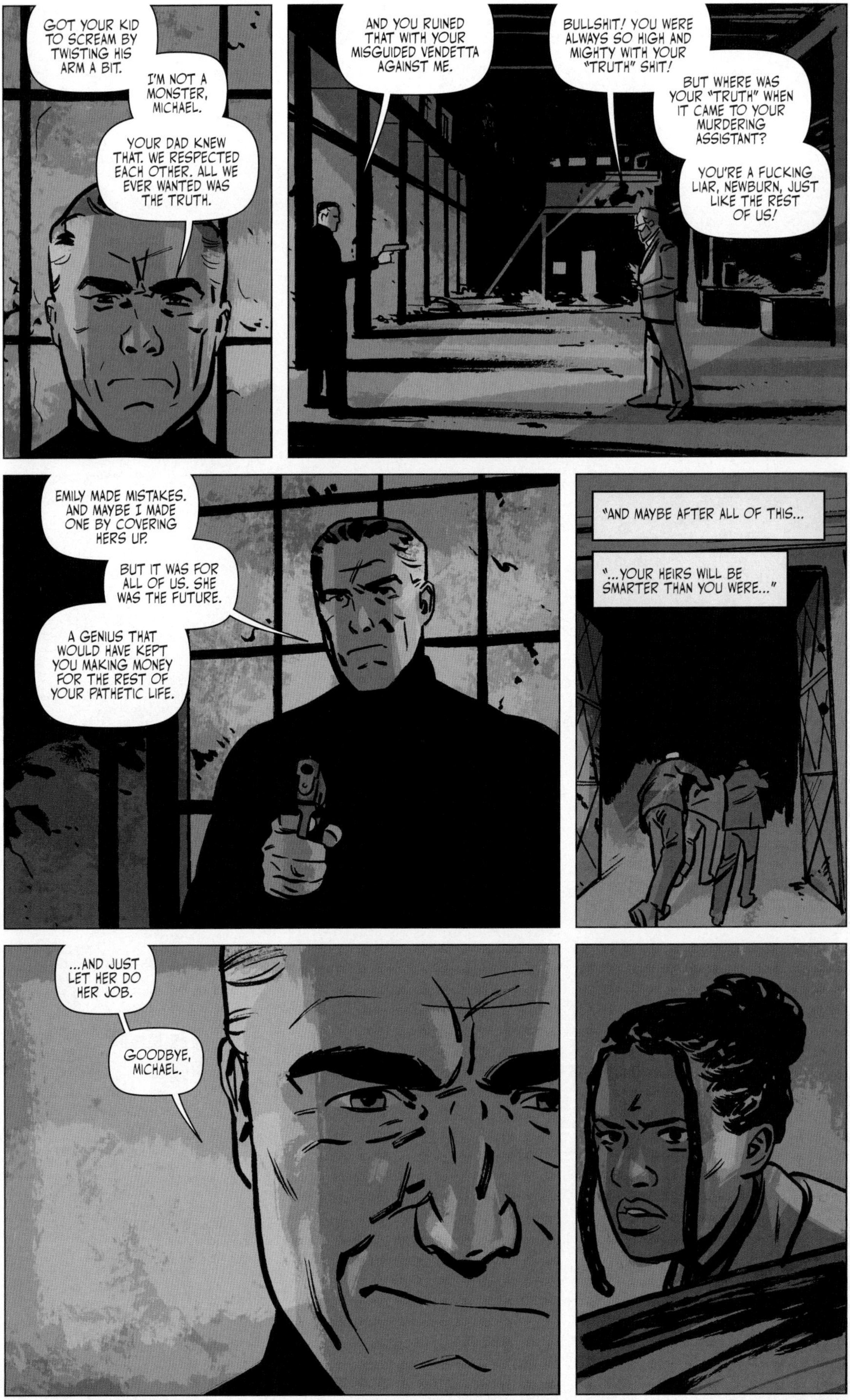
GOT YOUR KID TO SCREAM BY TWISTING HIS ARM A BIT.
I'M NOT A MONSTER, MICHAEL.
YOUR DAD KNEW THAT. WE RESPECTED EACH OTHER. ALL WE EVER WANTED WAS THE TRUTH.
AND YOU RUINED THAT WITH YOUR MISGUIDED VENDETTA AGAINST ME.
BULLSHIT! YOU WERE ALWAYS SO HIGH AND MIGHTY WITH YOUR "TRUTH" SHIT!
BUT WHERE WAS YOUR "TRUTH" WHEN IT CAME TO YOUR MURDERING ASSISTANT?
YOU'RE A FUCKING LIAR, NEWBURN, JUST LIKE THE REST OF US!
EMILY MADE MISTAKES. AND MAYBE I MADE ONE BY COVERING HERS UP.
BUT IT WAS FOR ALL OF US. SHE WAS THE FUTURE.
A GENIUS THAT WOULD HAVE KEPT YOU MAKING MONEY FOR THE REST OF YOUR PATHETIC LIFE.
"AND MAYBE AFTER ALL OF THIS...
"...YOUR HEIRS WILL BE SMARTER THAN YOU WERE..."
...AND JUST LET HER DO HER JOB.
GOODBYE, MICHAEL.

EMILY'S JOURNAL
01/17/23

Here we go.

And here's where we end.

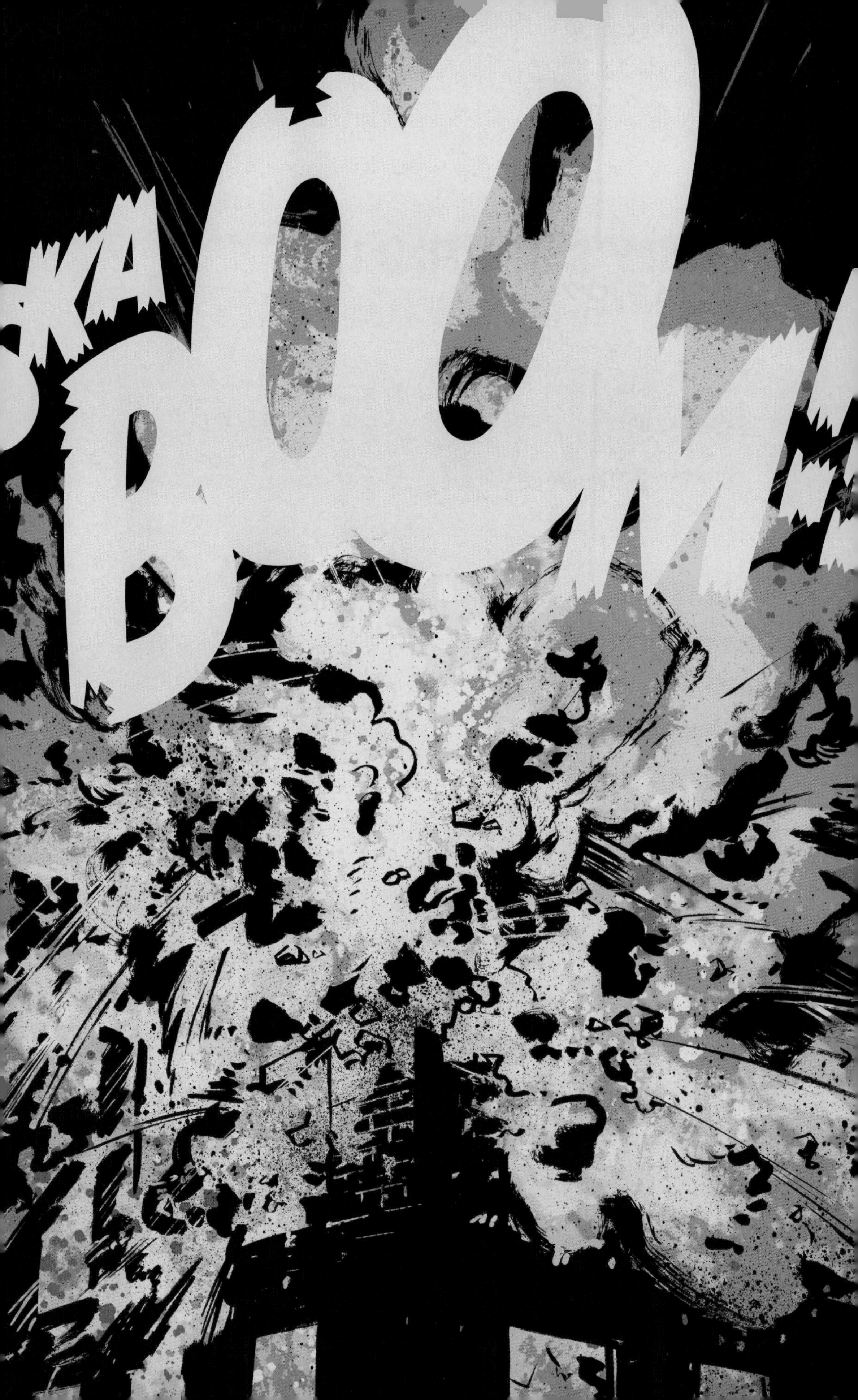
KA BOOM!!

16

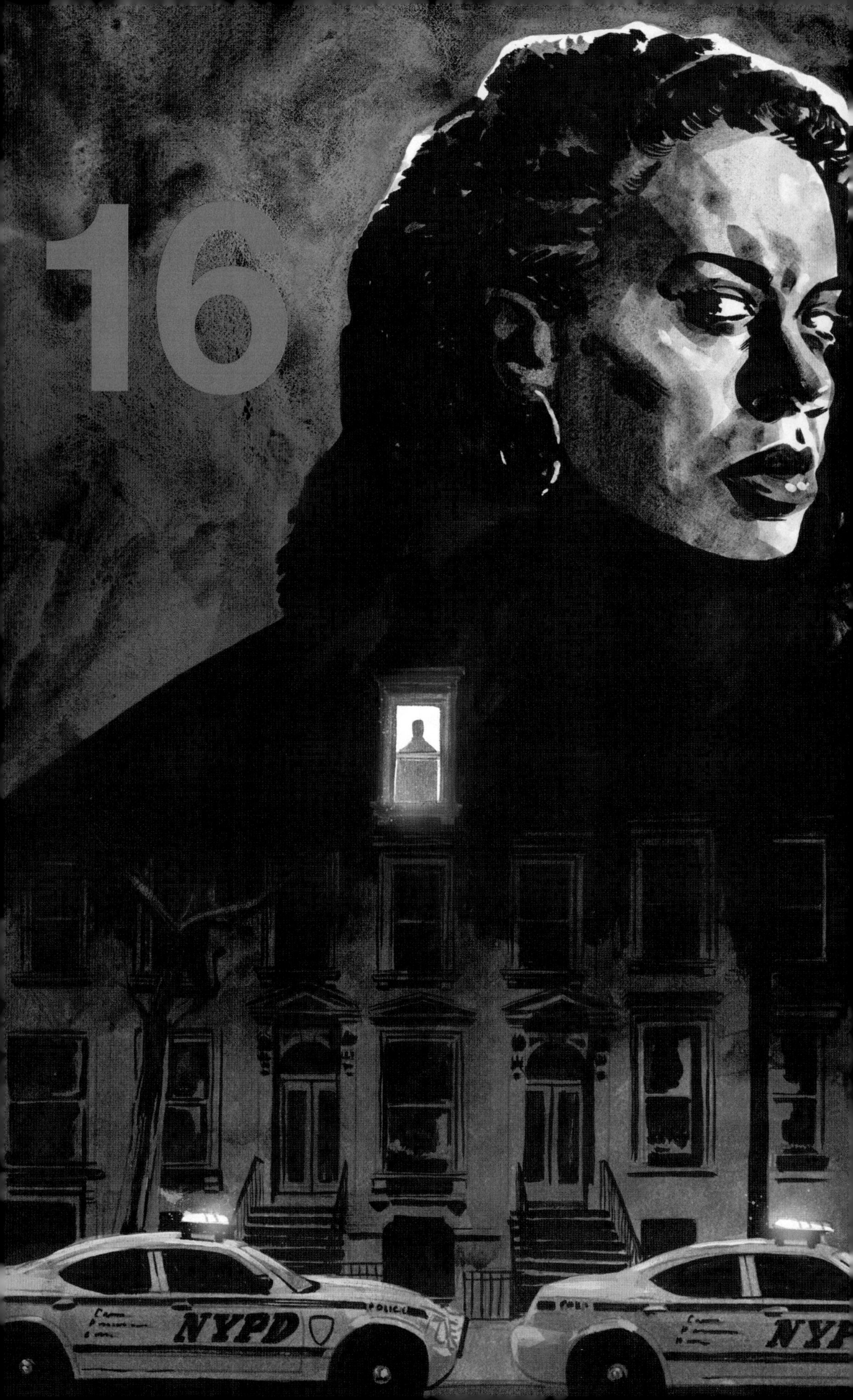
NYPD
POLICE

Here we go.

And here's where

01/17/23

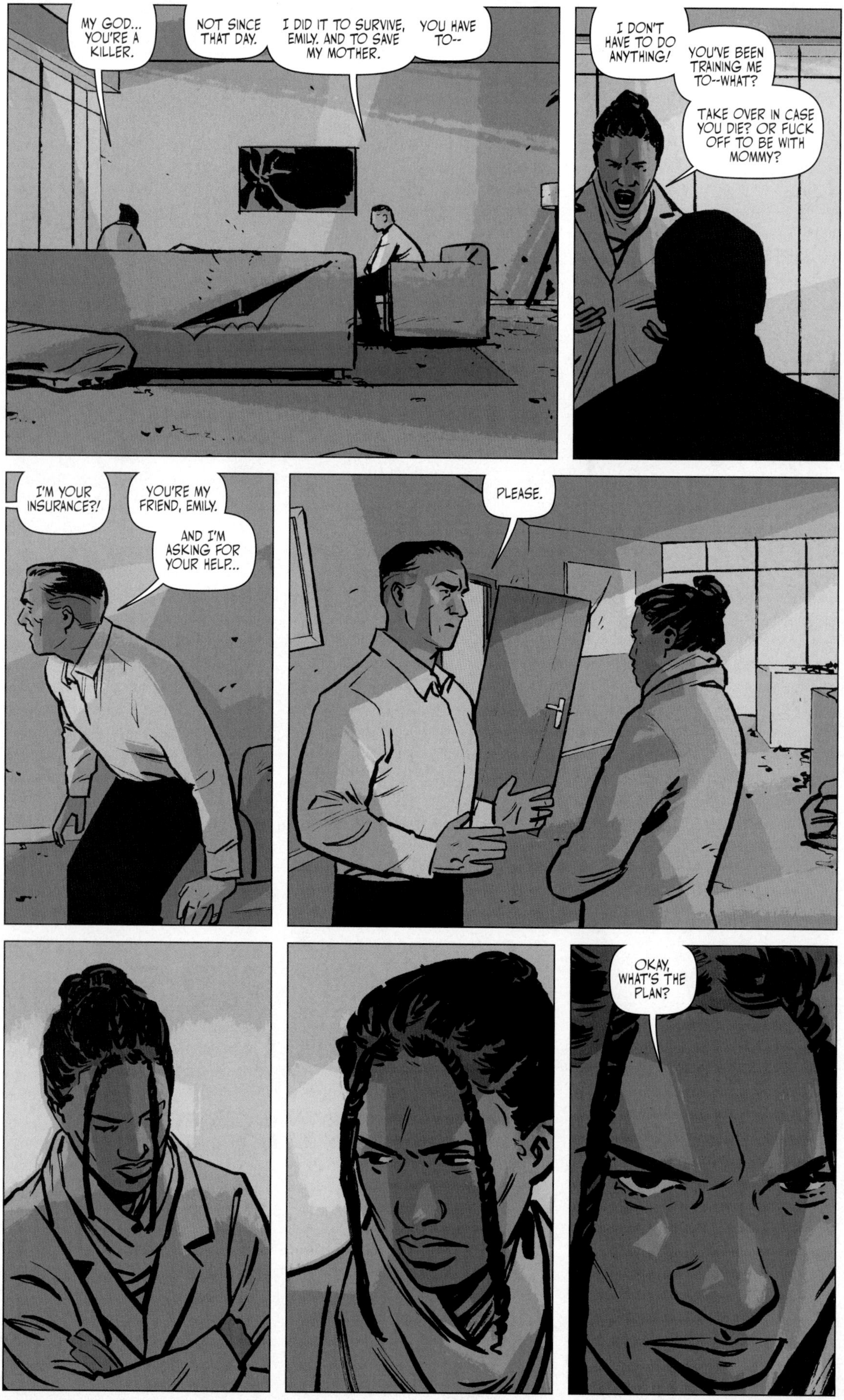
MY GOD... YOU'RE A KILLER.
NOT SINCE THAT DAY.
I DID IT TO SURVIVE, EMILY. AND TO SAVE MY MOTHER.
YOU HAVE TO--
I DON'T HAVE TO DO ANYTHING!
YOU'VE BEEN TRAINING ME TO--WHAT?
TAKE OVER IN CASE YOU DIE? OR FUCK OFF TO BE WITH MOMMY?
I'M YOUR INSURANCE?!
YOU'RE MY FRIEND, EMILY.
AND I'M ASKING FOR YOUR HELP...
PLEASE.
OKAY, WHAT'S THE PLAN?

There's an order to things. Will return to this always is, even in death. Today I h...... y me...... know what to expe...... s laid ...... it's still an odd feeling finally going through these steps.

You m... everything so ...cated and so simple a... ... he time ... on.

02
/14
/23

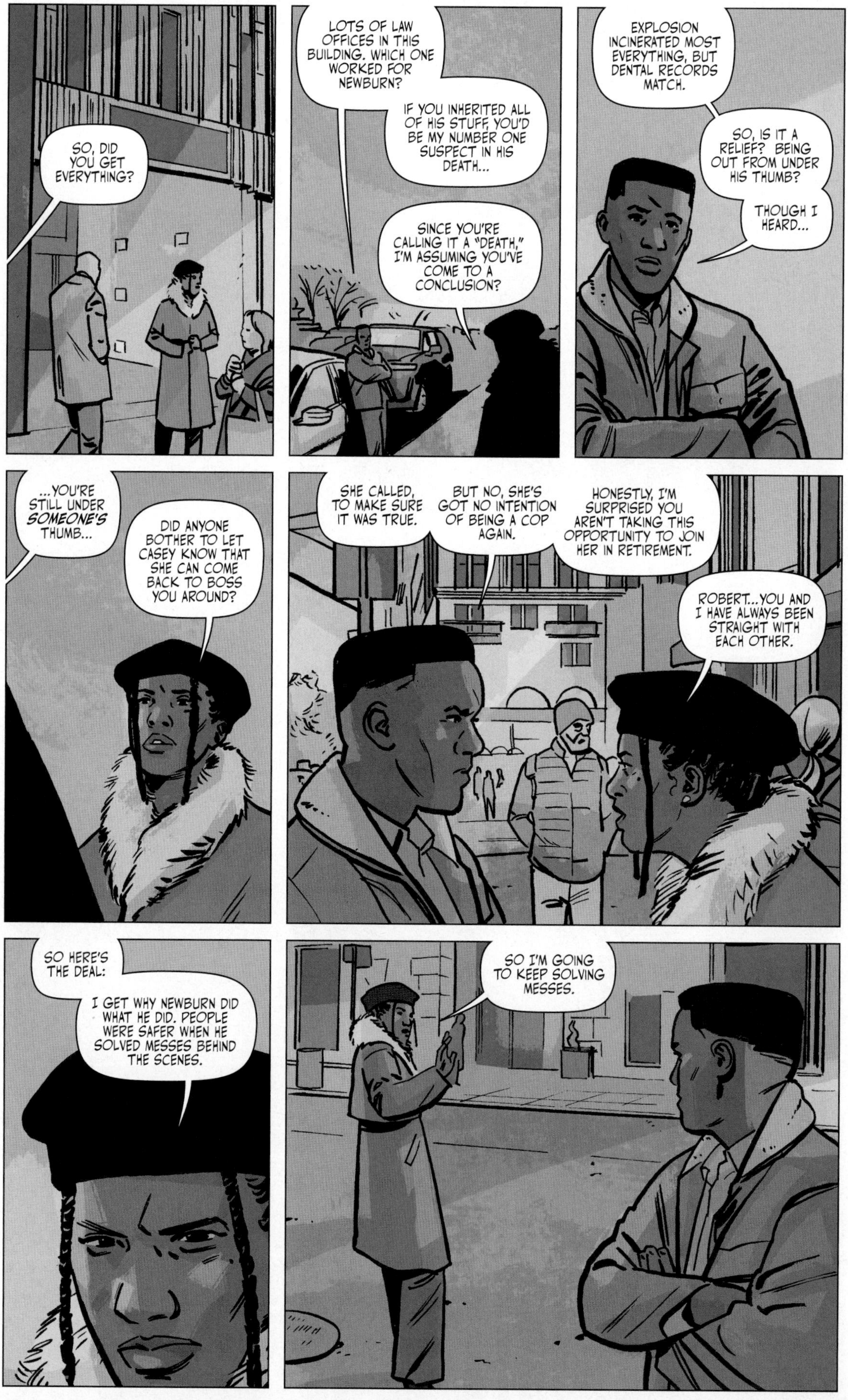

SO, DID YOU GET EVERYTHING?
LOTS OF LAW OFFICES IN THIS BUILDING. WHICH ONE WORKED FOR NEWBURN?
IF YOU INHERITED ALL OF HIS STUFF, YOU'D BE MY NUMBER ONE SUSPECT IN HIS DEATH...
SINCE YOU'RE CALLING IT A "DEATH," I'M ASSUMING YOU'VE COME TO A CONCLUSION?
EXPLOSION INCINERATED MOST EVERYTHING, BUT DENTAL RECORDS MATCH.
SO, IS IT A RELIEF? BEING OUT FROM UNDER HIS THUMB?
THOUGH I HEARD...
...YOU'RE STILL UNDER *SOMEONE'S* THUMB...
DID ANYONE BOTHER TO LET CASEY KNOW THAT SHE CAN COME BACK TO BOSS YOU AROUND?
SHE CALLED, TO MAKE SURE IT WAS TRUE.
BUT NO, SHE'S GOT NO INTENTION OF BEING A COP AGAIN.
HONESTLY, I'M SURPRISED YOU AREN'T TAKING THIS OPPORTUNITY TO JOIN HER IN RETIREMENT.
ROBERT...YOU AND I HAVE ALWAYS BEEN STRAIGHT WITH EACH OTHER.
SO HERE'S THE DEAL:
I GET WHY NEWBURN DID WHAT HE DID. PEOPLE WERE SAFER WHEN HE SOLVED MESSES BEHIND THE SCENES.
SO I'M GOING TO KEEP SOLVING MESSES.

03
/20
/24

The death of a man, Carraro, who the the man in charge of heroin shipment, was an accident, but murder. The fact that makes it a coverup, so it's not a "message sent."

Of course, Natalia, accident for bogus a smiles our

It's like the I actually n w

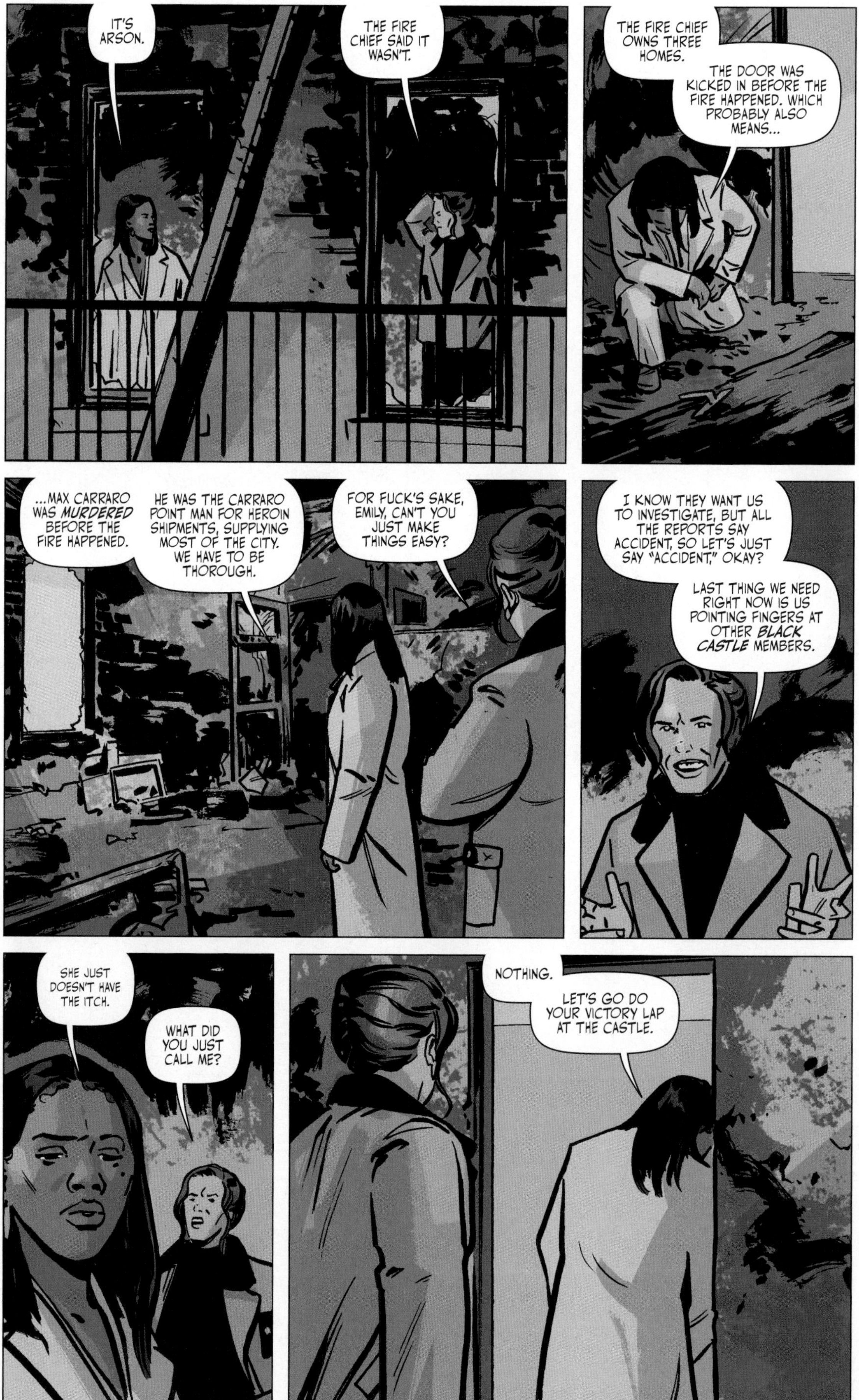
IT'S ARSON.
THE FIRE CHIEF SAID IT WASN'T.
THE FIRE CHIEF OWNS THREE HOMES.
THE DOOR WAS KICKED IN BEFORE THE FIRE HAPPENED. WHICH PROBABLY ALSO MEANS...
...MAX CARRARO WAS MURDERED BEFORE THE FIRE HAPPENED.
HE WAS THE CARRARO POINT MAN FOR HEROIN SHIPMENTS, SUPPLYING MOST OF THE CITY. WE HAVE TO BE THOROUGH.
FOR FUCK'S SAKE, EMILY, CAN'T YOU JUST MAKE THINGS EASY?
I KNOW THEY WANT US TO INVESTIGATE, BUT ALL THE REPORTS SAY ACCIDENT, SO LET'S JUST SAY "ACCIDENT," OKAY?
LAST THING WE NEED RIGHT NOW IS US POINTING FINGERS AT OTHER BLACK CASTLE MEMBERS.
SHE JUST DOESN'T HAVE THE ITCH.
WHAT DID YOU JUST CALL ME?
NOTHING.
LET'S GO DO YOUR VICTORY LAP AT THE CASTLE.

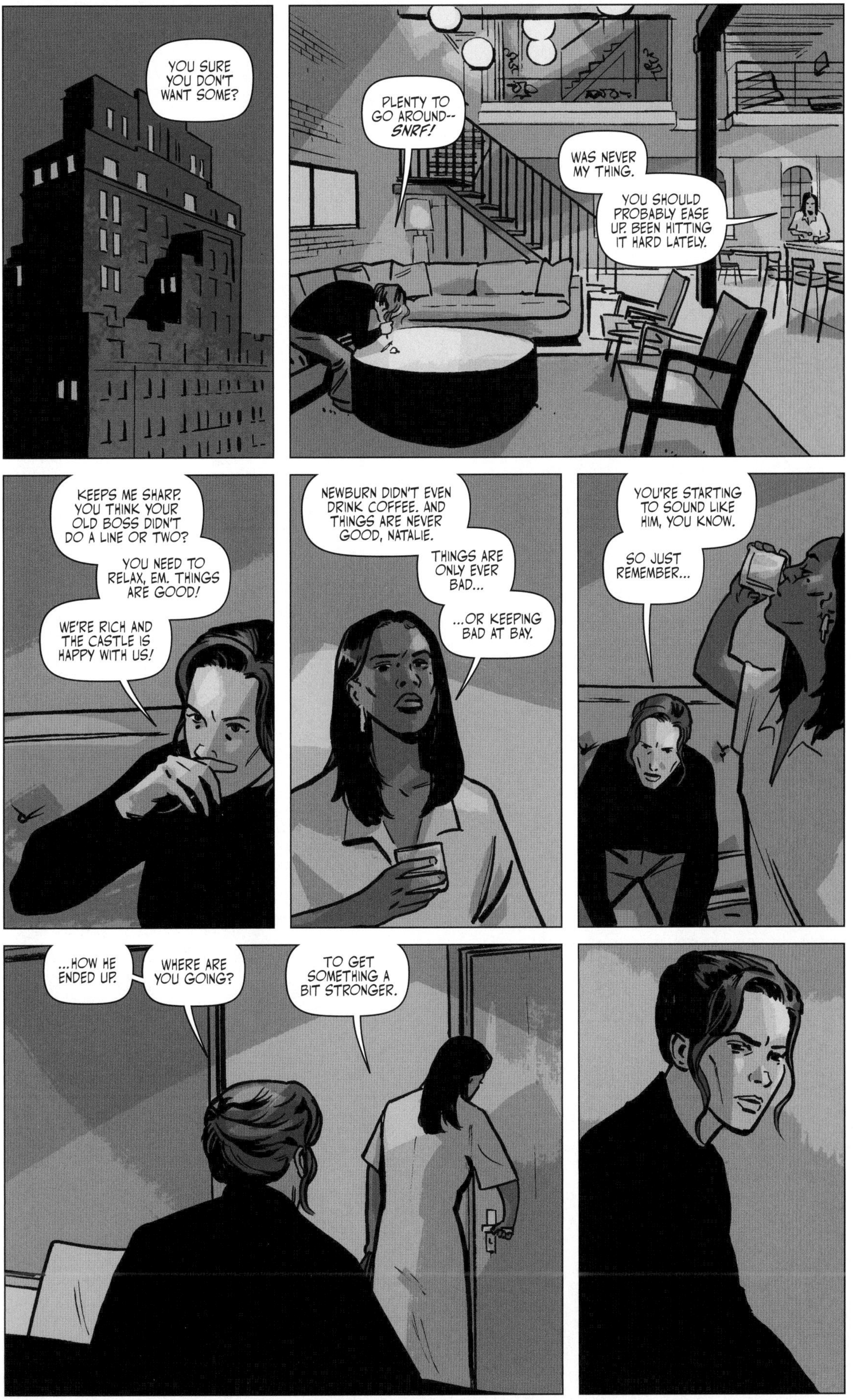
YOU SURE YOU DON'T WANT SOME?
PLENTY TO GO AROUND-- SNRF!
WAS NEVER MY THING.
YOU SHOULD PROBABLY EASE UP. BEEN HITTING IT HARD LATELY.
KEEPS ME SHARP. YOU THINK YOUR OLD BOSS DIDN'T DO A LINE OR TWO?
YOU NEED TO RELAX, EM. THINGS ARE GOOD!
WE'RE RICH AND THE CASTLE IS HAPPY WITH US!
NEWBURN DIDN'T EVEN DRINK COFFEE. AND THINGS ARE NEVER GOOD, NATALIE.
THINGS ARE ONLY EVER BAD...
...OR KEEPING BAD AT BAY.
YOU'RE STARTING TO SOUND LIKE HIM, YOU KNOW.
SO JUST REMEMBER...
...HOW HE ENDED UP.
WHERE ARE YOU GOING?
TO GET SOMETHING A BIT STRONGER.

The visuals on the main would ate in coming fro
Southeast Asia. howi
elements as before

Which y indicate Council has a lock on th lier
and w anythi

03
/24
/24

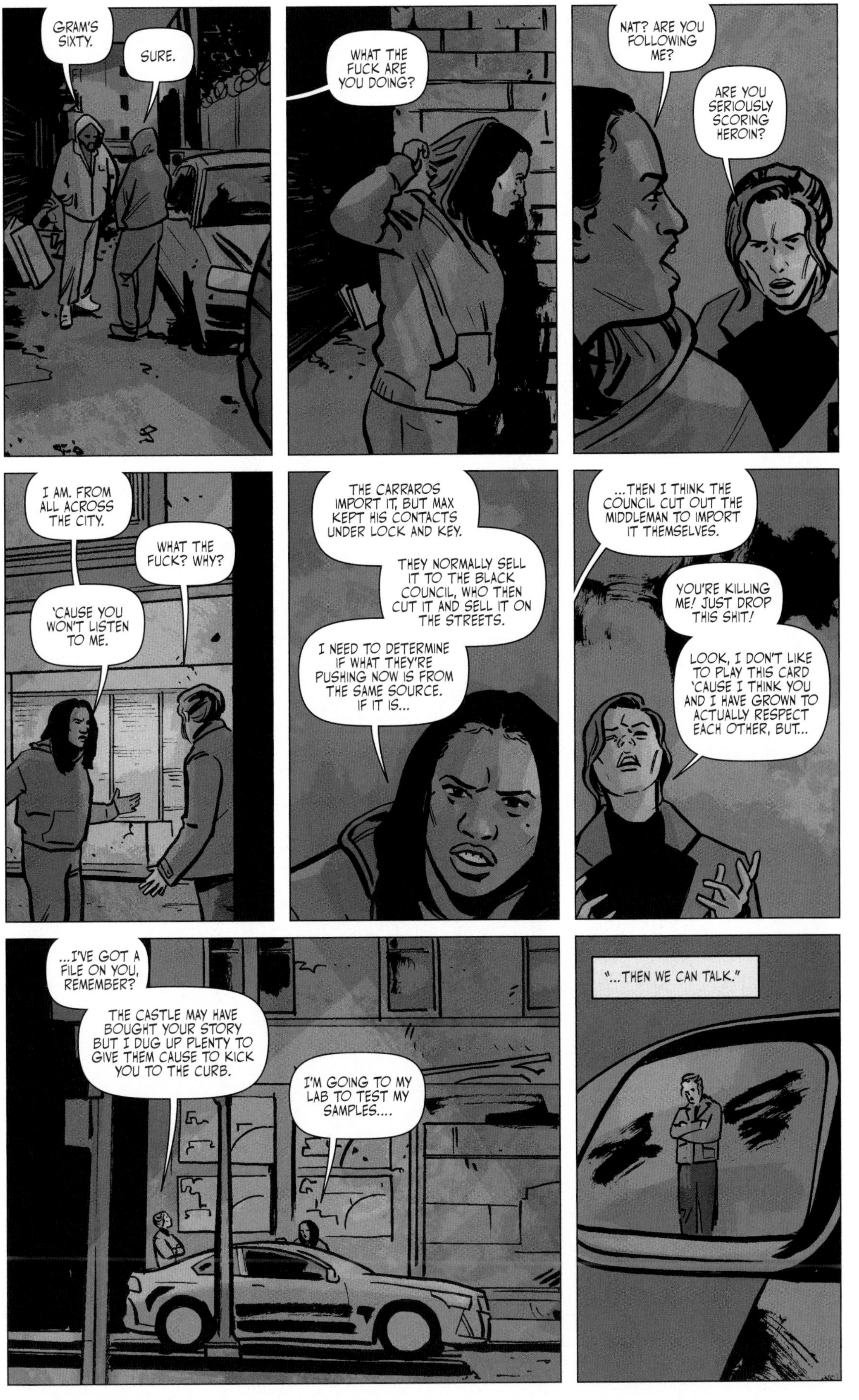
GRAM'S SIXTY.
SURE.
WHAT THE FUCK ARE YOU DOING?
NAT? ARE YOU FOLLOWING ME?
ARE YOU SERIOUSLY SCORING HEROIN?
I AM. FROM ALL ACROSS THE CITY.
WHAT THE FUCK? WHY?
'CAUSE YOU WON'T LISTEN TO ME.
THE CARRAROS IMPORT IT, BUT MAX KEPT HIS CONTACTS UNDER LOCK AND KEY.
THEY NORMALLY SELL IT TO THE BLACK COUNCIL, WHO THEN CUT IT AND SELL IT ON THE STREETS.
I NEED TO DETERMINE IF WHAT THEY'RE PUSHING NOW IS FROM THE SAME SOURCE. IF IT IS...
...THEN I THINK THE COUNCIL CUT OUT THE MIDDLEMAN TO IMPORT IT THEMSELVES.
YOU'RE KILLING ME! JUST DROP THIS SHIT!
LOOK, I DON'T LIKE TO PLAY THIS CARD 'CAUSE I THINK YOU AND I HAVE GROWN TO ACTUALLY RESPECT EACH OTHER, BUT...
...I'VE GOT A FILE ON YOU, REMEMBER?
THE CASTLE MAY HAVE BOUGHT YOUR STORY BUT I DUG UP PLENTY TO GIVE THEM CAUSE TO KICK YOU TO THE CURB.
I'M GOING TO MY LAB TO TEST MY SAMPLES....
"...THEN WE CAN TALK."

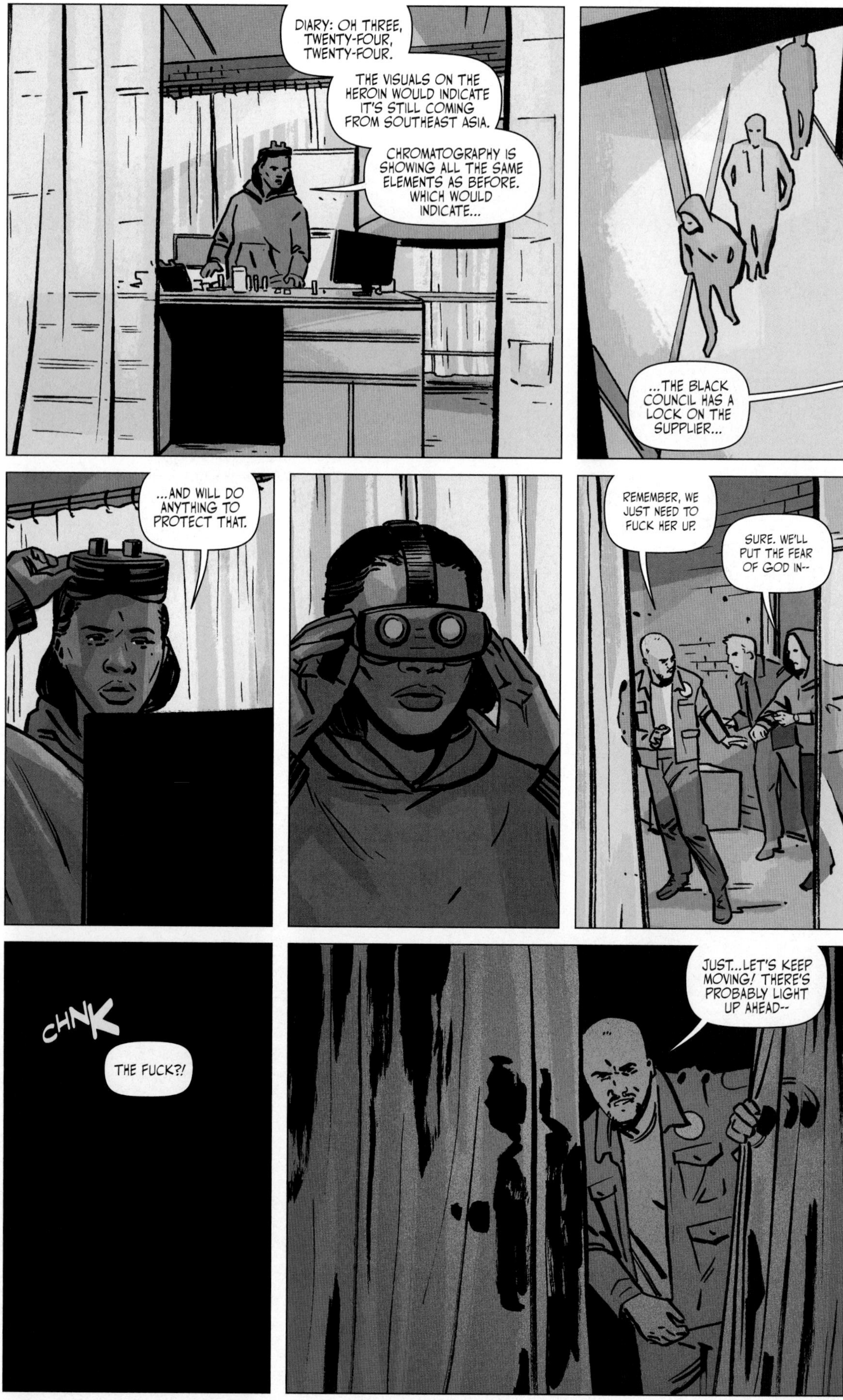
DIARY: OH THREE, TWENTY-FOUR, TWENTY-FOUR.
THE VISUALS ON THE HEROIN WOULD INDICATE IT'S STILL COMING FROM SOUTHEAST ASIA.
CHROMATOGRAPHY IS SHOWING ALL THE SAME ELEMENTS AS BEFORE. WHICH WOULD INDICATE...
...THE BLACK COUNCIL HAS A LOCK ON THE SUPPLIER...
...AND WILL DO ANYTHING TO PROTECT THAT.
REMEMBER, WE JUST NEED TO FUCK HER UP.
SURE. WE'LL PUT THE FEAR OF GOD IN--
CHNK
THE FUCK?!
JUST...LET'S KEEP MOVING! THERE'S PROBABLY LIGHT UP AHEAD--

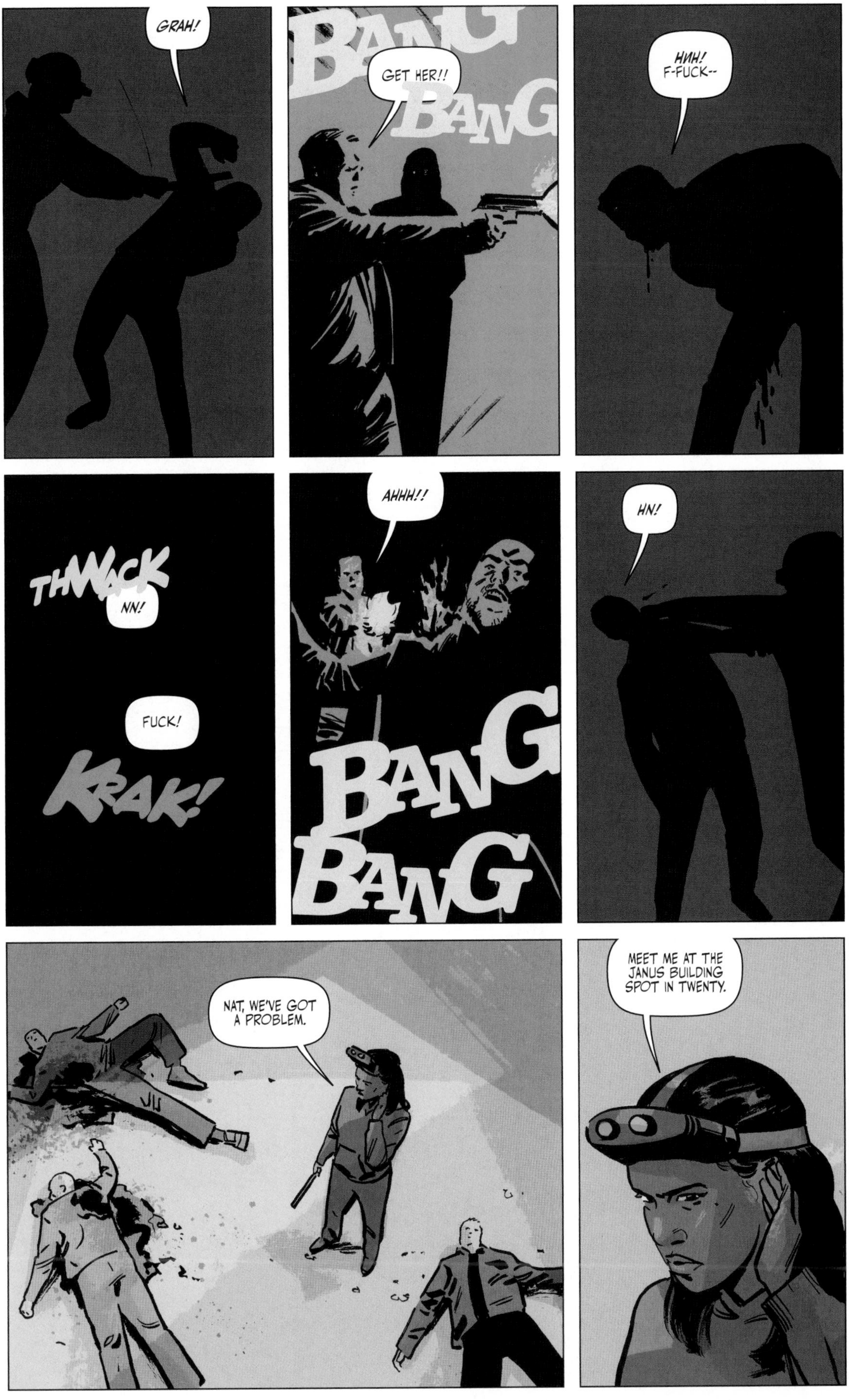
GRAH!
BANG
GET HER!!
BANG
HNH!
F-FUCK--
THWACK
NN!
FUCK!
KRAK!
AHHH!!
BANG
BANG
HN!
NAT, WE'VE GOT A PROBLEM.
MEET ME AT THE JANUS BUILDING SPOT IN TWENTY.

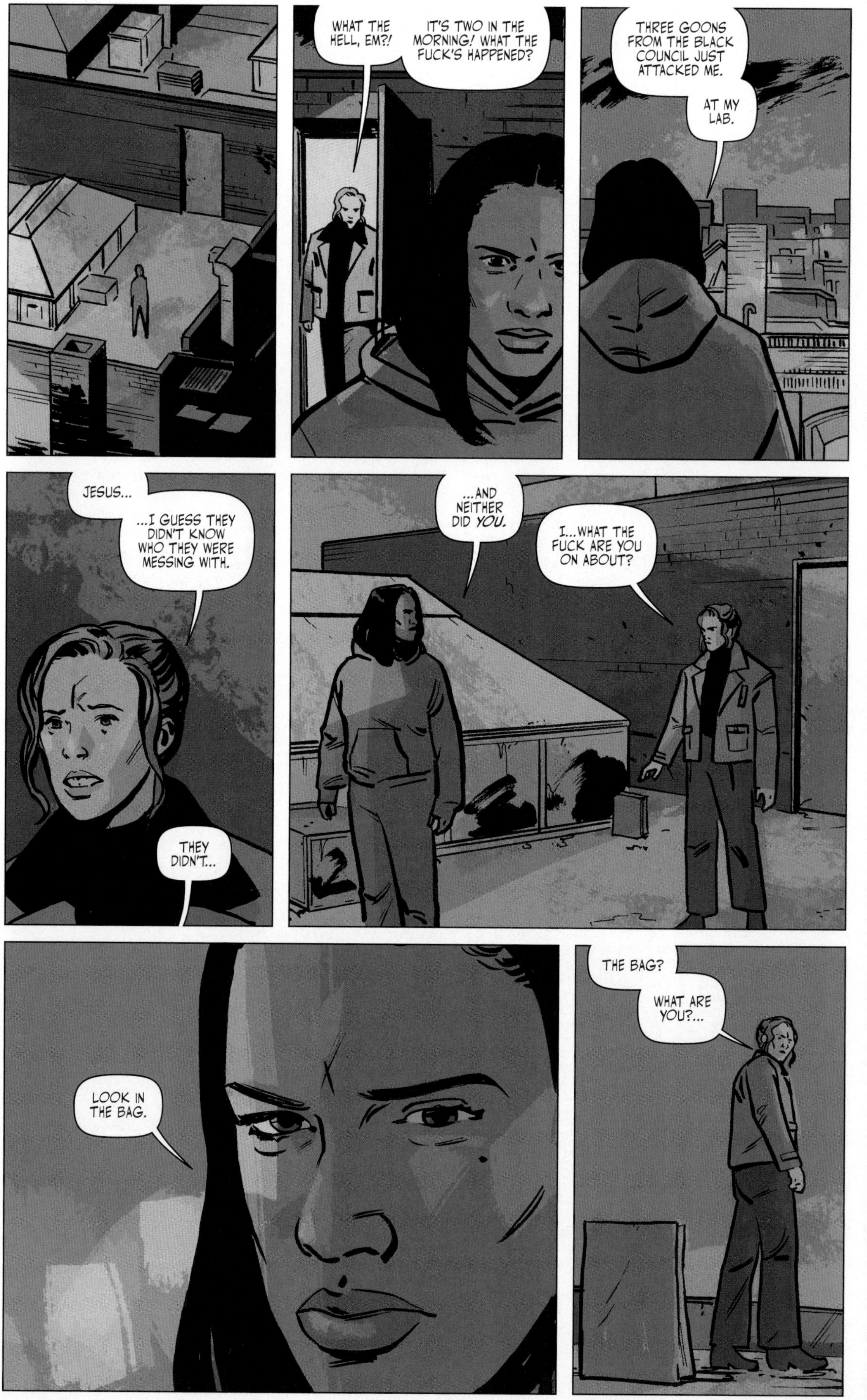
WHAT THE HELL, EM?!
IT'S TWO IN THE MORNING! WHAT THE FUCK'S HAPPENED?
THREE GOONS FROM THE BLACK COUNCIL JUST ATTACKED ME.
AT MY LAB.
JESUS...
...I GUESS THEY DIDN'T KNOW WHO THEY WERE MESSING WITH.
THEY DIDN'T...
...AND NEITHER DID *YOU*.
I...WHAT THE FUCK ARE YOU ON ABOUT?
LOOK IN THE BAG.
THE BAG?
WHAT ARE YOU?...

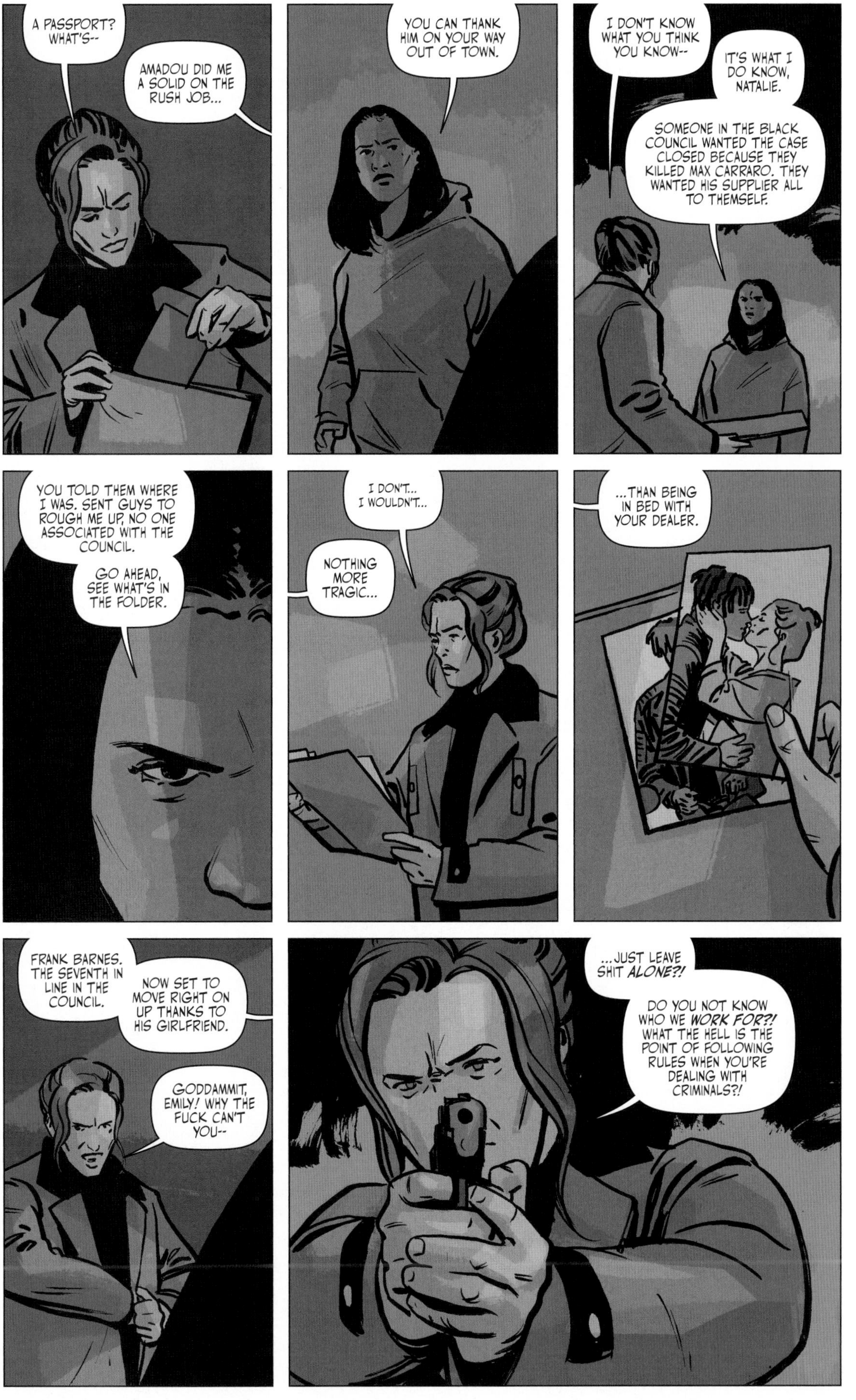

A PASSPORT? WHAT'S--
AMADOU DID ME A SOLID ON THE RUSH JOB...
YOU CAN THANK HIM ON YOUR WAY OUT OF TOWN.
I DON'T KNOW WHAT YOU THINK YOU KNOW--
IT'S WHAT I DO KNOW, NATALIE.
SOMEONE IN THE BLACK COUNCIL WANTED THE CASE CLOSED BECAUSE THEY KILLED MAX CARRARO. THEY WANTED HIS SUPPLIER ALL TO THEMSELF.
YOU TOLD THEM WHERE I WAS. SENT GUYS TO ROUGH ME UP, NO ONE ASSOCIATED WITH THE COUNCIL.
GO AHEAD, SEE WHAT'S IN THE FOLDER.
I DON'T... I WOULDN'T...
NOTHING MORE TRAGIC...
...THAN BEING IN BED WITH YOUR DEALER.
FRANK BARNES. THE SEVENTH IN LINE IN THE COUNCIL.
NOW SET TO MOVE RIGHT ON UP THANKS TO HIS GIRLFRIEND.
GODDAMMIT, EMILY! WHY THE FUCK CAN'T YOU--
...JUST LEAVE SHIT *ALONE?!*
DO YOU NOT KNOW WHO WE *WORK FOR?!* WHAT THE HELL IS THE POINT OF FOLLOWING RULES WHEN YOU'RE DEALING WITH CRIMINALS?!

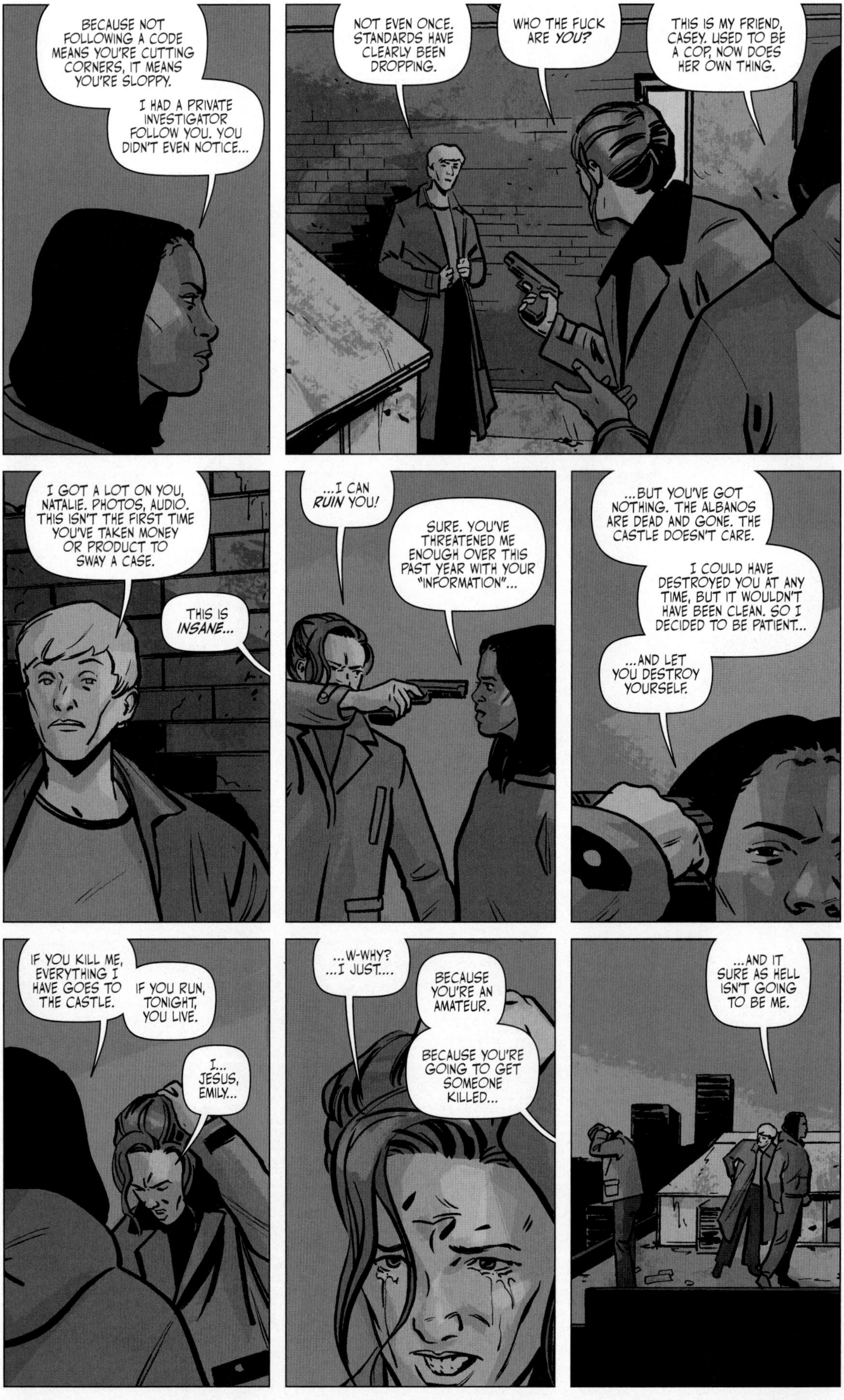

BECAUSE NOT FOLLOWING A CODE MEANS YOU'RE CUTTING CORNERS, IT MEANS YOU'RE SLOPPY.
I HAD A PRIVATE INVESTIGATOR FOLLOW YOU. YOU DIDN'T EVEN NOTICE...
NOT EVEN ONCE. STANDARDS HAVE CLEARLY BEEN DROPPING.
WHO THE FUCK ARE *YOU?*
THIS IS MY FRIEND, CASEY. USED TO BE A COP, NOW DOES HER OWN THING.
I GOT A LOT ON YOU, NATALIE. PHOTOS, AUDIO. THIS ISN'T THE FIRST TIME YOU'VE TAKEN MONEY OR PRODUCT TO SWAY A CASE.
THIS IS *INSANE...*
...I CAN *RUIN* YOU!
SURE. YOU'VE THREATENED ME ENOUGH OVER THIS PAST YEAR WITH YOUR "INFORMATION"...
...BUT YOU'VE GOT NOTHING. THE ALBANOS ARE DEAD AND GONE. THE CASTLE DOESN'T CARE.
I COULD HAVE DESTROYED YOU AT ANY TIME, BUT IT WOULDN'T HAVE BEEN CLEAN. SO I DECIDED TO BE PATIENT...
...AND LET YOU DESTROY YOURSELF.
IF YOU KILL ME, EVERYTHING I HAVE GOES TO THE CASTLE.
IF YOU RUN, TONIGHT, YOU LIVE.
I... JESUS, EMILY...
...W-WHY? ...I JUST....
BECAUSE YOU'RE AN AMATEUR.
BECAUSE YOU'RE GOING TO GET SOMEONE KILLED...
...AND IT SURE AS HELL ISN'T GOING TO BE ME.

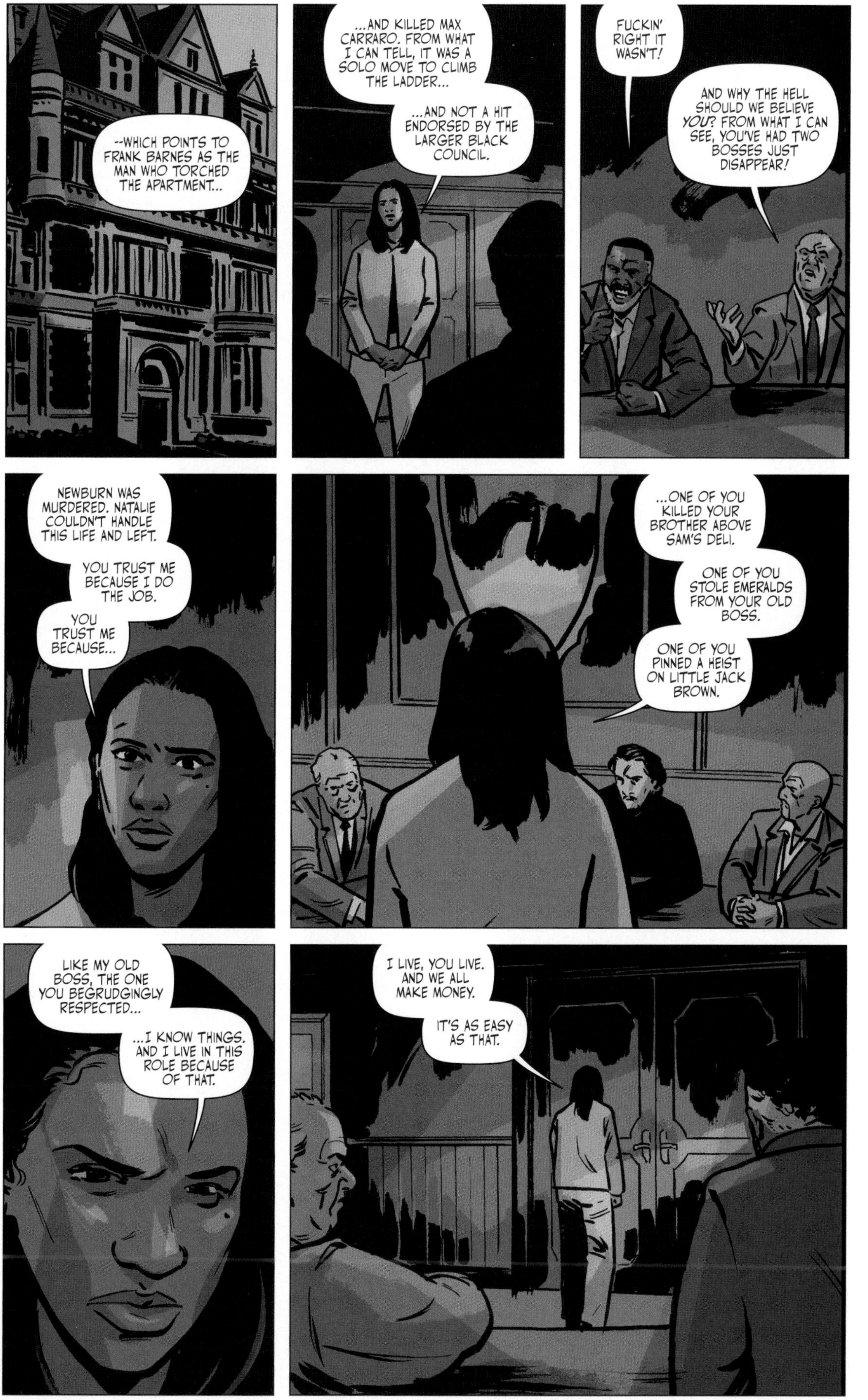
--WHICH POINTS TO FRANK BARNES AS THE MAN WHO TORCHED THE APARTMENT...
...AND KILLED MAX CARRARO. FROM WHAT I CAN TELL, IT WAS A SOLO MOVE TO CLIMB THE LADDER...
...AND NOT A HIT ENDORSED BY THE LARGER BLACK COUNCIL.
FUCKIN' RIGHT IT WASN'T!
AND WHY THE HELL SHOULD WE BELIEVE YOU? FROM WHAT I CAN SEE, YOU'VE HAD TWO BOSSES JUST DISAPPEAR!
NEWBURN WAS MURDERED. NATALIE COULDN'T HANDLE THIS LIFE AND LEFT.
YOU TRUST ME BECAUSE I DO THE JOB.
YOU TRUST ME BECAUSE...
...ONE OF YOU KILLED YOUR BROTHER ABOVE SAM'S DELI.
ONE OF YOU STOLE EMERALDS FROM YOUR OLD BOSS.
ONE OF YOU PINNED A HEIST ON LITTLE JACK BROWN.
LIKE MY OLD BOSS, THE ONE YOU BEGRUDGINGLY RESPECTED...
...I KNOW THINGS. AND I LIVE IN THIS ROLE BECAUSE OF THAT.
I LIVE, YOU LIVE. AND WE ALL MAKE MONEY.
IT'S AS EASY AS THAT.

SO, IS THAT IT?

YOU'RE THE NEW NEWBURN?

"NEWERBURN"?

I DON'T THINK *ANYONE* WANTS THAT....

...BUT HE LEFT ME WHAT HE HAD. HIS FAILSAFES. ALL HIS FILES ON THE BLACK CASTLE.

SO, I'M PROTECTED LIKE HE WAS.

IS IT WEIRD...

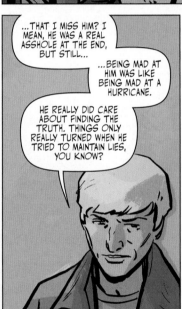

...THAT I MISS HIM? I MEAN, HE WAS A REAL ASSHOLE AT THE END, BUT STILL...

...BEING MAD AT HIM WAS LIKE BEING MAD AT A HURRICANE.

HE REALLY DID CARE ABOUT FINDING THE TRUTH. THINGS ONLY REALLY TURNED WHEN HE TRIED TO MAINTAIN LIES, YOU KNOW?

I...THOSE LIES WERE BECAUSE HE WAS PROTECTING *ME.*

I FEEL LIKE...IT WAS HARD TO GET A READ ON HIM, HOW HE FELT ABOUT ME.

BUT NEWBURN *COVERING A TRUTH...* IT WAS PROBABLY THE CLOSEST THING HE HAD TO SHOWING LOVE.

YOU SURE YOU DON'T WANT TO WORK WITH ME?

I CAN MAKE YOU RIIIIICH...

NAH. I'M CONTENT ON MY OWN THESE DAYS.

HOW ABOUT YOU? YOU GOING TO DO THIS FOREVER?

AS LONG AS I CAN. BUT FIRST I NEED A VACATION...

I follow everyth   he letter   only   ings wor
Criss-crossing t   ports, o
all times. I would   do it this way   t it
helps that someone else thought it through first.

Time   acation.

06
/16
/24

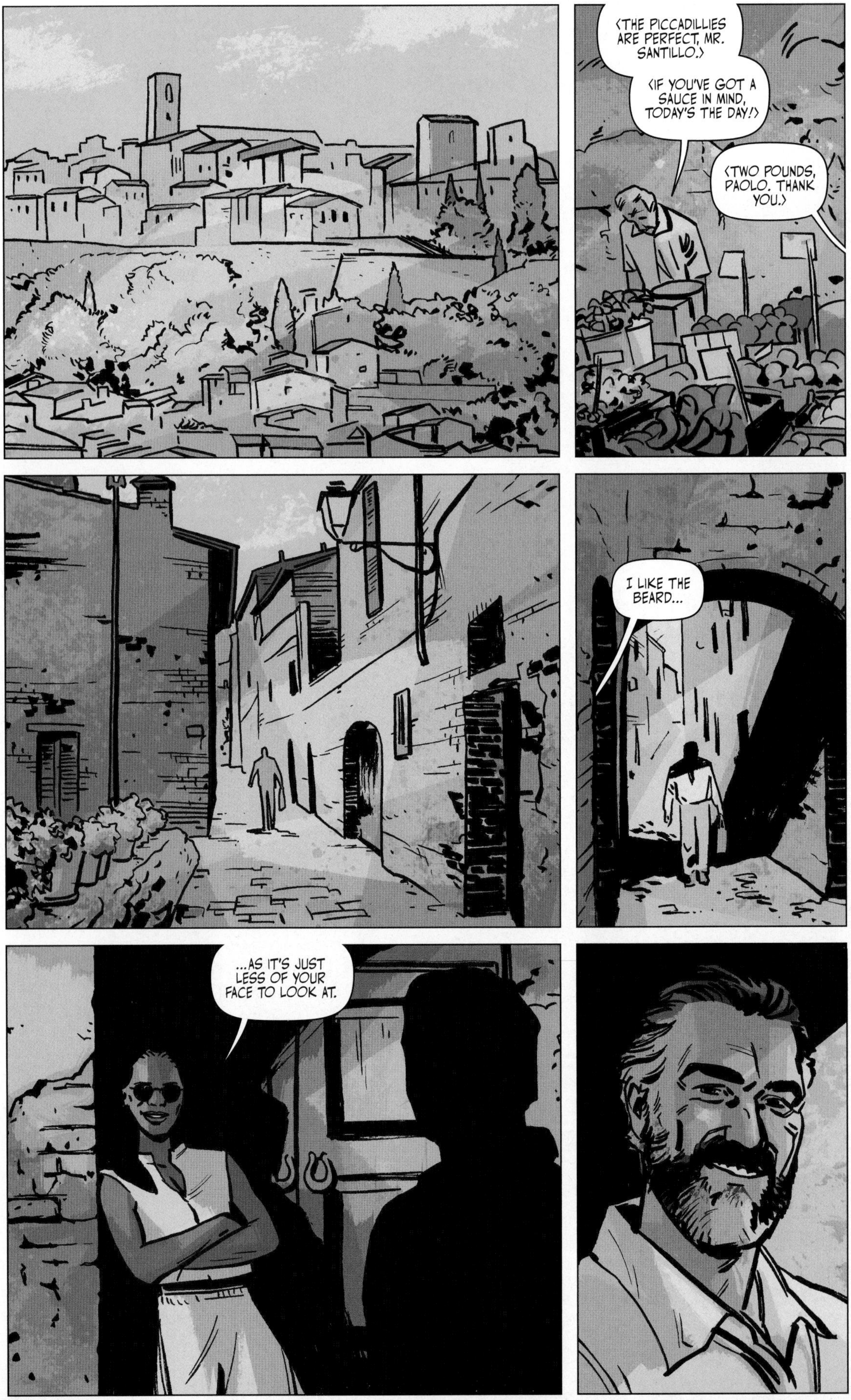
‹THE PICCADILLIES ARE PERFECT, MR. SANTILLO.›
‹IF YOU'VE GOT A SAUCE IN MIND, TODAY'S THE DAY!›
‹TWO POUNDS, PAOLO. THANK YOU.›
I LIKE THE BEARD...
...AS IT'S JUST LESS OF YOUR FACE TO LOOK AT.

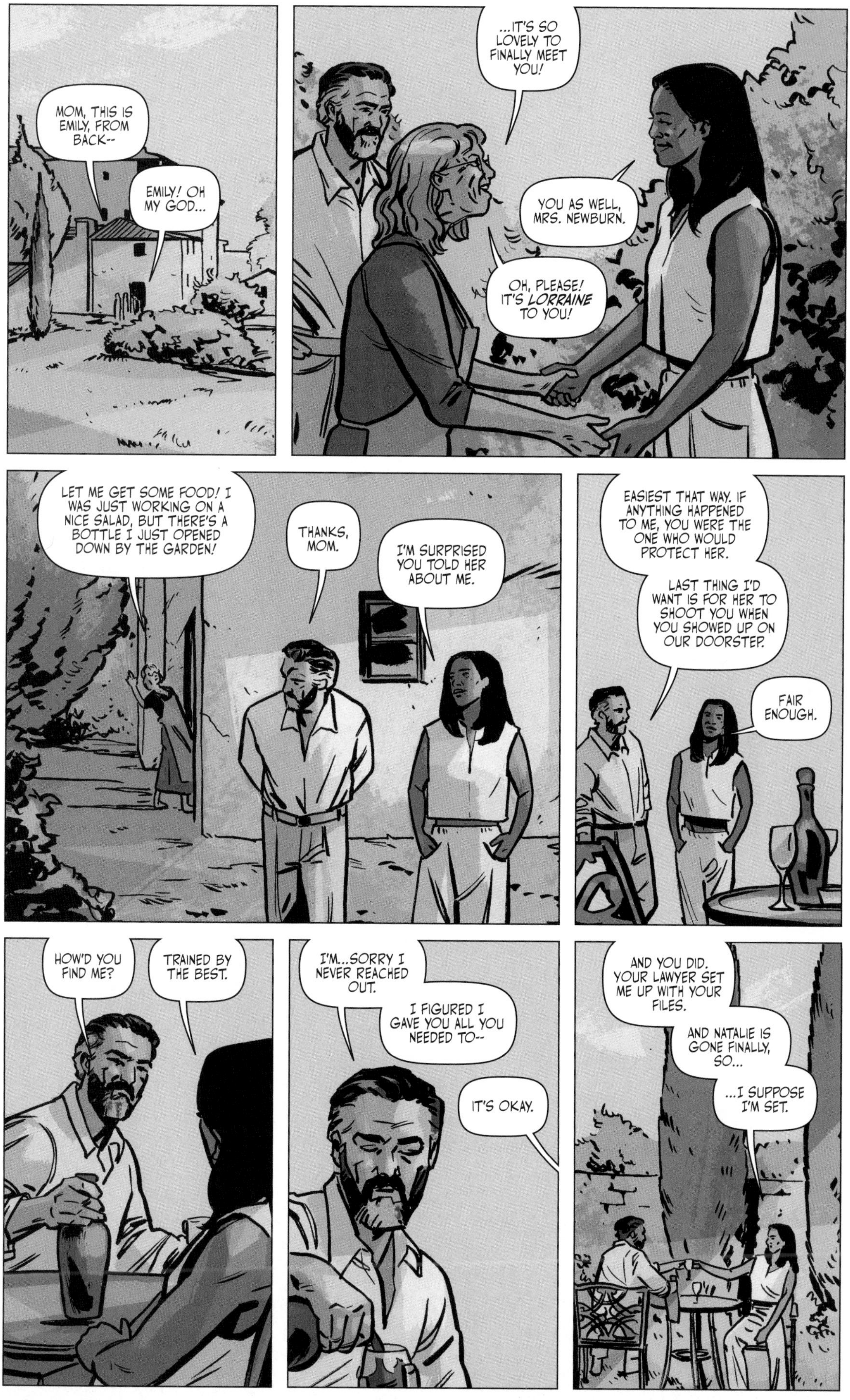
MOM, THIS IS EMILY, FROM BACK--
EMILY! OH MY GOD...
...IT'S SO LOVELY TO FINALLY MEET YOU!
YOU AS WELL, MRS. NEWBURN.
OH, PLEASE! IT'S *LORRAINE* TO YOU!
LET ME GET SOME FOOD! I WAS JUST WORKING ON A NICE SALAD, BUT THERE'S A BOTTLE I JUST OPENED DOWN BY THE GARDEN!
THANKS, MOM.
I'M SURPRISED YOU TOLD HER ABOUT ME.
EASIEST THAT WAY. IF ANYTHING HAPPENED TO ME, YOU WERE THE ONE WHO WOULD PROTECT HER.
LAST THING I'D WANT IS FOR HER TO SHOOT YOU WHEN YOU SHOWED UP ON OUR DOORSTEP.
FAIR ENOUGH.
HOW'D YOU FIND ME?
TRAINED BY THE BEST.
I'M...SORRY I NEVER REACHED OUT.
I FIGURED I GAVE YOU ALL YOU NEEDED TO--
IT'S OKAY.
AND YOU DID. YOUR LAWYER SET ME UP WITH YOUR FILES.
AND NATALIE IS GONE FINALLY, SO...
...I SUPPOSE I'M SET.

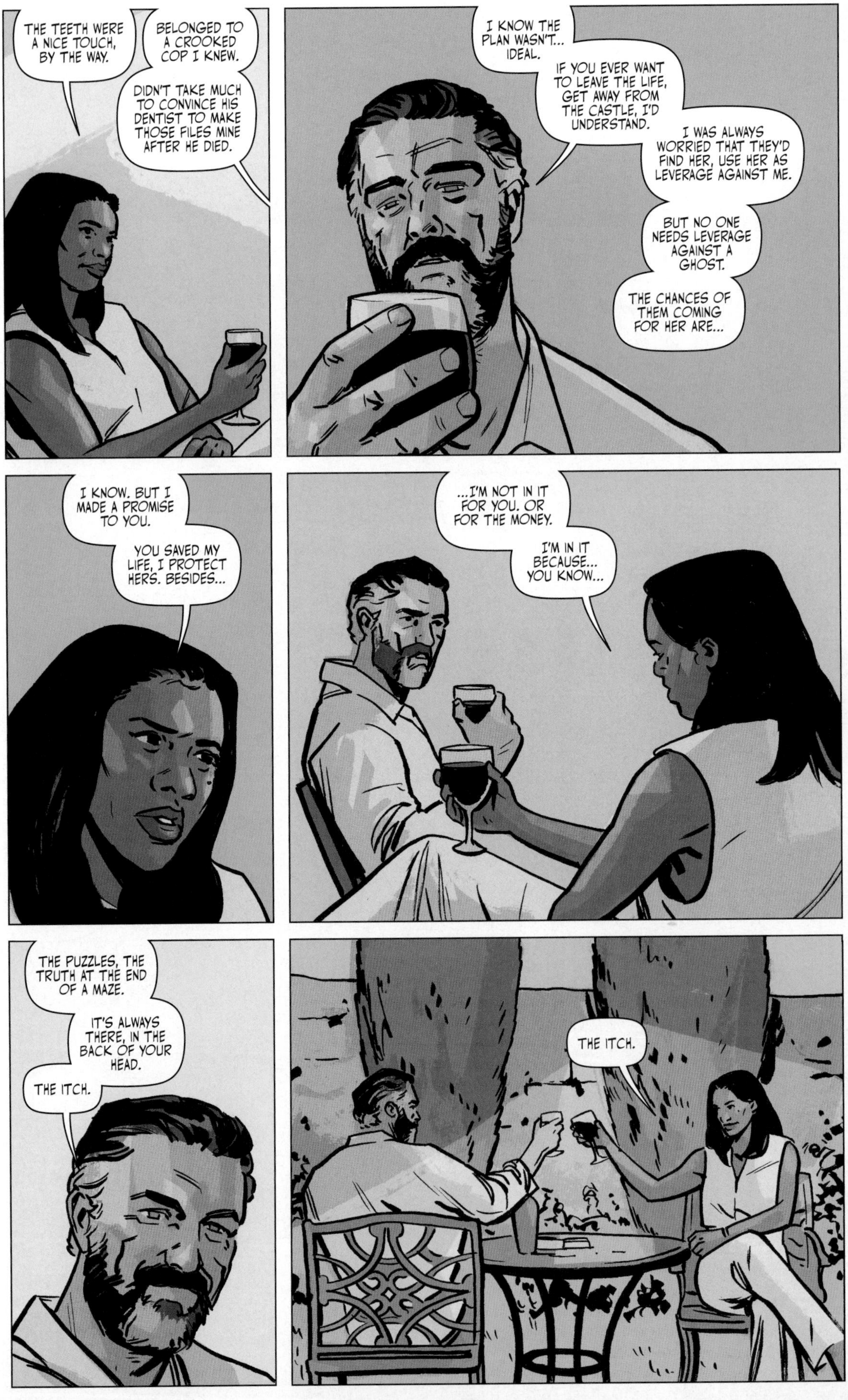
THE TEETH WERE A NICE TOUCH, BY THE WAY.
BELONGED TO A CROOKED COP I KNEW.
DIDN'T TAKE MUCH TO CONVINCE HIS DENTIST TO MAKE THOSE FILES MINE AFTER HE DIED.
I KNOW THE PLAN WASN'T... IDEAL.
IF YOU EVER WANT TO LEAVE THE LIFE, GET AWAY FROM THE CASTLE, I'D UNDERSTAND.
I WAS ALWAYS WORRIED THAT THEY'D FIND HER, USE HER AS LEVERAGE AGAINST ME.
BUT NO ONE NEEDS LEVERAGE AGAINST A GHOST.
THE CHANCES OF THEM COMING FOR HER ARE...
I KNOW. BUT I MADE A PROMISE TO YOU.
YOU SAVED MY LIFE, I PROTECT HERS. BESIDES...
...I'M NOT IN IT FOR YOU. OR FOR THE MONEY.
I'M IN IT BECAUSE... YOU KNOW...
THE PUZZLES, THE TRUTH AT THE END OF A MAZE.
IT'S ALWAYS THERE, IN THE BACK OF YOUR HEAD.
THE ITCH.
THE ITCH.

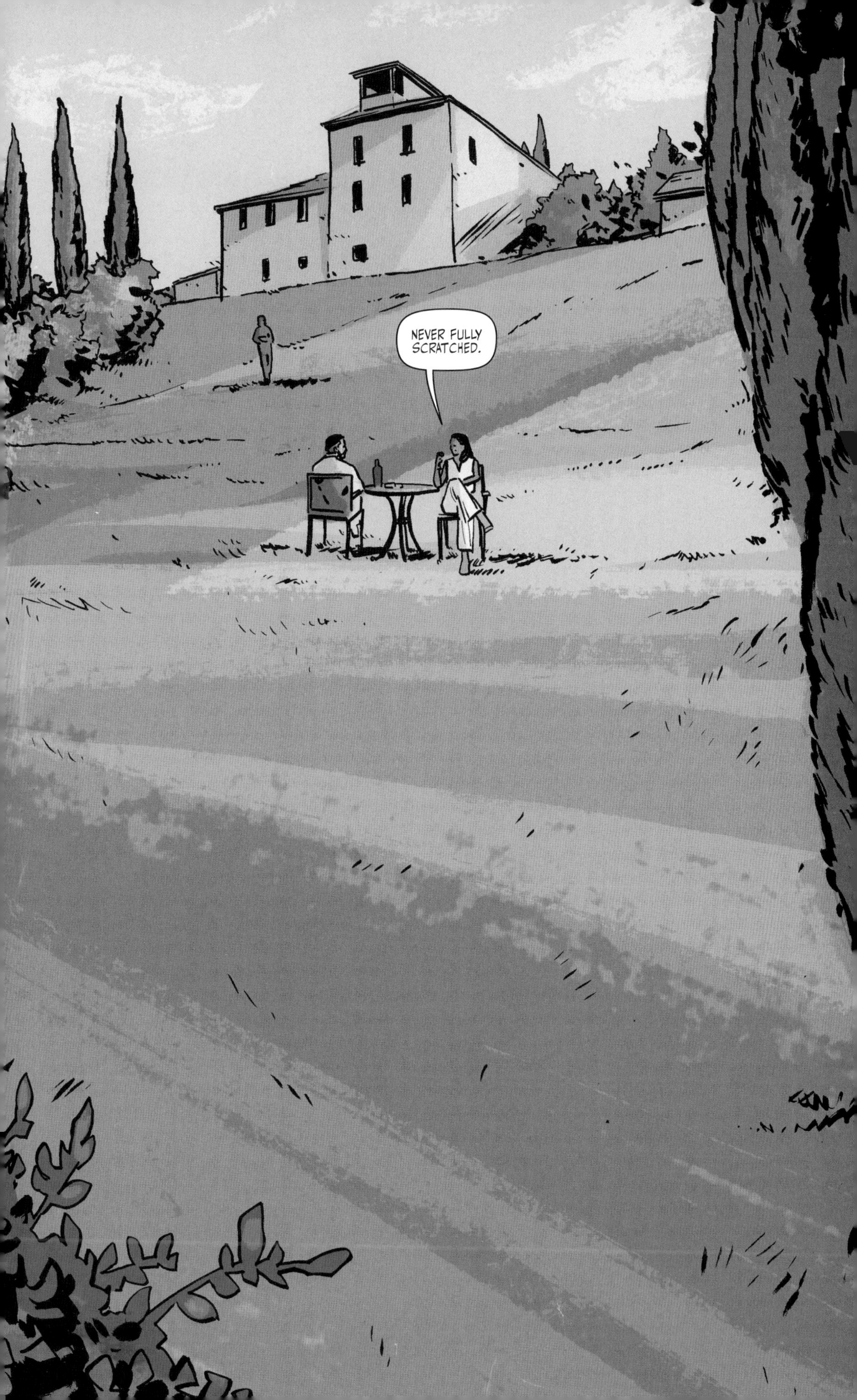
NEVER FULLY SCRATCHED.

Chip Zdarsky

is the award-winning creator of *Public Domain* for Image Comics. He's written such titles as *Batman, Daredevil* and *Spider-Man: Life Story.* His only crime is loving too much.

Jacob Phillips

is a comic artist and colourist residing in tropical Manchester. He has been drawing his whole life, self publishing first comic, *Roboy* at the age of 11 and selling it at Brighton Comic Con. Skip forward 19 years and today he is the artist on *Newburn, That Texas Blood* and *The Enfield Gang Massacre* from Image Comics as well as colouring projects such as *Reckless, MADI, Where the Body Was* and *Night Fever.*